A SEVEN SERIES NOVEL

DANNIKA DARK

All Rights Reserved
Copyright © 2014 Dannika Dark

First Print Edition
ISBN 13: 978-1495405914
ISBN-10: 1495405915

Formatting: Streetlight Graphics

No part of this book may be reproduced, distributed, or transmitted in any form or by any means, or stored in a database retrieval system, without the prior written permission of the author. You must not circulate this book in any format. Thank you for respecting the rights of the author.

This is a work of fiction. Any resemblance of characters to actual persons, living or dead, is purely coincidental.

Professionally edited by Victory Editing
Cover design by Dannika Dark. All stock purchased.

http://dannikadark.blogspot.com/
Fan page located on Facebook

Also By Dannika Dark:

THE MAGERI SERIES
Sterling
Twist
Impulse
Gravity
Shine

NOVELLAS
Closer

THE SEVEN SERIES
Seven Years
Six Months

ACKNOWLEDGEMENTS:

This book is dedicated to every person who has found their happy ending in a new beginning, and for those who seek it.

The first time I laid eyes on Reno,
I was afraid of him.

Six months later,
I was afraid of living without him.

PROLOGUE

RENO PARKED HIS TRIUMPH MOTORCYCLE off a side road on the outskirts of the city. He could smell the thick prelude to an oncoming storm mingled with the sweet fragrance of wildflowers. No better scent in the world.

It had been a grueling week and he'd just closed an important case. Reno was a private investigator and accepted jobs at his own discretion. Most of the time he turned down the petty shit like Shifters who suspected their mates were cheating. They'd offer Reno good money to stalk their women and capture damning evidence. He'd learned men like that didn't have good intentions, and Reno didn't want to do anything that would endanger a woman's life because of a jealous man. He'd relocate women when he suspected abuse, but he preferred jobs that led him on a chase, hunting down deplorable criminals. That's the kind of life he came from as a former bounty hunter.

Bounty hunters went after nefarious men with a price on their head, officially declared outlaws by the higher authority. But plenty of criminals flew under the radar. After years of getting his ass shot at and living out of a suitcase, Reno had decided to settle down and start up a new career. PI work wasn't as glamorous, but it had its perks. For one, he could hunt men who committed an act not punishable by Breed laws. Because there weren't many Breed jails, the laws were lax in order to fill their prisons with only the most depraved criminals who were a threat to society. If a man beat his wife, he wouldn't be arrested. Wolf packs didn't tolerate abuse and would make those men regret they had ever drawn breath. But not all Shifters followed the same code of conduct, and not all Shifters were wolves or living in tight family units. Reno worked for anyone who hired him, regardless of Breed. Sometimes a little street justice was called for on Reno's part, but in most cases, he handed the offender over to his client.

It didn't work like human investigations where evidence was gathered and they'd have a trial. Reno was a Shifter, and that meant he roughed men up in order to set them straight. Sometimes he was hired to find a person gone missing; other times he set up surveillance to help catch people suspected of fraud.

This last job had taken him on a wild-goose chase for two days to track down an embezzler up in Chicago. He'd gotten double the pay to compensate for the travel expenses. After closing the case, he decided to take a little time off because money was good and he needed a vacation.

Reno's personal life had been scattered for the past few months. His wolf itched to get out more, and on a number of occasions, Reno had woken up far from his bike, deep within the city limits. Humans had no idea Breed existed, so his wolf's erratic behavior could prove dangerous if someone were to catch him. Reno lived on a hundred acres of rural territory with the Weston pack—plenty of space for his wolf to run. But lately Reno's usually obedient wolf had been roaming.

To appease him, Reno had begun parking his bike closer to the city. Maybe his wolf was just curious about humans. Shifters had to make peace with their animal; there's nothing worse than waking up naked, fifty miles away from your bike and clothes because of a cantankerous wolf. So Reno made a compromise and began shifting in a wooded area near the population, establishing boundaries. The change satisfied his wolf's curiosity but did nothing to suppress his uncompromising restlessness.

Reno had never experienced this level of disobedience before, and it had progressively worsened over the last three weeks. Even after shifting back, he didn't feel the usual contentment that came with returning to human form. Something was up and he didn't like it.

Reno kicked off his motorcycle boots and unbuttoned his dark blue shirt. He had brought a waterproof bag to store his clothes in to protect them from the rain, so he neatly folded his shirt inside and stripped out of his jeans and shorts.

Damn, it felt good to be a Shifter. His muscles flexed as he drew in a deep breath, listening to the majestic stillness of the thick woods. Sprinkles of rain created a canopy of sound overhead, tapping against the fragile leaves. Fall was his favorite time of year to shift. He loved the feel of rain against his naked body, the crisp sting of clean air, and the heavy scent of winter trying to push its way in. Winter in Texas was a joke compared to the snowy hills of Colorado, but it appeased his wolf just the same.

Reno had everything a man could want: family, brotherhood, a home, a respectable job, a sweet bike, and life. Yet there was an unshakable emptiness in the center of his chest—one that gnawed at his heart like a ravenous beast whenever he thought of having a woman filling the empty space in his bed. One who could make him a better man, completing him the way that only a good woman could.

Not just any woman, but one in particular intruded into his mind in quiet moments. A girl he'd only met once, but the vision of her sweet eyes and delicate nature had branded his thoughts. Shifter men were notoriously attracted to strong women who spoke their mind, but this girl seemed strong in a different way. Inwardly. He could sense her resilience; it was something he'd acquired over his many lifetimes of witnessing war, famine, and poverty. A quiet strength that made a person keep walking forward in life, no matter what. Sometimes strength wasn't about brawn, but heart. It reminded him of a horse race he'd once witnessed years ago. Everyone had given the accolades to the impressive thoroughbred that soared through the finish line. But not Reno. He patiently waited and applauded the horse that came in dead last with a broken leg but not a broken spirit. That horse could have fallen and given up, but it pushed through the pain until it reached the finish line. That was the toughest damn animal in the race, whether or not the horse knew it would be his last run.

Reno needed to erase the thoughts he was having of this girl; they were from two different worlds. Aside from that, he remembered the fear glittering in her eyes when she looked upon him. He could hardly blame her because that wasn't an uncommon reaction when humans looked at Shifters. But for a fleeting moment, he also thought he saw a flicker of desire in the way she blushed and wet her mouth, quickly averting her gaze. Shifters were perceptive when it came to body language, and something about hers was conflicted. But he still felt it—a magnetic pull that threaded between them and piqued his curiosity.

After Reno tucked his handgun in a separate compartment on his bike, he carefully hid the bag beneath some brush.

In a fluid movement too fast to track, Reno shifted into his earthy-brown wolf. He lifted his snout and inhaled the fragrance of red cedar, yellow damianita, and autumn sage. He pawed at the wet dirt and let out a howl that stilled every living creature within earshot. A white rabbit scurried off in the distance and he lurched forward, disappearing into the wild woods.

CHAPTER 1

OMINOUS STORM CLOUDS BLACKENED THE autumn sky, and thunder growled like a savage beast. I looked at the Sweet Treats display windows in front and considered how dangerous it would be if they shattered from straight-line winds or flying debris. Spring storms in Austin weren't uncommon, but this was fall and I didn't like the dull green tint blanketing the street.

"We need to close the shop, Alexia." I tapped my electric-blue fingernail on the glass.

Alexia Knight had recently inherited the candy store when our boss, Charlie, died of cancer four months ago. Lexi had given me an unexpected promotion, despite the fact I was only twenty-two.

I'd never thought I'd be a store manager so quickly. After college, I had submitted my résumé to all the top companies in the area, hoping to get my foot in the door.

Unfortunately, I discovered many businesses preferred experience over education. I wasn't paid a great deal managing a privately owned candy store, but the position would look great on my résumé if the business became stagnant and I decided to move on. I liked my job because it not only gave me leadership experience, but I also rocked at it. Lexi had relinquished complete control of all the hiring and firing. Luckily our part-timers were reliable and I hadn't had to let anyone go yet. I not only worked the retail angle but also was in charge of scheduling days off for the staff, coming up with the work rotation, and monitoring inventory.

"April, I keep telling you to call me *Lexi*," she complained from a crouched position behind the white counter. "That's what my friends call me and I think you qualify. Where did you put those little coupon books?"

A clap of thunder rattled the windows and we shrieked in unison.

Lexi sprang to her feet, clutching her heart. "What the hell is going on out there?"

"*Armageddon*," I said in a jittery, singsong voice.

After securing the locks on the doors, I watched people scurry to their cars with shopping bags over their heads. I was thankful to be at work because the last place I'd want to be during a tornado was in my Airstream trailer. It looked like those old-fashioned models you hook onto a truck, only this one was bigger. I'd worked at Sweet Treats for over a year and Lexi didn't have a clue where I lived. There were nice trailer parks in the area, but mine had a reputation for housing drug dealers and ex-convicts. People often judged me on where I came from, not where I was going.

"Can you turn on the radio, Lexi?" My hands were shaking as I straightened a few packages of Japanese gum on the shelf. "Maybe if we have some music going it'll block out all the thunder."

Lexi lifted a portable black radio from beneath the register. I'd bought the radio a week after my car had died. My younger sister used to pick me up from work in her VW and I hated waiting in the empty store late at night—the silence rattled me. Rose, my sister, had recently wound up in a whirlwind romance with a guy named Shane. He had a counterfeit smile and sold plenty of cars at a dealership located just a mile up the road. A few weeks ago, they skipped town and moved in with his aunt in Arizona—something about him being promised a better job. I couldn't believe Rose ditched me on short notice, and I'd been walking to and from work ever since.

Lexi switched on the radio and stopped on a severe weather alert. After the intermittent squelching, an automated message came on. "Sounds like a tornado watch," she said in a distant voice, adjusting the antenna. The announcer confirmed the adjacent county was under a warning, although no tornadoes had been spotted.

"Do you think we're safe in here with all this hard candy?" I glanced at all the aisles filled with plastic canisters, laughing at the idea of being whipped to death by licorice.

"If the big one hits, I guess the firemen will have to eat their way to our rescue."

"*Not complaining*," I sang.

She slapped a hand over her mouth to smother her quirky laugh.

I threaded my long bangs away from my eyes and hugged my arms when the wind began stripping the leaves from a few pear trees outside. I should have been used to storms by now, but I just couldn't stay calm when it came to an all-expenses-paid trip to Oz.

Lexi switched the radio station to a classic rock song and belted out a few lyrics. I smiled when my boss swished her brown hair around a few times. Lexi had a sarcastic bite and enjoyed making me laugh. She'd recently hit a rough patch with some personal family stuff and had split with her ex, Beckett. I hadn't seen him in months, not since the night he drove by and tried to win her back. Lexi seemed like a changed woman ever since she met the new guy, Austin Cole.

Austin was easy on the eyes in every conceivable way. He had the kind of masculine body women fantasized about, except for the bold tattoos on his upper arms and shoulders. I'd never been a fan of ink, but Lexi loved tracing her fingers over the intricate lines whenever he wore a sleeveless shirt. Tall and built, Austin looked like a guy who knew how to take care of himself. Any woman would melt if his thick arms were protectively wrapped around her. His dark hair and brooding eyes made it seem like someone important had just walked into the room. Whenever he swung by the shop, his eyes stayed glued on Lexi. She usually had to leave him and assist customers, so Austin would lean against the counter, watching her with a molten gaze. Sometimes he put on a pair of fringed leather gloves and she'd scowl at him.

Lexi had once admitted she thought the gloves were sexy as hell, but Austin wasn't allowed to know that. I found out they'd known each other since childhood, but it had taken years before they were both in a place where being together made sense. I was surprised at how quickly she'd moved in with him, but then again, I wasn't exactly the spokeswoman for relationships.

My love affair was with paperback novels and hair lightener. I had natural blond hair, but I began dying it a platinum shade back in college to change my image and wore it short in back, tapered to the base of my neck. It worked with my fair complexion, and my best friend had told me it was fashion forward. I'd had a rough time in high school. A group of boys used to bully me right up until the eleventh grade, calling me a dumb blonde. Then one day they'd spray-painted "slut" on my locker and hung up a picture of a porn star who resembled me. Crying in front of them had only made it worse. After that, I kept to myself, studied hard, and didn't date. The less ammo I could give them, the better. My life had changed by college, but I still worried about running into those boys someday. Chances are I would, but I hoped by then I'd be able to outshine them in my achievements.

Thunder rattled the windows, and while we lowered the blinds, the Rolling Stones sang "Gimme Shelter" on the radio.

"Well, at least we can take a break," she said with a heavy sigh. "I'm not going to be able to serve customers if glass is flying around."

I gave her a sharp glare. "You should be used to it by now. I'm surprised my little fiasco didn't end up on the Internet."

Lexi snorted. "I haven't figured out how to use the camera feature on my phone yet. Seven years, April," she teased.

A week ago I'd attempted to straighten a large mirror on the wall. The mirror gave the illusion of extra space, and more importantly, allowed us to keep an eye on mischievous kids who liked to stuff candy in their pockets when they thought no one was looking. I should have just left it alone, but the mirror looked crooked and when I tried to straighten it, the cord snapped and glass shattered at my feet. Two guys laughed and turned away, not offering to help. So much for chivalry.

My mother had once said I was an accident waiting to happen and it started with my conception.

"Whoa, those clouds look *creepy*." Lexi cupped her elbows as she peered between the slats in the blinds.

The streets were black as sin, as if something hellish were preparing to crawl up from the underbelly of the earth. Fat drops of rain assailed the windshields of passing cars, and the wind began to bend the trees in the parking lot. I hurried to the back room, my heart galloping. I stood amid a wooden bench, a plastic chair, a vending machine, a silver water fountain, and a unisex bathroom. It was where I retreated at night, after hours. I'd lie on the bench and read one of my novels until my sister knocked on the front door after her shift ended at Sonic.

Lexi strolled in and examined the antiquated vending machine to her left. "You know what? I think I'm going to request a new line of snacks for this thing," she announced.

I sat on the floor to the right of the bench and stretched out my legs, crossing them at the ankle. We each wore matching uniforms: bright orange shirts with the store logo written in cursive across our chests and white skirts that stopped just above the knee. My legs looked ghostly compared to Lexi's warm complexion. She had stunning legs, a cascade of silken hair, a lean frame, and a beautiful shade of whiskey-brown eyes. I also had a slim figure, but more endowed up top and thicker thighs.

Were men more attracted to brunettes when it came to serious relationships? I had hazel eyes—sea green with brilliant flecks of copper. Smokey eyeliner made them appear larger, although it sometimes gave me the appearance of a punk-rock girl. I wanted men to notice me, but after having spent a good part of high school looking like a stereotype, I decided I'd rather be admired for my brains and heart. I worked with what I had, but not in a way that garnered negative attention.

"We need to dump out all these snacks we don't eat and change the inventory," she said, looking at the contents in the machine.

"Good. I want those little chocolate donuts."

"Do they still sell those?" She spun around and knitted her brows.

"Neither of us eats that junk and God knows how long it's been in there. Is it our machine, or does it belong to an outside vendor?"

Lexi twisted her mouth to the side. "Good question. I'm not sure. If it's ours, the key might be in one of the envelopes at home. I bet this bad boy is ours. I've seen those cute vendors in their shorts refilling the machines in some of the stores, so I know someone would have come around asking about it by now," she said, patting her hand on the glass. "The last time I bought something was two months ago. Only an idiot would put a snack machine in a candy store."

"We stare at sugar all day long and that's what Charlie gave us to snack on? May he rest in peace, but that man didn't have his head screwed on right."

We both laughed and Lexi fished out a few coins from a Styrofoam cup we kept on top of the machine. "Oh my God, wouldn't it be awesome if it's ours? We can put whatever we want in it. Cookies?"

"I like animal crackers."

She wrinkled her nose.

"Ding Dongs?" I suggested.

"Now you're talking. A *man* machine. My friend, Naya, would totally love that concept. What kind do you want? Dark and handsome, tattooed and dangerous, a sexy jock, nerdy and hot…"

"That's not what I meant." I removed a candy barrette from my pocket and clipped my bangs away from my face. The hard rain made a clamor against the rooftop.

"I know what you meant, April. We could always put PMS pills in there," she said with a snort. "Sorry, just having some fun. What's wrong with you today? You're always in a better mood."

"You're asking me what's wrong while tornado sirens are blaring outside?" The lights flickered and my heart did a quickstep. I felt an urge to run outside. Despite the fact it was storming, being in the open made me feel safe. I hated the dark.

Hated.

I'd been known to have panic attacks in a dark room.

Lexi sat on the bench and fumbled with her new phone, sending a text message. "Austin says everyone is okay at the house," she said in a distant voice. "The storm is south of them and all they see are a few dark clouds. He wants us to sit tight."

"Sounds like a man with a plan," I said facetiously. "What was our other option? Because I was thinking we could dance naked in the street with a few gumdrops stuck to our nipples."

Lexi burst out laughing and texted feverishly with a devilish grin. Then her brows popped up and I knew she was giving Austin the full visual. I could only imagine what his reply was.

A terrible thought crossed my mind. What if something happened to my trailer?

My grandma was sixty-five when she died from lung cancer two years ago. It didn't come as a surprise since her health had been declining. Some people inherited money, jewelry, or even a house when a family member died. I got a trailer and a stack of bills. The student loans weren't as bad as I'd imagined, and as tough as it was, I didn't drop out. Rose had worked part time and helped with some of the expenses until I got a job at Sweet Treats. Grandma had given us a roof over our heads and fussed a lot, but we were grateful she'd taken us in after Mom had left us. Each Friday, she made a trip to the gas station and bought a wad of scratch-off lottery tickets and a carton of Marlboros. I'd had no idea how much debt she had incurred until after her death. Maybe if she'd taken out a loan from the bank it might have gone away, but I quickly found out she'd dealt exclusively with loan sharks. These men didn't let a coffin get in the way of getting back their money. I had to ignore them for a while until the funeral was paid for, but after that, I squared away her debt. I was finally in a good place where I could put aside money and save for an apartment.

I bent my knees when something rapped against the glass at the front of the store. "Do you think the hail will blow out the windows?"

Lexi stood up and peered around the doorway. "Hail doesn't fly sideways. Well, usually. Someone's outside—be right back."

"Lexi, this is the part of the horror movie where I'm supposed to scream *don't do it!* But that's okay. Let the serial killer inside. Be sure to show him the cash drawer while you're at it!" I yelled at the empty doorway.

The bell jingled and I grabbed my oversized brown purse and dug around for my charcoal eyeliner. I flipped open a compact and did a little touch-up. Not that I needed makeup, but it kept me from going into freak-out mode. *Thirty more minutes*, I kept telling myself. Severe storms ended quickly unless there was a squall line.

"You're paying for those," Lexi grumbled as she breezed into the room. Her tennis shoes squeaked against the white floor when she spun around and sat on the bench to my right.

I lifted my eyes to a tall man with a mop of wavy blond hair. Not bright blond, but a sexy color with a few dark shades mixed in. He had the face of an angel and the indigo eyes of a devil. He could have been a male model in a fashion magazine. When he raked his fingers through his hair, he revealed a prominent scar on his forehead. But it just added to the allure.

He also had about twenty gummy worms shoved in his mouth. After chewing most of them up, he looked down and grinned. "I don't believe we've met, honeypie," he said with a mouthful. "I've heard a lot about you from Ben."

Oh. Ben.

Lexi's new boyfriend had a bunch of brothers. I'd met two of them a couple of months ago when the electric company shut off our power. Ben and Wheeler were identical twins—except Ben had a perverted mouth and Wheeler had tats and chin hair in the shape of a circle beard. The mean-looking one didn't say much and seemed like a guy who liked to pound people's faces in. Ben might have been clean-cut, but he couldn't take his dirty eyes off my ass. If I had to guess their age, I'd say around thirty. The man in the doorway had the same look about him—youthful and yet seasoned, but something flickered in his eyes and made me second-guess myself.

"I'm April Frost," I said with a subtle wave of my hand.

"Denver Cole," he replied, swallowing the last bite of candy. "I'm here to save the day, so you girls just sit tight and I'll protect you."

Lexi sighed and crossed her legs. "What are you doing on this side of town?"

"Austin sent me to check on you since I was in the area. Your mother ordered curtains," he grumbled. "Can't she just get them at Walmart like everyone else? No. She has to *special order* them," he said, using his fingers to make quotation marks. "They're in the back of the truck. I hope a tornado blows them all the way to Mexico."

"Why would you wish something like that?" I wondered aloud.

He quirked a brow. "They're lacy with flowers and shit on them. Sorry, but men outnumber the women in our house. Every time I see a doily or a new flower arrangement, my balls get a little bit smaller. Speaking of, you got any malt balls in there?"

Denver wandered over to the vending machine and put his hands on top of it, tilting it forward. The lights in the store flickered.

"Stop doing that," Lexi said, losing her patience.

Then it happened. Total blackout.

A rising tide of panic set in and I catapulted to my feet. Before I knew it, I was unlocking the main door and running into the street. Lexi yelled from behind me, and the wind funneled my short hair around my head, whipping my bangs in front of my face. A few grains of sand stung my eyes as the wind battered me with relentless force.

Suddenly, a strong arm hooked around my waist and lifted me off the ground.

"Are you a bag of nuts?" Denver shouted over the wind as he hauled me back inside.

The lights flickered back on and he set me on my feet. Lexi watched with wide, uncertain eyes as he shut the door and the bell jingled wildly.

My heart pounded against my chest like a drummer in a parade.

Denver grumbled and folded his arms. "Saving damsel in distress: check. Nearly crapping pants while standing in the middle of a fucking tornado: check."

Lexi wrapped her arms around me and we stood in the center of the room. "Sorry, April. I'm on the verge of freaking out too, even though it doesn't show much. My coping mechanism is denial. We'll be fine."

Denver stuck his hand in a bin full of chocolates and I walked over and grabbed the collar of his T-shirt, yanking him back. "Those are for *paying* customers. We can't afford to just give it away."

When he winked at me, I got flustered and let go.

Something hard jabbed into my back and I glanced over my shoulder at the corner of the shelf. I pivoted around and knocked several bags of candy on the floor. Denver chortled, pinching his chin as he watched me step on them.

A flush of heat stung my cheeks.

Handsome or not, I hadn't made up my mind if I liked him. I certainly didn't enjoy being a klutz in front of *any* guy. I possessed an inner monologue voice that *loved* to criticize. Now she was saying, *Smooth move.*

Why did I have to turn stupid around men? I'd been in a

relationship before. Then again, Nathan had cheated on me constantly, so maybe it hadn't given me enough experience with men. Who had time to date? I had to focus on work and savings before I ended up living under a bridge, which was a frightening possibility if I suffered one financial misstep. No guy wants a girl with that much baggage at the airport.

"You're kind of cute," he said with a handsome smirk. "If I had a tail, I'd wag it."

"Leave my friend alone, Denver," Lexi scolded.

"I don't wear a leash," he replied. "Nor a muzzle. Ah, hell. Looks like the storm's over."

We glanced out the windows and sure enough, sunlight sprayed onto the street through a break in the clouds. Denver angrily tucked the back of his thin T-shirt into his faded jeans, which were so frayed at the ends, long pieces of thread dragged on the ground.

"Maybe I can throw those curtains in the road and tell 'em we got hit hard."

"Do that and my mom will never cook you another seasoned pork chop again," Lexi said in an amused voice, folding her arms and tilting her head.

"Am I done saving lives now?" Denver said gruffly. "I came here to be a nice guy for a change and all I get is heat. I'm outta here. Tell Aus I'll be home later; I'm going to check out a new place up the road. I hear they got a three-story laser-tag room. If that's true, then we're going," he said, circling his finger to everyone in the room and invisible parties not present.

Denver had an easygoing personality with a flair for humor, and sometimes that was a good quality for a man to have. The only thing I didn't care for was how he'd walked in on a tense situation and had done little to keep me calm. I respected men who knew how to take charge, although I'd never known one outside of a paperback novel. Maybe they didn't exist.

"Oh, no," Lexi gasped, staring at her phone. "April, I need to go home early. Can you handle the rest of the shift alone, or do you need me to be here? I have an emergency."

"Not a problem," I said.

"What's wrong?" Denver asked in a serious tone, his brows slanting down.

Lexi's brown eyes flashed up. "Maizy's hurt."

His face tensed and he clenched his fists so tightly his knuckles turned white. "What happened?"

"She fell off the new swing and hit her mouth. They're taking her to the—"

The bell jingled and Denver jogged toward an old yellow truck. Lexi grabbed her purse and followed close behind.

CHAPTER 2

A FEW MINUTES AFTER TEN O'CLOCK, I decided to flip our sign in the window to Closed and lock up the store. The scent of rain hung heavy in the air, and I dreaded the walk home. I absolutely loved getting up early and walking to work, but after dark was another story.

Lexi assumed I rode the bus. She had no idea the bus didn't go that route. My house was close to a five-mile walk and it gave me plenty of exercise, which I enjoyed. I don't think my legs had seen muscle tone in all my life until the last two weeks after my car had broken down. The first three nights were a killer, but after that, I'd managed to build up my stamina and it gave me a boost of energy in the morning.

Most of the walk was along a busy street… until the turnoff just beyond the railroad tracks. Then I had to cut across open ground. I got spooked by sudden noises and shadows moving about. Each night, I'd slip on my dark track pants and hoodie so I wouldn't stand out.

I looked like a burglar.

After three miles of singing "Piano Man" by my all-time favorite singer, tiny raindrops began to dampen my cheeks.

"Shoot," I said, kicking a small rock as I hurried up the wet sidewalk.

At least we were having a mild October and the cold weather hadn't kicked in yet. While my goal was to get an apartment, I'd been giving serious thought to buying a car first. It all depended on whether or not I could find an apartment near a bus route. I didn't think I'd be able to continue walking once the temperature decided to drop.

The steady rain beat a staccato rhythm on the parked cars, and an SUV swerved so close to the curb that a wave of water splashed over me.

"Thank you!" I yelled with a laugh, waving my drenched arm as the car sped away.

Probably a decent guy trying to rush to the store to grab dinner for his wife and kids. I held my elbows tightly as a memory jostled loose in my head—one I'd just as soon not think about.

Every so often, I glanced over my shoulder at a strange clicking sound coming from behind me. Each time I stopped and turned around, I was confronted by a long stretch of shadows and concrete, but no boogeyman.

"*I'm hearing things, I'm hearing things*," I sang to myself—the sort of thing you do when you're alone and on the brink of running home like a frightened child. The streets were brightly lit and passing cars provided me with a sense of security, at least until I reached the wooded area.

"This is not my life," I said to my wet shoes. "I should be like all the other women my age—going to happy hour with friends and flirting with attractive men. Instead, I like to read and play Scrabble. Then again, I've never been successful with flirting. Just ask the last guy. He ended up wearing condiments on his shirt after standing beside me in the burger joint. I tried talking to him and wound up slinging a half-opened packet of ketchup on his white shirt. He actually walked off without saying another word! That was so mortifying. Maybe I'd have better luck meeting someone on the Internet."

I chuckled nervously and peered over my shoulder. A shadow snaked behind a building and my heart palpitated.

No one was there, but I quickened my step.

I pulled out my phone and sent Lexi a text message. She had recently purchased her first cell phone and so we kept in touch more often. She hadn't figured out all the acronyms, and I'd sometimes make up one just to drive her crazy.

When I finally reached the turnoff that led to my trailer, I was in a full sprint. My purse slapped against my back and my shoes slipped twice in the mud. A gravel road led through the park, but it was too far ahead and not worth the extra walk.

Panting for breath, I reached the door and scraped the mud off my shoes on a large cinder block. Sometimes I wondered how all three of us had lived in that thing. My sister had shared the bed with Grandma, and I'd snuggled up on the built-in sofa.

I stood on the step and tugged off my sopping-wet sneakers. When I unlocked the door and went inside, my nose wrinkled. I must have burned a million scented candles in there, but it's like the ghost of Grandma Frost was permanently fragranced within. She had a thing about using mothballs and it took five months after she died to get that funk out of there. I'd never been able to expunge of the smell of cigarettes. I think the tar had seared into the walls.

"Hey, little guys," I said cheerfully, tapping my finger on the round fishbowl sitting on the counter straight ahead.

Hermie and Salvador paddled in sprite little motions, alert and joyful that it was feeding time. I dropped a few pellets of food in the water and moved toward the back of the trailer.

Just to the left of the kitchenette was a hallway that led to the bathroom on the right, closet to the left, and the bedroom straight ahead. I peeled out of my shirt and pants and hung them on a towel rack in my tiny bathroom, which I'd painted a cheery color. I think the name of the paint was called Songbird Yellow. Someday I hoped to have my own garden tub where I could slip beneath a layer of bubbles and read by candlelight. But for now, I made the best of a home that was the length of a few cartwheels.

My cell phone rang and I answered the familiar pop melody. "Rose, I wondered when you'd finally get around to calling me."

"Hey, sis! You surviving out there?"

I tugged off my wet socks and tossed them by the door. "Couldn't be better. How about you? Is the weather hot?"

"You wouldn't believe it! Oh my God, it's like the freaking desert or something!"

"It *is* the desert, Rose."

"You're so literal, April. I'm just teasing. Are you still mad at me for taking off so fast? By the way, I'm coming down for Christmas.

I talked Shane into it and he said it's cool. We'll just need a place to stay. I um... *you know.*"

I knew.

Our trailer park had been featured on the local news more than once for drug busts. There were a few respectable people living there, but it always attracted the ones with questionable character. One time, an elderly gentleman had wandered down the road as naked as a jaybird and bleeding from his head. Grandma had pushed us inside the trailer and called the cops. Rose had never brought Shane over to visit. They always met up somewhere and I couldn't say a thing about it because I was guilty of doing the same. People judge.

"Are you doing okay, Rose? Do you need money?"

"Big news! We're getting married next month."

"Are you sure? It's so soon. Why don't you have a long engagement and enjoy each other before you take the plunge?"

Disappointment seeped in my heart and I hated my initial reaction to her good news; Rose had to live her own life. At least they were getting serious about each other and maybe this would be good for her. Rose had been a capricious child and I used to worry that she'd never settle down. I'd made a silent bet with myself that she'd return in five months and it would be the two of us again. Maybe a tiny part of me was jealous that she'd found someone else to share her life with. Rose had never had to take on the responsibilities I'd been forced to shoulder as the older child, and what a blessing that was for her.

I sat down, dressed in just my underwear, twirling a deck of cards in a circle. "Let me know if you need anything, Rose. I'm really happy for you. I've just had a long day, so I didn't mean for it to come out that way. Shane's a good catch and you know I'm always here if you need anything."

"Aces," she said with a giggle. "Gift cards are fab, but we're not doing the big wedding gig. Shane wants to drive to Vegas and have one of those drive-through weddings. Gotta run. We're heading out to the honky-tonk tonight. What kind of mess is that? I thought I'd left Redneckville and all they do out here is two-step." She giggled again and I knew Shane was in the room with her.

"You guys have fun and stay out of trouble! I love you, Rose."

"I'll have fun for the both of us, April. As *usual*."

I set the phone down and sighed thoughtfully as I lifted a heavy pot of water from the floor. Stupid rain. Water leaked in through a skylight and some dents on the roof and I had no clue how to fix them. The trailer was pretty old and my grandma had mentioned a tree branch falling on it years ago during a storm. She had done some work on it since then, but hadn't seemed concerned with a little water damage.

I was lingering in front of the sink in my cherry-red bra and panties, dumping out a pot of water, when a knock at the door startled me. The thick brown curtains were closed, so I stood still and waited another second. Nobody ever came over unannounced, and I wasn't on speaking terms with my loopy neighbors. The insistent knock sounded again.

"Is there an April Frost in there related to Ginny Frost? I have business matters to discuss with you of an important nature."

"Can you come back in the daytime?"

"I came by this afternoon and again around seven. I can tell you right now that sunshine doesn't make me any prettier to look at. Your grandma owes me some money. I don't have time to figure out what your schedule is, and my time is *your* money."

Oh, crap. "Um, just a minute."

I grabbed a white sweatshirt and pulled it over my head. The only pants I could find were yesterday's jeans, so I yanked those on and answered the door barefoot.

A man wearing a hat looked up at me with steel eyes—one boot in the mud and the other on a step.

"You can call me Maddox," he said in a burly, Southern drawl.

Maddox looked to be a seasoned man in his late forties. He wore a scruffy beard that was silver and brown. His wavy hair rested on the tips of his shoulders, and his faded brown boots matched the color of his hat. It wasn't a traditional cowboy hat, but more like what the guys in the Australian outback wore. Maddox looked like he'd stepped out of a time machine.

"Can I help you?" I said through the crack in the door.

"I'm going to cut to the chase. Ginny Frost owed me fifty grand and I know you're her granddaughter. Open up and let's have a friendly chat about business. I won't take but five minutes of your time."

I drifted away from the door and stood by the sink. Maddox ducked his head and moved inside, shaking water off his hat.

"You mind if I sit?" he asked, motioning toward the sofa on his immediate right. I shrugged and he sat down with his knees apart and forearms resting on them, leaving the door open. "Ginny was pretty good about settling her small loans. I know she died a ways back, and let's just say I have a soft spot for women and decided to give you a grieving period." Maddox stared at the hat in his hands. "One thing I've got is time. But time's up and there's no clean slate with my loans due to death. I'm not insured like the bank. Her debt rolled over to the next in line and that's you."

"Fifty? I can't pay you that much money. I don't even have enough to buy a car."

He obscured his mouth with his hat and glanced around the trailer with a contemplative look in his eyes. *Oh please, let this guy have a heart.*

"Tell you what. I'll give you a week to figure it out, then I'll come back for a visit and see what's what. You got something you can liquidate? You better do it."

"Why did she borrow that much?"

"I don't ask what people do with my money. I don't care. I baby-step them into my services to see how good they are about paying back the interest. You seem like a smart girl; you don't know what she would have needed that much money for?"

God. I did. To help put me through school. Grandma had helped pay for college, but I'd assumed she had money stuffed in a savings account or it was coming from her paychecks. Rose had saved up for her VW by working summer and evening jobs, and I shared a car with Grandma. The trailer had been paid off for eons, so I couldn't think of another explanation.

I never thought it was possible to hate someone for loving me so much.

He scratched his beard, staring at a short stack of paperbacks on the counter. "You got a boyfriend? To help you out, I mean."

"I think you need to go."

"I'm a reasonable man," he said in a smooth voice, rising to his feet. "You'll see that in no time. Charmed to meet you, April Frost." He opened the door and peered over his shoulder. "Stay dry."

Early the next morning, I had a banana for breakfast and decided to walk to the local drugstore to shop around before my afternoon shift began. Since morning sales were slow, we usually gave those hours to the part-time girls. That meant I could sleep in, but today my thoughts were in a scramble and I needed to take a walk and clear my head.

I slipped on a pair of black biker boots to keep my feet dry. Perish the thought I was making a fashion statement when I put on a pair of leggings and an oversized black shirt. In the summertime, I loved wearing Capri pants and fashionable sandals. But with the cold weather fast approaching, I began to dip into the bottom drawers and pull out some of my casual-crazy wear for gloomy weather.

An indie group played on my earbuds and I walked into Walgreens, humming along and tracking in a few streaks of mud behind me.

"Can I help you?" I heard a voice say over my music.

A middle-aged woman with a prominent mole on the side of her nose and heavy glasses stared at me impatiently. The small tag on her blue shirt displayed the name Patsy.

"Where's your perfume?" As if I didn't already know.

She pushed her glasses up her nose and stole a glimpse of my boots. "This way."

Sometimes they put the perfume samplers on display, but this was not one of those days. The boxes were sealed in plastic and locked behind the glass case. It was ludicrous to think someone would come into a store and steal a bunch of perfume when they had expensive makeup at their fingertips. So I wandered the store and scoured the clearance aisle for makeup, sifting through green eyeliner and whore-red lipstick. I'd learned to make things stretch; it's something my grandma had taught me. It's why I'd adopted the smoky liner look—that stuff went a long way and didn't require eye shadow. Rose had also showed me a neat little trick of using a Q-tip to get all the lipstick from beneath the barrel. We had become quite resourceful in learning how to save money when it came to expensive makeup.

I lied whenever someone asked how I was doing. People don't want to hear the truth. Lexi had given me a slight salary increase, but it wasn't enough to get me where I needed to be. One of Austin's brothers was helping her manage the business and analyzing her profit margin, so she'd told me to hang tight until she got a firm grip on the finances. Lexi'd really had a lot dumped on her at once and had taken it like a champ. There's a huge learning curve with operating a business, but she stayed positive, and to be honest, Charlie chose the right person. Lexi had been working there for years and knew what it took to keep things running. So I'd been putting aside all my money and living off the necessities. Things like junk food, movies, and books were temporarily cut out of my budget.

"April Showers," a bristly voice said.

Loud enough that I heard him over my music. I popped out one of my earbuds, knowing who it was before I looked up at his handsome face.

"You really need to stop calling me that," I said, quirking my mouth.

"When I'm near you, I feel nothing but showers of love, babe." Trevor offered a staggering smile and lifted me off the ground, embracing me in a tight hug. "Missed you."

"I missed you so much, Trevor. When did you get back in town?" I grunted as he squeezed so tight my lungs constricted.

"Last night. Should have known I'd find you perusing the makeup aisles or at the bookstore. Any good romances I should know about?"

I chuckled when he set me down. "Didn't you get my last e-mail?"

Trevor's razor-cut brown hair had an edgy style with dark

highlights. He liked combing his hair in different directions across his forehead. Trevor was the most fashion-forward guy I'd ever met—always in designer jeans and a button-up shirt. Today he sported a pair of black leather oxfords with his dark denims. A girl standing near the makeup counter ogled him; little did she know my best friend would be more interested in her boyfriend who was busy sniffing a bottle of body lotion. Trevor looked like an incognito celebrity with his sweet face and sexy lips. He had a commanding presence—like he was somebody important but didn't want people to know.

He was mysterious, and that's what I loved about him.

It's how we met. While riding down an escalator in the mall, I'd watched him going up in the opposite direction and had one of my *mantastic* episodes. I'd turned around to gawk at him, hadn't noticed the landing coming up, and had fallen flat on my back.

Little had I known that Trevor was a romance novel hero sprung to life. He'd performed a one-armed vault to the other side of the escalators and run down to make sure I was okay. I still remember the smirk on his face when he cradled my head and asked if I'd fallen head over heels for him.

He had walked me to a nearby bookstore and bought me a latte. After a long conversation, we found out we had a lot in common, including our love for reading. I'd always been a huge fan of romance novels, whether contemporary, paranormal, or something risqué. Trevor offered me a unique chance to hear a man's perspective on books, and I got him reading a bunch he'd never heard of. In return, he turned me on to indie music.

Trevor loved playing the acoustic guitar and had an appreciation for undiscovered talent. He wasn't in a band; singing and playing guitar was just something he did when we were lounging around with nothing to do. It was only later that I found out Trevor was gay—I hadn't had a clue until he brought up his boyfriend in conversation. I didn't make a big deal about it and neither did he.

"I've got news," he announced, taking my hand in his. "Do you need something in here or can I take you out for brunch?"

"You don't have to buy me anything. I had a banana for breakfast."

"I'm paying."

"I'm not hungry. Maybe we can…" I glanced around, trying to come up with an alternative.

He gripped my chin and looked down at me. "What's wrong? Do you need some money?"

"Rose is getting married."

"No fucking way." He tugged my arm and hauled me toward the door. "That's it. We're talking."

Instead of brunch, we sat inside his Honda hatchback and played catch-up. Trevor was shocked to learn about Rose's upcoming nuptials and he gave them a year. I lightly punched him in the arm for being pessimistic and he shook his head, saying all she wanted in Shane was a way out and that kind of relationship didn't stand a chance.

"Are you living alone in that shithole trailer park in the hood?" he asked. "Please tell me you have a boyfriend staying with you."

I shook my head.

"Jesus, why didn't you call me?"

"What's your big news?"

He shifted in his seat. "I'm moving in with you."

My eyes widened. "What?"

"My news is I broke up with James and decided to come home because I've never seen more repressed people in my life than in that tiny tinker town in the middle of bumfuck—"

"Seriously? What happened between you two? I thought it was going so well."

He shrugged and adjusted the vents. "That's why I haven't e-mailed in a couple of weeks. I was living in my car for two days before I decided to come back home. It just wasn't right. Now I'm here with no job, no place to live, and I have to start from square effing one."

"What about Lucy?" She was mutual friend we'd met at a party years ago who thought she could convert Trevor into a straight man with her magical vagina.

"No good. Long story short, her boyfriend thinks I'm pretending to be gay to get in her panties."

"She wishes," I muttered.

"I have to leave for a couple of days," he said, picking at the steering wheel with his finger. "I zipped out of there in a hurry, but now I regret the hell out of it because I left some personal shit there I need to get back—like my Gibson, all my plants, and my model airplanes."

Trevor was a curious guy. He played guitar, partied with the best of them, but in his downtime, he liked to unwind by flipping on a bright desk lamp and assembling model airplanes that came in a billion pieces. He once told me a hobby like that taught a man control and patience, and that's something he needed in his life.

"Will he give them back to you?"

Trevor sighed and grunted all at once, throwing his head back and staring at the roof. "James isn't a total jerk. I just didn't want to deal with seeing him again." He rolled his head in my direction and patted my leg. "You mind if I stay with you? Say no and I'm parking my car by the barbecue grill and setting up camp. Why don't you sell it and move to a safe apartment complex?"

"No one in their right mind would buy that old thing," I said with a laugh. "I wouldn't get anything for it and besides, it's paid for in full and I'm actually saving money by living there. Apartments are expensive these days with all those deposits."

"Seriously, babe, that's a scary fucking trailer park. And the guy with the gnome collection who lives down the road?"

"Mr. Potter?"

"He waters his lawn naked. That man needs to be introduced to a razor and a pair of pants. It's fucking creepy. If you say he's a nice guy, then I'm throwing your books in the river."

I frowned and gazed sullenly out the window.

"What did I say wrong?"

I watched a few stray sprinkles catch on the glass. "Last week it rained so hard that it leaked in the trailer when I was sleeping. Water got all over my favorite books that were stacked in the corner of my bedroom."

"Oh, shit no."

"Ruined about thirty of my favorites. Some of them I salvaged, but the rest wound up with wrinkled paper and warped covers. I had another stack in the living room, so it wasn't a total loss."

"E-readers, babe."

I rolled my eyes. "Books aren't a big priority at the moment."

"*Damn.*"

"What?"

Trevor leaned across me, so close to my face that I could smell his hair.

"It's like Jensen Ackles had a baby with a professional fighter and made *him*. Only he doesn't have Jensen's pouty mouth… more like Fassbender. Add a splash of Jason Statham's kickass attitude…"

"Who?"

Trevor grabbed my chin and turned my head to the right. "You need to watch more TV. I swear, sometimes I wonder if you even know who the president is these days. Why the hell did I ever leave Austin? Look at that fine specimen of a man. Tall, tan, and a little rough-looking in the face, but I'd forgive him. *And* a Triumph motorcycle; that's fucking hot."

The second I saw the man Trevor was salivating over step onto the curb and adjust his mirrored shades, it triggered a memory. As did his spectacular body beneath his tight, long-sleeved shirt—nary an inch of skin showing. Not to mention his chiseled face that had a light dusting of whiskers around the chin—a face I'd thought I'd never see again. Only now, fully dressed, he gave off more of a paramilitary vibe. Maybe I'd forgotten the scary aspects about him, but his looks still lingered in my mind all these months later.

"I think I know him," I said under my breath.

Four months ago, I gave Lexi a ride home. Reno Cole, Austin's brother, was outside throwing horseshoes in the yard without a shirt on. A thin sheen of sweat covered his broad torso, which was the only thing I noticed since he was wearing sunglasses and a baseball hat. I had a "stupid" attack and almost tripped in front of him. I'd never felt more intimidated by a man's presence in my life. I felt cowardly and my mouth refused to work, and when it finally did, I mentioned something about the heat like I was a walking weathergirl. Reno's fit body spanned just over six feet, but his expression was tight and menacing. I shamelessly fled the scene, but the tire on my car wedged into a pothole. He stalked over as if he might rip my car door off and pummel me for messing up their driveway.

But he didn't. He pushed the car free and I never saw him again.

Fingers snapped in front of my face and Trevor gave me a killer smile. "Nice to see you still have a pulse. I was beginning to think your libido took a permanent vacation. April, my mission this year is to find your Mr. Right."

Trevor was kidding, of course. He'd always been overprotective and never let a stranger approach me without giving him the third degree. He liked the *idea* of me finding a man more than the reality.

"I hope you find a place soon, Trev, but you can stay with me as long as you need to."

"At least you'll have someone to talk to besides those damn critters you keep taking in. You still got the squirrel?"

Picking at my blue nail, I shook my head. "Skittles didn't make it."

"Rabies?"

I slapped his arm and we belted out a few laughs.

Over the years, I'd gained a reputation for rescuing injured animals. Some I found along the road, while others wandered in from the woods. They were amazing creatures—like the garter snake my grandma had attempted to murder with a broom. It was a good feeling to help something wild and then set it free. As much love as I had for them, I learned you couldn't hold on to something with a wild heart. They live on instinct and they'll never love you back.

Trevor held my hand up to his mouth and kissed it. "I'll be gone a day or two—tops. And then we're roomies."

"My trailer won't fit all your stuff."

"Stuff?" he scoffed. "I won't have much to move because none of the furniture was mine except the couch, and he can keep it. I don't want anything his ass was on."

"The very ass you talked about endlessly when you first met?"

"The very fucking one."

CHAPTER 3

Later that evening, after a long walk home from work, I freshened up with a quick shower and went to bed in my bra and panties. I only ran the air conditioner for an hour or two and usually shut it off before bedtime. Despite the humidity, the days were beginning to get cooler. Thank God.

Trevor was right. The trailer park *was* creepy. It's something I tried not to think about, but late at night when I heard rustling noises outside, it made me curl up and pull the sheets over my head. I never thought about stuff like that when Rose lived at home. Things had quieted down since the drug raid last year that took out some big dealer. Now there wasn't as much traffic at all hours of the night, not to mention loud parties.

The third time I heard a high-pitched noise outside, I sat up with adrenaline pumping through my veins. The intensity of my heartbeat couldn't be matched as I tiptoed to the front door and grabbed a long knife from the kitchen drawer. I drew the curtain back and peered outside.

The orange light from the lamppost illuminated the area around the barbecue grill and I spotted a shadow moving.

"Oh, no," I whined. The shadow wasn't a man-eating alien but a wounded animal. A stray dog limped a few steps before lying down on the muddy gravel.

I threw on a silk robe and slippers, careful not to make any sudden movements as I stepped outside. I crouched down and placed my fingertips on the ground, avoiding direct eye contact.

"Hi there. Did someone hurt you?"

I shuffled forward and he lifted his head, his snout wrinkling as he bared his sharp canines. As soon as I spoke in a calming voice, his savage expression vanished. If it's one thing I knew about, it was how to placate an agitated animal. Years of practice.

"I'm not going to hurt you, sweetie. Can I just see? Bet I can help, and I have some leftovers inside you might like." I kept my voice confident and soothing, knowing animals responded to tone and body language.

He was an intimidating creature. His breed resembled a Husky, but fierce, like what I imagined a wolf might look like. From what I could tell, his thick coat looked earthy brown and his face had all kinds of dark markings on it. It was an unusual pattern for a dog, but boy, was he a looker. He was also well fed, which led me to believe someone cared for him and he was domesticated.

"Come inside?" I clicked my tongue three times.

He wasn't going to be a submissive fella, so I slowly backed up and walked inside my brightly lit trailer. It looked welcoming from the outside, and I'm sure he could smell the cheeseburgers I'd cooked up earlier.

"Come on, tough boy."

My grandma used to say I was crazy for letting wild animals in the trailer.

Bat crazy.

She'd made me keep them outside, which is why some of them had died. I'd been a fearless child who had a penchant for helping injured animals. Every wild thing deserves tenderness even if it doesn't want it. The thing is, I'd always been good about reading animals. My dad used to say I was Doctor Dolittle in a past life—that some people were born with more compassion for all of God's creatures. I felt more connected to animals than I did to people because I understood their basic emotions. I'd once saved a jackrabbit from a feral cat with a voracious appetite, but because I was forced to keep it outside, a red-tailed hawk had dined on him for breakfast the next morning. That had upset me, even though I couldn't blame the hawk for having survival instincts.

I kicked off my slippers and left the door ajar, breaking off a few pieces of meat and placing them near the door. Either he'd come in or he wouldn't. The choice was his.

Ten minutes later, a noise startled me. I turned my paperback facedown on the tiny kitchen table to the right of the sink. A steady growl rumbled in the quiet room. Not a menacing one, just the kind that told me he was hurt and too stubborn to admit it. Coming inside the trailer proved he wasn't aggressive; animals acted violently out of fear, and feral ones stayed away from humans. If he walked up those steps on his own, he had a fearless heart. He wouldn't be the first dog I had let inside the house. Trevor once suggested that I get a job working in a zoo.

I laughed and told him I already worked in one.

The dog's toenails clicked on the floor and I got an eyeful of his enormous size. I briefly entertained the thought of locking myself in the bathroom, but decided it wouldn't be in my best interest to show fear and run. After polishing off every morsel on the floor, he lifted his nose and sniffed in my direction, his tail wagging lightly. I kept my eyes glued to the table so he wouldn't perceive me as a threat.

"Change your mind?" I asked softly. "*Good* boy."

His wet nose glided across my left arm and I shivered. I sat motionless, allowing him to check me out even though a small voice in my head was whispering, *You're a certifiable idiot. You just let the Big Bad Wolf in, whetted his appetite with hamburger meat, and now you're going to become the main course.*

The poor thing limped in a circle and collapsed on his right side. He looked barely conscious, panting the way an animal does when it's in pain. I circled around him and locked the door.

"Oh, baby. What happened?"

I knelt down and ran my long fingers through his silky fur. His face relaxed at my touch and while I couldn't see any blood, his front leg was curled in a peculiar position. When I gently lifted his heavy paw and peered underneath, I saw why.

Instinctively, I began humming a made-up melody to keep him calm. Lodged deep in his upper leg was a screwdriver. It made me steaming mad to imagine that someone could have impaled him intentionally; we had sickos in the area notorious for animal cruelty. The brown handle protruded from the inside of his leg and the spike angled toward the back. I bent over to make sure it hadn't gone into his chest cavity, but it looked clear. His dense fur made a close examination difficult. I couldn't call animal control because they would only put him down.

My hands trembled and I took a deep breath. I had to pull it out, and that would snap him out of his placid state of semiconsciousness, and he'd be looking for someone to bite.

"How did this happen?"

He refused to answer the question.

I slipped out of my robe and decided the best thing to do was cover his head so he wouldn't see me when I pulled it out.

Kneeling before him in my bra and panties, I draped my silky robe across his back, sliding it over his face until it obscured his view. I wrapped my fingers around the handle, ready to pull it out with lightning speed. At least I had medical insurance, even though the deductible was outrageous.

"Here we go," I whispered. Then I did a mental countdown. *One... two... three!*

In a clean motion, I yanked the handle and pulled the screwdriver free.

He yelped and growled all at once. The wolf flipped onto his feet and the robe fell away, revealing one pissed-off animal. I scrambled backward, holding the bloody screwdriver in self-defense.

He limped forward, tracking blood with each step as his brown eyes locked on mine like a target.

This was it. I was going to be one of those sad-o'clock news stories about a lonely woman found mauled to death in her bra and panties. Then they'd go to commercial and talk about squeezably soft toilet paper.

"I'm so sorry," I said in a shaky voice, lying on my back as he reached my legs and then my hips. "You had a bad thing happen, and I'm... Please don't hurt me."

In that moment, I was either going to be ripped to shreds by an incensed wolf, or I was going to kill an animal to save my life—something I'd never done.

My fingers gripped the handle tightly and I tensed, preparing for the inevitable attack.

Tension mounted.

I couldn't breathe and kept thinking about my sister.

The wolf lurched forward and fell beside me, resting his chin on my left arm. After two short wags of his tail, his tongue stretched out and licked the bottom of my jaw. I sighed dramatically and stared at the ceiling in relief.

"Just another exciting night in the life of April Frost," I said, laughing with tears hovering at the corners of my eyes.

That was the night a fierce and beautiful creature walked into my life and changed it forever.

The next morning, I sleepily crawled out of bed and brushed my teeth. I made a mental note to pick up toothpaste on my next trip to the store since I had all but sat on the tube to get a smidge on my brush. My wild encounter the previous evening had slipped my mind and I went about my morning routine. When I suddenly remembered, I burst into the hall and found the wolf asleep in my kitchen.

Just as I'd left him. Lying on top of my grandma's blue blanket, a bandage wrapped around his wound, which I'd carefully cleaned before going to bed. He wasn't showing any signs of sickness and seemed to be almost smiling in his sleep.

I set a pan on the stove and heated up a few slices of sausage. If he planned to become a regular tenant, then I needed to pick up dog food from the grocery store.

He still had his eyes closed when I sat down to eat. What a gorgeous animal. His large, heavy paws were crossed in front of him, giving off a regal aura. I'd never seen such an unusual pattern as the dark mask that covered his face. He must have been a mixed breed, because wolves didn't live in Austin. I'd heard of coyote sightings, but they were smaller and more skittish of people.

"Are you hungry? I'll share what I have with you."

His brown eye popped open as if he'd been listening all along. The nose-twitching led me to believe he was famished, despite his indifferent demeanor. But when I held out my sausage, he made no attempt to lunge and gobble it up.

Peculiar.

Lexi sent a message on my phone asking me to hurry my ass up—in those exact words. Which meant I'd overslept.

"Shoot," I grumbled, scratching my wolf behind his ear. My life was just getting too weird.

"April, can I see you for a second?" Lexi tugged the hem of my orange work shirt and dragged me away from a customer. I knocked over a counter display of Pop Rocks, but we both ignored it.

"What's up?" I leaned against the vending machine and her eyes pretty much scraped me from head to toe. I tried to pretend I had no idea what she was about to say.

But I did.

"You *cannot* walk around the store looking like you just crawled out of a Vietnam War movie. Don't you have a change of shoes? It looks like you've been to boot camp and then ran through a jungle."

"I'm sorry. I'll rinse them in the sink again," I said, staring at my white sneakers.

Which were now my brown sneakers.

"Look, I have a pair of sandals in my car you can borrow. Austin's funny like that. He helped me pick out a new car and lately he's been obsessed with stocking it for every kind of emergency imaginable. Blankets, clothes, bandages, flares, and even food," she said with a roll of her eyes. "So if an asteroid wipes out the planet, I'm good to go because I have a bag of jerky and peroxide."

"I think I saw your boyfriend's brother yesterday," I said, changing the subject.

"Who, Denver?"

"No. The guy with the motorcycle."

A smile wound up her face and Lexi flipped her long hair behind her shoulder. "Ah, you mean Mr. Mysterious. Where did you run into Reno?"

"Oh, we didn't speak. He was walking outside a store."

"Did he talk to you?"

What she really wanted to know was if I went flying over a newspaper stand or knocked an old lady down.

"No, I was in the car."

Lexi folded her arms. "What car? You don't have one."

"Trevor's. He's a close friend of mine. He's been in the store a few times. You complimented his belt and he liked that. Nobody ever notices stuff like belts and it was one of his favorites."

"Yeah... I remember now. The belt is probably the first thing I notice on a guy, kind of a habit. He was pretty cool—sexy from what I recall, but polite. You two, uh..." She pursed her lips and her eyes slid down.

"Jeez, Lexi. Can't I just have a male friend and it not be a thing?" I peeled off my shoes and tossed them to the side. "You better grab those sandals for me; I don't want to keep our customers waiting."

Her smile waned. "Charlie made a good choice hiring you, April. Thanks for not bailing on me. I don't know what I'd do without you."

I sat on the bench, watching Lexi cut through the store.

When Charlie died, he'd left her a mess of legal documents to sort through. Lexi had e-mailed me some of the files since she wasn't sure what she was looking at. I'd found the inventory records as well as the vendors he worked with. Over the past few nights—perhaps out of boredom—I'd been examining those files a little closer. There were odd withdrawals in the account I couldn't find any explanation for. Maybe it was for charity, but it was always the same amount every time. Lexi had been given access to his house to pick up a set of keys and anything else she needed. Charlie had left a comment in his will that everything in the office was hers for the taking. She'd found a ledger, files, and a few extra flash drives I'd copied to my computer. It felt good to know she trusted me—partly because of my education, but mostly because Charlie had always touted that I was going to make waves someday with my skills.

He was the closest I'd had to a father figure in a long time. I'd enjoyed our afternoon conversations in the shop before he started working more from home. Charlie had a great laugh and loved to talk about history. My real dad was the most amazing man I'd ever known, but he'd died in a car accident when I was fifteen.

"I think that's a sexy look; barefoot really works for you."

I glanced up at Denver. He smiled at my feet and nibbled on his bottom lip. My first reaction was to pull my legs under the bench since I hadn't painted my toenails that week and the blue polish was chipping.

I frowned when I noticed his cupped hand holding a colorful assortment of sour candy.

"Where are your shoes?" he asked.

I tipped my head toward the corner of the room and he noticed the dirty pile.

"So you walk to work. No car?"

"The transmission died. At least, that's what the mechanic told me. I don't know anything about cars except how to turn them on."

"Hmm," he pondered, popping a green candy into his mouth with a sly smile. "I'd say knowing how to turn something on is pretty important."

Dang, I was *staring*. I lowered my eyes to his flat sneakers and noticed his legs. He had on a pair of knee-length cargo shorts and jeez, what calves! Denver must have spent time outside because he had a warm tan and strong legs. His frame was average, but he filled out just right.

"Are you here to save the day again?"

"I might," he contemplated, nibbling another piece of candy and staring at my legs.

"Denny! Lexi said I could have a bag of candy, but I can't reach the big round ones," a blond-haired girl whined, tugging at his shirt.

"No hard candy, Peanut," he said in a firm voice. "What did I tell you about that?"

"But it doesn't hurt." She pointed at her new missing tooth.

Denver rubbed a worried look off his face.

I'd met Maizy a couple of times; she was Lexi's six-year-old little sister with a candy obsession. She was charming and sweet, so I couldn't help but sneak a piece to her now and again. Maizy appeared so innocent compared to some of the kids who wandered in our store. She sometimes played by herself in a corner while her mom talked to Lexi, and a few times she'd brought in a wand. It seemed a little immature for her age, but I found it endearing. It's a sad day when children realize magic doesn't exist and they have to grow up.

"Hi, Miss April."

"Hi, sugar. You're getting so tall," I said with a dramatic gasp. "You grow faster than a wildflower!"

She laughed and ran back into the shop.

"You're good with kids," he said, complimenting me.

"Is she okay?"

Denver stuffed his free hand in one of his front pockets. "She banged her tooth hard enough they had to pull it. Good thing it was a baby tooth, but the dentist isn't sure if it's caused any damage for when her real tooth grows in."

I smiled softly. "She seems to like you."

He shrugged and turned his head to the side. "I look after her. Kids should be protected from the lowlifes in this world. Her dad's not around, and Austin's not in a position where he can devote that kind of time."

"That's sweet of you to do. I'm sure Lexi's mom appreciates a little help."

Denver inhaled sharply and the conversation shifted gears. "One of my brothers is missing. I dropped by to see if Lexi would watch Maizy for about an hour while I look for him. I had to take her to the dentist, but I don't want to drive her home and have to come all the way back into town. I know you've met the twins, have you ever met Reno?"

I chewed my lip. "Guy with the short brown hair who wears sunglasses all the time? Muscular arms and…"

Then I blushed and looked down so fast that my bangs covered my face. My inner monologue started up again. *Yeah, tell him just how hot his brother is. Then he might go for you because that's what every guy wants to hear.*

Denver lifted his cupped hand to his mouth and slid all the candy in, talking with a mouthful. He wiped his hand across his T-shirt. "That's probably him. He's not a man who falls out of touch, and we're a tight family who keeps tabs on one another. Seen him?"

"He was at Walgreens yesterday on his bike. Maybe he was at a party or left his phone off the hook. Sometimes I turn mine off when I just want to sleep in."

Denver sniffed out a laugh. "We all live together and his bed is made up so tight you could crack an egg on it."

"You all live in the same house?" Lexi had talked about Austin's brothers, but I'd assumed only one or two lived there, not the entire family.

He slowly ran a hand through his unkempt hair. "Yep. Don't you live with anyone?"

"My fish."

"Ah, is that so? Well, I hope he's a *fintastic* roommate."

"Here, April," Lexi said, tossing me a pair of sandals. "They might be too big for your feet, but that'll get you through the day. Did you walk all the way up here? I thought you took the bus?"

"I just stepped in some mud is all."

Maizy ambled in, chewing on a wad of red gum.

"Maze, do you feel like treasure hunting today?" Lexi asked.

Maizy ignored her and Denver shot Lexi a private glare. "You need to give that shit up," he said with a pop of his brow.

Lexi sighed and began tapping her fingernails against the doorjamb.

"Did Reno say anything to you?" Denver continued.

"No. I just saw him park his bike and go into the store."

"*The fuck?*" Denver exclaimed in frustration, throwing up his arms. Lexi covered her little sister's ear and had one of those pissed-off smiles that told me she'd tried a dozen times to get him to curb his language around Maizy. "He wants tabs on every single one of *us*, but he thinks he can just cut loose and..." Denver thinned his lips and made a sharp noise with them that made Maizy giggle.

Lexi didn't seem as worried about Reno as Denver was.

"I'll keep an eye out for him," I promised.

Denver stared privately at Lexi. "Did you invite her?"

"Oh!" she exclaimed. "We're having a house party on Friday. It took some time to settle in, but we wanted to have a big barbecue and throw on some music. You *have* to come. I know you don't normally do these, but you've been such a big help to me these past few months, April. If we're going to be running this shop together, then I think we need to hang out. What do you say?"

"Um, I don't know." I hesitated. I really wanted to go more than anything, but the transportation conundrum was a real party killer. "Where?"

She fed me the location and I knew I couldn't go. Buses didn't run out there and no way could I walk that far. Trevor might not be back by then and who knew if he'd want to go?

"I think I have something planned, but I'll let you know."

"I smell bullshit," Denver sang in a low voice. "If you don't have a ride, I'll come get you, but you're coming," he said, wagging a finger at me. "Let me know if you see Reno. He's always forgetting his damn phone, but it's just not like him to vanish."

"Sure thing."

CHAPTER 4

AFTER A LONG WORKDAY, THE evening crowd died down and I prepared to close the store. Lexi had gone home early to do some research on coffee shops, and I knew why. She'd always dreamed about buying the empty space next door and knocking out the wall to join two shops. That was a lot to take on, but the potential was there. The only downside was the noisy kids in the candy store would disturb the adults next door who were trying to read and enjoy their espresso.

One alternative would be to change the coffee shop idea into a pastry shop. Moms could relax with a croissant while their kids scoped out the candy next door. Lexi liked that idea and wanted to talk to Austin about it. She was a crazy-good baker, and if she were involved in baking the sweets, then we'd be a surefire hit. After eating eleven of her homemade peanut butter cookies with macadamia nuts, I could testify on her behalf in a court of cookie law. I didn't know how she'd swing that kind of money to start up a separate company, but she'd mentioned a couple of Austin's brothers might be able to help out for free.

God, no.

I could only *imagine* that tattooed guy scaring the kids. Then again, his twin might actually draw in some of the women because every mother on a bad day wants to feel like she's still got it going on, and Ben sure liked to let women know how sweet their asses were.

"Are you open?"

A nice-looking Hispanic man poked his head through the front door and I realized I had forgotten to flip the sign.

"I'm about to lock up. Is there something I can help you find real quick?"

He slipped in through the crack and the bell jingled. "Nice place."

"Thanks." I looked him over, trying not to be judgmental about the fact he was wearing saggy pants and I could see his red underwear. I had serious objections to men who showed off their drawers in public.

He scoped out the room. "I'm looking for something ah... vanilla."

"We have taffy and wafers over here," I suggested, leading him to an aisle on the right. I thought about offering the almond bark since a local lady worked with us to sell her candy, but I didn't think that's what he was looking for.

"That all you got in here that's vanilla?" he said, coming up behind me.

I spun around with a wafer in one hand and taffy in the other. "I'm sorry, but it is. We don't get that request too often. We do carry products that have vanilla flavoring in them, but they're diluted with other ingredients so it's not as strong. Is this for a special occasion? I might be able to look in our catalog and order it."

Up close, I noticed a teardrop tattoo on his brown face and a scorpion on his thick neck. He smiled with closed lips and grabbed each piece without removing his dark eyes from mine. I backed up against a shelf but didn't want to appear rude by weaving away from him. He placed the wafer in his mouth first and swallowed it after two bites.

"I'm Sanchez."

That's when I heard my inner voice *screaming* to get out. The main lights were off, leaving only the accent lights on near the windows and the sign behind the register. I was alone in the store with a guy hitting on me.

Not just that, but doing it in a creepy, roundabout way. I noticed a bandage on his arm and backed up a step.

"Nice to meet you, Mr. Sanchez. Let me grab something else I think you'll—"

"No," he said decidedly, wedging in front of the small space I was trying to squeeze through. I had the wall to my back and nowhere to go. "You look pretty vanilla to me. How do *you* taste?"

Something knocked off the shelf and rolled across the floor. My heart sped up when his tongue swept across his bottom lip. By the glittery expression in his eyes, he *liked* seeing me nervous.

"I'm sorry, you need to leave. I have to lock up the store," I said in a firm voice.

"What if I want you to *open up?*" he said suggestively.

Sanchez had rock-solid arms that looked eager to crush me in his grasp. He chuckled while chewing on the taffy. "I work for Delgado."

I blinked in surprise at the familiar name and cleared my throat. "I paid him."

Delgado was a loan shark my grandma had owed money to. We'd only met once because he'd wanted his payments in cash, so he always sent a guy to collect. I'd squared away the debt to him, though.

"Mmm, true." Sanchez pinched the tuft of hair below his bottom lip. "Delgado wants the interest. All you paid was what was borrowed."

My brows slanted in an angry line. "He didn't tell me that! All he said was that I owed him three thousand and that's what I paid."

Sanchez's eyes roamed down my shirt and he stared at the lettering that said Sweet Treats, written across my C-cup breasts.

"How much is the interest?"

I was relieved when he lifted his hand and held his fingers in the shape of a zero. Until he took his other hand and poked a finger in and out of the hole. "Pay me what *I* want and I'll buy you some time."

Guys like Sanchez thrived on intimidation. I grew impatient and narrowed my eyes. "I don't care what *you* want; what does Delgado want?"

A smile crossed his face and a silver-capped molar gleamed back at me. "Been a few years. Interest builds up. Now you owe more than you paid."

"That's not fair!" I shouted, pushing him away as I struggled to get around him. He walked me against the wall and slammed his left hand over my head, leaning in hard.

"Be nice." He bit his lip and lowered his eyes again.

I got scared. Sanchez stopped smiling and I cowered like a cornered animal, now understanding why they lashed out violently.

He bent forward and licked the tip of my nose. I wrinkled my face, turning away from him.

"Five large, or one night with me and I'll give you a discount. I'll be real sweet. But if you don't pay him what he's owed, then I start taking fingers," he said, lifting my right hand up between us. "Starting with the pinky."

Faster than a heartbeat, Sanchez shoved my pinky finger into his mouth and clamped his teeth down hard. I tried to pull it out, but when I felt them lock on the bone, the threat became vividly real. This man didn't really want to sleep with me—he wanted to mess with my head before he minced me up.

Sanchez closed his lips around my finger and eased up, so I quickly pulled it out and wiped my hand on my jeans.

"I'm not doing anything with you," I growled. "When does Delgado want his money by?"

He tucked his business card in the hem of my skirt. "Saturday," he said, backing up and stalking out.

"That's in three days!"

As he opened the door, Sanchez glanced unapologetically over his shoulder. "Noon, Saturday. If you bring half the money, then I'll... I'll just take your pinky toe," he said with a dark laugh, briskly walking out the door and into the night.

I slid down the wall. "Oh God, what did you get me into, Grandma?" I whispered.

That night, I made a desperate decision. I devised a scheme to deduct money from the company account to pay off Delgado. I had access to the account to pay bills and Lexi wouldn't notice the transaction right away. My plan was to redeposit my own paychecks until I covered the amount withdrawn. I knew it was wrong, but I didn't know what else to do.

When I got home, I refilled my wolf's water dish and poured him some dog food I'd picked up at the store. He lapped up the water but only sniffed the food before scratching to go out. He was acting peculiar since I'd walked in the door. When I had first sat down, he wouldn't stop smelling my right hand.

And growling.

Something deep, dark, and ferocious that made my stomach feel all fluttery and reminded me of how wild he might actually be. But his leg had improved, so out he went while I got on the laptop and transferred company funds over to my personal account.

It was one of the hardest things I'd ever done because I'd crossed an ethical line. I was stealing and could wind up in jail because of it, not to mention I was betraying Lexi.

Hermie and Salvador paddled around in their fishbowl without a care in the world. I stared between Sanchez's business card and the one Maddox had left behind. I wondered if borrowing money from one shark to pay off the other would get one of them off my back.

Which wasn't a bad idea.

I already owed Maddox more than I could possibly pay, but at least he wasn't threatening my life or my fingers. If my grandma had borrowed frequently from the man, she must have trusted doing business with him.

My cell phone rang, pulling me away from my thoughts.

"Hello?"

"How's my April Showers?"

"Hey, Trevor. Where are you?"

He sighed. "A Burger King in bumfuck nowhere. I wanted to eat inside, but a couple of rednecks were giving me the *Deliverance* stare. Did you ever see that movie? It gives me the heebie-jeebies about driving anywhere in the South. Not that I have much of a choice," he said with a snort. "I got all my stuff packed up."

"That was fast."

"Yeah, I did it porn style. In and out."

"Thanks for the visual," I said, rubbing my eye.

"I'm headed back tonight."

Shoot! I hadn't cleaned. Trevor had visited my home only twice before, but I wanted to tidy things up and make it special since he had been through a rough breakup.

"How long is your drive going to be? If I'm at work when you get here, I'll have to hide the key somewhere."

"Don't sweat it, babe. I'll be there in less than an hour. Just wanted to give you a heads-up so you don't freak out and pull a machete on me when I come knocking on your door. And by the way, don't bother cleaning. I'm not the queen."

I laughed and put my feet up on the sofa. "I have a new friend living with me temporarily, and I don't know if he's going to like you very much."

"Huh?" His clipped tone was serious and a little pissed off.

"Careful," I said in a teasing voice. "Jumping to conclusions is an Olympic event."

"I want that on a T-shirt along with my gold medal. So, who's this friend whose ass I'm going to kick?"

"A dog. Well, I think. Maybe a wolf."

"A *what*? I hope you're yanking my chain, April. If you brought a fucking wolf home, I swear to God."

"It's okay," I said, getting up to open the door. "He's just hurt and has macho issues." I poked my head outside and whistled but didn't see him. "I'll make sure he stays outside tonight. Do you want me to wait up for you?"

"Nah. Leave the key in the grill and I'll let myself in. Are you workin' tomorrow?"

"Actually, it's my day off. Um, I meant to ask you something."

An amused laugh crackled on the other end. "This sounds good."

"Do you want to go to a thing? I mean, it's a party. Not the club kind, just a barbecue at a friend's house."

"Will adult beverages be served?"

"Probably. It's a bunch of guys."

"Magic words, babe. I'm in. Look, I'm going to take a whiz and then head out."

"Too much information."

I whistled a few more times, but there was no sign of my wolf. I slipped on a pair of sandals and walked to the grill to conceal the key inside. "Can you pick me up something for breakfast?"

"Don't you have food?"

I chuckled. "Nothing I'm not already sick of. Might as well get something for yourself while you're at it and stick it in the fridge."

"Cool. Don't wait up for me."

With Trevor on his way, I put on a thin shirt and a pair of black shorts with a pink waistband. He didn't care what I slept in, but I wasn't comfortable enough with *anyone* to walk around half-naked.

Something roused me from my sleep in the middle of the night and I rubbed my face, staring down the length of my bed and through the open doorway. A dim light was on and cast a soft glow on the couch. Trevor was sprawled out with one long leg on the wall and the other bent at the knee. I couldn't see his face because he had his nose buried in a paperback.

"Hey," I said groggily, sliding my bare feet across the floor. "How long have you been here?"

"Ah, shit. Did I wake you, babe?" He set the book down and stood up, giving me a tight hug. "I got in about a half hour ago and holy hell, girl. You've been holding out on me," he said, pointing at my new book.

"That's book three."

His brown eyes sparkled. "Good. That means I get to read it again." He collapsed on the sofa, scrambling his fingers through his hair until it was sexy and all in his eyes. "First thing we're doing tomorrow is getting you some food." Trevor's voice was borderline angry.

I bent down, picked up his leather shoes, and set them by the door. "I've been eating out a lot."

"Don't lie, April. That shit pisses me off. I know you're not big on eating out because you have a thing about people putting boogers and spit in the food."

"They do! I saw a show on it."

He patted the space beside him and I sat down, curling up against him.

After a few quiet moments, I finally spoke. "It's been so quiet around here. E-mails just aren't the same. I miss our coffee-shop trips and our trashy-romance Sundays. Going to those garage sales in search of bad romance novels for a dime just isn't the same. I missed you, Trevor."

"Me too, babe. I don't let go of a good friend that easily. If I moved to Alaska, I'd still be calling your ass. You're like a ray of sunshine I've been missing all these months. Plus, nobody makes a tuna casserole like you do."

I laughed and poked him in the chest. "You hate my tuna."

We sat quietly and rain tapped on the roof like the impatient tapping of fingernails.

"It'll get better," he whispered. "Everything else going okay? Work?"

"Yep," I lied. "Sometimes I just want to run out of this place."

He sighed and held my hand, stroking his fingers over mine. "I can speak from experience when I tell you that running won't get rid of your problems. They always catch up with you, and if you've spent your life running from them, you'll be too damn tired to fight them off. Nobody's going to help you in life, April. You've got to help yourself."

"I just wish I had someone to take care of me."

"Don't be that girl, April."

"What girl?"

"The one who needs a man to take care of her."

I sat up. "Is that so wrong? I don't want a man to make decisions *for* me, take away my freedom, and not allow me to work. Sometimes taking care of someone is loving them enough that you want to ease their pain and protect them. I care for these unwanted animals because they have no one to look out for them when they need it the most. Is it so wrong to love something that's so far gone it can't be saved?"

"You're not a pigeon, April."

I gave him my doe eyes; Trevor didn't contradict me very often. He wasn't seeing my point.

"I'm not saying I'm weak, Trev. I'm just tired. Tired of living like this," I said, waving my arm. "Tired of working my butt off and walking miles to and from work each day because I can't afford a car. Do I complain about it? No, you've never once heard me complain about how unfair it is that some people get to live on easy street while others are struggling to make ends meet. But you know what? I'm tired of buying food at the dollar store, because the bread there sucks. I'm tired of seeing other girls my age going out every Friday because payday for them means dropping a hundred dollars on dinner and drinks while for me, it means clearing my debt and helping my sister. I'm tired of not having the things I deserve to have because that woman died and left me all her problems." Tears streamed down my face. "I'm just so *tired*."

Trevor wrapped his arms around my shoulders and whispered in my hair. "I'm so sorry, babe. I didn't mean to make you cry. I get it. Shhh. I get it. It's late and you're exhausted. I just don't want to see you give up so easily that the next guy who comes along thinks you belong to him. That he can push you around and walk all over you because he's taking care of things. Remember shithead?"

He meant my ex who'd cheated on me.

"April," he said, holding my face in his hands and wiping my tears away. "I don't want you to think that you deserve that kind of love. I don't want you to think it's okay for a guy to fuck around or talk down to you because he's paying your bills or letting you stay with him. You see where I'm going with this? If a guy loves you, he'll buy you fucking Jamaica and walk away. He won't hold that shit over you so you'll—"

"I think our conversation train derailed," I mumbled, sniffling as he looked at me and smiled. "That's a little deep, Trevor. All I want is someone to take care of me for a change. It doesn't have to be forever, just long enough for me to catch my breath. I've been doing good on my own, but I never wanted to grow up so fast. Even when my grandma was alive, I had to take care of the shopping and cooking. I've been more of a mother to Rose than a sister, and it shouldn't be that way. I just want someone I can count on—a man who will turn the world upside down to help me find a slice of happiness because he loves me that much."

"Damn, girl," he said, wiping my tears with the pad of his thumb. "You should have been a romance writer. I'm not going to tell you Mr. Perfect is out there, because that's a load of crap. But I will tell you that *I'm* here, and no matter what, I'm looking out for you. And tomorrow, we're going to pick up some shit to make this place a joy to live in."

I laughed hysterically and whipped the small pillow out from behind me. "What's the matter, you don't like the embroidered pillows?"

"For kindling on the barbecue grill? You bet. Otherwise, I don't want your granny's fart pillow beneath my chiseled face and lips of a Greek god."

"You must have left off on chapter six," I said, glancing at the paperback.

He snatched it off the table and thumbed it open. "Yep. And I'm reading it again, so go back to bed and leave Vexton and me alone."

CHAPTER 5

"Well, well. If it isn't Reno," Denver said in a disgusted tone. He was stretched out on the sofa wearing only a pair of loose sweats and eating a bowl of macaroni. "Been looking for you. Must be nice to ditch your pack without a word and not feel a shred of guilt."

Reno scratched his chin indifferently. Denver was a cool cat, but young (by at least a hundred years), so he could be a bigger prick than a cactus. Reno perked up his ears but didn't hear any activity. They lived in a massive two-story house that had been a hotel over a century ago. Now it was the official homestead of the Weston pack.

"Where is everyone?" Reno asked.

"Bowling. It's Shifter night at the alley and drinks are free for women." Denver rolled his eyes. "You better have my back when I bring up laser tag, because that new place kicks ass and we're all going. Period."

Shifters were one of many paranormals living in secret in the human world. Each Breed had their own culture and laws, but Shifters were a tight-knit group. Once considered lower-class citizens, they'd been sold into slavery, kept as servants, and the wolves in particular had been chained around the neck and made into guard dogs.

Shifters came in all types, but Reno and his brothers were wolves. They lived together in a pack run by their youngest, Austin. Only an alpha could act as a Packmaster—the leader of a pack. Not all couples will have an alpha child, but when they do, it's almost always the firstborn male. Somehow that gene skipped Reno and landed right on their baby brother. It hadn't been easy for Reno to watch the kid grow up, knowing someday he'd outrank him, but Austin was a born leader and Reno respected rules. Austin led the Weston pack alongside his life mate, Lexi. She'd recently discovered she was a Shifter after having gone through the change in her late twenties. Austin thought it had been delayed because she'd lived with humans her entire life. It's a damn good thing the pack had taken her in when they did, because female Shifters gave off a strong vibe that made human men turn stupid around them. Lexi's human mother and sister had also moved into the Weston house. They were like family to Austin, and it didn't take long before the rest of the boys felt the same way. Packs had strong bonding instincts, and anyone brought into the family was one of their own, regardless of Breed.

"What happened to your arm, bro?"

Reno glanced at his left arm that he'd bandaged up. "My wolf got tangled up in some shit, I guess."

What exactly that was, Reno didn't know. When a Shifter changed into their animal form, most could only remember the first few minutes, but nothing after that. Many alphas could remember it all, but that had to do with their power. The last thing Reno remembered was running into the woods.

"You don't know what happened?" Denver asked skeptically.

"Went for a run—the usual. My wolf knows the rules about going into the city and I woke up by my bike. How long has it been?"

"Two and a half days. Something must have gone down for your wolf to not want to shift back, because he's an obedient mofo." Denver set the bowl on the coffee table of their living room and slipped his feet into a pair of black flip-flops. "Maizy's staying with Lexi's friend for the night—her hot neighbor with the round ass. Want a beer?"

"Why not," Reno muttered. "Grab me one and I'll be right back."

Reno headed upstairs and down the hall to the last room on the left. It was in pristine condition, just as he'd left it. He peeled off his shirt and stood in front of the mirror on his right, staring at his body. He had acquired a few scars, and each told a story. Shifters lived an extended lifespan of several hundred years, and they could heal through shifting. But his wolf had been injured too long this time and the mark on his arm would become a scar. It was sore all the way through, as if he'd been stabbed with a blunt object.

He peeled the bandage down, examining the wound. The skin had sealed up and turned pink. He couldn't remember a damn thing about how he got it either. He rubbed his heavy stubble, in dire need of a shave. Reno was a man who took grooming seriously. He preferred long sleeves in public to keep his wolf in check. Something about the tight fabric worked like a fence against his skin. Reno also kept a gun strapped to him most of the time and drove a Triumph Bonneville because fuck it, the bike was a classic.

Something felt amiss.

Reno sat on the edge of the bed and rubbed his face as a knot formed in his stomach. Shifters had to let their animal out regularly, and most of them did it on a weekly basis, if not more. That's why owning private land was important, and Austin had secured enough acreage to broaden their territory. Sometimes they all ran together, but Reno had always been a lone wolf. He wrung his strong hands, trying to figure out why his wolf had been breaking his pattern and getting too close to humans. It didn't make sense.

Reno felt an impulsive urge to return to town, but for what? It was a fierce calling, as if he'd left something behind or unfinished.

After a hot shower, Reno skipped shaving and went downstairs to join Denver for a beer. His hair was still wet and he ran his hands through it a few times to shake out the water.

Denver was lounging in his favorite rocker on the front porch and had his feet on the wooden railing. The sun stretched across the grassy field in front of them, the clouds finally breaking up. "Damn, I love it out here," he said.

Reno sat in a chair and sipped his ice-cold beer, sharing silent agreement. He stretched out his legs and crossed one biker boot over the other.

"Do you think Austin will recruit anyone new in this century?" Reno asked. A pack was often defined by strength in numbers, and lately a few assholes had dubbed them *The Six-Pack*.

Denver belched and set his bottle on the arm of the chair. "Can't say. He's young and probably thinks he should take his merry time."

Reno snorted. "*You're* young."

"I'm fifteen years older than him and a hell of a lot more mature."

"Says the guy who wears cartoon shirts."

"Maturity is based on the decisions you make, not what's in your damn closet."

"That's debatable," Reno muttered, watching a hawk fly overhead.

"Get off my back. I like my style and if I want to be two hundred and wearing a Donald Duck shirt, then you're just gonna have to live with it."

Shifters physically aged slower than humans did, and they all ran at different speeds. Reno looked like a seasoned man of thirty-five, even though in years he exceeded that by a century. As the alpha, Austin naturally had gained a formidable appearance early on and would likely retain it for a while.

"There are still just six of us. Ten if you count the girls, and only Ivy and Lexi are Shifters," Reno pointed out. Ivy was the new blood in the pack, recently traded over by her father. It wasn't common for a woman to come into a pack unmated to a male, so they treated her as a sister to prevent any friction.

"Well, there are too many rogues around here I wouldn't trust," Denver said. "Some of the larger packs might want to trade over, but they like to pass off their problem children like hot potatoes. Funny how humans have no idea how many of us there are living around here."

True.

Shifters couldn't smell one another, but sometimes they could pick up on Breed energy if they got close enough. Not always, but it helped since alphas didn't have any tells like unique eye colors. The Packmasters usually got tattoos and made their identities known, so they were always easy to spot. Being an alpha was one thing, but a Packmaster held an important rank, and a hierarchy existed among their kind. There was even a pecking order among Packmasters.

"We should keep a close eye for candidates when going out," Reno said. "Maybe drop a suggestion in Austin's ear."

It's why clubs and bars often had a Shifters' night. They needed to congregate and socialize, not only to build alliances with other packs, but also to scope out potentials for their own family.

Sometimes friction existed in the packs with too many dominant males and that got resolved by a little pack trading.

"How's your arm? Did you shift again?"

"Yeah," Reno said, rubbing at it. The wound had been itching for the last two hours. "I did a quick shift in the bathroom, but that's as much as it's going to heal. It's just sore as hell."

Denver examined the scar and then sat back, touching the one on his forehead. "Well, if your wolf didn't shift back for two days, it must have been for good reason."

Damn, now Reno was thinking about it again. He took a slow sip from his beer bottle and had a strange feeling come over him. An alarming tingle raced up his spine and made the hair on the back of his neck stand up.

He fished his hand in his pocket and twirled a small object between his fingers. "I'm heading back into town."

"The fuck you are," Denver retorted.

Reno stood up and stretched his stiff back. "Tag along if you want, but I can't sit around here. My wolf was out for too long and now I'm restless; you know that feeling. I need to walk it out of my system."

"We could meet up and bowl with the guys."

"I don't bowl."

Denver rocked with laughter and raised his beer in a toast. "Oh yeah, I forgot. The only balls you play with are your own."

"Trevor, I can't afford that. Put it back!" I laughed as he stood at the end of the grocery aisle, holding a steak like one of those game-show models.

"It's on me," he said, tossing it into the cart.

"And where are you getting this newfound money, Daddy Warbucks?"

A slender girl in a pair of white jeans sauntered by Trevor and batted her long lashes. I peered over my shoulder as we passed her.

"She's looking at my ass, isn't she?" Trevor muttered.

"Can you blame her? Now, back to the money."

"I've got a little tucked away. The ex took care of all the bills," he said with disdain. "I had a part-time job, so I made enough to stash a few dollars in my piggy bank."

So *that's* why he'd reacted to my comment about being taken care of. Trevor hadn't hashed out the details of their separation, but maybe his ex had held that over his head and made him feel inferior.

"Well, just don't spend it all on food. You need to tuck it away for your future, not expensive cuts of meat."

"And that's exactly why someday you're going to be one of those rich old ladies with a million dollars stashed in the freezer. Most of us are impulse shoppers. We see it and got to have it." Trevor lifted a pack of tuna and glanced at the label, privately chuckling as he put it back on the shelf. "You can tell a lot about a person who fills their cabinets with *that* shit."

"What do you mean?"

"Nothing," he murmured, resting his elbows on the shopping cart handle. "Who's this party for?"

"You remember Lexi, my boss? Well, she just moved in with this guy *and* all his brothers, I guess."

"Sounds cozy."

We slowly walked down the aisle, Trevor leaning on the cart. "She's pretty serious about Austin and I wouldn't be surprised if he popped the question on her. They're having a housewarming party."

"Should we bring a gift?"

Crap, I hadn't thought about that. "Maybe a bottle of wine? I know Lexi loves red wine."

"Go pick out a cheap bottle and I'll get the rest of the stuff," he said. "You talked some sense into me and I'm putting the steak back. We're having Trevor Taco Delight for dinner." Trevor swaggered off in his signature denim and button-up shirt ensemble. He never tucked in his shirts, so it made him look casual and put together at the same time.

It was so wonderful having him around again. Trevor could be a little odd at times, but I loved him unconditionally. He often started up fights with other guys over petty things, and sometimes the verbal exchanges between them were weird and made no sense. In fact, *news flash*—men in general made no sense to me.

I hurried down the aisle and made my way to the back of the store where the cheap bottles were lined up on the shelves.

Guilt weighed heavily on my conscience from pinching the money out of the company account, and I'd come to a decision. It wasn't worth the risk. Maybe I'd get away with it, but I'd never be able to live with myself. The best way to handle it was to take out a loan from Maddox and immediately deposit all the money I'd stolen back into the business account. After I took care of Sanchez, that is. I didn't want to owe anything to that finger-chomping maniac.

Jeez, too many choices, I thought, staring at the display of wine. I narrowed them down by the catchiest names that were under ten dollars. My fingers touched the caps on the bottles as I held my hand indecisively over the top shelf. I recognized a familiar brand on the second shelf—I'd seen it at a few parties. When I pulled my arm back, my bracelet snagged the neck of a Merlot.

Three bottles toppled over and smashed on the floor.

Glass exploded and red wine splashed across my legs. I covered my head with my arms and squeezed my eyes shut. When I dared to open them, I glanced down at the mess. Red wine pooled across the floor and saturated my sneakers. The bottles had cracked in large chunks and shards of glass were scattered everywhere.

Nice job, sweetheart, my inner voice mocked. *Will you be paying by cash or credit?*

The sound of shoes crunching over broken glass came from my right and I cringed, expecting to see a store employee with a mop in hand and a frown on their face.

Reno stalked toward me wearing mirrored shades, a formfitting black shirt, and boots with a thick tread.

Without a word, he hooked his strong arm around my lower waist and lifted me off the ground with a *whoosh*. I draped my arms over his shoulders, uncertain of what to do as he swiveled and walked me out of danger. I was in the middle of deciding whether I wanted to tell him to put me down or succumb to *hero syndrome*.

He stopped in front of the freezer of beer with me still in his arms. I marveled at how easily he held me, as if I weighed nothing.

"Hi," I said, staring at my reflection in his glasses. Then I began to get my first close-up look at Reno.

There was something mysteriously sexy about his lips even though they weren't expressive like Denver's. A tiny scar on his bottom lip caught my eye.

"Are you cut?" he asked, still not putting me down.

I was having a little trouble focusing when my entire front was pressed tightly against his, and tingles were awakening from a long slumber. My God, his cologne was intoxicating and clouding all rational thought. My mantastic episode was on the verge of becoming epic.

"Put me down and I'll check."

"There could be glass on your shoes," he said matter-of-factly.

A grin curved up my face and I lifted the aviators off his nose and glanced into a set of coffee-brown eyes. They were so molten that I found my mouth operating without a license. "Well then, I guess you could just hold me in the imported-beer aisle for the rest of our lives." My best attempt at flirting was about to crash and burn.

Reno set me down and towered over me. I was average height, but he must have been over six feet.

"I remember you," I said stupidly, straightening my blouse. "I ran into your brother. He said you'd gone missing. You probably don't remember who I am." I stepped back and bent over, wiping the wine from my lower legs.

"April Frost."

I straightened up and looked at him, wide-eyed. "How do you know my name?"

"Lexi introduced us and I don't forget a name." Then he knelt down and ran his hand down my strong calves and around the edge of my shoes.

Wow. I hadn't had a man touch me like that in ages. The feel of his rough hands sliding up my skin made me shiver, which was embarrassing because all he was doing was making sure I wasn't cut.

And there I was, playing out a fantasy in my head. I couldn't figure out why a guy like him was so attractive to me, but he was. Maybe ten years older, rough around the edges, and serious, but he had the hands of a skilled lover. Hands I briefly thought about having all over my body before I felt a blush rising and I quickly extinguished those silly daydreams.

When he pulled back his hand, I could still feel his touch on my skin.

"You should take these off and throw them out. There might be a shard in there I can't feel," he suggested, tapping his finger on my shoe.

He had a rasp to his voice, and a sultry flow of words brushed over me like a slow caress.

"Denver was the one looking for you, in case you didn't know."

He glanced up with his shades still perched high on his nose. "I know."

What was I, his mother? Then I went blank. I had *no* idea what else to say and shifted around anxiously. How had he remembered my name all these months later? "So, you're Austin's brother?"

Brilliant. My inner voice chided me, clasping her hands together. *We've already established he's Denver's brother, who is related to Austin. Let's show him how dense you really are.*

Reno stood up and straightened his glasses. "Yeah. He's the baby in the family. Where did your friend go?"

"Um…" Had he been following me in the store?

"He's picking up a few things for dinner tonight."

Reno's jaw clenched. "Does he look after you?"

"Trevor's the best. He probably looks after me a little too much, but we've known each other for years."

Reno's hand dipped into his pocket and he fidgeted with something. It wasn't change, because I didn't hear a jingle. A half smile slid up his face when Trevor appeared.

He didn't just appear—he wedged himself between us with his back to Reno and glared at my feet. "What happened to you?"

It was the scary voice. Trevor was going into ass-kicking mode.

"The usual, Trev. I'm a walking catastrophe, so behold the mayhem." I waved my arm toward the mess on the floor.

He spun on his heel to face Reno. Trevor was not only leaner, but also shorter in stature, missing the six-foot mark by an inch or two. It didn't take away an ounce of confidence. "What's your business with April?"

Reno didn't flinch. "The kind that's none of yours."

Didn't matter that Trevor had been drooling over this man a couple of days ago, because now Reno was encroaching on my territory and this is exactly what Trevor did.

"Trevor," I said in a low voice, trying to defuse the situation. "This is Reno. He's Lexi's friend and her boyfriend's brother."

Trevor spun around and regarded me with serious eyes. "He's related to Lexi's boyfriend? Oh, this barbecue should be *real* interesting."

"What does that mean?" I whispered.

He shook his head. My eyes flicked back to Reno, who stood with a cool expression and a hint of a smile tugging at the corner of his mouth. I couldn't help but smile back. Just the idea of his hardened face softening made me a little weak, and Trevor noticed it, snapping his fingers in front of my face.

"Come on, babe. Time for us to go." He seized my wrist and tugged me around the corner.

Reno moved so fast I barely saw it happen. He snatched Trevor's arm and forced him to let go of me, inching in close in a way that intimidated even Trevor.

"That's not how you handle a lady by dragging her around like a… pet. Is that what she is to you, a *pet?*"

Trevor's eyes narrowed in slow motion, and I knew it was time to buckle up, because this plane was about to hit major turbulence.

CHAPTER 6

"How's your nose?"

Trevor lifted the bloody rag from his face and studied it for a minute. Then his head fell back against the headrest of his car, and I handed him a bottle of spring water.

"Don't ever tell anyone about this," he said in a thick voice, taking a sip of water.

"It's not the first time you've been in a fight." But *boy*, had Trevor gotten his ass served on a platter. I'd had to help him into the passenger seat of his car and drive him home.

"I didn't even get in one swing." He sulked, shouldering his door open and slamming it behind him. Trevor stalked up to the trailer, unlocked the door, and began yanking grocery bags from the back of the car to haul inside.

I'd never seen him so agitated. He wasn't an aggressive guy—but he had buttons like everyone else, and if you pushed the right ones, he went macho. Trevor liked to fight—it's something he seemed experienced at, so when he knuckled up, it became like a halftime show. He'd flirt with bystanders and dodge swings while laughing. Something about it had been different this time. Trevor had not only confronted Reno in the grocery store, but he'd placed himself between us as if Reno were a threat to me.

Then he called Reno a freak.

A second later, Trevor was lying in the cereal aisle with a busted nose and bloody lip.

"Don't be like that," I said, grabbing two bags and heading inside. "Maybe if you stopped trying to beat up every guy who talks to me, I just might actually find Mr. Right."

He slammed the paper bag on the counter and washed his hands. "I may give shit to some of the guys who hit on you, but I want to make sure they're man enough to take you out. I don't want him near you again."

"What's wrong with Reno?" I asked defensively, turning on the air conditioner and closing the front door. "You didn't seem to have a problem with him the other day. The guy saved me from a wine mishap that could have made my walks home from work unbearable had I cut up my feet."

Trevor leaned over the counter and looked at himself in an oval mirror, pinching the bridge of his swollen nose. "*Fuck*. Look, I need to go out for a bit."

"What about your tacos?"

"Have a sandwich to tide you over. We'll do a late dinner. I need a few hours."

"Wait a second!"

Trevor swung around and cupped my head in his hands, giving me his crazy-sexy smile. "Don't be mad, babe. I'm just looking out for you. Sometimes I can tell things about a person that you may not see because you've got blinders on."

"What blinders?"

He tickled my eyelashes with his thumbs. "Those long lashes you bat around. There's an invisible thing that all boys can see that girls can't."

"And what is that?"

Trevor backed away and walked out the door, glancing over his shoulder. "Intentions."

Since it was late afternoon, I put the meat in the fridge and chopped up the lettuce and tomatoes, thinking about what had happened at the grocery store. I'm not sure what had come over Trevor or why he took off, but whenever he got moody, he needed his alone time.

After I cleared off the counter and put the toppings for the tacos in the fridge, I went in the bathroom and scrunched my hair, staring at myself in the mirror. I briefly wondered what Reno thought of me.

My natural blond roots didn't look that bad against the platinum, but still.

Platinum was more stylish, especially with my long bangs. I had an experimental dark streak of dye that was fading. Maybe my natural color was more of a perception thing; I hated the idea of being called the *dumb blonde*. Some girls just rolled with the jokes or blew them off, but I didn't want a label on me that said I was the party girl who would get drunk and sleep around. Maybe because of my mother, I'd become more sensitive to that kind of thing than most girls.

Trevor was the one who suggested platinum because it had a tough image that most guys thought was more badass than sweet ass. When I threw on my dark eyeliner and mismatched clothes, men didn't know *what* to think about me.

I wondered what Reno's impression was.

The air conditioner cooled my neck and I opened up my laptop and tried to look him up on the Internet.

Jeez. Stalk much?

After closing the search window and choosing not to become one of those women, I opened up a few files that Lexi had given me. There were so many miscellaneous documents on the flash drive, and I hadn't even begun to sort through them all.

Then I thought about how arresting Reno's eyes had been when I'd lifted his sunglasses. How strong his arms felt when they'd crushed around me, and how close our bodies were when they'd molded together like a piece of art. I'd felt every solid thump of his heart beating against my chest. He had a strong heart—like a banging drum. He also hadn't shaved, and I thought about how sexy it made him look. Something had altered from my first impression of Reno when he'd scared the wits out of me with his formidable presence. It's something I could sense without explanation. Behind the façade of a tough guy was a devoted man. Devoted to what, I couldn't be sure. But I felt it just as sure as I'd smelled his skin and felt his arms encasing me.

In fact, I sat at my table creating a romantic scene in my head of our interlude at the grocery store.

Instead of Trevor coming up and starting a fight, I slide Reno's glasses away from his head and drop them on the floor. Then I run my fingers through his short hair and he mumbles something about kissing him, so I do. I plant my lips on his mouth and at first, he's uncertain. Not wanting to appear needy for his touch, I pull away, and that's when he turns me around, knocks the items from the shelf with a swipe of his arm, and sets me down on it.

My legs are spread and he moves between them. Everything about him is smooth and unrushed. No groping. Just the feel of his strong hands barely resting on my hips, and it makes me want him even more because of his remarkable restraint. No one else in the store exists because… well… there was an evacuation. A tornado. Yeah, and we're all alone because everyone ran into a ditch for cover. The wind is roaring outside, but it doesn't match the sound of my heart. He kisses my neck softly, trailing his mouth across my clavicle and even lower until I softly moan…

"All right, fantasy time is over," I said aloud, cracking open a can of soda. "I think all these books are going to my head."

My time with Sanchez was running out. The marks around my pinky finger had made it difficult to sleep the night before. It's not what I imagined him doing to me—it's what I *couldn't* imagine. I didn't want to guess what guys like that did to terrorize clients who didn't pay up. The sooner I could get him out of my hair, the better.

So I dialed the number on the business card.

"Sanchez."

"It's April. I have your money."

"Ah, Vanilla Frost. You got *every* penny? I don't deal with people who cut me short."

"I got it. How do you want to do this?"

I heard a bristly sound on the other line as if he were rubbing his chin. The only hair I remembered on his face was a square patch below his bottom lip. "That was quick. How did you come across that kind of money so fast?"

"I won the lottery. Tell me how you want me to pay you. I can wire it to an account, or—"

"Cash," he quickly replied.

Somehow I knew that's what he'd say. "Okay. We can meet at the mall in the food court."

Laughter cackled on the other end of the line. "You are one *dumb* vanilla. How about I come over to your place?"

"No," I said firmly.

"Fine," he said, his voice getting dark and serious. "Meet me tonight at eleven. We'll do it close to where you work so it's quicker. You know where the railroad tracks are?"

"Uh-huh."

"There's an abandoned building with graffiti just south of your store. You know the one?"

I could hardly miss it. I walked by it on the way home every day. "Yeah, but I'd rather not. Look, why don't I just wire it to you?"

"Because this is the only way I do business," he said in a curt voice. "You think I want someone around to snap a picture on their cell phone? Or an electronic record of the transaction? I spent enough time in prison and I'm not going back. So skirt your little ass up there *no later* than eleven. This isn't negotiable, little girl. I call the shots, and you don't want to know what the consequences are. Feel free to call the police. They won't do a damn thing about it and all you'll end up doing is pissing off Delgado and wasting my time. And don't even think about bringing someone with you. All you have to do is pay the money and I'll go away."

I hung up on him and panicked. I needed to haul ass to the bank and make a personal withdrawal from my account if he wanted cash. My wine-stained tennis shoes were going into the trash anyhow, so I just kept them on and ran out the door.

"Now you boys behave yourselves." Lynn brushed a speck of lint from her dark slacks. Reno chuckled to himself; he loved the way that woman kept them in line. "I don't want to come back and find any of my new curtains torn down."

Lynn had become the matriarch in the pack despite her human status. Lexi's mom could be a little controlling of what went on in the house, but women were the lifeblood of any pack and they all knew it. She loved taking care of them, but over the past few months, Lynn had begun to take notice of how different Shifters lived from humans.

Jericho smirked from his leather stool at the bar and patted out the butt of his cigarette. They had converted an upstairs room into a lion's den with alcohol, a television, video games, and a stereo. Jericho had hung up the dartboard from the old house, and rumor had it Denver was buying a pool table. God knows the boys were all for that. Shifters loved billiards because if you could get a woman to play, it was one of the most erotic wonders to behold.

Jericho admired one of the silver rings on his hand, no doubt feeling all eyes on him as he had a reputation for being the troublemaker when it came to parties. Reno sat to his immediate right and nudged his arm to pay attention. Lynn hovered in the doorway and anxiety bled across her face at what they might be scheming. Lynn was an amazing cook, an attentive mother, and one sassy woman with a fixation on upgrading their historical home. However, she had become a damper on game night whenever one of the men invited a woman or two to join them.

Not that Reno brought home women, but Jericho sure as hell wasn't happy about it. Most packs minded their own business when it came to mattress bouncing, but if that front door so much as squeaked, Lynn was all over it and wanted to know the life story of every person who stepped inside.

That's why Austin was sending her on an all-expenses paid vacation to Sea World with Maizy. Not only would Maizy get to see dolphins and whales, but it would get Lynn the hell out of the house so they could run the party that weekend, *Shifter style*. The Cole brothers liked to get rowdy; that was a fact. It could hardly be helped when Jericho's band would show up with groupies. They usually invited neighboring packs, taking advantage of the opportunity to form and keep alliances. Lynn wasn't comfortable around that many Shifters, so it was for her benefit just as much as it was theirs.

"Behave, boys," she said sternly, lingering by the door. Maizy grabbed a fistful of her mom's shirt and tugged impatiently, looking about as excited as any kid who was about to go see Flipper.

Lynn would make it there before sunset and looked relieved to be getting away for a spell. Human women just weren't used to living with that many men, let alone Shifters. She'd have to get used to it if she wanted to remain with the pack. It was likely they would gain more members as time went by. Not just anyone—the selection process took time. Austin made the ultimate decision as the Packmaster, and the new blood had to mesh with their group. Someone who would die for his brothers, protect their women, and guard their territory. Loyalty meant everything. So the toughest pack didn't have to do with size, but the strength of the family.

"What the hell happened to your hand?" Jericho took another sip of beer and Lynn went downstairs with Maizy to pack up the car.

Reno lifted his hand, staring at the discoloration on his knuckles. "Just one of those mysteries in life," he replied.

"Bet it ain't so mysterious to the face it ran into several times. One of these days I'm going to get you to smoke a little weed and then maybe you'll loosen up," Jericho said with a suppressed laugh. "Man, I'd love to see that shit. Bet you're one of those sissies who holds on to the grass because the planet is spinning too fast."

"You need to cut that shit out," Reno suggested, as if his brother hadn't heard it a million times before. "You're too old for that mess and I don't think we need to take another trip down memory lane, if you get my meaning."

"Maybe you should mind your own business. I don't do the hard shit anymore."

Shifters acted the age they looked like more than the age they actually were. Jericho was old enough to know better, but his talents as a musician had kept him stagnant in a partying lifestyle. Jericho had gotten a taste of fame years ago, and it ended in disaster. In fact, it almost killed him. He kept his act local now, but little had changed in how he carried himself. He commanded attention when he walked into a room, and it wasn't just his height. The women loved his long hair and aloofness. Whether it was onstage or off, that boy had been born to entertain. Breed had to stay out of the limelight; the risk of being discovered by humans was too great for those who lived extended lifetimes. So sacrifices had to be made, and maybe Jericho was a little bitter about that.

Reno sniffed and looked at their reflections in the mirror. "Maybe you should realize life is more than a party."

"The day you quit having fun is the day you resign yourself to getting old," Jericho retorted. He eased off the stool and grabbed his longneck. As he passed by, he leaned over Reno's shoulder and lowered his voice. "Tomorrow, we're getting you laid. I know just the girl, and she's had her eye on your swagger for about three years now."

Reno cut him a sharp glare and a smug grin stretched across Jericho's face, brightening his milky-green eyes. Jericho raked his tangled dark hair away from his face and winked.

"I know *I'm* getting laid," Denver announced from the black beanbag chair in the corner.

"Says who?" Jericho tilted his bottle and took a swig.

Denver pointed to his crotch with his index finger. "Says *this* guy." He had a bag of Cheetos on his stomach and his fingers were tinted orange from the cheese. "It's been too fucking long, and I don't give a shit if my wolf is the one who gets laid, but *one of us* is getting a little tail."

"Well, I know *I'm* getting laid," Austin announced as Lexi entered the room.

"Don't be so sure," she said with an air of confidence, walking indifferently toward the short fridge behind the bar.

Reno silently laughed. All the guys loved her to bits because she put that alpha in his place.

Austin eased up behind her. "That's the *one* thing I'm sure of, Ladybug."

She bent over and reached for a wine cooler, tilting her ass just a little bit. Reno had to turn away because it was instinctual for males to become aroused when a female turned her back. The men in that house would cut off their right arm before making a move on a mated female in the pack, but Austin didn't take kindly to a room full of erections, so they averted their eyes out of respect.

Austin gripped her hips and growled, leaning over to whisper in her ear.

Denver shoved a handful of chips into his mouth and folded the bag. "Well, I'm sick of *that* shit," he said, pointing at the adorable couple. "Ain't fair. I got needs."

"You also got dirty socks all over the bathroom," Lexi pointed out, turning around and nudging Austin away. "Women don't want to be a maid and pick up after you."

"Our mother did."

"Women you *sleep* with."

Denver's mouth turned down and his brows arched. "Maybe I'll find a girl who will want me for who I am."

Jericho lifted his bottle in a toast. "That's so precious I want to put it on a greeting card. Women look at a man like Lynn looks at this house: a fixer-upper."

"That's not true," Lexi cut in. "I didn't have to change Austin; he changed himself."

A fierce smile slid up Austin's face and he reached in his back pocket and removed his fringed gloves. When he winked at her with his ice-blue eyes, Lexi scowled at him.

"That's it! I'm going to get the scissors and cut those fringes off." She stormed out of the room and Austin put the second glove on his hand, swaggering toward the hall.

"Be back in two hours, boys. My girl loves it when I pull out the leathers. It gets her all fired up in the sack."

"You see?" Denver said, throwing his head back. "That's *killing* me. It was fine until she came into the house."

Jericho tossed a dart at the board, hitting dead center. "Bitch all you want, man. We know you ain't got game."

Denver's legs flailed as he struggled to get out of the beanbag chair his ass was adhered to. The bag of Cheetos spilled on the floor and his face bloomed red. "Why don't you just shut it?"

"Why don't we make it interesting with a friendly wager?" Ben suggested.

Reno turned his back, ignoring the ruckus.

Wheeler slid in the seat beside him at the bar, shoving a deck of cards away. "You okay?" He eyed the new scar on Reno's left arm as he reached in a plastic bag on the bar and pulled out a flat stick of spicy beef jerky. Wheeler was the only one in the house who ate that stuff and he could eat bags of it at a time.

"Just a scratch," Reno said dismissively, taking a swig of beer.

Wheeler and Ben were identical twins. They looked alike in almost every way: amber eyes with angled brows, a strong nose, and carved features. They had brown hair, but Ben kept his styled neater than Wheeler, who wore his short on the sides and long on top, combed upward and every which way. They were six feet tall, which was a smidge taller than Denver but shorter than the rest of the brothers. Their build was average, but Wheeler had a tougher stance. He had a no-nonsense mean streak and had quickly gained a reputation in the family as the black sheep. Ben, on the other hand, was easygoing and always enjoyed a game of cards. In fact, he had entered a number of card tournaments and played the circuit. Everyone got along with him better for the simple reason he was less trouble and joked around more.

It was as if Wheeler was trying to sever his connection to Ben. He'd inked himself up, grown facial hair, and developed a serious attitude problem. He used to be a whiz at finance, working for some of the wealthiest immortals, but now showed no desire to go back to work. Austin had once confided to Reno he thought Wheeler might have been involved in a financial scandal, but they didn't ask questions because everyone who decided to join with the Weston pack was each given a clean slate. They all had a past, but you can't force someone to show you their ghosts. When a man wants you to see his house of pain, he'll open the door and invite you in.

Everyone has a few dark years on them. At least with PI work, Reno didn't have to travel as much, but he still armed himself. Shifters didn't have official law enforcement, so PIs worked independently. Only proven crimes would go to the courts run by the higher authority, and that left the rest to good old-fashioned street justice. So Reno didn't exactly have clean hands, but it's not something he talked about. He'd seen a lot of shit go down in his life, and sometimes those memories haunted him in quiet moments. Like the fifteen-year-old runaway he'd found living under a bridge who'd revealed what her father had done to her. Reno could have driven her home and let her pack deal with it, but he'd understood the humiliation she would have to endure. No woman deserved to have a man's eyes look upon her with pity. He'd taken her to a respectable pack up in Colorado and given her a new lease on life. The Packmaster had owed him a favor, so he'd assigned one of his best men as her watchdog. Reno had driven home and couldn't sleep for weeks. Not until he'd tracked down her father and delivered a beating that man would never forget.

"I've got someone I need you to check out," Wheeler said in a low voice.

Meanwhile, Denver and Jericho were in a verbal argument about who had the bigger dick, and who *was* the bigger dick.

"What's it for?"

Wheeler leaned on his forearms, staring at their reflection in the mirror behind the liquor glasses. "Austin wants me to help Lexi get the business on its feet, and dammit, I can't get out of it until I review some of the documents that dead human left behind. I found a couple of wire transfers I can't account for. Large sums of money."

"So? Maybe her boss bought a few cars."

Didn't seem like breaking news for a business owner to spend money.

"No," Wheeler said. "I tried searching the name on the Internet and nothing came up. It's an unusual name."

Reno cocked his head, considering Wheeler's insinuation. All Breeds had alternate identities. It was essential to use their fake IDs in human establishments so the Breed could keep tabs on them. Reno had once fallen off the radar after being arrested by human law enforcement, and his partner was able to run a trace and bail him out. Unusual names were easier to spot as one of their own. The Breed functioned as a completely separate society from humans. They had their own banks to avoid dealing with the IRS, their own jails, and their own clubs.

"Give me his name and I'll see what I can find out," Reno said in a quiet voice. "Are you going to transfer the Sweet Treats money over to a Breed account?"

"It gets sticky," Wheeler said, chewing off a piece of jerky.

"They've already filed taxes and Lexi is making quarterly payments. The only way around it would be to sell the business and start over. I talked with Austin and she can run it until she gets old enough that it might attract attention, then we can move it. It would make more sense to open it up on the Breed side of town where we have more control on leasing and don't file taxes. Humans just love those taxes," he said with a shake of his head.

"I don't normally track down humans, but as a favor for a brother…"

Wheeler jotted down a name on a paper napkin and slid it over. "'Preciate ya," he said, slapping Reno on the back and strolling across the room.

Reno glanced down at the name.

Maddox Cane.

CHAPTER 7

That evening, Trevor and I whipped up some beef tacos with refried beans, guacamole, and tortilla chips on the side. Nobody cooked tacos like Trevor; he made his own seasoning and deep-fried the shells. When he had extra time, he'd make salsa from scratch and it was out of this world and over the moon.

As delicious as it all tasted, my stomach twisted in knots over the thought of meeting up with Sanchez later that evening.

Trevor and I sat at the tiny table, eating off our paper plates, listening to the radio, and chatting. We mostly talked about dream vacations. Trevor wanted to see a shuttle launch at NASA, and I'd always dreamed of walking along a sandy beach where the waters were as crystal blue as the sky. I'd never been to the coast and loved the idea of standing with my feet in an ocean that stretched across the world. Just the idea of it made me smile, close my eyes, and imagine the warm sun on my shoulders and the powerful roar of the surf.

"You're a romantic at heart," he said, pinching a heap of fallen lettuce and nibbling on it. "No one would ever know it because of the mixed signals you give out."

"What signals?"

"*Slippery When Wet* mixed with *Library, Next Exit*."

I swiped the last of the guacamole from my plate and licked my finger. "You're one to talk, Mr. *Public Recreation, Next Five Miles*."

"Oh, is *that* how it is!" he said with a boisterous laugh. Trevor's eyes danced with amusement. "At least I'm not falsely advertising. I knew you were a romantic the day you fell on your ass in front of the escalator and looked up at me with those dreamy eyes."

"They weren't dreamy!" I tossed a piece of chopped tomato at him. Well, maybe they were a *little* bit dreamy, but Trevor knew me too well. Sometimes people just get you, and those are the people you never have to explain yourself to.

"Your nose looks a lot better," I said. Remarkably so. I couldn't even tell he had been hit except for a tiny bit of swelling.

"I put some ice on it." He arched an eyebrow and glanced at me. "It wasn't broken after all."

"And your lip?"

He wiped his hands on a paper napkin. "That was just dried blood from where my nose dripped."

"You still want to go to the party?" I asked, picking a morsel of beef from my plate.

Trevor licked the guacamole from his thumb and crunched on another chip. "If you work with Lexi, then there's no avoiding it. You don't need my permission to go—it's your life. But if *you're* going, *I'm* going," he said reluctantly.

"It doesn't have to be like that. We don't have to go."

"Yeah, we're going. I know how you operate and you don't fly solo to these things. You need to get out and have some fun for a change. You've been cooped up and not socializing. I'm here to rectify that. All this," he said, pointing around at the trailer, "it's bullshit. It's not who you are or what your life is about. I don't want to find you twenty years from now, chain-smoking at this table with a stack of scratch-off lottery tickets, dreaming your life will get better. That's what your grandma was—a dreamer. Not in a good way. She couldn't accept the cards she was dealt and always wanted somebody else's hand."

"We all want something better."

"At what cost?" He lifted his brown eyes to mine and they softened. "Forget all this. Go out and have fun."

I lifted my plate and set it on the counter behind me. "So you want me to live in denial?"

He shrugged. "Nothing wrong with that."

"There is, Trevor."

He shook his head and scooped up another bite of dip. "Works for me. I go out, have fun, and don't think about all the bullshit that tethers you to a life you don't want. Better than walking around all depressed, and that's what I'm seeing in you lately. I don't like that, April. I hate seeing you change."

"I'm just going through a patch these past couple of days. It doesn't mean I'm changing, it doesn't mean I'll never laugh again or take a chance and go to a party. But this is my life, and I have to accept it even if I don't like it. You can't live in denial or it catches up with you."

"*Fuck me.* I feel an argument coming on," he said in irritation, walking to the sink and rinsing out his glass.

I glanced at the clock and it was fifteen until eleven. I had to get out of there but didn't want Trevor to get suspicious. "So then run away from your problems and go play some pool," I suggested. "That'll make it all better."

I hated being so cruel, but when Trevor got mad, he usually bailed. I wasn't sure where he went—probably the bar.

"April Showers used to be a pet name," he said. "Now it's just a shower of tears. *Woe is me, I live in a trailer.*"

I threw a pillow at him.

Hard.

"Go to hell! I'm giving you a place to stay and doing the best I can to work out my problems and make it right. I'm not the one who hooked up with a guy because he bought me tickets to Linkin Park. Oh, excuse me—backstage passes *and* a limo ride."

Trevor flipped my paper plate on the floor, grabbed his keys, and stormed out the door. As I heard the engine to his hatchback rev, I wanted to run out and say I was sorry. We never bickered like that, and I was certain that I might have fractured our relationship. But I was protective of Trevor. He was like the brother I'd never had, and it was more important that he didn't get involved in what I was doing.

I waited until his car drove off before running out the door. I had gone to the bank earlier for a withdrawal and stuffed the money in my oversized brown purse. If I had it my way, I would have just wired him the money. Loan sharks worked on their own terms, so I wanted to get this over with as quickly as possible and put it behind me.

The building where Sanchez wanted to meet wasn't far from where I worked, so I jogged most of the way. When I arrived, I slowed my pace because the road leading up to the warehouse had some major cracks and potholes that weren't easy to see in the dark. Out of breath, I warily looked around and observed nothing out of the ordinary, although I'm not sure what I was expecting to see. A tactical unit? Police dogs? A crowd of mobsters holding machine guns?

Just to the right of the road, the pale moonlight illuminated a white BMW in the parking lot.

I swallowed hard and approached the main door, clutching my purse tightly. Most of the windows had been boarded up or smashed in, and graffiti covered the dark brick on the exterior walls. It was an eyesore, but since it was away from the road, no one had bothered to have it torn down or painted. It probably cost more to demolish than it was worth.

I wondered how he'd gotten the key to open the door, or if it had always been open. Maybe squatters lived inside. I cupped my elbows and peered through the doorway to make sure no one was in there. When I saw it was clear, I headed toward a white glow of artificial light down the hall to my right.

The concrete floors were covered with pebbles, dirt, cigarette butts, and old soda cans. An acrid smell of filth infiltrated my nose and I couldn't identify the scent, but it reminded me of the time I found a dead dog in a ditch. My stomach knotted when I glanced behind me at the dark corridor. I thought about leaving the money right at the doorstep and taking off, because I had no business being out here by myself.

"I'm in here," he called out impatiently from a lit room.

I peered through the open doorway and Sanchez was sitting at a metal table, smoking a cigarette. He made little donut rings, which floated up to a hanging light and quickly broke apart. When I realized the room had working electricity, that's when I got the impression he used this location frequently.

"I have the money," I said.

He glanced at his gold watch. "Sit down."

Across the table from him was a dirty chair and I wiped the seat with my hand before sitting, despite his chuckles.

Sanchez narrowed his eyes as he took another long drag from his short cigarette. I reached in my purse to pull out the envelope.

"You're late," he said.

"I'm sorry. I couldn't get here any faster. Here's the money." I pushed the envelope across the table with a shaky hand. "It's all there." My eyes skated to the open door and back to him. I kept telling myself that my grandma had done this all the time, and she never came home missing a finger.

Sanchez bit the end of his cigarette between his teeth and tore open the envelope. Very meticulously, he separated the bills by denomination and counted the money. Then he eyed me closely and put his forearms on the table, patting out the butt of his smoke.

"Where did a vanilla girl like you come up with this much green so fast?"

"I had some tucked away," I lied. "That should square me away with Delgado."

He tapped a fingernail against his tooth as if contemplating whether to believe my story. "The man will be pleased he got his money."

"Good," I said, rising to my feet. "Let him know we're even."

"Not quite," he said softly, beating me to the door. "You were late. There's always a penalty for tardiness."

I stared at him dumbfounded. "I paid what I owed."

He clicked the door shut and leaned against it.

"I need to go home. Someone's waiting for me," I said calmly, reasonably. "If Delgado has any issues, he knows how to get in touch with me."

Sanchez grinned in such a way that all the muscles in his face relaxed, as if it were drug-induced. "Sit down."

Collecting my nerves, I said, "Open the door. You have the money and—"

"Sit the fuck down. Last warning." He bared his teeth and chomped down once, causing me to step back at the sound his molars made when they clicked together. "I know you walked here, because there's mud on your shoes and I didn't hear an engine. You think you can run away from me? Let's negotiate like civilized people and things won't have to get ugly." He folded his arms and waited for me to comply.

I did as he asked because the man scared me. He not only had a car, but I could never outrun him. Plus, the idea of being chased like an animal frightened me enough that I decided we needed to have the conversation. It would also give me a moment to recall if I'd seen any objects I could use as a weapon. The chair would be a last resort, but getting out of the room would be a smarter option than trying to take down a man who outweighed me. Since this was a business transaction, I kept my wits about me and calmly sat in the chair, folding my hands on my lap.

Sanchez strolled back to his chair and sat across from me. The light from the bulb that shone on the table wasn't soft, but harsh and sterile. The metal shade directed the light so that it didn't illuminate the outer walls of the room—just the table.

"I charge one hundred dollars for each minute my clients are late," he said, looking down at his watch. "You came in at 11:14 p.m. That means you owe me…" He tapped his finger on his chin, lifting his eyes to the ceiling.

"I'm not paying you $1400 for arriving a few minutes late. You never stated there was a penalty."

His eyes lit up, not having expected me to respond so calm and businesslike. Sanchez chuckled dryly while pinching the small patch of hair on his chin. "I like you, Vanilla Frost. You're a clever little girl. If you're as smart as I think you are, then I'm sure you can come up with alternatives for cash that would clear your debt with me. This has nothing to do with Delgado. When it comes to dealing with his clients, I have my own separate rules. So, what ideas can you come up with?"

My heart constricted and then galloped in my chest. I put my hands on the table to show him how in control I was.

"We'll negotiate a payment plan," I suggested. "But only on the condition you lower the amount to half. You didn't disclose the penalty up front."

A smile crept up his face. "I like that idea. But I don't do payment plans when it comes to cash." His brow rose and my stomach turned. "Some collectors will pound your ass to the floor and beat you with a wrench, but I'm a guy who sees opportunity. I like to build that trust between my client and myself. So take off your shirt."

Stunned, the words became caught in my throat and I didn't reply. I hoped my silence would erase the reality of what he'd just asked me to do. My eye twitched involuntarily and I had the urge to rub it, but kept very still. I'd read a book on body language hoping it would help me during job interviews. There were certain "tells" that would give away if you were lying, nervous, or feigning confidence. The wrong gestures created a lack of trust.

What if I fled? What would he do? Could I dial the police beneath the table without him noticing? Is the table bolted to the floor? God, I'm getting a gun license after this.

"What is your deadline for the cash payment?"

He replied with a stony expression. "Midnight tomorrow. Same place."

I couldn't swing it. Not without stealing from the business account again. I thought about selling my car, but that wouldn't scrape up more than a hundred bucks at a junkyard.

"What if we make it one week from today?"

"What if you take off your shirt?" he said impatiently. "If you don't want to pay me tomorrow, then that's your choice. But know this: By the stroke of midnight, if you fail to give me all I'm due, then I'll carve you up like a pumpkin. Starting with all your fingers. Then your toes. I like to save the nose for last."

The tacos had been a bad idea. I kept swallowing, on the verge of throwing up. "Fine. I'll have the money tomorrow."

"Take off your shirt," he said again.

"We have a deal."

Sanchez reached down and placed a large knife on the table between us. The kind that had all those serrated edges along the blade.

"I give you my word I won't get up from my chair or touch that knife. But I want a down payment for the inconvenience you've caused me by throwing off my schedule, you little *puta*. Take. Off.

Your. Shirt. That's *all* I want. You'll see I'm not the bad guy, April. Maybe if this goes well, you'll change your mind about the cash and do it my way."

"And if I get up and walk out?"

A crooked grin slid up his face, and that's when I noticed he had a small scar on the bridge of his nose. Funny the things you don't pay attention to. He wiggled the crook of his pinky finger while touching the knife and leaned back in his chair.

I waited him out, staring at the knife and then at the door.

CHAPTER 8

I WOKE UP TO THE FEEL of someone's hands gently stroking my hair. My lashes unwillingly pried apart, and soft lips touched my cheek.

"I'm sorry, April. I'm a jerk."

"Trevor," I grumbled, stretching out my legs and yawning. "I didn't mean what I said either. I must be having PMS or something."

"No, when you have PMS, you break out the serious books."

"Huh?" I rubbed my eyes and noticed he was fully dressed.

Trevor fell against the pillow on my left, tucking his hands beneath it. "You know—those bodice-ripping romance novels where the girl is in peril and the hero cuts off his right arm to save her and then spews out the most poetic words ever spoken. Then you drag me to the mall so you can hide at a back table and drink your cocoa while getting those sad puppy dog eyes and watching adorable couples holding hands."

"It's too early for this, Trev. I'm starving. Do you want me to make you breakfast?"

A plastic sack appeared and he waved it over my head. "Got you something."

"What is it? Bagels?"

"Open it."

I sat up and squinted, closing the curtain behind the bed. Too much sunshine and my morning face didn't go together. Trevor smiled dubiously at me, his fingers laced behind his head as he watched anxiously. Today he was in a crisp white shirt with faded denims and a rope necklace made of leather.

Reaching in the bag, I pulled out a rectangle that was wrapped in red paper. It was thin, heavy, and definitely not pancakes. I glared at him.

"I had to take it out of the box," he explained. "You'll see why."

I tore the paper open and gasped. "An e-reader! I can't believe you got this for me. Trevor! It's too expensive."

"Ah, bologna," he muttered, sitting up. "It's the latest model so you can jump on the Internet when you're out, and it lets you watch movies. It's fully charged and ready to go."

I flipped it on and scrolled through the images. "Books? There's books on here. Or do I buy those?"

Trevor laughed. "No, those are yours, April. I bought them all for you to replace the ones you lost. I looked around the trailer and figured out what was missing. The rest are just for fun. I'll show you how to shop for free books later on, but those should keep you busy for a while." He paused for a few beats and his voice wavered. "So, uh, is it okay? Do you like it?"

I tackled him and squealed against his neck. He belted out a satisfied laugh, and I felt like a kid at Christmas. "I love you, Trevor. You didn't have to do this."

"Yes I did. It's your early birthday present."

I sat up and held it between my fingers. It wasn't the cost of the item—it's that Trevor was the only person in my life who really knew me. My own sister didn't indulge me with books, but instead picked out things that she would have wanted for herself. God, I loved him so much and couldn't understand how someone with such an enormous heart didn't have a family or close group of friends. It almost made me feel guilty, as if I were keeping him all to myself.

Trevor glanced at his watch and grabbed the wrapping paper and bag. "Now take off that damn shirt."

I froze and felt all the blood rush to my face.

Trevor rolled out of bed, not paying attention. "I hate it when you wear Billy Joel, especially when I'm lying beside you. It's like I'm sleeping with him. You want a breakfast burrito with some of that leftover meat in the fridge or… April?"

Before he caught on to my mini panic attack, I set the e-reader in my drawer and scooted down the bed.

He seized my wrist. "What's wrong?"

"I need to use the bathroom," I said, jerking my arm free and locking myself in that tiny little closet that wouldn't even allow me the privacy to cry. Trevor was right. Everything made sense about shutting away all the gloom and just relishing life. I needed to compartmentalize my emotions and lock up the bad stuff. The party was just the thing I needed—barring Trevor going Bruce Lee on someone.

A door violently slammed and I jumped.

"Trevor?"

When I heard shouting, I yanked my jeans on and hurried to the door.

"April, get back!"

It took me a second to assess the situation. Trevor stood ten feet in front of me, barefoot and holding a butcher knife. Pacing toward us was the wolf.

My wolf.

"Trevor, no!" I jumped down and tried to run past him. He grabbed my arm and swung me around.

The wolf growled ferociously and bared his white fangs.

"*This* is your wolf, April? I thought you were talking about a dog, like one of those fucking sled dogs."

I shrugged. "I'm not an animal expert, Trevor. He won't hurt us. I haven't seen him since he took off and maybe he's hungry."

"Get off our property," Trevor shouted.

But the wolf narrowed his eyes and stepped forward, not allowing anyone to talk down to him in that manner. Didn't matter he was facing off with a guy holding a sharp blade in front of him.

"Don't you dare hurt him," I hissed. "That animal is not aggressive."

He gave me an "Oh really?" look as a stream of slobber dripped off the wolf's jaw.

"Wolves are territorial. You let him hang around here once and he'll think this is his turf," he argued. "Get outta here!" Trevor yelled again in a threatening manner.

"He can't understand you. Come inside and he'll leave."

Trevor raised his arm at the wolf. "That's your only warning." His eyes latched on to mine as he walked by. "I got bit once. You can't trust a dog, wolf, whatever."

Trevor yelled out a curse when I slipped around him and dropped to my knees, holding out my hands. "Come here, sweet boy. Let me have a look at you."

The wolf compliantly paced forward, flicking his eyes at Trevor but wagging his tail. He licked my nose and I ran my fingers over his soft ears. "Is your leg feeling better today, pretty boy?"

He sat down and lifted his paw as if he wanted me to shake it.

"April," Trevor scolded, and then he gave up and went inside.

"I missed you." Then the tears came. It was just easier that way, because he didn't understand. The wolf licked my cheeks and groaned. "I'm so scared," I whispered. "Someone is after me and I have a feeling that something bad is going to happen. I don't know what to do. I wish you could help me." It seemed childish telling all my troubles to an animal, but it's as if he sensed something was wrong.

"April!"

I kissed his nose and stood up. "I have to go. I'll put some food out in a few minutes, so don't wander off."

When he trotted off, I couldn't help but notice that my wolf walked away without a limp.

"Tell me the truth, April. You have good taste, so I'll believe whatever you say. I would have brought my neighbor to help me shop, but Naya would love nothing better than to dress me in something that would end up on the Internet later on."

Lexi emerged from the dressing room in a pair of cutoff shorts with all the frayed pieces hanging down. She did a little hip swivel to give me all the angles.

"Put your hair up in a ponytail and it works," I said. "That knocks five years off your age, but otherwise they're too hoochie with all the jewels on the back pockets."

Her shoulders sagged. "I want something fun for the party that I don't normally wear, but I sure as hell don't want to slut it up," she grumbled. "I have long skirts, jeans, and shorts—Austin has seen it all." She disappeared behind the mauve curtain.

"Try the cutoff jeans," I suggested.

"Something with more leg!"

Oh.

Ever since Lexi had been living with Austin, she had discovered her sex appeal. She usually dressed casual, but with a hot guy at her side, I could see she wanted to spice things up and make sure he only had eyes for her at the party. Although I personally think he didn't care what she wore, because whatever it was, he'd probably just want to tear it off with his teeth.

"Uh, definite no," I said as soon as she ripped the curtain open and I got a glimpse of her pink shorts with rhinestones on the pockets. "Try the loose skirt with the slit. That's sexy. Goes to the knee, tight, shows leg along the side."

"I want you to buy something," she yelled out. "It's on me."

"That's okay. I have something at home I can wear."

The last thing I wanted to do was take her money. I hadn't figured out what to do about Sanchez and my nerves were shot. Lexi had invited me to go shopping while the other two girls we worked with ran the store. They were scheduled to open tomorrow; that way we could have as much fun as we wanted tonight.

"You're going to buy something and that's that," Lexi declared.

"Why? So you can hook me up with someone?"

"No," she said, pulling the curtain away. "That's what my friend Naya likes to do. But you don't think Denver is spoon worthy?"

My eyes floated up. "Denver?" He was handsome, but hardly a man I could imagine spooning me from behind after a night of blissful…

"Come on, April. You need to break out of that shell a little. I'm not saying you have to marry anyone. I used to be cynical about love, but Austin changed that. Sometimes it's like those Cracker Jacks—you have to go through a bunch of nuts to find the prize."

"Nice analogy."

She shrugged and spun around in a powder-blue skirt with a black top.

"That's pretty on you, with your complexion and long hair," I said, admiring the outfit.

Lexi grinned and stared down at her tan legs. "I don't wear short skirts that often, except at work. I think Austin's tongue will roll out when he sees me in this. It's thin, stretchy, and more formfitting."

"I'm sure he'll be panting." I chuckled and noticed she bit her lip, averting her eyes in a way she sometimes did, as if she were holding in a secret.

"You ever wonder if things like Vampires and Shifters are real?" she blurted out, tossing me a dress to try on.

I switched places with her and closed the curtain, slipping out of my jeans. "Where did that come from? I don't know. Why?"

"Just curious. I was watching this show the other night and they talked about all the mysteries in the universe and how there are things beyond explanation that exist."

"Like hot firemen?"

She snorted. "You got that right. But seriously, it made me think about how maybe those kinds of things might be real, and maybe they're just regular people. People who are born different are treated different. What do you think about it?"

"I've never given it much thought. Except, from what I know of Vampires, they're not born different. They're bitten and turned. Same with werewolves, right? Why wouldn't they come out?"

"Maybe they're afraid the humans will kill them."

"Uh, yeah. If someone tried to suck on my neck, I'd stake 'em."

"Thus explains your dating situation, April," she said with a laugh in her voice.

I stepped into the dress and zipped up the back. The lavender color wasn't a shade I wore very often. The length fell just below the knee and was higher in the front, giving it a little swish when I walked. The straps on my shoulders were about an inch wide and it wasn't too low around the neckline, which I liked.

"This is lovely," I said with surprise.

The curtain ripped open and Lexi gasped. "That's it. We're doing this again. You look like a totally different girl! You're a girly girl! You've always had fashion sense, April, but I never get to see you all dolled up. Damn, the men are going to *fall over* when they see you in that dress."

I blushed with a little anger. "I'm not going to be the only single woman there, am I?"

An expressive smile brightened her face. "No," she said, folding her arms. "The party is growing. We have a few Shift—shift workers that Austin knows coming by, and they're bringing dates or their friends. Ben and Wheeler are filling in potholes with gravel, while Denver is having a heart attack because there's not enough beer. He had to call up a guy last minute to haul a few kegs up to the house. It's going to be a good time, so please don't back out on me. Hell, you know me—I'm not a party girl at all. But it's not going to be one of those obnoxious get-togethers where hookers are dancing on the tables and—"

I snickered. "What kind of parties do you normally go to?"

Her brow arched. "My friend Naya is a stripper. 'Nuff said. Anyhow, my mom and Maizy are out of town and Austin is setting up the music and a few other things. My job is to pick up some stuff for the burgers at the store, another reason I invited you. Sorry, I need an extra set of hands."

"What about Ivy?" I'd met her once. A pretty girl who was friends with Austin and Lexi, she had a long, beautiful braid and a warm smile.

"Ivy will definitely be there; she's excited to meet some of the neighboring… ah, some of the neighbors. She's busy decorating and locking up a few things so they don't get broken. She bought some Chinese lanterns to string up in the front yard and I think Austin is going to help her put them up. Shit!" Lexi scowled at her watch. "We have to hurry. Do you mind helping me with the groceries?"

My stomach knotted. This would eat up time I needed to find money, but in the back of my mind, I knew what I had to do. Call Maddox.

"After we finish shopping, I can drive you home to take a shower and change clothes."

"No," I said sharply, and it caught her attention. "You can drop me off at the store. I have to run a few errands in town."

She began folding up some of the clothes she had tossed in a pile on the bench. "Then how are you going to get home?"

"It's the first day we've had sunshine, Lexi. Maybe I want to enjoy it a little bit."

"It's not a big deal. It'll give you more time to get ready or even take a nap. You can always run errands tomorrow. Don't eat though; we'll have plenty of food."

I sat down on the bench and spun the price tag on my dress around. "*Holy smokes.* I've changed my mind on the dress."

"No, you haven't. How come you don't want me to drive you home?"

Silence fell like a curtain between us. I parted my hair away from my eyes. "What else are you having besides burgers?"

She watched me for a few beats and then changed out of her shirt. "Hot dogs and chicken. Austin wants me to pick up a few steaks, but they're only for certain people."

I laughed. "That might not go over well. All men like steak over hot dogs."

"Well, I can't explain it. Anyhow, dammit!"

I stood up and helped her out of the shirt before she ripped it apart. Lexi was definitely stressing out.

"Thanks. What was I saying? Oh, we're also having corn on the cob and beans."

A laugh pealed out of me. "That should go over well, Lexi. Beans? *No* one ever thinks about practical side items. While the women are picking corn out of their teeth, the men will be farting to the tune of an old Queen song."

Her lip twisted. "Good point. Austin said no salad. There's going to be more men than women, so I have to get something they'll like, not rabbit food. Something… *manly*," she said in a silly voice, flexing her biceps.

We laughed and I folded up a few of the clothes. "Macaroni. You can buy tubs of that stuff and it's already precooked. Or grab some cold pasta salad and that way it will be one less thing to heat up, not to mention you can buy that premade too."

"What would I do without you, April? You're a genius. I've never hosted a party like this, so I ran out of the house before I gave myself a heart attack. Austin was driving me nuts with his choices for music. Some things we can agree on, but I won't bend for Kings of Leon. Well…" Then she muffled a private laugh.

"I'm looking forward to it."

God, was I. Trevor was right. I needed to step out of my comfort zone for a change and enjoy myself. Sometimes I got so wrapped up in the serious stuff that I forgot to have fun.

"Just stay away from Jericho."

"Who's that?"

"One of Austin's brothers," she said. "I don't think you've met him. He looks like a rocker. He's not a bad guy, it's just that he likes to party. Hard. He's not the kind of guy I want to see you get mixed up with. I don't know if his band will be coming, but his version of partying and ours are not even in the same zip code."

"You don't think I need a bad boy?"

She *humphed* and swung her purse over her shoulder. "There's a difference between a bad boy and a boy that's bad for you. Jericho is bad for you. He's a one-night stand who drinks, smokes, and does drugs."

Definitely not my type. "What about dessert?"

"Shoot. I forgot about that," she said gruffly. "I'm not going to stress. Guys sit around eating popcorn and trail mix, so that'll work for me."

"Sounds good. Cheesecake won't feed an army like pretzels will. Plus, it'll melt. Cheese dip or salsa will stain your floor, so if you want dip, we can grab onion or ranch and a few bags of chips."

Lexi smiled. "I'm glad you're coming, April. I never get to hang out with you outside of work."

"I need to be home before three; I have something to do before coming over tonight. My friend Trevor is still going."

"Still? Was there a reason he wasn't?"

I cleared my throat and used my pinky finger to move away a chunk of bangs that kept sliding in front of my eye. "He got into a fistfight with Reno."

She gasped and ripped the curtain closed again. "What? He didn't tell me this! What happened?"

"I have no idea. Trevor thought Reno needed to mind his own

business and Reno punched his lights out. If you don't want him to come, I'll understand."

"No," she said decidedly. "I'll have a talk with Reno and make sure he stays away from you two. He's not someone I've warmed up to in the house as quickly as the others. A wealth of information, but not very social and way too serious. I'm just surprised he did that; I wonder if I should tell Austin."

"Don't start up any family drama. Come on, Alexia. Sorry, I mean Lexi."

She dramatically opened the curtain. "We're going to make some tails wag tonight."

CHAPTER 9

AFTER WE LOADED UP THE truck with groceries for the cookout, Lexi drove back to her house and showed me how to get there.

"Wow," I gasped, leaning my head out the open window. "This is *huge*!"

"That's what I said last night."

Her phone rang and I unbuckled my seat belt.

"Hold on," she said. "Hello? Hi, Maze! Are you having a good time, sweetie? You are? ... Wow. Your big sis misses you. Tell me all about the pool."

While Lexi carried on with her little sister, I grabbed a few paper bags from the trunk and glanced at the house again. It was gorgeous. Two, maybe three stories, and a balcony filled with yellow and orange chrysanthemums. White shutters bordered each window, and a long porch wrapped around the front and sides of the house. Lexi mentioned it had once been a hotel many years ago. I couldn't imagine who would have come out this far to stay at a hotel, but I guess some people have money and just like to get away from it all. Wooden wind chimes clacked together from a pear tree on the right, and a child's swing hung from an oak tree a few feet away. I wasn't sure what to make of it all. Horseshoes, rocking chairs on the long porch, a purple bottle of bubbles on one of the steps, a bunch of cars and a motorcycle to the left, and a giant wooden sign nailed on the house that said Weston.

"Austin! I need some help," Lexi shouted out.

The door swung open and Reno stepped outside.

My breath caught.

He didn't notice me as he jogged down the steps to help Lexi.

I just stood there mutely, peering at him from between two paper bags. The closer he got, the more nervous I became and I wanted to flee. He wasn't the kind of guy I imagined myself turning stupid over, but there I was, feeling a mantastic episode coming on.

My heart pounded against my chest with each step he took across the grass in his black boots. And then he noticed me.

And stopped.

My heart stopped too.

"Reno, you remember April. I heard you beat up her friend," Lexi chided.

"I'm sorry," I said, peering up at him between the bags. He squinted as if he didn't want me to see his eyes—his beautiful brown eyes that I had only glimpsed briefly in the store. He'd shaved since I'd last seen him. Not a single rogue whisker poked out from his jaw. It was so smooth that I had a silly urge to touch his cheeks. Reno had a brush cut—trimmed on the sides and longer on the top with short sideburns. Perfectly styled and brushed. Reno's gaze intimidated me, yet there was something familiar about him that I couldn't put my finger on.

"What are you apologizing for?" he asked in a rough voice. Reno had a gravelly pitch that was masculine. Most guys just didn't talk like that. Then again, Reno wasn't most guys. He was unlike any man I'd ever known.

"For Trevor calling you a freak. It was rude and uncalled for, but you still shouldn't have hit him."

Maybe it didn't excuse Reno for knocking Trevor out, but whoever made up the sticks and stones song was an idiot who had never been picked on. Name-calling hurt, and maybe it hurt tough guys too.

He lifted the sacks from my arms and walked away without an apology.

Lexi put her arm across my shoulder. "Are you staring at his ass?"

"No!" I shrugged off her arm and she chuckled, reaching in the trunk for a few bags.

"Sorry, April. It just kind of looked like you were checking him out," she said with a private smile.

Austin flew out the main door and cut across the lawn, dressed in a white tank top and jeans. I got an eyeful of the tattoos that marked his shoulders and upper arms with a tribal design. "How's it going, April?" he said more than asked.

"Hey," I said, greeting him. "It's going pretty good."

"Lexi, I need your help."

"What's up?" She pinched the cleft on his chin.

He kissed her softly on the mouth and growled. I saw his bottom lip pull out a little as she nipped it with her teeth. "Cut that out," he said in a low voice, sliding his hand over her rear as if I weren't even there. "I forgot to pick up gas and charcoal."

"So why do you need my help?"

"We also need a shitload of ice for the beer. Ivy just brought it to my attention, and I'll need you to park in front while I load up the back. She also thinks we need to buy or rent some large trashcans."

"Oh, shit. I didn't think of that," Lexi said. "There'll be bottles and plates all over the place." Then she gasped. "I forgot the plastic cups. Dammit!"

"Everyone else is busy and we need to get it together before they start showing up. There are a lot of important people who'll be here."

I wondered what he meant by that. It wasn't as if the mayor was going to show up at a keg party. "Lexi, I need to get home."

She knitted her brows. "The hardware store is in the opposite direction."

"Reno!" Austin shouted. Then he stuck his fingers in his mouth and whistled. I always admired a man who could do that.

Heavy boots clomped on the porch as Reno came out. The sun drifted behind a cloud and Austin stalked in his direction.

Lexi tapped her fingers on the hood of the car, lost in her thoughts.

Austin's voice boomed across the yard. "Lexi, change of plans. Reno's gonna take April home. We need two cars because it's not all going to fit in one."

"Well, we better get back in time, Austin Cole. I have to get ready."

He snorted. "To throw on a pair of shorts and a tank top? Come on, Ladybug. Let's get going."

She smirked at him with a "You just wait and see" look in her eyes. He caught it, analyzed it, and folded his arms as she strolled around the car and looked at him provocatively over her shoulder.

I hated to admit it, but I loved watching those two. They had an explosive chemistry that most couples didn't, and I adored it. Yet, somewhere in the back of my head, I'd convinced myself that it wouldn't last. Austin was all kinds of hot and I'm sure he had women coming on to him all the time. Lexi had a temper, and all it would take was one meaningless argument that would send him out the door and into the arms of another.

That was why I loved romance novels. The book ends and there's nothing to spoil it. In real life, love isn't about the fairy tale. Love is about not being alone. Sometimes we settle for less because that's all there is.

I almost jumped out of my skin when a heavy hand lightly touched my shoulder. I spun around and caught my surprised reaction reflected back at me in Reno's aviator sunglasses. He smelled amazing, and I leaned in without realizing it.

He sucked on his teeth for a nanosecond. "You ever been on a bike?"

Reno took me on a short spin around the property on his Triumph Bonneville so I could get used to the feel of a motorcycle between my legs. When he first throttled her up, the vibration sent a thrill through my body, tickling every nerve. It was the sexiest feeling. He showed me where to put my feet and what not to do. When I started to wrap my arms around him, he laughed, guiding my hands down to his belt loops.

The loud motor made me uneasy and I had to trust that he wasn't going to kill me on the turns. Reno secured a helmet on my head that was sized to fit a woman, and he didn't baby-step it one bit when we hit the main road. I let out a few shrieks when he weaved around a car, but Reno seemed like the kind of man who owned the road on that bike. He wasn't afraid of the raw power and knew how to handle it with cool confidence.

The wind cooled my legs, but my fair complexion wasn't

compatible with the afternoon sun and my thighs began to redden. When we reached a red light, Reno put his feet out for balance and revved the engine. It sounded predatory, and the seat vibrated beneath me. I rested my hands on my hot thighs and wet my dry lips.

God, I had to admit I felt totally *badass*.

A car rolled up on our right and I heard one of those "Yeows" that a guy makes when he's catcalling. It didn't come from the driver, but someone in the back seat of the car who leaned over to get a better look at my legs.

"Too bad she's with that fucker," the guy in the back said.

I got mad and gave them the finger. The driver laughed and I grinned, putting my hands back around Reno's waist.

Then I heard a thick voice in the back seat of the car call me a cunt. It should have fueled my fire like it would Lexi, but things like that embarrassed me, so I looked away and leaned against Reno's back, holding him as if he were my boyfriend.

Then I heard a click and looked to my right.

"Say you're sorry," Reno said in a deep voice. A *calm* voice, but I felt it vibrating through his back.

I sat up straight when I saw his right arm was extended with a gun in his hand.

"You can apologize, or I can track you across the city. How 'bout that?"

"Sorry, goddammit," a young man griped before the windows rolled up.

The light blinked green and the car sped away. My heart raced as Reno made the gun disappear. I glanced around, but we were the only ones at the small intersection.

My mouth was opening to say something when he glanced over his shoulder at me. "I'm proud of you." He throttled the engine.

"For what?" I yelled through the helmet.

He lifted my facemask. "For sticking up for yourself. I don't step in when a man is appreciating a beautiful woman, no matter how juvenile he goes about it. Let's just say he caught me on a good day, calling you a name like that." Reno lowered my visor. "Hang on tight."

The engine growled and we took off.

Through hand gestures and shouting, I directed him toward my trailer. Suddenly, the bike veered off the main road and pulled into a Sonic drive-in. As soon as we eased into a parking spot, he cut off the engine.

"What are we doing here?" I asked.

"Having lunch. Lexi is going to starve me to death waiting for the party tonight. A man's got to eat."

I got off and was fumbling with the helmet when he turned around and undid my chin strap. As he slowly pulled it off, my hair fell across my face.

He looked down at me, still wearing his shades. "You did real good, April. How was your first ride?"

"Unforgettable." I smiled, scraping my fingers through my bright hair, which was now a tangled mess.

He held out his arm, coaxing me to walk toward the outside seating area. It felt good to sit in the shade and feel a gentle breeze on my neck.

"I love all this sunshine," I said, wiping dirt off the mesh table with my forearm. "I hope we get to keep it for a little while." I turned around and stared at the menu that was sitting between the tables on a sturdy pole. "What do you feel like eating?"

"Double bacon cheeseburger, large fries, and a banana shake," he said without missing a beat.

I slowly turned my head to give him a surprised look. "Are you sure you don't want to just eat light? There's going to be a lot of food at the party."

"This *is* eating light. I burn off a lot of energy," he said, sliding his shades on top of his head.

I admired his rich brown eyes, which were deep-set and pensive. Reno had a serious expression with frown lines in his forehead and a clean-shaven jaw. His hair was shorter on the sides and long enough on the top that I could pinch it. So clean-cut, and yet so tough-looking—like a cop or a soldier in civilian clothes.

"Order whatever you want. I'm paying," he said, placing his leather wallet on the table. Reno wore a white undershirt with a blue button-up over it, but it wasn't buttoned. I could see part of a gun strap that went over his shoulder. He caught the direction of my gaze and closed it up to conceal his gun. Then he placed his forearms on the table and narrowed his eyes. "You don't say much. Most women talk a lot to fill in the silence."

I shrugged, grateful I hadn't tumbled into a trashcan by now. "Do you always carry a gun?"

His mouth turned down in a contemplative way. "Most of the time. It's part of my job."

That explained it. "You're a cop," I said.

Reno shook his head. "Private investigator. I'm not going to sugarcoat it for you—it's dangerous work."

"Do you normally pull out your gun and aim it at innocent people?"

His lips thinned. "Innocent is debatable." His finger tapped on the table. "There're things you don't understand, and I can't sit here at Sonic and tell you whatever you need to hear to feel better about what happened back there. Every man draws a line in the sand that determines what he's willing to stand for. I know exactly where that line is in my life, and nobody crosses it. So if you think a man calling you a filthy name like that means he's innocent, then we're not on the same page."

I'm not sure if what he said made me feel better, but I couldn't deny I'd liked that renegade moment when a man had actually stuck up for me. Trevor did it all the time, but his intentions were misplaced; all a guy had to do was flirt with me. Reno had minded his own business until they called me a vulgar name. He could have blown it off and ignored them.

But he hadn't. Reno had protected my honor.

Maybe after a warning like that, those men would think twice about doing that to another woman. Probably not, but I admired Reno for not having turned a blind eye like I'd seen people do so many times.

I pressed the button on the menu and the lady asked if we were ready. After repeating Reno's order, I examined the menu again. "Could I just get some tater tots?"

"And?" she said in a tone that irritated me.

"Um, a small lemonade."

"Is that all?"

"Yes. That will complete my order." I spun around in annoyance. What did she expect me to do—order a foot-long chili dog and try to eat that with class in front of a guy like Reno?

"Is that going to be enough?" He pushed up his brow with his index finger and I smiled warmly.

"At least it's not a salad. I'm saving my appetite for later. Plus, I'm not big on eating out anyhow. Especially fast food."

"We're going to have drinks and you shouldn't be running on an empty stomach with alcohol."

"I don't drink much."

"How about your friend? Does he drink much?"

"Trevor loves to drink and have a good time. I hope there won't be any trouble because he's coming with me, but I'm not going to the party without him. He's my best friend and that's the deal."

Reno scratched his jaw and glanced at a truck pulling out. "Well, he won't be my friend if he thinks he's going to drive you home after drinking."

"No, I'll be the designated driver."

"Then you're not drinking."

I frowned. "One beer won't—"

"Kill you? Make you a little relaxed and not pay attention when a car makes a sudden turn and you can't get out of the way? No, you're not drinking. But you'll still have a good time because Denver makes phenomenal steaks."

"Lexi said the steaks were for certain people."

He tapped his knuckle on the table. "If you want a steak, then you're getting a steak. Fuck certain people." Then his lips briefly pressed together. "You probably don't like swearing, but I ain't gonna church it up for you."

Now that was a funny thought. I wasn't big on cussing, but I wasn't Mother Teresa either. Reno lived in a house full of men; it was to be expected.

"Be yourself, Reno. There's no need to censor yourself around me."

His shoulders relaxed a little, and a gust of wind blew a strand of hair in my eye. With a swift brush of his hand, Reno moved it away and we had a little moment. Maybe it was just me, but he smiled with his eyes.

"How long have you known him?" he asked.

"Trevor? Seems like forever."

"Does he have family here?"

"They cut off relations years ago." It wasn't my place to tell Trevor's business. "He's a really good guy and a loyal friend."

"That I don't doubt," Reno muttered.

"Were you born here?" I asked out of curiosity.

"No. Nevada."

"Ah. That explains why you don't have a heavy accent. Hey, wait a minute. Austin, Denver, Reno... Your parents must have moved around a lot."

He suppressed a grin and leaned forward on his elbows. "Yeah, our parents had a sense of humor. What about your name?"

"Nothing special about my name."

"I happen to think it's a pretty name. How 'bout that?"

I felt my cheeks flush. "I think they were trying to pick baby names that sounded good with Frost. My sister's name is Rosebud, but I call her Rose."

"Do your parents live here?"

I hated talking about my parents. Instead, I listened to the classic rock 'n' roll music playing on the speakers. It was Elvis singing about a little less conversation. "My mom... she um, she's..."

"Sorry," he quickly said, clearly assuming she was dead.

"Don't be sorry for her," I snapped. "She's a prostitute living on the streets and addicted to heroin. She abandoned us after my dad died."

"Damn," he said through clenched teeth. "April, you don't have to talk about it."

"You brought it up," I said in a melodic tone that dropped an octave. I never talked about it with anyone, including Trevor. Why I was rambling about my life story to a man I barely knew was beyond me. "She started using when I was around twelve or thirteen. I just remember seeing pills and bags of weed. I guess dad didn't make enough to support her habit because she started staying out all night. I didn't understand what was going on at first, but then the fights began. I can't believe she did that to my father," I almost mouthed more than said.

"Users have no control. No one can help them if they don't choose to help themselves."

"She could have tried. She had a family, but she wanted to escape. None of it was ever good enough. *We* weren't good enough. I've never tried drugs and I never will. That's not the kind of person I want to be. I deal with my problems."

Not just mine, but I was cleaning up everyone else's.

Reno worked on rolling one of his long sleeves a little higher, keeping his eyes low. "Have you seen her?"

"It's been years. The last time I saw her, she borrowed a bunch of money from my grandma. She stayed in the trailer for two days shooting up, and when I hid her drugs, she called someone. He showed up and went ballistic."

Reno's face hardened. "Who's *he?*"

"Her pimp, boyfriend, dealer—who knows. He tried to hit on Rose and she was just fourteen at the time. There was a big scuffle and Grandma called the cops when he broke the folding door in her bedroom. They left and she's kept in touch with me, but only when she needs to borrow money. My dad was the only solid thing I had in my life, and he was killed in a car accident."

My bottom lip twitched along with my cheek and I covered my face. I was about to have a meltdown at Sonic.

A slim girl in a pair of roller skates wheeled in our direction and slid a red tray onto the table. "Here you are. Ketchup? Napkins?" Her blond ponytail swung from side to side.

"All of it," he said, handing her a bunch of bills. "Here. Keep the change, darlin'."

"Wow. Thanks, mister!"

She skated off and Reno's hand curled around my wrist. Not to pull it away from my face and make me snap out of my funk, instead he just stroked his fingers on the back of my hand and let me have a moment.

"I don't want kids," I blurted out, deciding to go all the way with my confessional to a total stranger. What did I have to lose? If anything, maybe someone would be honest with me for a change. "Do you think that makes me a bad person?"

When he didn't answer, I lowered my eyes. "Kids are great, but I'm just not wired that way. Just because I can have them doesn't mean I should. I don't want to take the chance of messing up someone else's life the way mine was." I wiped my finger under my lashes and stared at a smudge of liner on my finger. "Great."

Reno handed me a napkin and I wiped off my face.

"Don't let your parents' fuckups make that kind of decision for you."

After a deep sigh, I wadded up the napkin and put it on the table. "Sometimes it's okay to be honest with yourself, but not everyone understands it. They think you're selfish and missing out. But I've seen how it can go wrong, even with good intentions. Sometimes kids grow up to despise their parents. I just decided a long time ago that I was completely okay with not having a family. Rose will have kids for the both of us, and I'll love being an aunt to them. But me?" I shook my head, unable to explain where I was coming from.

I laughed when I noticed the mountain of tater tots in front of me. His eyes flashed up briefly and I wondered if he thought my laugh strange. Lexi used to say I sounded like a mischievous fairy.

Then I noticed what was going on over on Reno's side of the table. "Do you have OCD?"

Reno dramatically tilted his head to the side and I snapped my mouth shut. He continued to neatly squeeze ketchup onto the edge of a plastic wrapper and placed the empty packages in a straight line. It was as if everything in front of him had its place.

"Do what's best for you, April. I don't judge. I've seen a lot of bad shit if you want to know the truth. There are people out there unfit to parent, or maybe they're just stressed because they can't swing the rent and they have another kid on the way. Maybe they never got to have a life of their own before it all started. But yeah, some people just aren't wired that way. I get it."

"Thanks." I took a slow bite of my tot and then another. I never imagined I could be so open with a stranger and not be judged. "Now that I've slammed you with all the heavy stuff on our first date, maybe we should talk about the last movie you saw," I said with a laugh.

Reno held the burger up to his mouth and froze before taking a bite. His dark eyes were on me and a few pieces of diced onion spilled out of his bun. When he set the burger down, I put my hands in my lap.

Reno smiled wide, and it revealed lines in his face that were deep and wonderful. He had straight teeth. I couldn't help it—I was one of those people who looked at teeth. Trevor had a crooked bottom tooth, but it gave him that edgy look. I just liked to know that a man thought enough about himself to take oral hygiene seriously.

It took me a minute to figure out what he was smiling about. *Great job,* my inner voice said. *You just officially declared this a date. Desperation train, all aboard!*

"It'll be our secret," he said in a humorous tone. "I know you didn't mean it that way. Do you plan on moving out of the trailer?"

I frowned suspiciously. "What makes you think I live in a trailer?"

He shoved about six fries in his mouth and chewed slowly before answering. As his jaw moved, I got a chance to admire his sculpted face up close, right before he sucked the salt off his thumb and made me squirm in my seat. "You mentioned it a minute ago. I just assumed you're still living there since we're heading toward the parks."

"Oh." I tilted my head and shrugged a little. "I'm saving my money; it's just temporary."

Then his eyes squinted, and not because it was sunny outside. It was that look someone gives you when they know you're lying about something.

"Aren't you hot in that getup? It seems like every time I see you, you're wearing long sleeves."

"Not *every* time," he said in a throaty voice that rumbled from deep within his chest.

A shiver rolled through me and I ate a few more tater tots.

I had once driven Lexi to Austin's house. Reno had been standing in the hot sun without a shirt, his golden chest glistening with a sheen of sweat, and the muscles in his arms and pecs twitching as he turned a horseshoe around in his hand. I could hardly comprehend anyone looking as sumptuous as he did while looking as equally intimidating. I hadn't been able to take my eyes off him when I saw his thick arms and how his skin bronzed in the sunshine, whereas my pale skin just turned blotchy red. What I felt about him wasn't curiosity or admiration—it was a fever. One that caught me off guard—I'd never been attracted to a man like him before. At least, not in real life. The guys I dated were of average build and much younger. Now here I was, sitting at Sonic with a man who made my toes curl just by looking at me.

I felt a blush rising, so I grabbed the empty ketchup packets and stood up to toss them into the trash. My feet tangled around the long strap of my purse and I stumbled awkwardly, grabbing the menu stand just seconds before I did a face-plant. I steadied myself and threw the ketchup in the wastebasket. When I turned around, it was with the full expectation of seeing Reno silently cracking up at my blunder. I wasn't a graceful woman by any means, and most guys had no qualms about laughing at my antics. It was something I had grown accustomed to, but it still needled me.

Instead, he had shot around that table in a flash and was cupping my elbow, ready to catch me if I fell.

When he bent down to pick up the packet, I knew immediately that I wanted to see him again. He hadn't made a big deal about my clumsy ballerina act, and that meant a lot.

"You still drive that toy car?" he asked, taking his seat again.

I cleared my dry throat and sipped my drink. "No, that was Rose's VW and she took it with her to Arizona. I don't have a car."

Reno sucked on his banana shake and drew his brows together pensively. He set the cup down and folded his arms on the table. "You mean to tell me that you're walking everywhere?"

"Work is close by and I can't complain about the exercise. It's the rain I'm not crazy about."

Then he began rubbing his hands all over his jaw, as if he wanted to make that bristly sound your hands make when they rub against whiskers. But his face was baby-smooth and all it did was push his skin around.

"I'll lend you one of our cars."

"No."

"Yes."

"I get the last word, Reno. Borrowing means you owe, and I'm tired of owing people."

"Are you in some kind of trouble?"

"I barely know you. I can't borrow your car. Look, I'm sorry to rush, but I need to get home. There's something important I have to take care of before the party tonight. Would you mind eating a little faster?"

Reno stood up and dumped his food in the trash.

"Wait, I didn't mean that you had to—"

He walked around the table and tossed mine in the trash next. I sprang to my feet to confront him, but before I could say a word, he tucked a swath of hair behind my ear that had slipped in front of my eye.

Then I forgot my name and how to speak.

There's a buzzing sensation when you have chemistry with someone. It's like there are invisible threads connecting your bodies and igniting into sparks, and the residual pulse bounces back in shockwaves, growing stronger with each second.

I felt that with Reno. He stepped so close to me that I remembered how good it felt when he'd held me in his arms. The animalistic look in his eyes captured me like he was a predator and I was prey. He felt it too. I could tell by the soft breath he took before he spoke.

"I've always liked hazel eyes," he said. "Yours look like a sunset over sea-green waters."

I hit pause. This was a scene I'd be replaying in my head for weeks to come, and I didn't want to ruin the moment by saying something inane. I let him graze his thumb across my mouth. He pulled my lower lip down just enough that his thumb glided across the fleshy inside. Then he rolled his wet thumb across my lip, making what seemed like a casual gesture become the most intimate moment I'd experienced with a man outside of sex.

His eyes hooded.

I wanted to do something bold to get a reaction, like suck on his thumb. But that's something my prostitute mother would do. So I became immobile and just let him touch me.

And that was enough. Staring into Reno's chocolate eyes up close was like riding on that motorcycle. Intense, sexy, and addictive. When I felt his hand leisurely traveling down the curve of my back, my icy walls began to melt and I warmed to his touch.

I waited for him to make another move, but it never came. He looked at me like something unattainable—the same way I coveted the expensive perfume bottles behind the display counter, or the chocolate macadamia nut cookies at the gourmet shop.

I whirled around and he captured my wrist, gently tugging me back. "Something wrong with the way I touched you?"

"It's nothing," I breathed.

But Reno didn't let go. He stepped closer and lifted my chin. "Did you want me to kiss you?"

"No."

Reno grinned. "Liar."

"Do I seem like the kind of girl who would kiss a guy by a trash can with about fifteen cars watching us?"

His face reddened. "I wasn't trying to insult you."

"I know you weren't. I had a nice time, but I need to go home so I can take care of some errands and get ready for the party."

"Only if you save a dance for me."

I sniffed softly as we walked to the bike. "I can't dance."

"Good," he said. "Then I won't have to worry about someone else stealing that dance." He handed me the helmet and threw his leg over the bike.

"I'm not dancing with you, Reno."

"Climb on, April. And get used to holding on to me as tight as you can, because you'll be in my arms before the night is over."

CHAPTER 10

"Holy smokes, Trevor. You look like one of those hot, swanky models in the magazines!"

White dress shirt, slim grey tie, dark wash jeans with fading in the front, and instead of a pair of oxfords, he wore black Converse sneakers with white laces. It was an outdoor thing and he didn't want to ruin his good shoes. Trevor smelled amazing, and his hair was combed forward in that every-which-way style that made him devilishly handsome.

"Who were you talking to on the phone?"

"No one important," I lied. "Just a friend."

Whose name happened to be Maddox. He had agreed to loan me what I needed, which would cover the business account and pay off Sanchez. I didn't disclose what the loan was for, and true to his word, he didn't ask. Maddox said we still had an appointment to discuss the details of our arrangement, and that this loan would be tacked on in addition. He seemed like a reasonable man in comparison to Delgado.

An hour after our call ended, a knock sounded at the door and a delivery truck sped away. The package on my step looked like an ordinary yellow envelope with bubble lining.

Inside it was my lifesaver. Sanchez's cut was stuffed in a letter envelope in my purse and I put the rest in my bedroom drawer to be deposited at the bank. Trevor knew I wanted to head back no later than nine o'clock and he seemed content with my request. Then again, it didn't seem like he was overly excited about going in the first place.

I, on the other hand, was looking forward to a night of music and fun. My nails were polished lavender, and I'd spent an hour washing and styling my hair. I swept my bangs to the side and away from my eyes, securing them with a few pins. My hair barely tickled my shoulders and I liked the *no fuss* aspect. Plus, it suited the shape of my face. As I put on my dress, I wondered if I had gone overboard. I felt as if I didn't deserve something so beautiful. A few stretchy bracelets covered my wrists and completed the outfit. I debated wearing perfume and finally decided against it since the barbecue grill would be going. I couldn't think of anything else, and so I declared myself ready.

Trevor was thick with compliments from the moment I emerged from the bathroom. We sat at the table staring at each other, genuinely impressed by how nice we cleaned up. All we needed were horses and a carriage.

"I'm your date," he announced.

"Of course you are."

"No, I'm your *date*. I have a feeling some of the jerk-offs there will want to get in your panties, and I don't want you tangled up with that kind of drama. You're not about to become a one-night-stand girl because of that sexy dress. Also, don't tell anyone about me."

"When have I ever done that?" I lifted my oversized brown purse from the table and glanced around to see if I'd forgotten anything.

"Robert's party."

I gave him a scolding glance. "That was *two* years ago. How long are you going to hold that against me? I didn't know better."

"Yeah, well, when I want people to know I'm gay, I'll pass out flyers and hire a fucking band to sing a song about it. Otherwise, you're my date."

"What if someone has gaydar and they find you out?" I smothered my laugh.

"Babe, that's one radar I can fly under when I need to. You should know that by now."

"In that case, you're going to have the girls swarming all over you."

He smiled wolfishly and we stepped out of the trailer. "No complaints here. What was in the package that came by this morning?"

"Oh, just something I ordered on the Internet." I quickly

changed the subject as I locked the door. "I don't want to stay there all night, but do me a favor and don't start any fights. Please?"

He kicked up a clump of dirt and tucked his hands deep in his pockets. "I can't promise."

"*Yes,* you can."

"What if *they* are the ones who start shit?" He looked nervous and twitchy, which was so unlike him.

"Then let me do the fighting."

Trevor gave a boisterous laugh. "Now that I'd like to see, babe."

I wore a pair of slingbacks and carefully walked down the steps. He held my hand as we strolled to his car. "We look pretty swank."

"Maybe it's your swag," I suggested.

"Maybe it's your swing," he replied, waggling his brow. "I promised I'd find you a Mr. Right, April. I just don't know who the hell deserves a stunner like you."

The car radio blared a song by Pearl Jam and he turned it down.

"Trevor?"

"Yup."

I stared at him for a second, unable to verbalize what my heart was feeling. Total admiration, but also fear. I had no idea what was in store for me later that night when I planned to meet up with Sanchez to deliver his money, and I kept wondering if something were to happen to me, how would Trevor react? He'd once said I was the only family that mattered.

"Nothing. I just love you is all."

"See? April Showers, always showering me with love." He kissed my hand and turned over the engine. "Hold on to your panties."

By the time we arrived at the party, it was in full swing. Multicolored Chinese lanterns were strung up along the porch and in one of the nearby trees. The skies were clear and the sun had just set. Dark clouds loomed on the horizon. As soon as we parked the car and walked up the long stretch of driveway, I began to get butterflies. Trevor took my hand and lent me some of his confidence.

"April!" Lexi shouted, hobbling across the grass in her heels. "Oh my God. I should have never worn these shoes," she said in an exaggerated voice. I gave her a hug and she whispered, "Hot damn, girl. Where have you been hiding this one?"

"Lexi, you remember Trevor? We're old friends."

He cleared his throat. "I'm her date," he announced.

Oh yeah.

"Is that so?" Lexi said wonderingly.

She looked beautiful with her hair pinned up. Her silver necklace stood out against her black top, and the powder-blue pencil skirt showcased her long legs.

"Who are all these people?" I asked, sweeping my eyes across the large crowd that covered the lawn and spilled into the house.

"Austin's friends, neighbors, and just about everyone else with a pulse," she said, smoothing out her hair.

I could see Lexi was in a good mood from the way she kept swinging her left leg back and forth so that it peeked in and out of the slit in her skirt. Austin must have been showering her with compliments all evening—she glowed with happiness. Or maybe the glow was from the shimmery blush, or the fact she was going to get laid by a man who worshipped her.

The music was loud, but not obnoxiously so, and an old Aerosmith tune had a few people singing along. I didn't listen to classic rock, but Lexi played it in the store during downtime. My guess was that Austin had given her full control over the music playlist.

It fell silent for a moment and the crowd chattered and laughed. The sky quickly darkened and the smell of barbecue and smoke hung heavy in the air.

"Come grab a cheeseburger and beer before it's all gone," she said, strolling toward the house. "Denver's been barbecuing out back and people didn't waste time fixing their plates. Not everyone here knows each other, so just mingle and have a good time. If you need anything, scream. Literally. I have no idea where I'll be." She laughed and Austin appeared, scooping her into his arms and planting a kiss on the curve of her neck.

"Missed you, Ladybug."

"I was only gone for a minute."

"A minute too long," he said, inviting her lips into a sultry kiss.

Suddenly, a Kings of Leon song came on. Austin gave her a wolfish grin and swaggered off.

"Austin Cole!" She flounced after him with quick steps.

Trevor's palm was sweaty and I glanced up at him. "Are you sure this is okay? We can go if you want."

"I'm here to have a good time, babe. Don't worry about me."

He bent over a metal tub filled with ice and beer and grabbed a couple of bottles. I waved away his offer, so he tucked one under his arm and cracked open the other, downing half the bottle in one swig. I scanned the lively crowd and noticed a disproportionate ratio of men to women. What seemed odd was how none of the women had formed their own separate groups like I'd usually seen go on at parties.

"April?"

I looked over my shoulder and recognized a pretty brunette with a long braid coming my way. Ivy lived with Lexi and had helped me with a situation we had at the shop many months ago during a power outage. She was a thoughtful girl who was probably my age but seemed wise beyond her years. Ivy carried herself in an elegant manner with radiant, sun-kissed skin and earthy-brown eyes. She had to be part Native American or Spanish, but not full-blooded.

"I love your outfit," I said, admiring her turquoise earrings and the chocolate-brown dress that fell to her ankles. It made me wish I hadn't gone overboard—sometimes simple was classy.

"Thank you," she said, smiling at my dress. "You look like a delicate flower that some of these men would like to pluck the petals from. Come with me and we can put your purse in a safe place so you don't have to lug it around."

"Trevor?" I asked, turning around. "Are you okay on your own?"

He glanced at Ivy and then back at me. "Go have fun. I'll catch up with you in two shakes."

I leaned up and kissed his cheek. "Be good. I'll be inside if you need me."

Ivy led me up the wooden steps and through the main door.

Several men looked me over as I passed them and Ivy grabbed my hand. I grinned because it was flattering to receive warm smiles of admiration. We climbed the staircase on the left side of the room and reached the second floor. One hall went toward the back of the house, and another to the right.

We walked toward the back. "This is my room," she said, opening a door on the right. She took my purse and set it near the door. "Your things will be safe in here. Closed rooms are off-limits; everyone here knows the rules."

"And how are you going to monitor that?"

She closed the door and leaned against it. "No need to. If anyone breaks the rules, we'll find out. That wouldn't go over well. Are you feeling okay? You look nervous."

Loud voices boomed from downstairs and the outside music seeped through the walls.

I shrugged and swiped a strand of hair away from my eyes. "I don't go to many parties—not as big as this one. I've never seen this many people gathered in one place."

"Austin has a lot of friends," she replied, touching the end of her braid. I caught the strange way in which she said it. Like there was a hidden subtext. "Are you hungry?"

"Famished."

"Great! How's a cheeseburger sound with some potato chips?"

"Um, I think I'd like some of that pasta salad we brought over instead of chips."

"Oh, that's already gone."

My mouth hung open. "Already? Jeez, I guess we didn't buy enough."

She snickered. "Oh, you bought *plenty*. But these are hungry men who know a good thing when they see it. Everything you suggested has been a hit with the crowd. Don't worry; we have a backup plan if the food runs out. Denver volunteered to pick up a couple dozen pizzas from an Italian place up the road. He's a bit of a Nazi on the grill and was hoarding some of the meat in a futile attempt to make it last. Austin chewed his ear off, so the burgers are on the fire again. Austin is the kind of Pack—person who doesn't care about cost. He wants to make sure all his guests are fed and taken care of. The game room's a few doors down to the right if you want to relax and have a drink. Denver just bought a new pool table and they're practically glued to that thing. I'll go downstairs and fix you a plate with something cold to drink."

"No beer," I said adamantly. "I'm the designated driver."

"Lemonade," she sang, floating down the stairs.

Voices echoed from the game room and I gripped the edge of my dress as I approached the open door. *Holy smokes.* The television on the wall to my right was humongous! All they needed was a couple of leather chairs in front of it instead of the oversized beanbag. There weren't many places to sit, although most of the guys were just standing around by the dartboard and bar. A couple of men stood beside an impressive billiard table with a green felt top that looked brand new. A cylindrical lamp hung from the ceiling with a red shade, illuminating the table. A couple of guys clinked their glasses together at the bar on my left. It was a spacious room full of men.

Attractive men.

Not that all of them were physically good-looking, but there was an air of confidence about them—something magnetic I couldn't put my finger on.

I targeted a barstool and quickly went to claim it. Someone whistled and the boisterous chatter fell to a murmur. I tucked my skirt beneath me as I took a seat.

No bartender. *Great.*

"Hey, April. Glad you made it," Denver said with a welcoming smile. He walked behind the bar and patted his hands on the smooth surface. "You want a drink? Anything you like; this is what I do for a living."

"Do you have any soda?"

He shook his head, and my eyes wandered down to his faded red T-shirt.

"What's that supposed to mean?" I pointed at the cross on his shirt that had *Lifeguard* written below it.

Denver poured ginger ale in a short glass and leaned close on his elbows. "It means if someone needs any mouth-to-mouth, I'm your man."

"Even that guy?" I suggested, pointing a few seats down.

He reached out and touched the ends of my hair. "You're really pretty."

His directness flustered me and I sat up straight, almost knocking over my drink. It splashed on the bar and he leaned over and grabbed a rag, wiping it up casually with a private smile.

"Is Reno around?"

He frowned a little. "Maybe you should stay away from him."

"Why?"

Denver slanted his eyes to the left and then back. "He's rough with women in bed."

"I didn't say I wanted to sleep with him." This took me by surprise and piqued my curiosity. "What do you mean by rough?"

"I mean, unless you like being tied up, blindfolded, and submissive to his every command, then you should keep away from Reno. He's got control issues and plays them out in the bedroom. You don't seem like his type. *At all.*"

Why did a tiny thrill move through me as I got a visual? I had never done anything adventurous in bed, but a small part of me was a little curious. Then again, Denver was probably yanking my chain. That's what brothers did.

When I turned around, my heart almost stopped. Reno filled the doorway, arms folded, his sharp eyes taking in my every move. And he looked *all kinds* of hot—from the shine on his boots to the neat way in which his white button-up shirt was tucked in. My heart thumped harder and harder until I had to take a deep breath. Even worse, Reno didn't move. He just kept watching me and I couldn't read his expression. I thought he wanted to dance with me? Why didn't he come over?

Because you look desperate, my inner voice said, mocking me. *Men don't want a woman that clings to them like a sock fresh out of the dryer.*

I swiveled my chair toward the pool table. One man leaned over and took a shot, while his friend with the trimmed goatee hung back. He had his pool stick standing on end and rolled it slowly between his fingers.

Eyes on me.

"Motherfucker!" the man taking the shot barked out as he missed. The white ball bounced around the table and clipped a green ball.

I knew nothing about pool outside of what I'd seen in the movies. What I did know was that tough guys looked sexy holding a big stick.

With slow precision, I crossed my legs. It gained an immediate reaction from the man with the goatee across the room, but my interest was in Reno. I swept my fingers through my hair and casually swung my eyes in his direction.

That's when I saw her. A brunette strutted through the doorway wearing wedge shoes that boosted her four inches taller, white shorts, and a silk blouse. The kind that was low-cut in the front and looked like a gust of wind from the snap of a finger could make it evaporate.

Not to mention she was grossly endowed and had porn-star lips.

So that's your competition? my inner voice wondered. *Looks like your chance just went from slim to none.*

Had she just walked into the room and mingled, I wouldn't have given her a second glance. But she had her eyes all over Reno as if she were memorizing his DNA.

She crossed in front of him and turned around so that he could admire every angle of her curvaceous figure. When they engaged in conversation, I sulked.

How could I compete against someone like *her*, an ambitious woman who didn't take no for an answer?

"Want to play a game of pool?" Denver winked and offered me his hand. "It's my table; I can kick them out anytime."

"I'm sure that'll go over well," I said apprehensively.

Denver whistled through his teeth by curling in his lips. The sharp sound caught the attention of the men and he gave them the universal thumb that said, "Get the hell out."

To my astonishment, they obeyed, setting their pool sticks on the rack and shaking their heads. Denver retrieved the balls from the pockets and placed them in the triangular rack. "You ever played?" he asked.

"This'll be my first time."

"Okay then, I'll break." He handed me a stick and stood close, rubbing the chalk on the tip. "Solids and stripes. If a solid goes into the pocket, then that's what I need to sink for the rest of the game, and you'll target the stripes. Don't sink the black ball until you've cleared your balls, or else you'll lose the game. First person to clear the table of all their balls plus the black wins. Each time you sink a ball, you get another turn. Whenever you miss, you lose your turn."

"Why don't you show her how to *hold* your balls?" someone razzed.

Denver snapped his fingers at them without turning away from me. "Shut it," he yelled and continued his billiard lesson. Excitement flared in his indigo eyes and I wondered if it was the game or me. "If you sink the white ball then you lose your turn, even if it goes in with your target. Make sense?"

"I think so."

"If you sink the wrong ball, well, you just did me a favor. Ready?"

He whirled around, leaned over with his right arm pulled back, stroked the stick over the knuckles on his left hand, and made his shot. A loud crack filled the room and balls scattered across the table, sending a solid red in the pocket. Denver took another shot and sank a blue.

"Why do I have a feeling that I'm getting hustled?" I said, walking around the table.

Denver missed the next shot. "Your turn, honeypie," he said quietly. "Aim for the stripes." The music cranked up outside and the room became noisy again. Denver stepped up close and spoke privately. "Look, I can see you got a thing for Reno. You want to know why he won't talk to you?"

"Why?" I whispered.

"Some dogs don't like to be handed a bone; they want to work for it. Reno's the kind of man you need to make jealous to get his full attention. He likes the challenge. Keep that in mind. Your shot."

I nervously stepped up to the table and felt a sea of eyes watching me. I mirrored how Denver had held the stick and when I took my shot, the stick scraped across the felt top.

Denver hissed through his teeth. "Careful, it's a new table. Here, let me show you." He came around and took my left hand, curling my index finger. "Slide it gently through that hole."

"That's what she said." It was our heckler again.

"Get the fuck out," Denver said in clipped words, his biceps tightening as he threw back his shoulders.

The men shook their heads and stood by the bar but didn't leave.

I'd been so caught up in the game I hadn't realized Reno had his eyes on me. Not only that, but the girl with the Dolly Parton rack was still talking to him.

Grrr. Maybe Denver was right. I'm not sure why I'd sought Reno's attention out of all the available men in the room, but because of the things I had told him about myself, I felt a connection with him that went beyond physical attraction.

"But *you* didn't hold it like this," I argued.

"No, but I have more control," Denver pointed out. He'd held the stick across the base of his thumb but hadn't looped his index finger.

I bent over and Denver leaned across the table next to me. "Your angle is all wrong and you're in too much of a hurry to hit the shot. You have to line it up and take your time."

"I can't do this," I said disparagingly. "I'm just no good at games."

"If there's one thing that all women are good at, it's games. Let me show you." His eyes lit up and he got behind me. Denver's arms came around me and his hands slid up to my wrists. "The corner pocket is the easiest shot," he said roughly in my ear. "You're too close to the table, so step back a little. That's it. Now bend over a little more."

When I did, he walked around and readjusted my fingers to hold the stick properly. As he leaned over my back, I thought I heard a growl, but the music kept a steady beat that drowned out the low sounds. Denver stretched across my back and placed his chin on my right shoulder, holding my right arm and lining up the shot. His breath slid across my neck and when I flicked my eyes around, I saw the men watching with hooded eyes and whispering to each other.

I'd seen guys showing women how to play pool before, so I didn't understand their interest. The pool stick gently glided between my fingers. In and out. In and out. In and out.

"Take your aim," he said, settling over my back.

I stretched out my leg, causing some friction between our bodies. He released a hard breath and I focused on the ball as if my life depended on it. All eyes in the room were watching; I couldn't mess this up!

"Concentrate on the ball. You're too high. That's it, honeypie."

I thrust my arm forward and after the loud crack, the white ball sank the stripe. "I did it!"

An exhilarating rush filled my veins and suddenly pool was a game I wanted to learn more about. I turned around with a broad smile beaming across my face. Denver looked feverish—a look I'd seen on men before. His eyes lingered on my mouth as if memorizing its shape.

"That's a pretty color of lipstick on you," he said, licking his lower lip. "What's it taste like?"

I shoved the pool stick against his chest and frowned. "Thanks for the crash course, but I should get back to the party."

Disappointment flared in his eyes and he stepped back. When he did, I noticed the empty space where Reno had once stood.

Great going, my inner voice said. *Looks like your plan to make him notice you backfired. Or was the goal to make him livid by hitting on his brother?*

I mentally gave her the finger. Part of it *was* to make him jealous so maybe he'd walk over and talk to me, but I guess Dolly Parton had more to offer a man like Reno. I left the room and lingered in the empty hall, feeling uncharacteristically defeated. I hadn't realized how much I liked Reno until I saw how little he liked me. Only then did the sting of rejection fill me up like venom.

"Hey, prettylicious," a smooth voice called out. I looked up at a tall man lurking in the hall. He popped open the lid to a plastic container tucked under his arm. "I'm Jericho. I don't remember seeing your sweet face around here before."

This was the guy Lexi warned me about? I had imagined a musician with yellow teeth, nose rings, and gaunt features. Not a man with lush lips, razor-cut hair that fell to his shoulders, and an amazingly firm body. It was apparent the Cole brothers had been blessed with the *hot and sexy* gene, each flaunting it in their own unique way.

"I'm Lexi's friend, April. We work together at the candy store."

"Ah," he said with a brisk nod, a look that indicated he "got" something that I didn't. I wondered what Lexi had told them about me. "I have a private party going on in my bedroom. Want to join?"

I walked up and peered in the room. A woman was sprawled out on a beanbag chair with her legs open, holding a guitar and plucking the strings. Lying on his bed was a busty blonde in a pair of leather pants and a black top that tied in the back with a little string. She was on her stomach reading a magazine, her legs bent at the knee and crossed at the ankle.

"Um, no thanks. I'm waiting for Ivy to bring me a plate."

"Here," he said, offering the plastic container. "Tide yourself over with one of these. They're abso-fucking-amazing. A friend of mine makes them for a living and I brought over a bunch of containers, but most of these pigs have already cleaned them out. I grabbed these for myself," he said with an orgasm-inducing grin.

I reached in and politely took one of the cupcakes, licking the mint-cream icing off the top. "Mmm. Not bad. Is that buttercream?"

Jericho's broad smile had a glimmer of mischief—the kind that could make a woman's panties damp and give her a feverish glow. He seemed harmless and I didn't know why Lexi had presented him with all the warning labels like he was some kind of a prescription drug. Jericho looked like a rock star, but he didn't act cocky or rude.

"So you're the guy Lexi warned me about."

"Shit, really?" He shook his head. "I personally think she doesn't dig my music."

I peeked in the room again and noticed Led Zeppelin and Pink Floyd posters, a black amplifier, and three guitars sitting on stands.

"Anyhow, if you change your mind and want to get away from those jerk-offs, I'll be in here. Some of those assholes get a little rowdy as the night wears on, so watch yourself."

He winked and closed the door, abandoning me in the hall to devour my chocolate cupcake. I patiently waited at the top of the stairs because it would have been rude to let Ivy go through all that trouble and then disappear on her. When I licked the last crumb from my finger, I wadded up the wrapper and placed it on the floor beside me. *Why didn't I just talk to Reno like a normal person?* Maybe all that stuff he had said to me about saving a dance was just talk.

A door swung open behind me and a cacophony of sound headed my way. A man stormed out, pulling a shirt over his head as if he were getting dressed. I recognized him as the one who'd made all the lewd comments in the game room. A few spatters of bright blood stained his shirt, but his face didn't appear broken or bruised.

"I don't give a shit," he said to his buddy. "That motherfucker is going down, so don't you even try to stop me."

"If you go after the host's pack, then you'll get buried in a shallow grave. I'll be sure to stop by and piss on it to water the daisies," his friend said. "Packmasters don't like trouble at peace parties. Get a grip."

"Fuck off. A swing for a swing is all I want."

They tromped down the stairs in a hurry and I wondered what drama I had missed.

As the front door slammed, I rubbed my finger on a piece of icing staining the fabric on my dress, disappointed by the growing smudge. I had a hunch this would be an uneventful night.

CHAPTER 11

RENO WATCHED AS APRIL HANDLED her pool stick like a novice. He felt an inexplicable attraction to this human, as if he knew her better than he did. Maybe it was how straightforward she was about her life, especially given how Reno was a closed book when it came to his own past. An unexpected protectiveness flooded his veins, and he needed to get a grip on it. The second he entered the game room, he'd wanted to go to her. But he played it cool and took a moment to soak her in. That's when a ball of nerves hit him right in the gut. *Shit*. Men like him didn't get nervous over a woman, especially a human. All he could do was notice how radiant she looked in that delicate dress. Reno realized he didn't know a damn thing about humans. Maybe they didn't like the same abrasive approach he would give to a Shifter. He had to play this cool. Then she turned away and showed an interest in Denver.

Reno sighed deeply. Maybe she wasn't that into him.

None of these assholes knew April was a human. You could only pick up on a human's distinct lack of energy when you stood close to one. When April leaned over the table—her dress hitching up in the back and showing more leg—it became an open invitation to every man in that room. Reno had no claim over this human, but damn, it burned him nevertheless to see all those eyes leering at her. She was an innocent amidst a pack of ravenous wolves.

When a female Shifter turns her back on a man and bends over, she's signaling her interest. April didn't know better and was giving mixed signals to every male in that room.

The man in the pale blue shirt who kept shouting lewd remarks at them was three ticks away from getting his ass kicked if he didn't keep it in check.

And then there was Crystal. Reno was pretty damn sure she wasn't on the invite list, but Wheeler or Jericho must have added her. She'd been stalking Reno at every public function. He thought he could lose her by heading inside the house, but she had a talent of hunting him down.

Persistent little bitch, and he didn't mean that in a derogatory way. Among Shifter wolves, females were affectionately referred to as bitches. It didn't have the same negative connotation as it did among humans.

Reno had spent a lot of time getting ready that afternoon. He'd shined up his black boots, put on new laces, and picked out a white shirt that looked good on him, carefully rolling the sleeves to the elbow and unbuttoning the first two buttons. The leather belt he wore was one of his favorites and had a silver buckle. Reno even splashed cologne on his face and neck. He was a little surprised at the care he'd taken, but he wanted to impress April.

"You smell delicious." Crystal let out a little growl, twirling her fingers around one of his buttons. "What color is your wolf?"

Personal, he thought. Unlike Jericho, who thrived on winning over the ladies with his wolf, Reno kept that shit locked up. He'd been told his wolf had a mask, and a lot of people thought that meant he had something to hide.

"I bet you're famished," she said. "I'll go fix you a plate, so stay *right* here."

Shifters loved a good woman who kept them fed; it was a nurturing characteristic. Other Breeds, like Chitahs, believed a man should cook for a woman. Not Shifters. They revered a strong-willed woman who looked after her family, took care of her man, earned a living, and kept the pack in line. In return, a good pack protected that woman and made sure her needs were met. Some packs lived outside the new laws and followed the old ways of some of the rogue packs. Those Shifters saw women as subordinates and treated them like whores. It disgusted him because it wasn't the true way of the Shifter. Those were traditions spawned from corrupted Packmasters.

Crystal was submissive, and that was an attractive quality to Reno. She was the kind of woman he'd normally take to bed without hesitation. But tonight he didn't give her a second glance.

"Be right back," Crystal said in a soft breath, slowly easing around him and letting her hand slide across his chest. "I'll take real good care of you."

Meanwhile, two men drifted toward the bar. Reno's wolf paced within him as Denver positioned himself behind April. She had *no clue* that letting a Shifter come up from behind was as good as giving him the green light to pursue her for sex. Denver knew, and he was taking advantage of her naivety. Something he was going to be sorry for after this damn party was over.

"I saw her come with a date," the man in the blue shirt said. "Looks like this bitch needs a leash. Look how she's slutting around and letting him mount her over the pool table."

Reno clenched his jaw, grinding his teeth in the process.

His buddy gave him a friendly jab on the arm. "I want a piece of that when he's done."

"Not before me," Blue Shirt said. "I got my eye on her, and I'm going to have my turn later on after this party kicks into gear. She can play with my balls and stroke my pool stick." He laughed and walked out the door.

Fuck. That. Shit.

Reno pivoted around and stalked into the hall. He cracked his fist into Blue Shirt's face so hard that the man hit the ground in less than a second. Reno didn't break stride and went down the stairs.

"Austin," he yelled out.

"Reno, get your ass out here and join us," Austin said from the end of the porch. He sat casually on the railing with Lexi standing between his legs, his arms wrapped around her. That was one lucky alpha.

"Need to talk to you," Reno said, jogging down the steps and cutting across the lawn.

Austin kissed the top of Lexi's head and hopped down. "Be right back. You boys watch over my girl," he said in warning, half kidding, half not.

No one ever assumed an alpha was joking when it came to his woman, and with him being a Packmaster, they fenced her in and continued talking over beers.

"What's up?" Austin put his hands in his pockets and they walked to the side of the house for privacy.

"Why is a human here?"

Austin jingled some coins in his pockets and shrugged. "We don't have rules about that kind of thing and you know it."

"It's an unspoken rule," Reno argued, folding his arms. "She doesn't know how to behave and—"

"She… You mean April?"

Reno kicked up a tuft of grass. "She's leaning over a pool table with Denver right behind her. He's answering to me later on, but it's getting some of the men worked up."

Austin rubbed his bristly chin, pushing the skin around as he glanced up at one of the lanterns. Out in the sticks, the night lit up as if someone had thrown a million diamonds into an obsidian sky. Reno noticed a few people lying on their backs, stargazing.

"Lexi's been debating on telling April about our world since they work so close together running the business. I think she wants her to hang out with us first to prove we're normal or some bullshit. You want April to leave? That's going to be awkward as hell, and you can bet Lexi's going to make a scene."

Someone hollered and they both turned their attention toward a group of men out front who were pointing as a wolf ran by. Austin slid his jaw to the side. "They know better than to shift," he said in a gruff voice. "That's a big fucking rule of a peace party."

Shifting created too much opportunity for the wolves to attack one another and instigate conflicts among the packs, so it was against the rules whenever Packmasters were present. Shifters had to stay in human form at all times during a peace party.

Another wolf sprinted by, his paws kicking up tufts of grass.

"*What the fuck?*" Reno said, stepping out in the open. "Austin, you need to get this shit in check before it gets out of hand."

A man lying on his back flopped around, laughing hysterically. No one seemed to get the joke, but after a quick scan of the crowd, other people were acting peculiar.

"Let me find out what's up," Austin said, briskly stalking away.

"You boys got it under control?" a voice said coolly.

A Native American with long, silky hair and high cheekbones that intensified his dark gaze strolled up. Lorenzo Church. Personal enemy to Austin, but not technically a foe.

Not a friend, either.

But to keep up civilities, all neighboring packs had been extended an invitation. Lorenzo had once had a thing for Lexi, but she'd lost interest after finding out they were related. Not by blood, but through marriage. Plus, he'd made the mistake of trying to cut in on Austin's action. Lorenzo's pack was established and wealthy, making him one of the most eligible Packmasters in town. While he had a few women in his pack taking care of his needs, Lorenzo wasn't mated. Nor did he have children, which was extremely uncommon for someone of his status. No woman could tame that wolf.

"We've got everything under control," Reno said in a flat voice, not showing any signs of incompetence. "Anyone who shifts will be escorted off the property and reported to their Packmaster."

"Hmm," Lorenzo purred. "Seems easier said than done." A smile hovered on his lips as he watched a black wolf taking a piss on a nearby oak tree. "You should have invited more single women. There never seems to be quality bitches at these functions, and I deeply enjoy selecting new blood for my pack," he said, his tone arrogant.

Reno had to agree with him for the most part. Women balanced things out, and a bunch of men getting together became nothing but trouble. Packmasters were attracted to large gatherings so they could strengthen alliances and the pack could find new mates. But it sounded more like Lorenzo was looking to add to his personal collection.

Reno paced the grounds, shoving a few guys who were acting sketchy. It smartened them up for a fraction of a second before they trailed off again. Beneath the aging oak tree on the front lawn, Ivy stood on the new swing that Austin had put up for Maizy. It was one of those old-fashioned rope swings with a flat board to sit on. She had decorated it earlier with a strand of ivy and battery-operated twinkle lights wrapped around the ropes. Her shoes sat at the base of the tree and she gracefully swung forward, gazing at the canopy of branches overhead.

"What's going on out here?" Reno asked.

"A beautiful sky that's been smiling over us for a billion years," she said in awe. "An old tree that's putting up with me tugging on its arm. The wind giving me a breath to float on."

The branch creaked above as she continued pulling and pushing on the ropes. Ivy had a way with words, but this wasn't Ivy talking.

"What's wrong with you?"

A gust of wind lifted her dress at the hem, showing a little leg. She smiled as she glanced down at him, looking like an enchanted being out of a fairytale. Strands of mahogany hair had come loose from her long braid, not that she cared. Reno didn't know what to make of it and turned around to see where Austin had gone.

"Is everything under control?" Lorenzo interrupted, slowing his stride until he stood beside Reno.

"You can't control life," Ivy interjected, her eyes wide on the night sky above.

Reno noticed Lorenzo watching her in a way that made his wolf want to bite him in the ass. Had Lorenzo been anyone but a Packmaster, Reno would have knocked him down for looking at his pack sister that way. He had no problems confronting a rogue alpha male, but rules were rules, and you never put your hands on a Packmaster.

"Who is this woman?" Lorenzo wondered in low words.

"My *sister*, so if you would respectfully back the fuck off, I'd appreciate it," Reno said, warning him through clenched teeth. At least, as much as he could warn a Packmaster.

"I'm the tree fairy," Ivy sang in a beautiful voice, the swing really going now and the wind undoing her braided hair. "I'm here to grant you three wishes," she said to Lorenzo. "Don't tell me what they are, just think about them, and if it's something you truly want, then it will be planted in my heart. It will grow branches and leaves and bear fruit."

Lorenzo's jaw slackened as he was completely enthralled by her words.

"Tell me," she said, her eyes fixed on Lorenzo. "What do you think trees dream about?" Her hair blew forward and backward with each soft swing, one tendril getting caught on her full mouth. "Do they miss their acorns when they fall to the ground and are scattered away from their reach? Trees are strong and immovable, but they sway. They are rough, but their leaves are as soft as kisses. I think they dream about love. I think they're jealous of free spirits who can run, and that's why we fall from their branches. We think they are protecting us because we are beneath them, but their arms do not wrap around our bodies."

Reno grabbed Lorenzo's jaw and turned his head. "You need to help us get some of your pack under control," he said firmly. "One of *yours* just took off behind the house."

That snagged Lorenzo's attention and his eyes darkened. Lorenzo had zero tolerance for insubordination.

"Who?"

"Handlebar mustache, tats on his hands, and his wolf just ran by. White with a black leg."

"Saul," he said with a scowl.

Three seconds later, Lorenzo spun on his heel and stalked across the grounds to kick some Shifter ass back in line.

"I think he's an old oak," Ivy said in a distant voice, watching Lorenzo with an enigmatic gaze.

"Who listens to Pink Floyd anymore?" I said with a laugh, staring at a poster on the wall. It seemed to be shifting colors all on its own.

"Blasphemy," Jericho replied, still kissing on the blonde he had pushed up against the wall in his bedroom. The chesty girl with the leather pants was on the bed, engrossed in a magazine.

Meanwhile, I sat in the beanbag chair after having invited myself in to escape from the men ogling me in the hall. *Okay, maybe I was hiding.*

When Trevor had come knocking, Jericho had slipped out of the room and told him someone had given me a ride home. I felt rueful when I heard him running down the stairs. Poor Trevor, always trying to save the day, even if it meant raining on my picnic. For some reason, I wasn't as upset about it as I should have been.

"Where are my shoes?" I whined, glancing at my bare feet and wiggling my toes. Then my head fell back and I stared at the ceiling, searching for shapes and faces. It was the first time I'd ever sat in a beanbag chair and I had to admit I liked it. Might consider getting one. Pink, or maybe purple.

Where would it fit in the trailer? Hmm, conundrum.

I lifted my head when I heard the sound of buckles. Jericho was pressed up against the blonde's back and a low growl rose from his throat as he kissed the nape of her neck. I couldn't help but stare. It was an erotic visual, and nothing like my ex who did everything under the covers with all the lights off. Never any spontaneity, although I'm sure he had plenty with my friends.

Jericho lifted her skirt, yanked down her black panties, and the next thing I knew, his hips were moving in a steady rhythm. She moaned, reaching around to hold on to his neck with her hand.

Movement caught my eye and I turned around, planting my knees into the beanbag chair as I stared at the red lava lamp. Melting, misshapen blobs rose to the top and it seemed never ending.

"Cool lamp."

Two hands were on my hips, rubbing in slow circles. "Little girl, you just don't have a clue what this does to me."

I kind of did. It had quite an effect on Denver.

"Tell me if you want to play," he asked, doing nothing more than softly touching my hips with his fingertips. "I'm going to lie down on the bed and you can stay right here if you want, or join in."

The door swung open, hit the wall, and his hands instantly came away from my hips. I glanced over my shoulder and my eyes played tricks on me as two men moved like the little blobs in the lamp.

"Reno?"

He punched Jericho with a hard fist and I gasped when something unbelievable happened. Jericho transformed into a beautiful brown wolf with sea-green eyes.

Everything was magical.

Floaty.

Bubbly.

I crawled on the floor toward him. "Pretty puppy!"

"April?" Reno appeared in front of me and pried my eyelids up. "Ffffuck," he hissed. "I'm going to *kill* you, Jericho."

Then I leaned in and kissed Reno on the mouth.

Soft. Wet. Familiar. Why did Reno seem so familiar to me? His delicious cologne filled my senses and he tasted like sin.

Reno pulled back, hooked his arm around my waist, and hauled me off the ground. He gave me a hard shake and speared me with his eyes. "You're stoned."

Something licked my hand and I petted the wolf. Reno smacked him on the nose and the wolf leapt on the bed, letting the blonde stroke his cream-colored ears.

"Why did Jericho change? Is he a magician?"

Reno bit his lower lip and I touched his smooth face. "We're Shifters, April. That's what we are. You're coming with me; it's too dangerous for you to be alone right now. Austin's clearing out the party. Jericho, your ass is dead meat," he reiterated, staring at the wolf. "You can hear me in there and I know you were behind this. Think it's funny? Well, one of the Packmasters got into your cupcakes and his mate is not happy. This is damage control I don't even want to deal with," he muttered.

I wriggled free from his grasp and flew out the open door, dashing down the hall in my bare feet.

"April!"

"Catch me if you can!"

I hurried down the stairs with a giggle on my lips and… Oh, another pretty wolf!

"Hi, sweetie," I sang, stroking his soft grey fur. When I heard Reno drawing close, I flew out the door with a flurry of laughter, cutting straight across the lawn until I tripped in the grass.

When I rolled over and glanced up, I saw Dolly Parton looking down her nose at me. "Hi, Dolly. Didn't get lucky with *Reno Machino*?"

She looked mad enough to spit nails. I stared at her cheap shoes and noticed she had a corn on her toe.

"He didn't give me the time of day. *Every* man gives me the time of day," Dolly huffed. "That can only mean one thing. Is he gay?"

I sat up with a deadpan expression. "Flaming. You didn't know?"

She looked up at the sky and flapped her arms once, slapping them against her hips. "Figures. It just figures! You can *never* tell with Shifters."

Dolly stomped off and engines revved in the distance along the private road. I fell back against the high grass on the edge of the property. I'd never seen such a serene sky as what was blanketed above me. It made my life seem miniscule in comparison to the infinite depths of the universe.

A black wolf trotted up to my side, tongue hanging out and panting. He bent down, sniffed, and licked my neck. I stroked my hand down his side and in a fluid movement, he inexplicably transformed into a man.

A very *naked* man.

And there I was, stroking his side. Horror swept over me and I realized that Reno was right—I must be hallucinating. But was the wolf real, or the man? Before I could formulate a word, he covered my mouth with his hand.

"Shhhh. I just want to look at you. I've never seen a human up close."

He was stoned. I could see it in his pale eyes. I knew that look because I'd seen it in my mother's face a million times. He twitched his pudgy nose and tilted his head, studying me like a bug beneath a microscope. My extremities were numb and I felt glued to the earth.

"I can't breathe," I mumbled against his palm. *Couldn't anyone see?* No, because after a quick glimpse around, all I could see through the high grass were wolves, naked men, and people dispersing from the property. I was too far from the crowd.

He settled his weight on me, looking deep into my eyes. "Shhh, pretty pet. Pretty little human pet."

When he lifted up in the air, I barely registered what was happening. It was as if he were elevated by an invisible force.

I gasped, able to breathe again. I couldn't see Reno's muscles through his white shirt, but I knew they were sculpted and hard like granite. He had a dangerous look on his face and his hand was clamped around the naked man's throat. "Tristan! Get your mutt before I kill him myself." Then Reno knocked him in the jaw, causing the man to spin around and hold his mouth.

"I just wanted to look at her!" the man whined. "I didn't break any rules."

Reno stepped forward, every muscle tensing. "You broke *my* rule."

A man with long blond hair jogged over and looked between all of us before he grabbed the naked man by the hair. The man immediately shifted, and Tristan slapped the wolf on the snout before they walked off.

My hands trembled as I sat up, disbelieving what I'd just seen. What kind of drugs did I take? Everything seemed so vivid and I couldn't tell what was real and what wasn't.

Reno flexed his fingers, making fists and then opening his hands again.

"Reno?"

"Yeah," he said in a cracked voice.

"I'm scared. What's happening to me?"

And then his arms were beneath me, lifting me, holding me. Reno cradled me protectively against him and made his way to the house.

"You'll stay in my room tonight. No one will come near you. No one."

I believed him. There was a promise in his voice, and I remembered he was a man who had guns.

"Why didn't you kill him?" I asked, remembering how easily he'd aimed the gun at the car of men for simply calling me a name.

"Because of pack rules I'm bound to," he ground out. "Had he been a rogue, his ass would have been mine."

I didn't understand what he was talking about, but I quickly became distracted. "I'm hungry." I'd never been so hungry in my life. I snatched a bag of chips from a table we passed and pulled out a triangle dusted in orange cheese.

Crunch, crunch. Mmm.

CHAPTER 12

I OPENED MY WEIGHTED EYES AND glanced around a bedroom blanketed in darkness. A filter of dim light trickled through a curtainless window to my right. The sheets were cool against my hot skin and my memory drifted back. I'd thrown up after eating two hamburgers, and then Reno had forced me to drink water. I didn't know if people could die from water overdose, but on the second glass, I spit it in his face.

Which had officially murdered my chances of ever seeing him again. My inner voice was too irritated with me to complain about it, so she gave me the silent treatment.

I began crying, overcome with emotion.

Reno emerged from a small chair in the left corner. "Go back to sleep, princess."

My arms flew out at him angrily, slapping at him as he tried to touch me. *What did it matter?* He'd never want to see me again after an embarrassing display from a woman stoned out of her mind.

He caught my wrists and held them. "Settle down," he said in a thick voice.

"You let this happen to me!"

"Dammit," he roared. "I tried to run after you and lost track. I would have been there sooner if—"

"Not that! My *mother*."

He sat on the edge of the bed and his voice softened. "What are you talking about?"

Reno still held my wrists as tears spilled violently down my cheeks. "I said I'd *never* do drugs, Reno. I've spent my whole life trying to be a better woman than that. Going to school, working hard, paying my bills—but none of it matters. No matter how much I try, I'm no different. I'm just like her."

But my words failed me somewhere in the middle and broke into pieces. Maybe it was the drugs still in my system, or maybe it was almost twenty-three years of pain causing my heart to shatter. Maybe it was the realization that I was my mother's daughter after all, and the apple doesn't fall far from the tree.

He let go of my wrists and turned away. Then he kicked his shoes off and crawled in bed beside me, wiping my tears with the pad of his thumb.

"Listen to me, and listen good. You're not your mother, so erase that thought out of your head. One time isn't going to make you an addict any more than one beer makes someone an alcoholic; that comes from a weak person who's not willing to face their problems, and you're not weak. We all hit a rough patch and sometimes need to disconnect from the real world and get our head together. But a user is someone who can't live in the real world anymore. You're a strong woman."

"You barely know me. How can you say something like that?" I gasped three times, having one of those terribly embarrassing cries.

His hand came away from my face and he rubbed his chin. "Crying doesn't make you weak. I have a good sense about people. You're a shy girl, but you've got a strong will."

"But not someone you want to dance with."

Reno inched closer to me until I felt his entire body against my left side. "You were busy with my brother."

He had me there. "Sorry, I didn't know the protocol for ungluing your eyes from mammary girl."

I heard a smile in his voice. "Maybe the protocol doesn't involve letting my brother grind against your backside."

I flew up and pushed him away. "What time is it? I have to go!"

Oh my God. *Sanchez*. I had to pay him off by midnight.

"Lie down," Reno demanded, tugging at my dress.

I slapped his hand away and leapt off the bed. "I have to go home, Reno. *Now*."

His eyes were sharp and alert in the dim light. "You're stoned as hell, and where do you think you need to be at this hour?"

"I need you to drive me home this second."

He didn't get a chance to argue because I was already running barefoot down the hall.

"What's up?"

"Nothing, Denver. Get your sorry ass back to bed. April, get back in here," Reno called out from behind. "I'm warning you!"

Didn't hear him. I was out the door and running down the driveway, wincing as the gravel bit at my feet. I had no sense of time and hoped it was still early. Behind me, Reno's motorcycle thundered to life. The light flipped on and flashed on the road as he rolled up beside me and yelled over the throttling engine.

"Get on."

Reno's bike cut through the night, and a delicate mist began to wet the streets. I wore the helmet, but my lavender dress was ruined. The air felt uncomfortably cool and I began to shake, my teeth chattering as I held him close. I curved my hands around him, drawing in his heat and using his body as a shield to protect me from the wind.

We arrived at my trailer and before he could get the kickstand down, I ran up to the door and yelled out, "Thanks! Good night."

I'd left in such a hurry that my purse with Sanchez's money was still in Ivy's room, along with my keys. I decided to test the handle before knocking. Strange. He hadn't locked the door. "Trevor?"

Holy smokes. The digital clock by the fridge said 1:19 a.m.

My heart beat wildly as I raced to my room to retrieve the money in my drawer, which I'd set aside to put back into the account. I grabbed a small purse and counted out the bills. It wasn't until I walked out of my bedroom that I noticed something that had failed to grab my attention when I'd rushed into the trailer.

"Trevor!" I screamed.

And *screamed.*

He was propped up on the sofa, head hanging to the side, a note safety-pinned to his chest. His *bare* chest.

Vanilla Frost,
I took a down payment.

"*Please, please, please*, don't be dead," I cried. My trembling fingers pressed against his neck and I felt a weak pulse. "Oh, thank God. Trevor? Can you hear me?"

He had been beaten to a pulp. His eyes were purple and swollen, a large gash ran along his cheek, and even his arms were bruised—as though someone had hit them with a heavy object. Horror gripped me when I noticed his misshapen arm.

Strong hands moved me to the side. Reno knelt down and turned Trevor's chin, getting a good look at his face. I stared at the drops of blood on his white shoelaces and winced.

Reno got on his phone. "Austin, level red. We've got a rogue and I need your help. Sunny Breeze Trailer Park, the one near the store. Second turnoff; last trailer on the right."

"We have to call the hospital," I said in a shaky voice. I grabbed Reno's shirt and water dripped from the ends of my trembling hair.

"He doesn't need a hospital," Reno said, carefully removing the note. "Do you want to tell me what this is all about?"

"I don't know." How could I tell him? If it had almost gotten Trevor killed, I sure didn't want to bring trouble to Reno's doorstep.

He scorched me with his gaze, his disbelief clear. "We'll talk about it later."

Trevor moaned. I hurried to the sink and ran a towel beneath the water, then rushed back to his side and pressed it against the gaping wound on his head.

"Trevor, can you hear me? I'm here, okay? I'm so sorry." My words came out broken and breathy.

"I need you to take a step outside and calm down," Reno said, taking the rag from my hand.

I stared at him wide-eyed. "I'm not going anywhere. What are you going to do?"

"Help him. His arm looks broken and I might need to set it. That's some disturbing shit for you to see, so I want you to wait outside. Right by the door," he said, making it clear he didn't want me wandering off.

Reno had some kind of command over me and I put on my shoes.

"April."

I looked at him from the open doorway and he nodded toward the wall. "Take the umbrella. I don't want you to get sick."

Sure. A cold was at the forefront of all my problems. Like a zombie, I walked into the misty rain and sat in a lawn chair, holding an umbrella over my head. Raindrops tapped against the fabric and it felt like the life had been sucked out of me. I didn't have a phone to call the hospital, and Trevor didn't have insurance. I'd help him pay for it. Somehow.

I nodded off, probably because of the residual effects of the drugs still lingering in my body. A loud motor revved up the driveway and I jolted awake, watching a black Dodge Challenger pull up beside Reno's motorcycle. Austin hopped out, glanced at me, and went inside the trailer.

I sprang to my feet and raced to the door, tossing the umbrella aside. As it opened, Reno blocked me from getting in.

"Need you to stay outside," he said.

"Then come out here and tell me what's going on. I'm feeling more lucid now, so don't lie to me. Is he going to be all right? Why can't I just sit in the back room? Did you call the police?"

The door closed to a crack and Reno said something to Austin. "I don't know; he won't do it for me. Do your thing. I need to step outside for a minute."

Reno opened the door and jumped down, mud splashing from beneath his biker boots as he walked me to the chair. I didn't feel like sitting down anymore. My arms were shaking, my teeth chattered, and the cold air sank deep into my bones. But it wasn't the temperature making me tremble.

It was the fear that Trevor might die.

Reno's brown eyes softened when he figured it out, and he stepped beneath the umbrella and wrapped his arms around me. "Here, I'll keep you warm."

Minutes passed as Reno held me in the rain. It was better than some meaningless dance because of how intimately close our bodies were, not to mention the emotion of it. The door finally swung open and I whirled around.

"Trevor!"

He stumbled down the steps, wearing only his jeans and shoes. Trevor's expression was volcanic and when I ran up to him, he waved me off.

"Trev, are you okay? Please talk to me."

He turned around and penetrated me with his gaze. "I thought you fucking *left*," he spat out in slow words. "It wasn't my idea to go to the party; that was *all you*," he said, shaking his head.

"I didn't make you go! Are you all right? Your bruises, your cut—"

I reached out to touch his head and he flinched, pivoting around and stalking toward his car. "Time for me to find a new place," he said. "Call ya later, *Showers*."

He put a negative emphasis on the last word, and it sank into my heart like a sharp blade.

Austin knifed by me and spoke to Reno in harsh words. "We'll talk later about this. I have to get back and do some damage control at the house."

I fell to my knees as Trevor sped off. He blamed me for what had happened, and maybe he had every right. He just didn't understand. I'd had no idea Sanchez knew where I lived since he'd come to my work and not my home. Had Trevor known what was going on, he would have gone with me to the warehouse. Trevor had a temper and Sanchez carried a deadly knife. I shuddered as the horrific images of Trevor lying unconscious infiltrated my thoughts.

"Get up," Reno said, cupping his hands beneath my arms.

When it didn't work, he simply bent down and lifted me. Reno carried me into the trailer, kicked the door shut, and took me to the bedroom. He set me on the edge of the bed and opened a few cabinets, searching for something. I'd never had another man besides Trevor in my bedroom, and here he was, wiping the mud from my feet with a clean towel.

"What do you wear to sleep?" he asked, opening a small set of drawers. It didn't take him long to find my nightwear. It should have tickled me to see Reno turn five shades of red when he lifted a pair of my pink panties with the white lace trim, but I didn't feel human anymore.

He handed me silk pajamas and I tossed them on the floor. I'd be sweating by morning if I wore those, so I reached around to unzip my dress. "Can you give me some privacy?"

Reno obediently stood up and closed the curtain. I threw my dress on the floor, and after changing into a new pair of panties and a white tank top, I hid beneath the sheet.

Rain dripped in through a leak, tapping loudly into an empty pot. Reno reappeared and tossed the towel in the bottom. "That'll muffle it," he said, sitting on the floor at the foot of the bed to my right. "You want to tell me what's going on, or do you want me to find out for myself? It's what I do for a living, April. I can. And I will. So what kind of trouble are you in?"

The kind a virtual stranger didn't want to know about if he knew what was good for him. He was a PI; what if he turned me in for theft?

"So that's how it is?" he said. "Your friend said he didn't know who attacked him."

My voice was monotone and low. "Reno, if you keep talking, I'm going to lose it. I'm going to scream at the top of my lungs and just... lose it. I'm not feeling well, and I can't talk anymore. I can't think anymore. Please, just leave. You don't want to get mixed up with someone like me."

All I could think of was Sanchez showing up in the middle of the night with a carving knife. I tried to forget all the hallucinations from the party and the fact I had been on drugs. God, what had happened to me? I used to be on the right track until my train jumped the rails and began heading toward a cliff.

"Is someone after you?" he pressed.

I rolled over with my back to him and he stood up, lingering in the doorway. "I'll sit outside if you don't want me in here, but I'm not leaving you alone tonight."

He closed the curtain and went out the door. I listened to the rain hammering against the trailer for what seemed like an hour before it tapered off. Then I crawled out of bed and went into the living room. I flipped on the light and noticed my fish, Salvador, was floating at the top of his bowl. I scooped him out and held him in the palm of my hand.

"Sorry, little guy," I said, wrapping him in a napkin and putting him in the trash.

My hair hung in my face in tousled clumps. I couldn't even run my fingers through it. Trevor was never going to speak to me again after this.

How did he manage to walk out on his own two feet?

My eyes floated over to the sofa. His arm *had* to have been broken. His face had been beaten to a pulp, but when he walked out, the gash in his forehead was gone, and his arm was fine!

Something put a fright in me when I heard a tap against the door. Or a scrape. I peered out the window but didn't see anyone. Then I heard a familiar whine. I unlocked the door and glanced down at a masked face.

"Hi, sweet boy. Where have you been?" I opened the door and knelt down before my wolf. My fingers brushed through his dry fur and I frowned. "Have you been sleeping under the trailer? Do you want me to fix you something to eat?"

I stood up and reached in the fridge, pulling out leftover sausages wrapped in foil. He trotted inside and shook hard, making himself right at home. I glanced down at his paws and knelt beside him with a towel, cleaning them off.

"You don't smell like a dog," I said, kissing him on the side of his snout. "Most dogs get that pungent smell when they're wet, but… so weird. You just don't smell like a dog." My wolf smelled like early mornings in springtime.

He sat down and gobbled up the cold sausages. It gave me a chance to inspect his wound to see how it was healing. Although I couldn't see anything through his mass of brown fur, he didn't appear to be in any pain.

I crawled over to the door, locked it, and then wiped up the tracks of mud off the floor.

"Last chance to go back outside," I offered. As if understanding me, he sprawled out on the tile and yawned. I touched his soft ears and looked into his dark, familiar eyes. "How come nobody loves you? It seems like someone should be out looking for you by now. You're so handsome. Anyone ever tell you that?"

I tried to keep my focus on the wolf and not the area by the sofa. There were still spatters of blood all around and the crumpled note in the corner. Tomorrow I would clean up the mess and call Trevor to check on him. Once I locked the door, my nerves took over and I found myself wiping down the counters and picking up a few clothes. I placed a tattered blue blanket in a heaping pile by the door, and almost immediately, the wolf circled around on top of it and settled down.

Finally exhausted, I switched off the light and went back to bed, heavy with sleep. Tomorrow I would replace the money I'd taken from the business account. Then I'd contact Sanchez and pay him off before he came after me or hurt someone else.

Not long after, when I was half-asleep, the wolf crawled up in the bed beside me. I nestled my face against his silky fur and held him tight.

CHAPTER 13

WHEN I WOKE UP, IT was still dark and I felt the warmth of the wolf radiating against my back. I blinked, allowing my eyes to focus. It wasn't predawn like I'd first thought. The sky was overcast and dawn was full of dark, rumbling clouds.

I reached over my hip to pet my wolf and froze. My fingers met with skin—more specifically, someone's ass. A hard ass, and as I pulled away, I felt the familiar hairs of a man's legs and peered over my shoulder at Reno. He moaned and hooked his arm around my side, caging me against him.

It didn't make sense! The doors were locked and the only one in the house was the… Oh. My. God. What if last night hadn't been a hallucination? Lexi had mentioned Shifters and Vampires conversationally and… No, this *can't* be happening.

The idea of Reno curled up behind me—completely naked—did a number on my stomach.

A flip-flop, somersault with a twist.

Girl, are you really complaining about waking up next to a sumptuously naked man with a sinful body? my inner voice asked with a delicate yawn. *Go back to sleep. Or better yet, don't. Wake him up*, she said with a wicked laugh in her voice.

"How did you get in here? This can't be real."

"It's real," he murmured in that sexy don't-wake-me-up bedroom voice against the back of my neck. "You're staying in bed for at least three more hours."

"Why three?"

"Because you didn't get enough sleep."

I pushed at his arm. "Let me up. Let go of me!"

Then his hand slid between my legs and cupped my sex, lightly stroking as he answered me in a defiant voice. "No."

"Yes."

Then he inched up closer behind me, as if that word incited something in him.

"No," he said firmly.

Then his fingers worked a little harder, pressing against my panties until I found myself getting wet. He felt it. I felt it.

"*Yes*," I said in a breathy voice.

Then everything changed between us.

Not like I had expected it to. Reno stopped and curved his arms around me so tightly that I couldn't tell we were even separate bodies. I felt him everywhere, from the nape of my neck to the tips of my toes. Reno's naked body against mine was insatiable.

A tremor rolled through him. Subtle, but I felt it. He lightly nipped my shoulder as if it meant something.

"Do you remember what happened last night? It wasn't the drugs, April. We're Shifters, and I belong to a pack of wolves."

I laughed at first. My heart raced at the admission of what I had already suspected but couldn't quite believe. "Don't be absurd. That kind of thing isn't real."

"You saw it, and I can prove it if you still want to hide beneath a cloak of doubt. There are things in this world that are real whether you want to believe in them or not."

Deep down, I knew it to be true. It explained something I thought I had imagined as a child—a man running toward the woods and transforming into a deer. For years, I'd assumed I was an imaginative child, but part of me knew what I had witnessed actually happened. But having seen a man transform right in front of me—I didn't know how to process it. Maybe the drugs had given me hallucinations, but then why would Reno lie? *Perhaps he left his straightjacket at home*, my inner voice suggested.

Reno's body felt like a hard mass of muscle behind me, and I had to confess I liked it. For the first time in a long time, someone made me feel safe and protected. Before I considered doing something I'd regret, I quickly sat up and pushed him away. Reno was as naked as a jaybird and shifted his left leg forward to hide a little bit of that fact.

Didn't hide much.

"You're the wolf? *My* wolf?"

Maybe I shouldn't have said the last bit because his pupils dilated and he got that heated look in his eyes—a possessive look.

"The wolf that got hurt," I corrected.

Too late.

Reno sat up and slid his hand around the nape of my neck and his eyes turned stony. "How do you know about my wolf getting hurt?"

"He's been hanging around here lately. He showed up at my doorstep with a screwdriver in his leg."

"A screwdriver," he breathed. Reno turned his arm, looking at the scar, and that's when I noticed it for the first time. "So that's what it was. Do you know what happened?"

"No. I can't believe I'm having this conversation. It's animal crackers, Reno. You can't be a wolf! *Can't!*"

In a blur of motion, he shifted into a brown wolf and I flew out of the bed, stumbling to the floor and covering my mouth. The wolf barked and showed me his sharp fangs as he shook his coat. Before I could formulate a thought in my head, he shifted back.

A shrill scream flew out of my mouth and I shut my eyes, as if that would make him disappear. "This can't be real. Can't be. *Can't be!*"

Reno was on all fours and quickly sat back, wrapping the sheet around his waist. My God, he looked all kinds of hot. He had strong cords of muscles in his arms, no tattoos, and defined abs like male models I'd seen on the Internet. Not that I looked up male models on the Internet, but sometimes a girl accidentally stumbles across pictures when she's searching for… um… recipes.

"You can't tell anyone, April. That's the rule. No one. I'm entrusting you with a secret and it's the kind with consequences if you break that trust. I'm not kidding around. They'll get a Vampire to scrub your memory if you betray us, and even worse, I've seen humans just disappear."

The last thing I needed in my life was more trouble. "Vampires? I've finally gone crazy. I'm having one of those mental breakdowns."

"Then I'm on the crazy train with you. It's real, April. I'd do it again, but I don't want to frighten you."

My hands trembled and I hugged my knees, staring apprehensively at him. "Is Lexi one of you?"

Reno rubbed his hand across his chest and sighed. "She should be the one telling you all this. Lexi just went through the change a few months ago. You were going to find out one way or another. If you two form a long-term business relationship, then you have a right to know. Austin disagrees and thinks you won't stick around at the shop—that you'll take off and find a new career. Is that what you plan to do?"

I shook my head. "I don't know. Can we not talk about my career path while you're shedding on my sheets?"

He threw his legs over the bed and planted his feet on the floor. "Is someone after you, April? I can't help unless you talk to me, and I'm the kind of man who can help." He stepped into a pair of boxers and crouched in front of me. "I can offer you protection," he said, cupping my cheeks and giving me a solid stare.

"Why was your wolf hanging around my house to begin with? Isn't it a little out of the way from where you live?"

"You're good at evading answers with questions." He let go and placed his hands on my knees. "I don't know. Shifters have to share the same spirit with an animal and that means we have to let them out regularly. I usually go for runs in the wooded area on the outskirts of the city. He knows not to go near humans, but maybe he sensed you were in trouble. I don't know why the hell he would have shown himself to you. We're not that different from humans. Wolves form packs and live together as a family. We protect one another and get jobs to take care of our home."

"Except you also have a tail."

Then his eyes went molten. "You saved my wolf, April. That's a big fucking deal in my world, and you're not even a Shifter. That's an act of valor that earns you respect among my kind," he said, his eyes focusing on my mouth. "I owe you my life."

"You need to leave, Reno. I want you out of my house. I don't want to see you again."

"Let's talk about—"

"No. There's nothing to say. You lied to me and I'm…"

"What?"

"I'm scared of what you are. Besides that, did you think it was okay to just strip out of your clothes and snuggle up in my bed? You must not think much of me. That alone gets you thrown out of my house because I can't believe you thought I'd be down with spooning someone I barely know! And I go to *one* party, and the next thing that happens, your brother is giving me drugs. How can I trust you? You weren't there to protect me. Then some naked guy, drugged out of his mind, decides that he wants to climb on top of me and make me his pet."

Reno stood up in a violent motion and stalked to the side of the bed, yanking on his jeans. "I'm going to take care of *that* problem." His voice grew cold and deadly. "And just so you know, my brother is going to get what's coming to him, but he wouldn't have hurt you. If you say no, he'll back off. Didn't look like you were saying no to Jericho," he pointed out.

"I was stoned!" I screamed, catapulting to my feet.

He tugged on a shoe and laced it up. "Another reason his ass is in the doghouse." Reno buckled his belt while holding his sunglasses between his teeth. "Call your friend and check on him, but be sure you're here at five."

"Why?"

"We have a date."

"Oh, we do?" I made a sound with my lips like a horse and flounced into the kitchen, where I poured a glass of apple juice. "I don't seem to remember you asking."

"I don't need to," he said, coming up behind me. Then he planted a tender kiss on the back of my neck and I wilted like a willow tree. "If you can't handle this because you think I'm a freak, then I get it. Humans aren't able to deal with finding out there's more to life than what they see on the news—it's why we keep it a secret. Less trouble. But if you're just pissed off at me for everything else that happened last night, then we're talking. I'm not turning my back on you."

I turned around. "You're not a freak." I'd never want anyone to feel that way.

His lips twitched. "Good. Five sharp. And put on a pair of jeans and a T-shirt."

Okay, a little weird. "You don't want me dressing up?"

"You looked... damn sexy in that dress last night, April. Couldn't take my eyes off you. But that's you trying to look good for a bunch of strangers. I just want you to be yourself around me. Got it?"

Hmm, my inner voice thought. *Then pink lace panties and a black bra it is!*

"How come nobody knows you guys exist?" Still skeptical, I folded my arms and refused to believe any of this could be real. Perhaps if I buried my head in the sand like an ostrich, the logical side of my brain would win. I used to pretend when I was little that we lived in a world of magic, but finding out Shifters were walking around Austin, Texas? Yet how could I dismiss what I'd seen with my own eyes?

"What do you think? You're a smart girl, April. Think about what it would mean if we came out to humans. I can't explain *why* I exist, but here I am," he said, briefly raising his heavy arms before dropping them again. "We live longer than humans, but we're not immortal. I've served in three wars, traveled outside the country seven times, watched this world change in the blink of an eye, and I've witnessed a lot of senseless shit. It's why I got into PI work. I feel like I'm on the right side of the law and I can make a difference. Whatever happened here last night had nothing to do with your friend, and I'm gonna find out the story whether you tell me the truth or not. Now get dressed because I'm taking you to work."

"Wait, what? It's my day off."

"Not anymore."

My hair looked like scrambled eggs and he wanted me to go to work on my day off?

"I don't feel good."

"Then you're going to drink water and sit down a lot, but you're going to work. That's the Shifter way; you dust yourself off and move on."

"I'm not a Shifter."

Reno's face flushed with anger. "I'm not leaving you alone knowing that asshole who almost killed your friend could be coming back for seconds. I'll pick you up from work, so grab a change of clothes," he said, sitting in a tiny kitchen chair that creaked beneath his weight.

I turned around and stormed down the hall.

"Princess?"

When I peered over my shoulder, Reno had his fist tucked against his cheek.

"Anyone ever tell you how pretty your hazel eyes are when you're mad?"

I blushed, and that made me even madder. "Are you goading me?"

"No, just sweet-talking."

"Don't be nice to me, Reno. I'm not in the mood for nice."

"Music to my ears," he said with a chuckle as I yanked the curtain closed.

When Reno walked in the Weston house after dropping April off at work, a sigh of disgust blew past his lips. There were muddy paw prints across the floor, scuffed-up rugs, and scratches on the doors. Guests had left their plates everywhere, so the girls were frantically trying to clean it up before Lynn returned from her vacation. That woman wouldn't just have a cow if she saw this mess—she'd have a herd.

"Shoes off!" Lexi barked as she hiked up the stairs. Reno kicked off his boots and followed behind her.

"Where's Jericho?"

She didn't bother to turn around. "After the shit he pulled last night? Austin is having a little chat with him. You know what he actually said? He said that our peace parties were lame and all he was doing was livening things up."

"Your friend knows about us now," Reno confessed.

Lexi gracefully spun around, a mixed expression of anger and relief on her face. "Well, maybe that's a good thing. Although now she'll think we're all batshit crazy and will probably turn in her resignation at Sweet Treats."

"Not likely," he said with a soft chuckle. "She's up there now."

"I gave her the day off." Lexi swatted at a fly buzzing around her leg, then turned around to climb the stairs.

"Long story," Reno said. "Any damage?"

"Uh, besides our reputation?"

Yeah, that was going to be problematic. Not keeping a peace party under control in front of the Packmasters wasn't a shining example of Austin's leadership skills and dependability as an ally.

Denver emerged from the game room wearing knee-length cargo pants and a threadbare T-shirt. He held a white kitchen trash can filled with beer bottles and paper plates.

"You could stand there or help out," Denver said, setting the bin by the wall.

"Let's get something straight," Reno began, approaching him with a menacing stride. While Austin was the alpha of the pack, they all had their rank, and Reno was second-in-command. "I don't ever want to see you putting your hands on April again. I don't care if she's naked and leaning over your truck with a wet sponge and a bucket of suds. You keep your distance and we'll be cool."

A smile softened Denver's face. He tried to mash it into a frown, but it wasn't working. "Well, thanks for implanting that erotic visual of April in my head for the rest of my life. I'll never look at a car wash the same again. Calling dibs? Looks like someone has a pet," he said in a smartass tone, wiping the sweat from his forehead with his forearm. "Didn't know you went for humans. That's cool. You got nothing to worry about with me; I was just trying to get some game last night and I didn't see anyone else stepping up to stake his claim." Then he pinched his chin and frowned. "Now, why do you think that is? Maybe you need to back off and stop getting territorial over something that isn't yours."

Reno's irritation level spiked. Denver walked off and began opening the bedroom doors, peering in.

"Looks like the rooms we kept closed off were left alone," he called out to Lexi, who had disappeared in the bathroom at the end of the hall. "Christ almighty! What the train wreck is going on in here?"

Lexi burst into the hall, clutching her chest. "What's wrong?"

Denver stood before the open door that went into Lynn's bedroom. "It looks like a Smurf exploded."

Her shoulders sagged and she rolled her eyes, closing the door. "Jesus, you scared me. My mom likes the color blue. Don't say anything to her or she'll be furious you were in her bedroom. Good thing she didn't do this to the rest of the house, so just let her have her space."

He threw his hands up defensively. "I'm *all* for Lynn having her own space if *that's* the end result. Has she seen a professional about that problem?"

Lexi smacked him on the arm and he let out a snort as he picked up the trash and jogged down the stairs.

"Do you want to help?" Lexi asked, looking weary. "We've cleaned the trash off the lawn, but I'm getting tired, and there's still a lot to do inside."

Reno felt a surge of protectiveness begin to surface. Packs looked after their women, even the mated ones. "Go lie down and take a nap for a few hours. Have you eaten today?"

"Yeah. Austin cooked breakfast burritos about an hour ago. Leftovers are on the stove if you want any. If Austin asks why I'm not cleaning, tell him I'm overheated and underappreciated."

Reno waited until she went into the bedroom and closed the door. Then he jogged downstairs and ate three of the burritos on the stove. They were already cold, but the eggs and sausage hit the spot.

Austin came through the back door in the kitchen and kicked off his shoes at the entrance. He tossed his baseball hat on the table and despite the agreeable weather, he was beet red beneath his tan.

"Damn Jericho. One of these days he's going to get us in serious hot water with the other local packs."

Reno licked the grease off his thumb and leaned back. They had a spacious kitchen with tall windows along the back wall. The table from the old house had ended up on the curb and they'd bought a new one that could seat twenty. Ivy had found a child's table at a rummage sale and placed it in the right corner of the room against the wall by the doorway. Lexi's little sister enjoyed sharing a meal with a doll or her invisible friend. It was nice having a six-year-old in the house; it reminded Reno what packs were all about.

Family.

"Where's Jerko?" Reno asked, finishing the rest of his juice. "Shouldn't he be the one cleaning up this mess?"

Austin took a seat across the table and laced his fingers together. "Jericho's staying with a friend for a couple of nights. I told him he needs to get his act together."

"So you kicked him out?" Reno shifted in his seat. He'd have a real problem if that were true because you didn't turn your back on family for something like this.

"No," Austin grumbled, sliding his jaw to the right. "If you fuck up in my pack, fine. You'll answer to me, and I won't go easy. But you'd have to do something serious for me to give you the boot. Jericho needs to clear his head and I don't want you boys messing with him while the dust is still settling. We need time to cool off and see what the situation is with the neighboring packs. I've spoken privately with three of the Packmasters, and we're still in good standing with them. Plus, I think Lexi's wolf is itching to take a bite out of Jericho for ruining the party," he said with a private chuckle. "That woman is something else. Someday she'll give me strong sons, of that I have no doubt."

"Are you two starting up a family soon?"

Austin scratched his jaw. "The pack is new and I want to put a few years behind us. Lexi loves kids and told me she's ready when I am. I think she'll say anything to get me to have sex with her while she's in heat, so I'll take that with a grain of salt."

Lexi was an excellent bitch, even though she'd kick your ass three times over for calling her that. Heck, Austin would take care of that for her. That was a rule in the house—one word they couldn't call Lexi. While the word didn't carry a derogatory meaning among their own kind, they were aware it did among humans. Lexi had grown up with humans, and for her, it wasn't a nice word to call a lady.

Reno privately thought to himself that he'd make a concerted effort to avoid using that word around April. Then the thought of another man calling her a bitch stirred a venomous fire in him.

Reno lowered his voice. "You ever heard of a man named Maddox?"

Austin's eyes flashed up with suspicion. "What do you want with him?"

"His name came up for a job I'm on. It has me curious because I didn't think he'd turn out to be a Shifter."

"Not a wolf," Austin corrected. "But yeah, he's a Shifter. Maddox has a thick reputation as a favor-trader, but I heard he branched off into monetary loans. I've never met him, but when I was a bounty hunter, a few of the guys I brought in had dealings with him."

"Is he dangerous?"

Austin wiped the sweat from his face and ran his fingers through a tuft of dark hair. "Who can say? I didn't get much information from the men I busted—only that they were trying to scramble up cash to pay him off."

Most Breeds didn't get financially tangled up with humans, so it was an unusual situation. Reno's connections had recognized the name and identified Maddox Cane as a Shifter. While Reno had bigger things on his mind, like who was after April, he owed Wheeler to help him sort out this mess with Sweet Treats. Wheeler didn't work for Lexi, but she needed someone with experience in accounting. Wheeler had no choice in the matter. A good Packmaster knows that a man needs work to feel dignified, so Austin had voluntold him for the job.

Lexi shuffled into the kitchen in a pair of loose shorts and a brown T-shirt, her long hair bound in a ponytail. She lingered by the stove and sleepily glanced at the empty plate where the breakfast burritos used to be.

Reno felt a pang of guilt for not having left her one. "I thought you were upstairs taking a nap."

She shrugged. "I can't sleep. I'm too hungry."

Austin crossed the room and came up behind her, wrapping his arms around her and kissing the side of her neck. "Me too," he murmured.

"You're all sweaty," she complained.

"Mmmhmm," he agreed, kissing her some more. "I think I need someone to wash me off."

Reno took that as his cue to head out. He had a few errands to run before picking up April at the store. One of them being a quick visit to the sonofabitch at the party who had put his hands on her.

CHAPTER 14

I was irritated with Reno for driving me to work on my day off. I organized the displays to keep busy, but I felt detached and anxious. The residual effects of the night before still plagued my thoughts. The worst part was I had no idea which part made me want to run into the streets screaming. Sanchez? Trevor? Shifters? Drugs? Waking up next to a naked man?

Well, maybe not so much the last part. Reno was undoubtedly the sexiest alarm clock I'd ever snoozed on.

After five failed attempts to get in touch with Trevor, I called Lexi and barricaded myself in the bathroom for three hours. When she heard how shaken up I was, she insisted on coming to the store to talk to me in person. But I told her I was on the verge of checking myself into an asylum and maybe that wasn't such a good idea.

In a calm voice, she explained how she'd gone through exactly the same thing, only her situation had been ten times worse since she hadn't known she was a Shifter and had to get used to sharing her body with a wolf. While she'd known Austin most of her life, he'd never spoken of his family because it would have opened the door for more questions. In fact, Lexi's mom thought he might have come from an abused home, which is why she'd always asked him over. In any case, he had been Weston's friend, not hers. She admitted she'd done the bathroom meltdown too, so that made me feel less crazy.

Each Shifter was born to one type of animal. Some lived together in packs, prides, or herds. Other animals, such as wildcats or hawks, preferred to live on their own terms. Wolves had a natural instinct to form packs, and each was led by an alpha male referred to as the Packmaster. Shifters had Councils comprised of different animals so there was no favoritism, and they worked to keep the peace. There weren't just Shifters out there either. I didn't know what to think when she started talking about the Mage her father had worked for and how they weren't magicians but creatures who could harness energy. Then she confirmed Vampires were real and started going on about things I'd never heard of, such as Chitahs and Sensors. My head was spinning. Some lived extended life spans, while some Breeds were immortal. Lexi told me about the division that existed among all the Breeds because of wars that had happened in the past.

She divulged some personal details about their sex life that made me laugh. Shifters are seemingly normal until they go through the change in their late teens or early twenties. That's the first time they shift into their animal. After that, their bodies acquire built-in immunity and they no longer carry or transmit human diseases. Their children can get sick and die, and she suspected it was nature's way of controlling the population. Most female Shifters went into their heat cycle once every year or so, and that was the time their bodies were ready for conceiving a child. In fact, she said an unmated Packmaster's duty was to make sure single women in the pack were kept away from the men during their heat cycle. In some cases, the alpha might help them out in ways that didn't involve sex in order to speed things up and get them out of heat, but that's something Austin didn't know much about firsthand since he hadn't grown up in a pack. Decisions like that always depended on the Packmaster.

Lexi empathized with the emotional roller coaster I was on, reassuring me that I had nothing to fear. She mentioned Jericho had been placed on punishment and was temporarily out of the house. With that being said, she had extended an invitation for dinner that evening.

But I had other plans.

Reno plans.

Her efforts were in vain, and after some prodding, it became evident that Reno hadn't filled her in on his plans to take me out. Suddenly, for whatever reason, I became upset. *Was he ashamed of me?*

Two minutes before five, the brass bell on the main door jingled.

"Welcome to Sweet Treats," I heard Bethany say in a bored voice.

I'd changed into a pair of faded denims with a hole in the knee and an oversized black shirt with quarter-length sleeves. He asked for casual, so I was giving him *casual*.

"Is April here?"

"Uh…" I heard Bethany stutter. "April?"

I peered around the corner and my inner voice did a *meow*.

Reno wore a black sleeveless shirt with a pair of black cargo pants. I took a moment to appreciate his firm biceps and his masculine stance because Reno was a man in every conceivable way. The kind of guy that made heads turn when he walked down the street. He looked like he'd just stepped away from fighting street crime, minus the gun holster. A sexy five-o'clock shadow dusted his jaw and his eyes were obscured behind mirrored aviator sunglasses. It had been cloudy all afternoon, so the shades made him look more like a cop.

Except when he was naked in my bed.

"Hi…" I greeted him shyly.

His predatory grin was so subtle I barely saw his lips move. "You ready, princess?"

I studied Bethany, who lingered behind the register, catching flies with her open mouth, which was full of braces. I'm sure Reno was nothing like the kind of man she'd imagined me with.

"Where are we going?" I asked.

He held the door open and we walked out onto the busy sidewalk. Reno stepped up to an oversized blue truck and opened the passenger door.

"Whose truck is this? Where's your bike?"

"We'll need the truck tonight," he said, helping me inside the cab. "It smells like rain."

After he buckled me up, Reno slammed the door. I held my breath and squeezed my seatbelt strap as he strolled around the front of the truck, deliberately tracing his finger along the hood. It reminded me of the courtship rituals of wild animals. I usually didn't pay much attention to a man's posture, but he stood up straight and walked with his shoulders back, like a man who owned his confidence. I liked that he wasn't covered in tats, because I wasn't really into body art. Reno hopped in, cranked on the engine, and a guitar riff blared through the speakers with AC/DC singing "Thunderstruck."

"What happened to your face and hand?" I glanced at a small cut on his cheekbone and noticed the knuckles on his right hand were bruised.

He lifted his shades and his resolute eyes looked sharply at me. "I took care of someone who needed taking care of."

Reno pulled onto the street and I shifted my gaze out the window, wondering where he planned to take me. Maybe it would be an outdoor patio at a Mexican restaurant. What did Shifters do for fun? Reno wasn't human, but it felt wrong to turn my back on him for something he couldn't help just because I didn't understand it. Maybe that's why I had agreed to go—I was curious to learn more about him. I'd known Lexi for over a year and she seemed normal, so maybe I needed to be more open-minded.

After a short ride, we parked in front of a Target and got out. *Well, this is classy*, my inner voice remarked.

Inside the store, I eyeballed him as he pulled out two red shopping carts. "What are we doing here?"

Reno took off his sunglasses and tucked them onto the collar of his shirt. "I need to buy a few things, and I want you to help me. I have an open credit line, so anything goes. I want you to take one of these baskets and fill it up with decorations. The necessities are full sheets, a comforter, uh… pillowcases and all that junk. Something with a feminine touch. I also need sofa pillows, decorations for a bedroom and living room, and small area rugs. The whole tamale. Don't look at price tags. Like I said, it's all taken care of."

Wow. They must have really messed up his house. "So I'm basically redecorating your house?"

"You have taste."

"And you got that from my trailer?" I leaned on the cart and glared at him skeptically.

He rubbed the corners of his mouth. "I saw the little touches in there that were all you." Then he glanced at his watch. "If I don't find you first, then meet me back here in an hour. I have to grab some things on the other side of the store. Like I said, go all out."

I wondered if they had a new woman in their pack. I'm not sure why, but the thought sparked jealousy in me. How could they live with a single woman in the same house and keep it platonic? Maybe this was for Ivy and they all shared her. I hadn't thought to ask Lexi every intricate detail about their lifestyle. Reno said they outlived humans and he had seen three wars. Three? I wondered how old that made him. Recent wars, or were we talking Civil War?

"Don't let me down," he said. "We've only got an hour to get it all together."

This was the weirdest date I'd ever been on. Maybe it wasn't a date—had he even used that word? He'd just said we were going out, hadn't he? *Mental eye roll.* I was jumping to conclusions again. If that were a board game, I'd be the undefeated champion.

"Gotcha. Shall I buy her some lingerie as well?" I angrily rolled my basket down the aisle and heard him chuckling behind me.

At first, I was irritated by the idea of shopping for another woman. But soon it became liberating to fill the cart and not look at the price tag. Reno could sift through my stuff later and decide what he couldn't afford; my assignment was simply to fill the basket. I picked out a trendy set of lavender sheets that matched a purple and black comforter. After I'd selected the bedroom set, I specially chose accessories so her bedroom wouldn't look like a purple nightmare. I found two lightweight mirrors that were classy and modern along with candleholders, candles, and a white vase with capiz shell flowers.

Then I hit the sofa pillows. Without a clue of what color the couch was, I went for neutral browns and a maroon. I also snatched a fuzzy maroon throw that could be put on the back of a sofa to match the pillows.

This was fun! Okay, maybe I went overboard when I spotted an adorable little bookshelf table, but it was too beautiful to pass up. I could put Hermie's bowl on top and fill the lower shelf with my books.

Except the only problem being it wasn't my table, and I was buying it for another woman.

Another woman.

Then my inner voice said, *Wait a minute. Hold the phone. Little decorations with a feminine touch? Missy, I bet he's seeing how into this lifestyle you really are. Those Shifters probably have harems.*

Had I ever asked Reno if he was married or had a girlfriend? What if Shifters practiced polygamy? I sure as heck wasn't going to be someone's second wife if that's what he had in mind. Or even a girlfriend on the side.

"April?"

I whirled around with my arms folded. "Do you have harems?"

His lips twitched. A slow chuckle rose, growing louder until Reno was rocking with laughter. I'd never seen him laugh and it unnerved me. So much so that I turned around and bumped into a man, causing him to drop an armload of towels.

"Oh, jeez. I'm so sorry," I said, bending down to pick them up.

Reno's laugh died down and he began clearing his throat.

The man knelt in front of me and winked. "It's fine, sweetheart."

Then Reno's laugh cut off and his boots clomped on the floor until he was beside me. The man's eyes flicked up and he scooped the unfolded towels from my hands and hurried away. I was left kneeling on the floor.

"You did good," Reno said, peeking into my cart. "Real good."

"You might want to look through it all and check out the prices. I was going to get that table up there, but the box was too heavy," I said, pointing at the end table as I stood up.

Reno lifted the box with one arm and slammed it over his cart. "You done? Or do you want me to wait?"

"No, I got everything and then some." I reached in the cart and held up a few things. "You weren't specific, but these mirrors are fifty dollars, so—"

"Put them back in," he said. "She needs mirrors. We're not thrift shopping, so if there's anything you were holding back on, then grab it. We need to head out."

I glanced at his cart and there was a mix of odds and ends. Lots of food, but also a toolbox, sealant or whatever that gooey stuff was that guys liked to buy in giant tubes, a lamp, paint, mops, and even a few small appliances.

"Let's go," he said. "Before the rain starts up again."

After we loaded up the bed of the truck, Reno agreed to head back to my trailer. I wanted to check if Trevor had decided to come back home.

A burden had been lifted from my shoulders after I'd deposited the money back into the business account early that morning. I stuffed Sanchez in my mental closet and locked the door so I wouldn't let the fear drive me to doing something stupid, like using the money to skip town. It wasn't worth the risk of hurting anyone else around me. My grandma had raised me to clean up after myself, and Sanchez was going to require a tremendously large mop.

I dashed inside my trailer and looked around. No sign of Trevor. Disappointed and a little concerned, I took a seat on my sofa and tried calling him again. No answer. He wasn't even responding to my text messages. It broke my heart because I loved Trevor and didn't want him to despise me. I couldn't have imagined Sanchez would hurt one of my friends. I shuddered to think that had I not gone to the party, who knows what would have happened to me.

Reno walked in with two sacks and set them on the table.

"Is it raining?" I asked. Reno didn't have a cover on the bed of the truck and the rain would ruin some of the items.

He returned with plastic sacks hanging all the way up his arms and set them down on the floor. I got up and reached outside the door with my palm up. No rain, but the clouds were darkening.

Reno went out to the truck and returned with the shelf under his arm and several more of the larger bags.

"We can head out now if you want. You don't have to bring all this inside; it doesn't look like it's going to rain just yet," I said.

He stepped inside and set everything down. "This is all yours."

Hand to God, my heart stopped in my chest and I made a soundless gasp. "What are you talking about?"

Reno put the flat of his hands on the ceiling, as if he were trying to make more room for his height. His head just touched the ceiling, so he made it a point to lower his chin when walking around. "I'm talking about the fact that I don't see any need for you to be living in these conditions. You were dealt a bad hand, but I don't like waking up in the morning and finding nothing in your cabinets but a bag of cheap rice and cereal. I don't like seeing a blanket on your bed with stains, or a leak in your roof and windows, or one sorry-ass pillow on your sofa—if you want to call that a sofa. As long as you have to live here, I'm going to make sure you got what you need."

He went out the door and I sank onto the small couch in complete and utter shock. What I had in my cart alone was in the hundreds! Reno hadn't just taken me out to dinner on our first date—he'd bought me *groceries*. Just the thought of it brought tears to my eyes and I covered my face. Bags rattled and then he knelt in front of me, spreading his arms across my legs.

"I'm going to look after you. No more walking to work, because I'm lending you the truck. I bought a strong lock for your door and I'm going to fix the leaks in your roof. It's a tight space, but I'll make room for the microwave. This isn't a bad place; I've seen a lot of poverty in my time and this doesn't even come close. But it's not safe, and it could be a whole lot better with a little work. So I'm going to make it better, and that's the deal. I'm also going to stay with you until I feel like you're not in any trouble."

"But Reno—"

"No buts."

Without pause, I held his jaw tenderly and kissed him on the mouth. Our kiss tasted like tears, but it was beautiful. His hands found my hips and slid beneath my shirt, stroking the small of my back. I'd never been so forward with my affection, but Reno did something to me, something I couldn't explain. Maybe it was pheromones, or maybe it was the fact that he'd bought me a houseful of decorations to make my self-made prison into a palace. My body ignited and I gripped his strong shoulders.

His mouth scraped away from mine and down my jaw, kissing my neck. I tipped my head up and moaned quietly, my breaths heavy and my body insatiably hungry. Then he broke contact and leaned back.

"What's wrong?" I asked.

He stood up and lowered his eyes guiltily. "I don't expect payment, April. That's not why I did this."

My eyes widened. "Do you think that I'm paying you off with a sexual favor?"

"Then why would you kiss me?"

"Because I'm attracted to you, Reno. No one does stuff like this," I said, waving my hands around the room. "No one's ever done anything like this for me before and it shows me what a big heart you have. But you're right. We shouldn't do this because it's all wrong. I can't keep any of this stuff."

"You're keeping it," he decided, unloading more groceries and putting them in the fridge. "I'll stay outside at night so it won't be weird for you."

"Oh sure. There's nothing weird about you sleeping outside my front door in the mud."

He shrugged and put a bag of Oreos in the cabinet. "My wolf doesn't mind and I can always sleep in the truck."

"Can I have some of those?"

He turned his head and his eyes danced with amusement. "These?" he asked, holding up the blue bag as the plastic rattled.

I nodded and returned an impish smile. I hadn't had cookies in forever. "Is there any milk?"

"Right here, princess," he said, opening a jug and pouring me a tall glass. He peeled open the bag and sat down beside me, putting the cookies in my lap. "So where do you want the table I'm going to build for you?"

I twisted the cookie apart and scraped the filling off with my teeth. There seemed little point in resisting his kindness; Reno was dead set on doing things his way and it was hard to stay mad at him. "Right there," I said, pointing to the left of the door. "I'm going to put Hermie on top and my books on the shelf below."

Reno set my glass on the table and lifted up a paperback book with a bare-chested man on the front. "This book?"

My face turned six shades of red when he began thumbing through it. "Give me that!"

A laugh pealed out and he leaned to the right, out of my grasp. Then he began reading a passage from the page I had marked. Well, what *Trevor* had bookmarked.

Oh. My. God.

"'His shaft glided into her velvety canal, exploring deep inside her like a man discovering new depths of passion. She moaned, rocking sweetly against him, their bodies marrying and clashing like waves in a violent storm. He laved her sweet nipples and they hardened against his tongue. His blood heated and his thrusts spiraled out of control…' *Hot damn*, April," Reno said, looking at me with an astonished expression. "You read this?" He glanced over his shoulder and I stuffed another cookie into my mouth.

"Trevor."

"And I suppose *you* read Shakespeare," he said sarcastically, setting the book back down.

"Why are you trying to make me ashamed of what I like? It's a novel. There are stories in there about love and adventures, and yes, sometimes there's sex."

"I'm not judging you, April. I think it's sexy as hell you read this kind of stuff. I don't know about these word choices, but it sounds classier than some of those magazines."

A laugh burst out of my mouth. "Magazines? Exactly what kind of literature are *you* reading?"

"A man has needs," he said in a low voice.

"You don't strike me as a man who has trouble getting women. I didn't picture you as the magazine type. Do you order them off the Internet or buy them at the gas station?"

His brow arched and he grabbed a cookie, shoving it into his mouth without any twisting, licking, or nibbling. "So, are you trying to make me feel ashamed about what *I* read? That's a little hypocritical."

"Are we *reading* those magazines, or just admiring the racy photographs?" I gave a spirited laugh and Reno handed me the milk. Then I realized I probably had chocolate teeth and took a long sip, putting the cookies aside.

"What's it like? Shifting, I mean. Does it hurt?"

"No. It feels like… I don't know how to explain it," he said, rubbing his chin. "It's like sliding into a pool of water or something. I can only remember a few minutes into my shift—after that, my wolf takes over."

"And you don't remember anything after that?"

"Zip. Total blackout. It's like that for most of us. Alphas are more likely to remember the entire shift because they have control of their animal, although I've heard stories about others who weren't alphas having the same talent. I don't know how they do it. I personally enjoy having a break."

I pulled up my legs and twisted the frayed edges surrounding the hole in my jeans. "Were you born that way?"

"Yeah. I'm a different species than you."

"Can you turn other people into one through a bite?"

The room grew silent and I kept playing with the strip of fabric, pretending I didn't notice he was watching me closely.

"I can't make you one of us, if that's what you're asking. This isn't a curse that's transmitted like a disease. You need to erase all those fictional werewolf stories you've watched in movies made to vilify what humans don't understand. We're *not* werewolves; Shifters are the spirits of man and animal inhabiting one body. Long ago, humans knew what we were. Man kills what he fears or doesn't understand. Sometimes they kill out of jealousy. It's why we've separated from your kind and live in secret."

"Just curious."

"That's fine. I don't expect you to wrap your head around it all at once. It's not every day you learn that the big bad wolf is real," he said with a dark chuckle.

Reno stood up and unloaded several cans of vegetables into an overhead cabinet. I got the rest of the bags out of the truck and decided to give the trailer a deep clean like it had never known before. I turned on a small radio and we listened to Billy Joel and some blues while we worked. Little did Reno know that I worshipped Billy Joel, although after me singing every word without missing a beat, maybe he figured it out. But he didn't complain about my taste in music and I liked that. It was romantic listening to John Lee Hooker's "Boom Boom" while Reno stripped out of his shirt and fixed my trailer in nothing but his black pants and socks.

Once I had my fill of eye candy, I closed the curtain to my bedroom and began to decorate. I was so excited when the comforter was spread across the bed that I leapt on top of it and let out a squeal.

I took out the e-reader that Trevor had bought for me and read a few chapters. Then I dozed off for a few minutes. Or maybe it was an hour.

When I opened my eyes, Reno was hanging up a new curtain. He had stripped down the makeshift one I'd made from a sheet. His was made from white lace—so breathtakingly delicate and beautiful. I reached over and flipped on my new orange lamp, softening the glow in the room.

"This'll look better," he said, sliding it along the track. "You like it?"

"Love it," I said sleepily.

Etta James sang "Misty Blue" in the background and the rain created a symphony of sound against the roof overhead.

Reno pointed to the corner by the door. "No more leak," he said proudly.

"Thanks so much for your help."

I wanted to freeze-frame that night and make all the bad things disintegrate into ashes and blow away.

Reno scratched his shoulder and crossed his arms, standing in the corner and looking uncomfortable as hell. "What are those?" he asked, pointing to a small shelf on the wall.

I looked at the low shelf on my right and smiled. "Snow globes. My dad used to give them to me when I was little, but I stopped collecting them after he died. The water evaporated in a couple of the smaller ones."

I had a total of fourteen. My dad had initiated a tradition when I was born where he gave me one every Christmas. He always managed to make it have a personal connection or a special meaning. Like the father-and-daughter one on the left. It was only after his death that my grandma told me that he had made them. She said it was his secret hobby and that he'd search for just the right pieces and put them all together to personalize it.

Reno's eyes lit with interest as he looked between all of them.

"Will you lie beside me?" I asked. "Keep me company for a little while?"

Without a word, he crossed to the left side of the room and sat on the edge of the bed. I glanced up at his back, tempted to touch it, but kept my hands folded across my stomach. Then he threw his heavy legs on the bed and reclined onto the fluffy pillow. Our arms touched and a grin eased across his face.

"This is nice. The mirrors look good up there," he said, pointing to the left.

"I didn't think you'd be able to get them up because of these walls. Makes the room seem bigger." They were small mirrors and he had bought some strong adhesives to mount them.

I glanced down at his socks and sat up. Wet socks, the closer I looked. "You are not wearing wet socks in my new bed, Reno Cole."

I peeled one off and he hooked his hands around my waist, trying to pull me back. I giggled and grabbed his foot, tickling the bottom.

I'm not sure if tickling a man is ever a good idea, because he had a knee-jerk reaction and almost bucked me off the bed. He gripped the hem of my jeans and pulled me fast into his arms. I curled up beside him, my head resting on his shoulder and my right arm draped across his bare chest like a sash. I tried to be subtle as I inhaled so Reno wouldn't notice I was sniffing him, but I couldn't help but think he smelled inexplicably wonderful.

"Why do you have a man on your wall?"

My eyes skimmed over to the poster. "That's not a man. That's Billy Joel."

"Old boyfriend?" he asked.

"That would be some serious cradle robbing if that was true."

He paused. "How old are you?"

I wondered if age mattered to him. Reno looked to be in his thirties. "I'll be twenty-three soon. What are your favorite foods?"

"Mexican, and sometimes Thai," he said.

My ear pressed against his chest and the rumbling vibrations tickled my cheek when he spoke. It was comforting to feel and hear him up close.

"Thai is unusual. I had Vietnamese food once."

He chuckled. "Not the same. What about you?"

"My favorite is home cooking. Beef stew, casseroles, greens—

all that good Southern food. Not many restaurants around here specialize in that unless they're a chain. It's all fast food."

Reno mumbled in agreement. "How many men have you dated?"

"One." I replied quickly before my inner voice piped up and I chickened out.

He stopped breathing. "*One?*"

I could feel his heart pounding against my forearm. "I didn't date until I went to college. One Saturday, I went to the movies with my sister and ran into this dashing young man in the lobby and spilled his popcorn. We talked for a few minutes before the movie started and exchanged numbers, but I didn't think he'd call me."

"How serious was it?"

Did I hear jealousy in his voice?

"He was… well, he was my first. Things were beginning to get serious between us, or so I thought. But then he started cheating on me. I know a lot of men cheat, but he did it frequently with my best friend and we haven't spoken since then."

"I don't believe that. Only one man has ever seen you naked?"

That was an embarrassing way to put it. It felt like a hot spotlight was burning down on me.

"Do Shifters get married?"

Reno rubbed the side of his nose and angled his body toward me. A burst of tingles moved down my body, and I thought about the restrained passion in our kiss. "Something like that. All a man has to do is declare a woman as his mate and his pack will respect their union. We don't use rings or tattoos to prove we're mated. If someone asks, we tell them. Usually what happens is the couple will gather with the local Packmasters to witness their vows."

"What are the vows you say?"

Reno shrugged. "I've never been to one. I don't think there's a script or anything," he said with a chuckle. "They probably take a vow to protect and die for each other. They sign a document to keep it on record in case there are disputes within the pack or other troubles. Word usually spreads and most of us don't encroach on someone's territory. We mate for life."

"So no dress or church?"

"Our customs aren't the same as yours. Being life mates isn't about a party."

I smiled and thought about how much money humans spent on weddings. "Did Lexi mate with Austin?"

His breath warmed the top of my head as he spoke. "Yeah. Austin's claim on her is as good as gold, but her mother wants a wedding. I didn't ask if they signed the papers, but all the local packs know they're life mates. Nobody messes with a Packmaster's woman."

"Well, if she has a wedding, I hope I'm invited."

"April? Do you want to get serious with me?"

The music faded and thunder rolled outside. My finger traced a small circle on his chest. "I won't live as long as you will, and I'm guessing by how old you implied you are that you age slowly. I don't. Let's enjoy tonight, because I'm not sure if by tomorrow I'm going to feel the same way as I do right now in your arms. We're too different for this to work."

"I like different," he said, brushing his right hand through my hair.

"And in thirty years when I'm fifty, are you still going to like different?"

Reno didn't answer.

CHAPTER 15

WHEN I OPENED MY EYES, I found myself bathed in a pool of sunlight. The magic of the night before with the soft orange glow of the lamp, the feel of Reno's warm body beside mine, the newness of my life, and the sound of blues music had melted away into a distant echo. It brought a pang of sadness because I had fallen deeply in love with a shining moment in my life, one I would treasure in my mind for years to come. Not just discovering that the world wasn't what I thought it was, but allowing someone to give me hope again.

When Reno had fixed my leak, bought me food, and hung a pretty curtain in my doorway, it returned a normalcy that I had long desired. I'd spent so much time focusing on getting away from my life, and Reno made me see that I could have everything I wanted right here. Living better was a state of mind that only required a few extra dollars, not a fancy job that paid a lot of money. It reminded me that I wouldn't always have this debt, and if I worked hard enough, I'd eventually have a place of my own, one that wasn't a hand-me-down, maybe even a house.

Last night had surpassed anything I had read in my romance novels or imagined in my fantasies because it was real, and it was mine.

I stretched out my legs beneath the crisp sheets. I had no recollection of how my jeans got removed, but my socks and black shirt were untouched. Reno's side of the bed was neatly made—the bedspread was pulled so tight I could bounce a quarter off it.

I reached for my phone to check my messages. Nothing from Trevor.

Reno hadn't left a note, but the keys to his truck were on my kitchen table in front of a red apple. I snatched the fresh fruit and took a few juicy bites. With the money deposited into the Sweet Treats account, I now had to turn my attention to Sanchez. Instead of calling, because I'd go ballistic at him for what he did to Trevor, I left a text message of where to meet me for the exchange.

My terms.

If he wanted more cash, then he needed to tell me before our meeting. I had no intentions of showing up only to find out I was going to be short on my payment. No more negotiations; this would be the *final* transaction.

Screw his abandoned warehouses and screw his mind games. If he wanted his money, then he'd have to meet me at the *mall*. I wasn't about to get myself chopped up into pieces, never to be found again, because I'd decided to meet a maniac alone. I'd learned my lesson after the first time and wanted to take every precaution. This wasn't something I had any experience doing, and if he continued coming after me, I'd either buy a gun or call the police. I had little faith the cops would do much outside of filing a report, and I was uncertain if I'd done something illegal in doing business with a loan shark. I didn't know the laws, but if they found out I'd taken money out of the business account, I'd really be in legal trouble. The most I could get against Sanchez would probably be a restraining order, and a lot of good that would do me living alone in the parks.

I took a quick shower and put on a pair of knee-length shorts, sneakers, and a sweatshirt. A clip held some of my bangs away from my face and I passed on the perfume and makeup. I had no desire to look or smell attractive for this man. Unfortunately, his money was in my brown purse, so I headed over to Lexi's to pick it up.

An hour later, I arrived at Austin's house and knocked on the door. I heard the sound of heavy footsteps approaching and the door swung open.

My eyes traveled upward, landing on a stern-looking man with lots of tattoos on his arms. A wolf, justice scales, a dagger—a myriad of images were married to his flesh and created a staggering display of imagery. A black sleeveless shirt hugged his body and it was then that I noticed his eyes. They were the palest of brown with flecks of gold in the irises. They glittered like amber and warm honey, standing out against his dark features and brooding expression. I glanced at his bare feet as he leaned on the doorjamb and stared down his nose at me.

"What a pleasure to see you again, April," he said insincerely.

What the heck did I ever do to this guy? Ben might have been a flirtatious handful, but Wheeler was too belligerent for my liking.

"I left my purse upstairs and came by to pick it up."

His eyes scratched down the length of my body with a judgmental sting. "Speaking of pickups, is that *our* truck you're driving around?"

A flush of heat touched my cheeks. "Reno lent it to me."

"That so?"

I looked directly into his eyes and stared. Didn't blink, didn't look away. I wasn't in the mood for games—not after everything I'd been through in the last twenty-four hours. I also didn't like imperious jackasses who sought to deflect attention from their own problems by instigating verbal warfare against someone else. His brows sloped down at a menacing angle and he tipped his head to the side, neither of us speaking a word as the sound of a distant airplane flew overhead.

"Wheeler, you're letting all the cold air out. Who's at the… oh, April! Please come in," Ivy insisted, nudging Wheeler out of the way and taking my hand. "Would you like some tea? I just took it out of the sun."

"No, thanks. I can't stay. I left in a hurry and forgot my purse, so I stopped by to pick it up."

Her full lips curled in as she licked them, and she glared at Wheeler with intolerant eyes while he held up the doorframe, still scorching me with a heated gaze.

"Then you'll join us for dinner," she insisted. "Lexi feels terrible about the party and talked about having you over for dinner. I make a delicious pot roast and I'd love to have you join us." She briefly glanced at Wheeler. "I think it's no secret what we are. We're no different from you, April. We have our own issues and disputes, but we also have unity and value a family environment. A pack in itself is a family, but we mate for life and work out our differences. I'm sure if Jericho had laced cupcakes at a human party, it could have gotten out of hand very quickly, but the Packmasters kept us in line and broke up the party at the first sign of trouble. *Please,*" she said, reaching out to hold my wrist. "I insist we make it up to you. Will you give us a second chance? You're a loyal friend to Lexi and she thinks highly of you."

Wheeler turned around and muttered, "Didn't take you for a pet lover, Ivy."

Her serene face showed that he hadn't ruffled her feathers. "Is seven o'clock okay? We'll have white wine and talk on the porch after supper. It'll be a relaxed atmosphere and a good time, so what you're wearing is fine. Come with me. Let's get your purse and you can think it over."

Ivy had been blessed with the gift of convincing people to do things they didn't want to do. At least she wasn't asking me to go skydiving. I agreed to stop by later that evening and have dinner with the pack, and she extended the invitation to Trevor.

When I arrived at the mall to meet with Sanchez, I looked as if I'd just rolled out of bed in my long shorts and sweatshirt. All the teens were glammed up, parading around in their satiny lipstick and designer jeans, hoping to grab the attention of one of the hot boys hanging out by the music shop.

My purse strap bit into my shoulder and I nervously turned a bracelet on my wrist as I glided up the escalator. Once I reached the top, I walked past the pizzeria and hamburger vendors. We needed to complete the exchange in a more private area, so I'd instructed Sanchez to meet me by the barbecue station at the far end. This felt like something out of an espionage movie, except there was no James Bond and my hands were shaking like an epileptic's.

My heart skipped like a stone when I saw Sanchez sitting at one of the plastic tables with an empty plate in front of him. I glanced at the clock wondering if I was late, but I was early this time.

"Take a seat, Vanilla," he said in a curt tone.

I bit my tongue for all the things I wanted to say to him about Trevor. "Here's the deal," I began as my inner voice sank down in her chair and covered her face. "None of this is legal. I'm sure you have a little leeway from your boss to garner a tip, but Delgado might not be too thrilled with how much extra cash you're making on the side."

Sanchez rubbed the patch of hair on his chin with his middle finger, showing me his bottom teeth.

I cleared my throat and reached in my purse, pulling out a small box with a bow on it. "Happy birthday. Every penny. And not that you even care, but I had a good reason for not showing up. If you ever touch my friend again, or anyone else I care about, I'll kill you." My face hardened like stone, and his eyes sharpened like razors as he watched me deliver my threat.

I slid the box in front of him and he glimpsed inside.

"It's all there," I assured him. "I'd be foolish to short you, given everything that's happened. I'm not threatening you, but I'm stating a fact about your boss. You know the guys running the show don't like to find out they're losing money. Don't come by my house. Don't call me. Don't accidentally run into me at a music store. You're getting *more* than enough, and you've already taken more than enough from me. I have nothing left to give you and this has put me in further debt. You'll get nothing else—money or otherwise. I'm sure you saw an opportunity with me being young and naïve, but I'm not playing that game anymore."

I folded my arms and sat back, waiting for him to pull out a butcher knife and put me on the six-o'clock news. There had come a point in my unprepared speech when I'd realized that I could never appease a man like Sanchez. Begging or bartering would only maintain a relationship with him I no longer wanted. The only way out was to be firm and show him my verbal middle finger. Then I could decide how many states I needed to move away.

He peered in the box again and leaned in tight. "You think you're one smart bitch, Vanilla. But you know what I see? A loser with cheap nail polish and a bad dye job. You're nothing but a secondhand girl who's going to wind up working one shitty job after the next and marrying an alcoholic who uses you for a punching bag. So you're going to get what you deserve, one way or the other. There's nothing special about you." He stood up from his chair and tucked the box beneath his arm. "You're going to live and die in that trailer."

Sanchez tipped his chair over when he walked off with an intentional swing in his step, trying to convey how tough he was.

He looked more like a man suffering from hemorrhoids.

I blew out a breath and felt an overwhelming sense of relief. I almost regretted not having someone there to witness how well I'd handled myself.

"It's over," I whispered. Now I just had to pay off Maddox for the rest of my life. My inner voice might have fainted, but I was proud of myself. Trevor would have been proud too.

"I'm so glad you came!" Lexi greeted me in a casual pair of black shorts and a cotton shirt with quarter-length sleeves. I was glad it wasn't formal because all I had on were a pair of jeans and a pretty blouse. She swung the front door wide open and smiled warmly. The Weston house smelled like heaven—a mixture of delicious meat in the oven and potpourri from a small vase on a table by the stairs.

I noticed a pile of shoes in the hall and kicked my sandals off. I hadn't heard from Reno all day and I wondered if he would be joining us.

Lexi led me through the living room and into the kitchen. The cabinets and appliances were straight ahead, and to the right by a wall of windows was a long wooden table with bench seating. Most people these days just grabbed dinner and went to their corners, but it looked as though they made a concerted effort to have family meals. Someone had strung up tiny white lights above the tall windows behind the table. The windows were curtainless and probably brought in an ample amount of sunlight. A clamor of noise made me jump and I glanced at an overflow of pans pouring out of a lower cabinet.

"Sorry about that," Ivy said.

I admired the white daisies on the table that were in clear jars filled with water. The room had a restaurant atmosphere with all the casualness of home. The kitchen appeared significantly larger than the dining room, and then I remembered this had once been used as a hotel. Perhaps people had eaten in their rooms.

"Smells heavenly," I said, glancing toward the stove on my left. Ivy scooped something onto a plate and turned off a burner.

"Here, try this," Lexi said, handing me a glass of wine. "This is the first white wine I've ever loved. Tell me what you think."

I took a short sip to be polite. "Mmm. It's more sweet than dry."

"Exactly. Austin thinks it tastes like fruit juice and should be served at the kiddie table," she said, rolling her eyes.

"I do," he agreed, ambling into the room barefoot with a closed-lipped smile. "I'm afraid the wine doesn't match the sophistication and complexity of my alpha female."

Austin had on a pair of loose jeans and a blue button-up with the top two buttons undone, revealing a medallion he always wore around his neck. He wrapped his arms around Lexi's waist from the side and kissed her on the neck, brushing her long brown hair away.

"When's dessert?" he murmured.

"Hi, Miss April."

I turned around and smiled at Maizy. She had on a pretty blue dress with white flowers. Someone had combed her blond hair back in a ponytail and secured two rainbow-colored hair clips on either side. Maizy also wore a scowl on her face.

"What's wrong, hon?"

"I hate blue."

"April! It's been too long since I've seen you," Lynn said from behind me in the hallway. Lexi's mom came into the shop every so often to take Lexi out to dinner with Maizy. I envied the relationship she had with her mother—they were a tight family. As it should be. She gave me a brief hug. "How are you, honey?"

"Hi, Lynn. I'm doing good." She didn't like going by Miss Knight and had always insisted that I call her Lynn. Even though I wasn't a child, it still didn't feel right calling her that since I'd been brought up to address my elders respectfully. "Have you changed your hair? It looks a little shorter, but I love how you're styling it." I reached out and touched the ends of her blond hair.

"Just a trim," she said. "The long hair was becoming too much to manage. Did Lexi tell you we're having pot roast?"

"Ah, yes. Ivy did, actually. Can I help with anything?"

A laugh bubbled out and she headed toward the cabinets and began slicing bread. "You're the guest; of course not! Put your purse on the table by the door and have a seat. We're almost ready."

Austin claimed a spot at the head of the table while I lingered, uncertain of where to sit. I hadn't grown up in a home where we ate together at a table, but I knew most people had regular spots where they liked to sit, and I didn't want to impose. He watched with amusement and steepled his fingers in front of his face.

I carefully walked around the table and finally chose a spot facing the windows that I thought no one would want.

Austin let out a short "humph" and leaned back. "Lexi told you all the rules, I take it? About our secret."

"Yes, she did. It's a little hard to swallow," I admitted. "Just don't shift in front of me or I might freak out."

"We don't live that way," he said. "Our animals are a part of us and we let them out when they get an itch to run. But we don't walk around shifting at will for the hell of it; we have no direct control over our animal, so it's important not to give them too much power. Just keep in mind that entrusting you with this knowledge is a privilege, so just take care not to—"

"Austin, we discussed this," Lexi sang from the kitchen. "Let's just have a nice dinner."

He averted his eyes and dropped the subject.

The place settings were gorgeous, with mosaic plates and cloth napkins—each person had a different color. I ran my finger along the yellow plate in front of me. Ivy set two bowls, one of mashed potatoes and the other of peas, on the table. The steam rose from the large bowls and my stomach growled.

Denver waltzed in wearing a shirt with a tie printed on the front and dark pants. "Damn. It smells like heaven down here. I can't wait to dig in."

Austin locked his fingers behind his head. "Word is you've been digging in *all* day. Stay out of the kitchen when they're cooking and wait like everyone else."

Denver stood with his arms folded and glanced at Maizy, who was sitting at the tiny white table to my right. "C'mon, Peanut. You eat with us tonight."

"Can I sit next to you?"

Denver sat on the edge of his bench and left about an inch of space to his right. "Can you fit right there?"

Maizy giggled and he scooted over, allowing her to sit beside him. When the twins walked in, Ben changed direction and grabbed a beer from the fridge, delivering a toothy grin as he strolled around the table and sat across from me.

Wheeler, the one who'd given me the stink eye earlier, sat to his left. Ben wore a white polo shirt with red sleeves and a collar, while Wheeler was in his usual cutoff black shirt. I didn't like the way he kept staring at me, so I sipped my wine and turned away to watch Lexi in the kitchen.

"Are you sure I can't help?" I offered.

Two strong hands gripped my shoulders and I stiffened as a deep voice barked, "Someone's in my seat." My heart raced and I glanced up at Reno.

Holy smokes, he looked *amazing*.

The room was a little warm for a long-sleeve cotton shirt, but if he was aiming for sexy, he nailed it. Reno's charcoal shirt was tight all over, showing off his impressive physique. I glanced down at his dark jeans and the leather belt with a square silver buckle. It seemed strange that only Austin could lead the pack when Reno was an alpha male in every way. Even his dark hair was styled as neat as a pin. I took a deep breath, flooding my senses with his cologne, which I loved so much.

"Is this your seat? I'll move."

But he held my shoulders firmly and stepped over the bench to my right. I wondered if anyone in that room knew about Reno hanging around my house. Did he talk about me with them? Had he told them that he'd slept naked in my bed and kissed me?

Just sitting beside him and remembering the feel of his body against mine gave me goose bumps. Especially when his arm brushed against mine and I began to feel the heat from his nearness.

"Jericho's not coming," Lexi said, setting two baskets of bread on the table. Austin immediately snatched the end piece and buttered it. "He's still in the doghouse."

"He also has a gig tonight," Denver added. "Jericho showed up at Howlers and we talked for a little while. I think you need to sit down with him, Aus. You know how Jericho is, always playing jokes and trying to liven up the party. He does stupid shit, but it's not with bad intentions."

"Do you have to work tonight?" Lynn asked Denver, sitting to Austin's right.

Denver plucked a pea between his fingers and set it in the center of Maizy's plate.

"Eww," she said with a giggle.

"I go in later," Denver replied, elbows on the table. "Jake moved me to a later shift so I can earn higher tips. He seems satisfied with how I keep the alcohol moving and the customers happy. Our peak time extends after midnight, so that works for me."

"You should go full time," Lynn suggested, her tone laced with judgment.

Denver huffed out a breath and scooped a spoonful of mashed potatoes on his plate. "I make a shitload of money just working four nights a week, Lynn. We don't give cheap tips like humans. Most of these rich immortals have money to burn and Packmasters pay well when they get good service."

"Watch your language around Maizy."

"*Shitload*," Maizy sang, and Denver quickly snaked his arm around her head and covered her mouth with his hand, smiling sheepishly.

Lynn turned to watch Ivy carry in the pot roast.

"Do you guys always eat together?" I asked Reno in a quiet voice.

He nodded and leaned in close. "When our pack gets bigger, we'll eat in shifts to make sure no one eats alone. That's how a family maintains a good foundation. You look pretty tonight." He spoke quietly and no one heard him over all the chatter. His bedroom voice made my belly flutter.

I smiled and put my hands in my lap, turning my ring around my finger. It suddenly popped off and rolled beneath the table. *Nice job*, my inner voice said. *You managed to walk in the room successfully without tripping, so you decided to throw your jewelry underneath the table? Smooth.*

Since I couldn't scoot the bench back, I squeezed between the gap and crouched underneath the table. The ring had rolled by Wheeler's foot and he must have noticed, because he appeared under the table with me.

Everyone chattered at the table and I froze as Wheeler held the ring between his fingers. "I know what you did," he whispered. "I have access to the account, and I don't know what the hell you're up to, but Lexi is going to know about it."

"Please don't," I begged.

"You okay down there, April?" Lexi asked. "Or do we need to call a search party?"

A few laughs overlapped and someone started coughing.

"Sorry, just a second. My ring fell off," I explained in a loud voice. "*It's not what you think*," I whispered back to Wheeler. "Please don't say anything."

His eyes narrowed and he handed me the ring, holding it between his fingers until he finished serving his warning. "You tell her the truth or I will. It's her business and livelihood—not your Monopoly money to play around with."

When I climbed through the gap and sat in my seat, I was certain my face was the color of a tomato.

"Is something wrong?" Reno said in a low voice.

"No, I'm fine. It's hot under there."

I smiled mechanically and slipped the ring on my shaky middle finger, afraid to make eye contact with anyone.

Wheeler knew I had stolen from Lexi. Wheeler knew I was a thief.

The roast came out delicious. Spirits were high as we drank, laughed, and shared wild stories of childhood. It seemed like an ordinary get-together and I could hardly believe that these people were Shifters. Since Maizy and Lynn were comfortable with these guys, it made it easier for me to trust them.

After two glasses of wine, I had forgotten about Wheeler's threat. He kept his eyes on his plate while explaining to Denver how to replace a part in his truck.

"Are you dating anyone special?" Lynn asked me, leaning around Ivy who sat to my left.

I had no idea how to answer that in front of Reno, so I held my wine glass in front of my mouth and bit on the rim.

"Mom…" Lexi chastised her in that voice that implied she was getting too nosy.

"What? I'm only asking what her situation is," she said conversationally. "It's a perfectly legitimate question to ask a single girl her age. We're not getting any younger."

Denver laughed and pushed his plate forward.

"Can I be excused?" Maizy asked, standing up from the table. "I want to read my new book about Peter Pan."

"Skedaddle!" Denver barked out. Maizy giggled and disappeared around the corner.

"Well, April? Who are you seeing these days?" Lynn folded her napkin and placed it on her plate.

Lexi cleared her throat and shook her head at her mom.

Time froze when I felt Reno's heavy hand rest on my right thigh. He gripped it firmly and our elbows touched. Something about being in his presence felt electric, and the warm sensation of his hand on my body almost made me spill my wine. I set the glass down and touched my hot cheek.

"There's someone," I finally answered to end the bickering between mother and daughter.

"Is it serious?" Lynn pressed.

"I'm not sure yet."

Lexi's brows popped up in surprise and she smirked at Austin. He frowned and rubbed his jaw as I'd seen him do before when in a contemplative mood.

Reno slid his hand up and tucked his fingers between my inner thighs. I quietly gasped and began tugging the ends of my hair, noticing my bangs were longer than the length of my nose. It was time for a trim.

My frantic attempt at distracting myself was in vain. All I could think about was the private touch of Reno's hand beneath the table. His body leaned against mine in such a way that no one could see what he was doing. It felt as if he were privately claiming me in front of his pack.

Lynn didn't relent from probing further and exposing my dating situation in front of everyone. "Do you know your way around the kitchen? I taught my girls well and Lexi will make a good wife someday if the right man ever asks for her hand," she said with a pointed look. Apparently the woman didn't consider mating to be an official union. "Learn how to cook, April. You can still have it all with a family and career, but a man wants a woman who knows her way around the kitchen—one who can take care of him."

"True that," Denver agreed.

"That's because you're a lazy bastard," Wheeler grumbled at him.

"At least I'm an *employed* bastard," he retorted, leaning forward with a look that dared Wheeler to keep riding him.

Austin cleared his throat and they backed off the topic.

"Some men like independent women," Reno said, giving my leg a light squeeze. "A good woman who raises a family and keeps order in the pack is admirable, but a woman doesn't need to cook a meal to prove her worth any more than a man needs to kill a spider."

Lexi raised her eyebrows and sipped her wine. "I wouldn't go that far. I'm not touching those creepy-crawlies, so you boys better man up."

"I do a little cooking," I admitted. "I have my signature dishes." A smile crossed my face when I thought about my famous tuna casserole that always made Trevor gag, but everyone gobbled it up at parties.

"What dish is that?" Wheeler asked. "Money cake?"

Reno's hand vanished from my leg and he slammed his fist on the table in front of Wheeler, causing a few forks to bounce up.

"I don't like the way you've been eyeballing her tonight," he ground out through his clenched teeth. "I expect someone like Ben to leer because she's a pretty girl and he's an asshole. But the way you're looking at her isn't the same," he said, pointing a heavy finger. "You got something to say?"

I touched Reno's arm, not wanting to start any family drama. "Don't worry about it. We've all had a lot of wine. Let's not fight."

His arm didn't move from pointing at Wheeler, who leaned back in his chair and folded his arms. "April stole five thousand dollars from Sweet Treats by transferring funds into her personal account."

A veil of silence fell over the room and all eyes settled on me.

"I put it back!"

A smile ghosted Wheeler's lips. "And boom goes the dynamite."

I sucked in a sharp breath, realizing my admission. I shouldn't have had the second glass of wine.

"You *stole* from me?" Lexi said in an angry voice, blinking with wide eyes. "Is that true?"

When Reno leaned away, I teared up. "I put it all back, Lexi. I swear. Every cent of it."

She shook her head slowly, rising to her feet. "I can't believe you did this. You *stole* from me! I thought I could rely on you, April. Here we are, inviting you over to dinner, and we're entrusting you with an even bigger secret. *Why* would you do something like that?"

My forehead ached from frowning and I refused to give her what she wanted: answers.

Austin's chair scraped back as he stood up and dropped his arms to his sides. A dizzying wave swept over me as her eyes glittered with betrayal and anger.

I lowered my head. "I'm so sorry. I never meant for you to find out."

"So you were going to steal my money and cover it up? That's even worse! You're not even going to tell me why?" She covered her eyes with her hands. "Oh, my God. I can't believe this. I gave you *all* those financial documents and files. You have full access to the account. If Wheeler hadn't have told us, then what?"

"Let her explain," Reno said.

But I couldn't. They were all staring at me expectantly and I knew I couldn't provide a reason that would excuse my behavior—not in their eyes. At this point, nothing I could give them would justify my actions. Their whole lives as a pack revolved around trust, and I had broken it.

Wheeler shook his head and threw his napkin on the table as he stood up. "Can't trust anyone around money."

CHAPTER 16

When I grabbed my keys and fled toward my loaner vehicle, Reno came after me and hauled me by the waist to his truck. He said I'd had too much wine and he'd drive me home.

I was mortified. What had started out as a lovely evening had ended up as one of the worst moments of my life. What had made me think I could cover up my crime and everything would be okay? Even if they hadn't found out, the guilt of that secret would have eaten away at my conscience.

Did I even have one anymore?

Even worse, Reno was taking me home to a trailer he'd filled up with his own hard-earned money—all for a girl who'd stolen from his family. I hadn't just embarrassed myself in that room; I'd seen the judgmental stares Reno's brothers had given him. I gazed out the truck window and suddenly didn't want to go home. *Anywhere* but there. The vehicle bounced over a bump and we slowed at a light in a familiar part of town. Just a few blocks away, Trevor was probably crashing on a friend's sofa. I knew his go-to people and was certain that's where he was hiding out.

I also knew that I could run remarkably fast—walking to work had built up my endurance. While Reno fumbled with texting a message on his phone, I quietly unbuckled my seatbelt and threw open the door, flying down the street at a breakneck speed before he could put the truck in park. My lungs were about to burst as I gasped for oxygen. It felt so good to run that hard, and maybe if I ran fast enough, I'd leave my problems behind and they'd never catch up with me.

I turned down an alley and scaled a chain-link fence. My face heated as I cut through a stretch of land behind an auto repair shop. I no longer heard Reno's footsteps behind me and when I reached the apartment complex, I pounded my fist on one of the doors, gasping for breath.

An overweight guy with a mustache answered.

"John, is Trevor here?" I panted.

"Jesus. Did you run here from the hood?" he said with a hard laugh. "Get inside. Trevor's takin' a piss. Been a long time since I seen you, Apricot."

"Don't call me that, Long Johns," I said with a smile in my voice. But no smile crossed my face as I entered his living room and set my purse on his musty leather sofa. John used to work with Trevor in a landscaping business and they'd remained friends over the years. He'd always had connections in getting Trevor good tickets to rock concerts. I think he knew a DJ at one of the radio stations.

I wiped my face, still breathing heavily. John plopped down indifferently in the recliner propped in front of the TV and turned up the volume.

Trevor appeared in the doorway to my right, surrounded by a halo of light from the hall behind him. His face hardened and he crossed the room with a menacing stride.

"Trevor, please don't kick me out. I—"

He cradled my head in his hands and something dark flickered in his eyes. "What's wrong, April? Did that man come after you?"

I blinked a few times and couldn't speak.

"Trevor, I thought you were dead." Then I couldn't see him anymore because tears flooded my eyes and all I could see was the misshapen blur of his face.

He kissed my forehead. "Shhh, I'm fine. Looked worse than it really was because I'd been drinking and passed out. I'm sorry for what I said, babe. I didn't mean a word of it. Now tell me what's wrong."

John leaned around. "Can you two take that shit elsewhere? I'm trying to watch—"

"Shut up, John," Trevor said in a voice so thick that it cut through the room like steel. John turned back around and Trevor led me upstairs where the bedrooms were.

After giving me a glass of water, he sat me down on a computer chair and knelt before me. "What's going on with you? What kind of trouble are you in?"

"None."

His eyes narrowed skeptically and he leaned on my knees. "You're an expert bullshitter, April. You should have gotten a degree in it."

"It's not bullshit. You won't have to worry about that guy who beat you up, because I took care of him."

His mouth wrinkled. "What do you mean... took care of?"

I rubbed my face and sighed. "He's a loan shark. Not the one who attacked you—that guy works for him and picks up the collections. My grandma ran up a bunch of debt and I thought I'd paid it all off years ago. But he came back and said I didn't pay the interest, so I had to come up with the money. I paid him off, so he won't be coming back."

He shot up to his feet and stared down his nose at me. "Your grandma was a real piece of work. Holy hell. That bitch—"

"Trevor, *don't*. She's dead, and—"

"And you could have been lying in the cemetery beside her. That asshole was going to do something a hell of a lot worse to you if I wasn't there. He kept asking where you were, but I didn't tell him jack. He looked like a stalker, but now I see the big picture. Do you know what guys like him do to girls like you?"

"Cut off our pinkies."

He blanched and gave me a puzzled look. Trevor's bruises were faded and not nearly as serious as I remembered.

"Is your arm okay?" I asked.

"Is my arm okay? You show up here looking like the Terminator is hunting you down and then tell me all this business about a loan shark," he shouted. "And you want to know about my *arm*?"

I sprang to my feet.

And lost my mind.

I grabbed a lamp and launched it across the room. It crashed against the wall and then I blindly reached for a box of junk beside the bed and threw that too. Tiny guitar picks and CDs went flying like shrapnel. After that, I threw everything on that skanky bed onto the floor. My arms were flailing in violent motions as I pulled open a drawer and tossed out all the stuff inside—including a box of condoms and pack of cheap cigarettes. Then I tried pulling out the drawer.

Trevor's arms wrapped around me from behind. I struggled, screamed, kicked, and made feral sounds like an animal caught in a trap.

"*Shhhh. It's okay.* I got you. I love you, babe, and no one is coming after you. We're going to work it out because we're family. I'm not going anywhere, do you understand? I'm a jackass for running off and leaving you like that."

My fingernails dug into his arms and I kicked, but the energy deflated like air from a balloon. I slumped in his arms. "Oh, Trevor. I'm so sorry he did that to you," I said, heavy with guilt. "Please don't hate me. I had no idea he would come after you and I wanted to die when I saw you lying there with no life in your eyes."

"It's not your damn fault. You got that?" Trevor spun me around and lifted me up in his arms—my feet dangling off the ground. He didn't seem like the kind of guy who would sweep a woman off her feet.

I rested my head on his shoulder, tears wetting his neck. "I'm so sorry."

"Babe, if you say that one more time, I'm throwing you out the window into the dumpster below. People make mistakes in life and sometimes shit happens. Share some of that burden with me, April. You can't control everything, but I admire the hell out of you for trying. Now stop wiping your snot all over me and let's go home."

Trevor was back for good and I had someone to lean on. Explaining my refurnished trailer didn't go over well, and he especially didn't like Reno's involvement.

"We're taking all this shit back," he declared.

It saddened me, but he was right. Keeping Reno's money would be selfish and insensitive. I could only imagine what it looked like to him—secretly stealing from his family and then relaxing on my brand-new bedspread like a princess, all while he filled my house with expensive things and fixed my leaks. I felt sickened by the whole thing, and worst of all, I'd lost him.

Trevor neatly folded up every last item and placed them in the living room. "You don't want a guy like that thinking you owe him something," he said, preparing to take a shower.

He grabbed his guitar from the sofa and propped it against the kitchen counter where some of his model airplanes were sitting. Trevor had brought over most of his belongings and used a few available cabinets and corners as storage. I smiled when I heard him in the bathroom cussing, maneuvering around as he tried to figure out the shower.

I was draping a thick blanket over the sofa when a light knock sounded at the door. Trevor enjoyed long showers with the music on, so he didn't hear it.

I lifted the corner of the curtain and peered outside. Maddox stood away from the door, holding his hat in his hand and scratching his beard.

I opened the door just a crack.

"Got a minute?" he asked in a gentle voice.

Maddox took several steps back and looked off toward the road as I went outside and stood in front of the door.

"Have you had time to figure things out on how you're going to pay?" he asked.

Without a word, I shook my head.

He wiped his hand over his mouth and stroked his facial hair. "You know about Shifters, and no sense in denying it because I know it to be a fact," he said, slanting his eyes inside the trailer. "Your grandma didn't know what I was because I deal with everyone, including humans. I'm not exclusive like some morons are. Money is money. But it's not always about the money," he said, his voice softening. "We're partial to favor-trading."

I crossed my arms while Maddox scanned the property.

"Your grandma was always good about her payments, even if it took her a while. She started doing business with me exclusively in the end, although I knew she was having trouble with a few other sharks who were trying to take a bite. Are they bothering you?"

I bit my lip and he scrunched his mouth as if he'd gotten the answer he wanted.

"I can offer you protection."

"For how much?" I said with disgust.

"I'll clear you of every last penny you owe with me and anyone else. Free and clear—I'm good on my word. I can offer you the safety of going to bed at night with both eyes closed."

My shoulders felt lighter. "How?"

His brow quirked and he smiled bashfully. "Well, being my pet."

"Pet?" I didn't like the sound of that.

"It's just a loose term for some of the humans who are... *friendly* with Shifters." He chuckled warmly and fidgeted with his hat. "It doesn't have to be sexual if you don't want it to be. I get lonely at the house sometimes and would enjoy the company. Someone to talk to, cook up a meal, and occasionally work a jigsaw with me. You like those? I've got an addiction and spend hours at the table. But a man gets lonely and craves companionship. I'm not askin' for you to be my woman—not unless you want to. But there are rules. You'd have to live with me, wear a collar, and not bring any men to your bed."

My eyes turned into razor-thin slivers. "You want me to put on a collar?"

"Necklace," he quickly corrected. "Fashionable-looking thing the ladies wear now that looks like a choker. Only it has my name on it. It's just a way to show my claim so that no one will mess around with you. It's a form of protection more than ownership. Look," he said, putting his foot on the lower step and leaning on his knee. "I'm not a bad guy. I've never done this before, but I've seen a few women take a shine to it. I don't live in a mansion, but I sure as hell don't live in a trailer. You'll be taken care of and if you want to go to school, I can help with that too. You see where I'm going with this? Whatever you want."

"Feels like prostitution."

"If you were giving me sex in exchange against your will, it might be. Except this isn't a one-time transaction. I'm not asking for sex, but you're free to give it should you take a liking to me. I treat ladies the way they should be, and I don't raise a hand or bully them around. This is a second chance I'm giving you—one that won't come around again," he said, leaving the thought out there.

"And if I say no?"

"If you decline my offer, you'll owe me full payment. I'm not showing up at your door with a crowbar, but you'll probably be in debt for a long time unless you find yourself a rich fellow. You've got my number and I want you to call me in a few days and let me know how you decide. If I haven't heard from you by Sunday, I'll assume we're still on track for payment. I'll tell you how much for the first installment, but my interest rates are high and I don't see how you're going to clear this."

I rubbed my face in frustration. "You just want me to live with you? No sex?"

"I'm a man. I'd love sex to be part of the deal if you're okay with it, but it's not expected. I'm not forcing myself on you and you're free to leave at any time, but that debt will travel with you like a shadow. As long as you stay with me, it's clear. Think it over, and stay dry."

Maddox walked across the yard and disappeared through the trees.

I went back inside, dumbfounded. How had I managed to run into so many of these Shifters? How many had I known my entire life without having realized it? Lexi said the Breed population was high in some cities. She also said there were some Breeds that wanted to exterminate Shifters because they felt threatened by their numbers.

Trevor finally emerged from the bathroom with damp hair and an irritated look on his face. He opened up one of the cabinets and found a bag of sour-cream chips. "When is the last time you had a bubble bath?"

"Maybe the time we had a blow-up pool and Rose put dishwashing suds in the water and ran the hose."

He sat beside me on the sofa and kissed the back of my hand before ripping the bag of chips open with his teeth.

"Do you want to see me living better than this?" I asked.

"Hell yeah. Nothing wrong with living in a trailer, April. But this thing is run-down and the neighborhood is one of the worst in the city. Especially with that a-hole on the loose," he said, crunching on a chip. "You may have paid him off, but guys like that don't surrender. Men have a weakness called pride, and they don't get over it easily when someone bruises it."

A motor cut off outside and a door slammed.

Gravel crunched outside as footsteps approached the trailer and Trevor launched to his feet—hands balled into tight fists and ropes of muscle on his arms tightening.

The tiny door shook when a fist pounded against it. "April, open up this door or I'm breaking it down."

Trevor glanced at me. "The big bad wolf?" Then he pushed the door open and shoved a giant trash bag into Reno's arms. "Take your shit. You're not welcome here anymore."

Reno tried throwing down the bag, but Trevor kept grabbing stuff by the door and thrusting it into his arms. "Think you can buy her like a golden retriever and that'll make her loyal? She doesn't know what you're doing, but *I do*. April's naïve to these kind of intentions because she's young, but you're a real piece of work for taking advantage of that," he said, tossing a box of mirrors at him.

I heard the glass break when Reno threw them to the side and filled the doorway. "Get out of my way."

I swiftly rose to my feet. "Don't you dare threaten my best friend. Trevor is a brother to me, and if you put one little finger on him, then I'll…"

Damn, girl, you're on a roll! Threaten him with something good! my inner voice cheered.

I glanced around and grabbed the nearest thing I could find.

A spatula.

"I'll cut you up."

My eyes slimmed down and theirs widened.

Reno's lips twitched and Trevor tried to contain his laugh beneath his pissed-off face, but it slipped out and he turned his head away.

"April, I need to know you're safe. You broke out of my truck and I've been searching the streets for hours."

Trevor sliced me with a cold stare and I shrugged. I knew he didn't like the idea that I'd been running the streets, especially after two glasses of wine.

"Can we talk?" Reno wasn't looking at me, but Trevor. He was asking permission to speak with me. "April has a right to make her own decisions. You're looking out for her, and I respect that more than you know. That's why I'm asking if we can settle what's between us once and for all."

"It's okay, Trevor," I said, tossing the spatula on the counter.

He threw up his hands and sat down on the couch, angrily grabbing a magazine and snapping it open.

"Come inside and we can talk it over," I said.

"Not here. Neutral ground where kitchen utensils are not within arm's reach," Reno said with a handsome smirk.

CHAPTER 17

"Where are we?" I asked, cupping my elbows as I stood behind Reno on the front porch of a rural house in the dark woods.

Reno slid his key in the lock. The hinges stubbornly creaked when the door swung open. I took a breath of stale air and warmth touched my skin.

"This was our old house before we moved into the big one. Austin's keeping it around as a retreat," he said, flipping on a light. "We've still got power."

It was semi-furnished, as if someone still lived there. Reno closed the door behind us and hung his key on a nail that had the letter *R* below it. When he kicked off his shoes in the corner, I did the same and followed him around the wall and into the living room. While he went into the hall to adjust the thermostat, I checked out my surroundings. The walls were bare. Aside from a ratty maroon recliner and an old sofa, the room was empty.

"Thirsty?" His voice reverberated off the walls.

Reno walked around a built-in bar on my left, which connected to the living room. A light clicked on and he bent down, pulling out a few drinks from the short fridge. He handed me a can of soda and I cracked it open, grimacing as the carbonated soft drink burned my throat.

Reno threaded my hair away from my face with a single sweep of his hand, centering his eyes on mine. "Tonight was rough. Are you hanging in there?"

"I didn't mean to jump out of your truck and worry you like that. I was scared to go home by myself and too embarrassed to tell you after what happened at dinner. I needed to find Trevor."

"You think I haven't seen what people will do when their ass is on the line? You're mixed up in some serious shit and I want to help. People who steal money and bolt out of a truck into a busy street are running from something—or someone. If you owe someone money, I can help."

"No, Reno. I can't stay in this vicious circle of owing people; that's what I'm trying my best to fix. I owed a man and I paid him off—the one who hurt Trevor. It's done."

His chocolate eyes were pensively searching mine. "Are you sure about that? Say the word, April, and I can make your problems go away."

"That's not a promise anyone can make."

He took the soda from my hand and set it on the floor. Then his thick hand slipped around my neck and he stepped close. He smelled intoxicating—a mixture of cologne and his natural scent.

Reno backed me up against the wall and slipped his hands beneath my shirt. He cupped my breasts through my thin bra, placing his thumbs on each nipple and rubbing in slow, methodical motions. I gasped, every nerve awakening as I struggled to suppress a moan. Reno ignited my body with his skilled touch, one that left me desiring more.

His knee abruptly slid between my legs, forcing them apart, and his lips brushed against my mouth as he spoke. "I wonder if I could make you come like this."

I was certain he could.

His mouth lingered against mine with just the lightest contact of skin. He didn't kiss me, but pressed his thumbs sweetly against my nipples until I moaned from the delicate friction. My breathing became erratic and he abruptly stepped back and dropped his arms. "Take off my belt," he said in a throaty voice.

An electric buzz ripped through my body at his command. He lightly held my wrists and guided my hands to his waist.

As he stood there watching me, his eyes hooded. I tugged at his belt until the metal prong came free from the hole.

"Slide it out," he said. "Do it slowly."

Holy smokes, my inner voice exclaimed as she had a mental orgasm.

I pulled his belt and listened to the hissing sound it made as it slid out from the loops. When it was free, his mouth parted slightly and his breath caught.

"Drop it."

The buckle clamored against the wood floor. Reno placed his hands on the wall above me and leaned in hard. "I've wanted you since the first day we met. Austin tried to warn me when he saw the way I looked at you, but I can't stop looking."

"Why did he warn you?" I asked in a breathy voice.

"Shifters and humans don't mix. We can't have kids with your kind and we live longer." His breathing grew heavy with need as he looked down at me. "Pick up my belt."

I tried to look down but my chest was pressed against his. "Step back; I can't move."

"Yes, you can," he urged, his eyes dripping with lust.

I found the belt with my foot and had begun to lift it up monkey-style when Reno's mouth came against mine.

"With your hands." He kissed me softly and leaned back, waiting for me to make a move.

Not one to back away from a challenge, I placed my hands around his waist for balance and slid down the length of his rock-hard body. Every inch of me rubbed against him and Reno reduced the space between us to nothing. I got an eyeful of his crotch on the way, and wide-eyed, I grabbed the belt and tried to stand up. There wasn't any room, so I practically had to climb up his body as if it were a mountain.

Mount Reno, an expedition that left me wondering if I needed a harness.

When I felt a tremor go through him, I knew he was turned on.

His body pinned mine against the wall. "Can I lock this around your wrists? I'm not going to do anything you don't want me to do. We can stop at any time; just say the word."

I looked up at him with quiet eyes.

"Never mind. We don't have to—"

"No," I quickly said. "I want you to. *I trust you.*"

He took the belt from my hand and, without breaking eye

contact, looped it around my wrists. Not too tight, but it left a lot of slack with the holes at the end of it. His pupils dilated and I was getting so turned on by the thought of his hands on my body that I could hardly think. He pivoted around and led me by that belt into the hallway.

I remembered Denver's warning about Reno. Something about him being rough or tying women up. *What exactly did he do with them afterward?*

My guess was that I was about to find out.

Reno led me into a bedroom and shut the door. He lifted his arms and slid one of the holes in the belt over a hook secured to the ceiling. *Who has a hook in their ceiling?* So there I was, standing with my arms tied up above my head in Reno's bedroom.

I'd never felt such a wave of anticipation come over me. I fought to get my panting under control when he slowly walked behind me, snaking his hand across my breasts and the flat plane of my stomach. Then he slowly unbuttoned my pants, tugged down the zipper, and got on his knees behind me.

Every move was methodical and slow.

I peered under my arm and watched his fingers grip the hem of my pants and slide them down. I bucked a little and when they fell around my ankles, his mouth feverishly began kissing my upper thigh.

"Oh, God," I breathed. *Moaned.* My ankles were tangled and I tried to kick the pants away, but Reno gripped my legs and held them still.

"Don't move unless I tell you to."

His mouth moved higher, his tongue stroking and tasting my inner thigh. When his hand cupped my ass, I gasped. Reno quickly stood up and broke contact.

He paced around front and examined my hands, checking the tightness of the belt. "If it hurts, you let me know," he said. "Don't put all your weight on that belt. I'll be upset if you bruise."

I nodded.

Then he stepped in close and kissed my mouth salaciously. His fingers lifted the hem of my shirt higher until it was over my head.

He pulled it high enough that my mouth was free, but I couldn't see anything.

Before I could ask that stupid "What are you doing?" question, he tugged down the cups of my bra and his mouth came around my left nipple. Desire licked over my body as he flicked his tongue and sucked in tight pulls.

I couldn't see through the heavy material of my black shirt. All I could feel was his hot mouth; even his hands weren't touching me. It was the most erotic sensation—wondering when he pulled his mouth away where it would end up next. He surprised me with a warm kiss to my neck, and then his tongue circled around my navel before moving to my breast, where he flicked his tongue so maddeningly, I felt it to my core.

I needed him. *God, how I needed him.*

I could hear his heavy boots pacing in circles, but he didn't touch me. I pressed my cheek against my right arm, breathing heavily.

Then his finger slid across my panties and I bucked hard—but not in a good way.

It was a panic-stricken feeling that came over me, and I started gasping for air. "I'm scared of the dark, I'm scared of the dark," I chanted.

Reno yanked the shirt away from my eyes and unhooked the belt, eyes brimming with concern. He bent down and removed my jeans so I wouldn't trip.

My hands shook with embarrassment. I looked away as he freed my wrists from the belt and tugged the shirt off my arms. His hands cupped my inflamed cheeks and I'd never felt more exposed than standing in front of Reno in my underwear while having a panic attack.

"Breathe, April. Look at me and breathe. In through your nose and out through your mouth. That's it… nice and slow. I'd never hurt you. What's wrong?"

"I just don't like the dark."

"Why?"

"A phobia thing."

"Tell me."

I shook my head adamantly and he held me in his arms so tightly that I was unable to get dressed and leave. Maybe he could sense it, because that was exactly what I was thinking of doing.

His bristly cheek scratched against my temple and he whispered, "Tell me why you're afraid of the dark. We're not born with fear, April. We're exposed to it."

"No, you don't really want to hear all this."

"The hell I don't," he bit out angrily. Then his voice softened like molasses. "Talk to me."

Don't do it, my inner voice warned. *No man wants to hear personal baggage and you're going to extinguish whatever fire you had going if you open your mouth.*

So as I stood in the arms of a man who wanted to take me to new sexual lands, I exposed a dark part of my past that I'd never once told a living soul except my mother.

"I was… molested."

Reno froze, as if his entire body had transformed to granite. I tried pushing him away, but he didn't budge.

"Let me go," I said, feeling shame and guilt for even saying the word. "I shouldn't have said anything, but you asked."

When I felt his tender lips kiss my forehead, I stopped struggling.

"Who?" he asked in a chilling voice.

"I don't know. I was little. It happened in a department store. I don't remember why, but I had separated from my mom and wound up in the bathroom. I wasn't alone—a man came in behind me. He flipped the switch and shut off the lights."

A tremor rolled through him, but not in a good way. Fear rose in me and I pushed at his chest.

But Reno held me tight, whispering in my hair. "How old were you?"

"Five, I think. My mom gave me a spanking when she found out I'd wandered off and when I told her what happened, she called me a liar. I guess she thought I was making up a story to get out of trouble. It was so long ago that it almost feels like a dream, so it's not like it's fresh in my memory. I just remember bits and pieces of what happened. I can tolerate low light, but sometimes I get scared in the dark. Not all the time, but I'm sure that's where it stems from. I don't even remember what he looks like," I said, not believing I was telling him all this. "When the lights came back on, he told me that I'd get in big trouble if I told anyone and he'd come find me. I thought I'd done something wrong to make him do that to me. For years I thought he was going to come after me because I'd told my mom."

"You didn't do anything wrong. *Fucking bastard*," he whispered. "They never caught him?"

I shook my head.

"Do you remember the store?"

I nodded.

"Wonder if they have surveillance archives," he muttered.

My hands pushed hard and I leaned away. "Don't you dare dig up my past. It could have been a whole lot worse. I was fortunate that none of my mom's pimps or dealers ever got a hold of me as a teen. I scraped out of my childhood with only a few skinned knees. He just touched me."

"Just? He *just* touched you? No big deal?" A vein pulsed on his forehead. "Do you have *any* idea what we do to Shifters who abuse children? It's not only a crime punishable by death, but you can bet your ass they'll have the entire pack going after them with the law on their side."

Anger sparked in his dark brown eyes.

I relaxed and took a calming breath. "Look, Reno, I don't need a therapist. I'm scared of the dark and I shouldn't have let you tie me up. Apparently, I have limits. My ex liked to have sex in the dark, missionary style. So my sex life has been pretty bland and—"

"No wonder," he said, leaning against the door and shaking his head as if a revelation had hit him.

"No wonder what?"

"The only sex you've had is with a guy who throws you in the dark so that you can relive your childhood fears. You freaked out over a blindfold; I'm willing to bet you weren't much of a willing participant when it came to sex. You've got control issues."

Was he serious? "Oh, *I've* got control issues?" I folded my arms.

"For you, sex is giving up control. You go about your day trying to control everything. I get that. You're compensating for what you don't have in the bedroom with men because of one fucking pervert. So you fix your own problems, make your own money, and keep things running smoothly. Take back your life, April. You need to take back total control—that's the only way you're going to prove that you didn't let him get the best of you."

"Is that why you tie up women, because you lack control in your life?" I asked, lowering my gaze to the belt.

Confronted with the truth, Reno averted his eyes. I didn't expect an answer because if there was one thing I knew about Reno, his fault was that he didn't open up and share his pain with others. He was the eldest brother, and yet the youngest in the family was the alpha, which Lexi told me was rare in a family of Shifter wolves. Not only that, but Austin had decided to become a Packmaster. Reno had to give up what leadership and control he'd once had over his family and relinquish that to his baby brother.

Reno was the opposite of me. He *lacked* control in his daily life, so he made up for it in the bedroom by making his women submissive. He didn't need to tell me; I could see it in his eyes.

"Maybe this isn't going to work out," I said, looking up at him. "We're too different in what we need. Maybe this just isn't the kind of thing I'm into."

"Do you even *know* what you like?" he threw out there. "Because it seemed like you enjoyed what was going on in the other room, and I doubt your ex ever got that kind of reaction out of you. Am I right?"

My mouth parted to argue when he kissed me again, hard, his hands cupping my face. "Tell me you don't like this," he said against my lips, walking me backward. "Maybe we need to make some compromises. Let's do this different." The back of my legs bumped against the edge of the bed. "Get in, princess."

A dull ache throbbed between my legs and I crawled onto the bed, aroused by how eager he was to please me. Despite my past, my present, and everything I had confessed to him—Reno didn't care. I wasn't damaged goods.

He collected two scarves from a bottom drawer and tied them

around my wrists before securing them to the posts on the bed so my arms were spread out.

When he finished, Reno stood motionless to my left. The animal attraction pulsed between us, and his fervent gaze traveled down the length of my half-naked body.

"What are you doing?" I smiled and winked, but he didn't budge or say a word. "Can you loosen the left one? It's pinching my wrist."

He obediently leaned down and loosened the material. Then he stood erect and lowered his gaze.

When your hands are tied up, things start to itch as if by magic. I began rubbing my left leg against the sheet. "My leg itches. I can't do this tied up, Reno."

He walked to the end of the bed, rubbing his fingers down my leg in a scratching motion.

"Higher," I said.

His hand roamed higher to the spot behind my left knee.

"To the left. Higher..." I hissed and squirmed, releasing a satisfied sigh. "That's it."

When he resumed his position with hooded eyes, it clicked. I figured out *exactly* what Reno was doing. He'd placed me in a helpless situation but had given me full control over what happened to my body. Yet it still gave him the illusion of being in control. My heart warmed at the idea that he would change his pattern for me. Maybe it was a little kinky and out of the norm, but he understood me better than anyone else did. Tingles of excitement swept through my core and I wanted to kiss the man. He was empowering me by making sure that everything happening would be only what I allowed by my own command.

"Touch me," I whispered.

"Where?" The sound of desire rumbled in his chest.

That was the best question I'd ever been asked. I gave it some consideration. "Kiss my neck."

Reno sat on the bed and trailed his lips down my neck, kissing below my jaw, sucking a soft patch of skin, all while keeping his hands to himself. God, I'd never felt so adored by a man's mouth.

"Take off my bra."

He reached around to unlatch it, but the straps created a hindrance and prevented him from carrying out the order. He leaned over, opened a drawer, and pulled out a small pocketknife. Maybe I should have been scared, but I trusted him. With a careful swipe, Reno cut the straps and threw it on the floor.

His eyes fell heavily over me and I could tell he was using every bit of willpower to restrain himself from sucking on my pink nipples. Reno seemed smitten with them as they began to change shape and harden, as if by command of his heated gaze.

Was giving me control hurting the experience for him? I thought about a way we could do this that wouldn't make it all about me. Reno needed some amount of control, and I wanted to entrust him with that.

"What do you want to do to me?" I asked him.

"Taste them," he bit out, licking his lips.

"Strip out of your clothes, lie on top of me, and suck on them."

His pupils were engorged as he shucked his jeans off so fast I barely saw him move. Reno's boxers went next and I turned my head away.

When I didn't feel him crawling on the bed, I peeked through my lashes at him. "What's wrong?"

"Eyes open," he said in a gruff voice. "I'm about to make you feel real good, April, and I want you looking in my eyes while we do this. Don't shut me out. Deal?"

I nodded as he crawled on top of the bed, warming me with his heavy body. When his mouth came around my nipple and the wet heat touched my skin, I gripped the scarves and pulled, making the bed creak.

Upon my command, Reno slid his hand inside my panties. He pleasured me until I came close to the brink and then he stopped. He kissed me long and hard, lips melting against mine, sliding his tongue deeper until his arms trembled from holding up his weight. He only did what I asked of him. Pulling down my panties with his teeth took longer than I had expected, but Reno was a persistent and patient man who aimed to please.

After a long seduction, Reno untied me and lay on his back,

pulling me astride him. I'd never been consumed by a man's gaze until that night, and I'd never felt more intimate with anyone as when he slid deep inside me. The measure of his restraint was remarkable as he gave up control, allowing me to pin down his arms and ride him until my thighs began to tremble. I loved every imperfect thing about him. The way the thin trail of hair below his navel brushed against my belly, the faint scars on his body, the way he'd grimace when I hit a sweet spot, and even his musky smell. My hips went into a wild rhythm that had him groaning and straining beneath me. God, now I knew *exactly* how he felt riding that motorcycle—the raw power between his legs and being in complete control.

He threw back his head and every muscle clenched, turning to granite. The cords of muscle on his arms had never been more evident. When he captured my attention with his magnetic gaze and called me princess—I came.

Or quaked.

Either way, my body rocked from the first orgasm I'd ever experienced with a man. I'd had plenty on my own, but Reno made me feel alive in ways my ex never could. But if he hadn't allowed me to take over, I would have never been able to reach my climax. Someone like me was too messed up; no man would ever be able to *give* me one.

Reno proved my theory wrong when he flipped me over and we did it the Shifter way. My knees pressed against the sheets as his hips slammed into me from behind. I gripped the headboard and my body hummed with pleasure. Then he stopped and allowed me to move—an act of give and take. Reno made an animalistic sound and dropped his head on my shoulder as I rocked him into a sweet orgasm. As I neared climax, Reno roughly grabbed my hips and pounded into me so relentlessly that he made me scream his name.

And I'd never screamed out any man's name before.

Except for the time I got fifth row tickets to a Billy Joel concert.

CHAPTER 18

"**WHAT IS THAT NAUGHTY GRIN** all about?" Trevor remarked. "And where the hell were you all night?"

"Well, I think you might have answered your own question," I said, hardly able to conceal my smile. I closed the door to the trailer and locked out the sunshine before heading to my room to change clothes. I'd taken a shower at Reno's house that morning, but I wasn't about to skank around in yesterday's panties. Not to mention I wasn't wearing a bra because he had cut it off with a knife.

After my fifth orgasm I was spent, and Reno had encased me in his arms and held me all night. He'd questioned me about my trouble with Sanchez. I told him everything I knew about him and Delgado. I didn't know what trouble it could bring, but it was time for me to come clean and start being honest with those who cared about me.

"If he wants a pissing match, he just fucked with the wrong guy, because I've got the longest dick," Reno had declared.

I wanted to let sleeping dogs lie, but I couldn't talk him out of going after Sanchez. It didn't matter; Reno said Sanchez was going down on sheer principle for messing around with his girl.

His girl.

It wasn't an epic moment of poetic words, but that one declaration made my heart flutter. My feelings for Reno were blossoming into something I didn't have a grasp on because I'd never felt anything like it before. After he did some heavy cussing, I kissed his chest and he settled down, stroking my arm until I fell asleep. That morning, Reno had dropped me off at home so he could have a talk with Austin and smooth things over with his pack. I had doubts Austin would accept what I'd done, regardless of the reason. Lexi probably wanted nothing to do with me, and I didn't blame her. But a pang of remorse struck deep when I realized I'd lost a friend.

Trevor came into the bedroom while I changed into a pair of jean shorts and long sleeves.

"I'm sorry for leaving you alone all night, Trev. I should have called, but I was a little... tied up," I said with a mischievous smile.

"You got whisker burn on your face," he pointed out, shaking one of my snow globes.

I ignored him, tying my shoelaces into double knots. "Don't ruin my morning with a fight."

"That good, huh?"

I fell back on the bed and smiled at the ceiling. "Blissfully good."

He crawled next to me and relaxed on his side, poking his finger in my exposed belly button. "Just don't fall in love with sex."

"Why do you have to be so obtuse? I know what I'm doing."

"It means you're young and maybe this is the first best sex you've ever had. Don't translate that to love, and trust me, it's easy to do."

"Trevor, you're two years older than me. I hardly think that makes you wise beyond your years about sex and love. So you can drop all that young and naïve business. It's time for me to start having relationships with men instead of reading about them."

"Yeah, but why does it have to be *him?* Anyone but him."

I sat up and frowned. "Just because he knocked you out? Bruised pride. Yeah, I get it." I hopped off the bed and made my way to the kitchen.

He trailed behind and leaned against the wall by the fridge. "Look, babe, he's bad news all around. I know exactly what his game is and you're..."

I slanted my eyes. "I'm what?"

"Just a plaything to him."

I poured milk into a bowl of cereal and sat in the chair. "Maybe he's a plaything to me, ever think of that? I'm not the victim here, Trevor. It's what I want. I'm finally heeding your advice and taking control of my life."

"One night of phenomenally great sex and she's taking back her life." He swung the door open and leaned outside. "You hear that, world? April had great cock and now she's turning over a new—"

I reached around him and slammed the door. "Cut that out! My neighbors will hear you."

"Who? Mr. Dongshlonger with all the gnomes?"

"Great, now I've lost my appetite," I said, whirling around and taking a seat at the table. I watched Hermie making bubbles at the top of the waterline.

Trevor snorted. "I'd ask what's got into you, but I think I already know."

A laugh bubbled out and I shook my head as he flashed an amused wink at me. I swirled the spoon in my cereal bowl, stretching out my legs and crossing them at the ankle. "You're so childish."

"Well, now that I'm speaking with the new and empowered April, I hope she'll know when to cut off the bootie calls," he said, peeling a banana and leaning against the counter. "Taking control also means learning when to let go of something that isn't healthy. It was hard as hell for me to leave my ex, but what we had wasn't right and would have eventually destroyed us."

"So why did you stay together?"

His cheek puffed out when he took a generous bite of the banana. "Sometimes you just want to hold on to the fantasy and the only thing you end up with is the reality. The reality was, James made me feel like shit on a regular basis, and as a result, I spent his fucking money just to piss him off. It was toxic because he didn't want to accept who I was."

"What do you mean? I hope you at least told your boyfriend you were gay," I said with a crooked smirk.

"Never mind," he muttered, dropping the half-eaten banana in the trash. "I have a few job interviews lined up for today."

I flew out of my chair and wrapped my arms around his neck.

"Hey," he laughed. "What's all this lovey-dovey business for?"

"Because it means you're staying. I was afraid you'd eventually go back to him and leave me here by myself."

Trevor gave me a big squeeze. "You're family to me, April. I look after my family. Look, I can't leave you by yourself all day, so let me drop you off at the mall."

"The mall?" I laughed and pushed away.

He held my wrist and arched his right eyebrow. "Yeah. *The mall*. That place we met at, remember? Don't act like you're so high and mighty that after one night of blistering sex, you're too good to mingle with the passionless sheep hitting the clearance racks."

"Okay, it's getting less funny," I said, glaring up at him.

Trevor smiled devilishly and leaned against the counter. I don't know how he managed to get every hair on his head combed in such a way that it looked messy and neat all at once. "Then where do you want to go? The candy store?"

"No, I'm not working there anymore."

"What?" He stood up straight and crossed in front of me. "What happened?"

"Retail isn't helping me with my career goals."

"You suck at lying."

"Cut it out, Trev. It's my life."

"So when are you going to tell me what kind of trouble you're in?"

"How about tonight? I promise. Give me one day to float around like a girl who just had the best night of her life, then I'll let you anchor me down to the depressing reality after we have tacos. Deal?"

He cupped the back of my head and pulled me in tight. "Sorry," he whispered softly against my hair. "And PS: your roots are showing and it's appalling. I'll pick up some dye later on and fix you up."

"Maybe I should just let it go natural."

"It's up to you," he said. "Or I'll dye it black." Trevor held me at arm's length, studying my face and hair. "Shit, that would look awesome with your complexion. You'd look like a badass heroine from one of those urban fantasy books who wears tall lace-up boots and ripped tank tops."

"Think I can find some of those at the mall?"

Trevor dropped me off at the mall and actually stuffed fifty bucks in my pocket. I had to laugh because he knew I wouldn't spend a dime of it. Since it was close to lunch, I stopped over at the sandwich shop and ordered a grilled panini with an avocado smoothie. It was relaxing to sit at my square table and watch people. A redheaded boy hopped in a circle on one foot, a teenager with mischief on his face flew by on a skateboard as an overweight security guard ran after him, and one exhausted mother had her hands full with five kids who all wanted something different to eat. I played a game with myself, guessing what everyone was doing at the mall.

I wondered if anyone sitting around me was doing the same and had guessed I was hiding from a pinky-chopping maniac who worked for a loan shark.

Halfway through my shake, I spotted a familiar face. I think she recognized me more than I did her. Naya James had breezed into our store on a few occasions to purchase pinwheel lollipops, but she was also a close friend to Lexi.

"April? I almost didn't recognize you!" Naya shouted, running in short steps to my table. Her black pumps made her bronze legs look impossibly long beneath her powder-blue skirt. Naya was all kinds of beautiful with thick curls of brown hair and exotic eyes.

She leaned down and kissed my cheek.

"Hi," I said, feeling at a loss for words at her unexpected appearance. "Did you find anything good?"

She threw a large bag onto the adjacent table and set her purse on the chair beside her as she sat down. "Whew! I've been shopping for an hour and my feet are killing me."

"What did you get?"

"Oh," she said with a sly grin. "Nothing I can pull out in front of all the children. It's for work. When I buy real clothes for me, I go shopping with Lexi. Girl time," she explained. Naya was a stripper, or exotic dancer. I wasn't sure which term was politically correct. She had a bubbly personality that was fun to be around, not to mention Naya was drop-dead gorgeous.

"Oh, girly, what is *that?*" she asked, staring at my green drink with her red lips scrunched.

"Give it a taste. It's an avocado smoothie," I said, sliding it across the table.

Naya pushed it back. "The only thing green I put in my mouth is Ben Franklin," she informed me with a suggestive wink. "So where is Lexi?"

I felt a flush rise on my cheeks. She had no idea what had gone down between us, and I was a little relieved. "Work, I guess."

"You guess? Don't you know her schedule?"

I glanced around to think of an answer.

Oh. My. God.

My trip to the mall had just escalated from awkward to epic fail when I saw Wheeler strut by with his sleeveless black shirt, showing off his tats that wrapped all the way down to his wrists. A woman walked by him and did a double take, snapping a picture of him with her phone. He lingered in the pizza line and I sank down in my chair. Naya caught on and turned to look around.

"I have to go," I blurted out.

"Already, chickypoo? Don't you want to hit the shoe stores on the lower level with me?"

"No, but I appreciate the offer," I said, untangling the strap of my purse from the chair. When I sat up, my elbow knocked the smoothie over and the cup clacked all over the floor. Several people turned to look.

Including Wheeler.

The moment he spotted me, he slammed his tray on the counter and stalked toward us with a venomous look on his face. His brows slanted fiendishly and his lips were tight. Wheeler's dangerous streak might have turned on some women, but it intimidated the heck out of me. He'd trimmed up that beard, which is more than I could say for the tangle of brown hair on top of his head. I guessed it to be about two inches long and hoped it would be enough to grab if this confrontation turned physical.

Wheeler's shoe stepped in a puddle of green liquid and he slammed his fist on the table.

"Stay away from my brother before you break up the pack," he said through clenched teeth, leaning forward with both hands gripping either side of the table. "You hear me? Being with someone like you is nothing but bad news for him all the way around."

Naya's chair scraped back and she stood up as straight as an arrow, throwing her shoulders back. "Don't you talk to her that way," she snapped, lifting a defiant chin.

I stared in shock between the both of them. Wheeler cannibalized me with his gaze, and then I noticed a fresh bruise on his eye.

"You may be fucking him, but you're not welcome on our property."

Wheeler hissed and recoiled when Naya swiped her hand and sliced him on the arm with her nails. He stood up and peeled his lips back angrily.

Without warning, Naya slapped him in the face.

Hard.

The crack snagged the attention of several people and they stopped to watch.

She wagged her finger angrily at him. "Didn't your mother teach you to treat a woman with respect?"

"And who the fuck are you?"

"Naya James," she said in the most badass way a woman could say her name. She looked like a heroine with her brown curls spilling across her broad shoulders and her fists resting against her shapely hips.

"You're Lexi's friend," he muttered, rubbing his cheek.

Naya stepped forward and before Wheeler could flinch, she gripped the back of his neck. I waited for her fist to smash into his nose. Instead, she kissed him softly on the mouth. As she did, her body moved until it was flush with his. Her tongue swept out in a subtle motion as her fingers tenderly caressed his neck. When she leaned in once more with an even softer kiss, his body went lax and his expression altered. Wheeler stood catatonic, looking down at her and not reciprocating. Naya casually stepped back and my eyes were wide and unbelieving at what just happened.

Wheeler turned as bright red as the lipstick stain on his mouth. A few people nearby chuckled and went back to eating.

"What did you do that for?" he asked in scattered words, his voice cracking mid-sentence.

Naya's full lips turned up in a smile and she snatched her shopping bag off the table, batting her curled lashes. "Because it's the only time you'll ever feel my lips on your body. I like my enemies to know two things about me: what they're up against and what they'll never have." She winked at me and pulled the strap of her purse over her shoulder. "I'll be sure to tell Lexi how you're treating her friend."

"By all means." He attempted to sound pissed off but failed miserably.

"Yes. By *all* means," she said with a purr, swinging her hips like a pendulum as she strutted off.

Wheeler watched until she disappeared around the corner. He licked his lips and sliced me with his gaze as if he wanted to let me have it. Instead, he pivoted around and stalked off, leaving a one-footed trail of green juice. His exit wasn't near as sultry as Naya's because his hands were curled into tight fists, and he looked ready to pummel the stuffing out of a punching bag.

I wanted to give that woman a high five for standing up to him. Wheeler had every right to be upset with me about the money, but my personal relationship with Reno was none of his business.

Which also planted another seed in my head: Reno must have said something to give him the impression that we were an item.

And that made my toes curl in my sneakers, just a little bit.

CHAPTER 19

"You're talking nonsense, Reno." Austin shifted on his barstool and rubbed his jaw pensively. "April is a human and our worlds collide. She doesn't know anything about our lifestyle any more than you do about hers."

An hour ago, Reno had dropped April off at her trailer after a night of passion that had seared into him like a brand. When he arrived back home, he called the boys upstairs and broke the news to the pack that he was claiming April. That was a big fucking deal among Shifters. Human or not, he wanted every man in that house to know that April Frost was off-limits. When the discussion became heated, Austin told Lexi to take the women out of the house. Sometimes when arguments got out of hand, Shifters would change into their animal, and that could be problematic.

Reno looked around their game room with distant eyes.

"Mom, let's go," Lexi coaxed from the hall.

"I don't see why I can't just stay in my room," Lynn protested, their voices growing distant.

Reno folded his arms and leaned against the pool table, his brothers scattered in various spots in the room.

"That woman you want to claim is a thief," Wheeler spat. "A conniving little human thief."

Reno unstrapped the gun from his holster and placed it on the pool table. "Say that again."

"Hold up," Austin interjected, moving between them. "Reno, you've got an infatuation. I get it. But she's a *human*. Think about it. No one here is saying you can't have your fun, but at the end of the day, you can't spend your life with one of them. Don't claim something you can't have."

Long term wasn't exactly how Reno had presented his intentions, but that's how they'd taken it. Maybe it was the dead-serious look in his eyes. "Who do you think we've got living under our roof, baby brother? Humans. We care for two human women."

"But not as *mates*," Wheeler said, folding his arms and pushing out his tatted biceps. "Lexi's mom and sister are a package deal, but that's not what we're talking about here, is it? You know public opinion about having pets."

Reno tensed. "Did I say anything about her being a *pet?*" he ground out slowly.

All gazes darted between one another.

Austin took a deep breath and sighed. "You'll be targeted by a lot of assholes who want to give you their two cents on the matter. Are you up for that?"

Reno lifted his chin and challenged him with silence.

Austin centered his eyes on Reno and his voice became grave. "That also means no kids. And you're going to watch her grow old and die."

"Only got a couple hundred years left on me if I'm lucky."

Reno's comment was met with derision as Denver tilted his head and leaned against the bar. "Reno wants to have a sexy grandma in his bed."

He cut a sharp glare at Denver who immediately lowered his eyes. "I'm going to let that slide this once." Reno lifted his index finger. "*Once.* If you ever disrespect her again, then you can tell my fist all about it." He studied the stern faces in the room. "That goes for every one of you. A woman shouldn't come between brothers. How I live my life is my choice, and I didn't say anything here about mating, kids, or any of that. I'm simply laying down the fact that I've got claim on that woman and I want to know that you have my back. That means out of respect for the brotherhood, you don't allow anyone to mess with her and you treat her with respect."

Wheeler stepped forward and his face tightened. He was lean muscle and could hold his own in a fight. They'd all seen him go at it and Wheeler was a man who didn't hold back on his swing. Austin used to say anytime Wheeler was the underdog, he'd bet on him.

"You're not getting my support on this, Reno. You'll never be able to trust her—she stole from the family."

Ben turned away with an apathetic expression and threw a dart at the board.

Meanwhile, Jericho lounged at the bar, half turned around, smoking a cigarette and watching the whole affair. Austin had finally buried the hatchet and let him back in the house, so Jericho chose to keep his mouth shut on controversial matters and fly under the radar.

"I already explained why she did it, and you're forgetting she replaced the money so it's more like an unauthorized loan. And you should be helping me find the sonofabitch who's been threatening her," Reno said in a gravelly voice.

"Not my problem," Wheeler countered, tilting his head defiantly.

Reno stepped forward. "My problems should be your problems, *brother*."

Wheeler slimmed down his eyes. "Why don't you take your problem somewhere else? We have enough of our own. 'Preciate ya."

A hard tap sounded to the right as Ben threw another dart at the board.

"Since when do you give a damn about the business, Wheeler? Austin had to force you to help out his woman and now all this sudden interest."

"Lexi's one of us," he said. "Your bitch ain't."

A hard crack sounded when Reno's fist struck Wheeler in the eye. He spun around and staggered before catching himself on the bar.

"How 'bout that?"

Austin pushed Reno back by his shoulders. "That's enough! I can see you're not backing down on this one, so on my order as Packmaster," he said loudly, "every man in this room will treat April with respect. Reno's made his claim, and we'll stand by his decision. But as long as she's on the outs with Lexi, she's not welcome in this house. Sorry, but that's the way it goes, Reno. Regardless of motive, she stole from my woman's pocket, and I have to respect Lexi's feelings. My pack always comes first. If Lexi forgives her, then April is welcome in this house. But if not, then you see her on the outside. That's a compromise and I think it's fair to all parties present and not present."

Reno could agree to that. Austin had made the call and he had to abide by the rules. The second-in-command remained steadfast, supporting the decisions of the Packmaster. Friction between the two would inevitably break apart a loyal pack.

"Agreed," Reno said tersely. "But just so we can make this fair, I want the women to talk to each other and settle it. Women go on too long holding grudges."

"Amen," Denver said as he plopped his ass in the beanbag chair.

Reno ignored him. "April didn't have a fair shot to explain her situation to Lexi. She should get that chance—*then* let your woman decide how she wants it to play out."

Austin curled in his bottom lip while scratching his chin. "Yeah, I'll agree to that. Lexi's been carrying around an attitude and it's killing my action."

Denver barked out a laugh. "The bubonic plague couldn't kill your action." He tapped his bare feet on the floor when all the men turned to glare at him.

"A horny plague couldn't *help* yours," Jericho said, taking a long drag of his smoke.

"Shut it, dickhead," Denver snapped. "I get enough action."

"Not much action going on at the library," Jericho said matter-of-factly. "I've seen you go after those good girls, but you know what? They go for guys like me. Quit holding out for Miss Perfect." He smashed out his cigarette and rose from the stool. "Good girls always have a dark secret. That secret is going to chew you up and spit you out once they realize they can do a lot better than you."

Denver rolled his eyes as Jericho headed out of the room. Jericho might have been the ladies' man of the house, but he was the least likely of all the men to settle down. Aside from Wheeler, but that was a given. Denver talked a lot of game, but saw little action from what the guys noticed. His standards were too high, as if he were always looking for faults and no woman was good enough.

That's why when Denver hit on April during the party, Reno had felt his wolf trying to come out. April was a good girl and that was an attractive quality to Denver, even though he didn't go out with humans.

Reno thought about the trust she had given him in the bedroom the night before. She needed to get past some of the bullshit that had happened in her past. He'd lived a long life and figured out some hard lessons on his own, but April had shown him that it was okay to give up some of that control. He'd never had a woman who understood him or sought to please him in the way he needed in order to move past his own issues. After she fell asleep in his arms, he'd decided they weren't using belts or ropes in the bedroom anymore. That was a one-time deal. Maybe kinky worked for some women, but for Reno, it had always been less of a game and more of a necessity. Next time he was going to be real sweet to April. A woman like her deserved more than the bondage and submission he had required of all his past lovers. She inspired him to be something he'd never been before.

Romantic.

Wheeler grabbed his wallet off the bar. "I'm heading out to the mall. I have to meet someone."

"Next time you see my girl, you treat her with respect," Reno said.

Wheeler shot him the middle finger as he walked out the door.

When Trevor picked me up from the mall, I didn't say boo about running into Wheeler and the drama that ensued. Naya slapping Wheeler and then delivering a smoldering kiss that left his knees shaking? It was the most incredible moment I'd ever witnessed.

Aside from Reno turning into a wolf.

Before going home, Trevor took me to a double feature at a movie theater across town. Afterward, we swung by a Mexican restaurant for dinner. I ordered the cheese enchiladas, and Trevor chowed down on tacos, chimichangas, flautas, and I don't know what else. Our table transformed into a buffet and we shared food and a pitcher of cold beer. He was surprised to see me eating because I'd always had a fear of people spitting in my food. But because Trevor was super flirty with the waitress, I didn't think we'd have to worry about that. He knew it was one of my quirky little hang-ups but had once told me that it's what made me adorable. Nobody could have asked for a better friend than Trevor.

We made up for lost time and he told me a few jokes that had me in stitches. One girl flirted with him shamelessly from a nearby table, and Trevor was just as shameless flirting back. He loved attention and didn't care who it came from. But he still played for one team, and it was interesting to see how no one could figure it out.

On the way home, we could barely buckle our seatbelts. "Babe, you can really put it away. I don't think I've met another girl who can eat an entire serving of nachos before the meal arrives and then have room for dessert at the end," he said as the car zoomed around a corner.

"Thank God you had coupons for dinner or I would have been embarrassed to pay that bill, as much as we ate."

His contagious laugh filled the small space, and he flipped on the radio. "That was the most fun I've had in an eternity. We should call up some old acquaintances and get together one night. Maybe hang out at Lucky's Bar or have a barbecue at the lake."

"Don't count on anyone showing up. Most of our old friends are married or they can't stay out late because they have to get up early and beat rush-hour traffic to their corporate job," I said, ending my complaint in a mutter. Mostly a complaint, because I felt left in the dust while everyone else was getting their lives in order.

We turned onto the road that led home and I shivered. My eyes went wide when I glanced around my lap. "Holy smokes, Trev. You're going to kill me." I reached in the floorboard and shot back up, looking at him apprehensively. "I think I left my purse at the restaurant."

"Oh, you're kidding me," he groaned. "Are you sure it's not... Check by the door."

I stuffed my hand in the crevice and felt beneath the seat. "No, Trevor. I can't find it. The last place I remember having it was in the bathroom... I think. You should have let me pay for everything. I would have noticed my purse was gone if I had to pick up the bill."

"If I had let you pay, we'd be in jail for skipping the damn check."

I snorted. That was probably true.

Trevor fumbled with the keys and handed me the spare to the trailer. "Go inside. I'll head over before they lock up."

"You sure?"

"I'll be back in fifteen. Just don't leave me standing outside too long with that wolf running loose on the property."

"Sorry, Trev. I feel rotten about ending our night like this. Check in the booth, just in case it's not in the bathroom. I can't believe I did this," I said, getting out and heading toward the trailer.

Trevor volunteered to pick up a sack of bagels for breakfast on the way home, so I had a feeling he didn't mind so much.

I shut the door, flipped on the light, and tossed the key on the table.

Just as I reached for the fish food, I heard a car pull in and the engine cut off.

"Trev, did you find it?" I yelled out, opening the door.

It swung open and the force pulled me off-balance as I was thrown back in a violent motion.

I crashed against the table and hit my head on the wall. Dizzy, I rolled to the side and looked up from the floor. A sunburst of pain radiated at the back of my head, causing me to see tiny flickers of light.

"How's it going, Vanilla? Miss me?"

Sanchez loomed in the doorway, dressed in all black. What scared me was the lighter fluid in his hand that he was spraying all over the floor, the curtains, and the table Reno had built for me. Hermie swam sporadically in his bowl.

"Wait, wait," I said. "What do you want? Please don't."

"Ahh, too late, Vanilla. You want to sit and whine about it now? You think you can talk smack to me and I'll let you get away with it? Bitch, you don't know me." He sprayed the sofa while holding a box of matches in his left hand. It rattled as he pooled up the fluid and finally threw down the empty can.

"I'll do what you want," I said, hands shaking, voice wavering. The thought of burning alive terrified me to the core of my being. *Thank God Trevor isn't here*, I thought. *At least he's safe.*

"Of *course* you'll do whatever I want. You know what I want?" he said, backing up toward the door. Sanchez held up a match and a malevolent grin spread across his face. "I want you to *scream*."

The wooden stick scratching along the rough edge of the box sounded like an attack.

And it was.

I screamed before the flame hit the accelerant. Sanchez lunged forward and stomped on my foot. A feral scream poured from my mouth as pain exploded up my leg. He closed the door behind him after he ran out, and the fire engulfed the sofa, floor, and doorway, forcing me to scramble into the back room. The pain in my head and foot became blinding and I fell on my knees and crawled through the noxious smoke that was quickly filling the room.

Years ago when the riffraff had moved into our neighborhood, Grandma had sealed up the windows, afraid of someone trying to snatch one of us girls in our sleep. One of them she had completely covered. The searing heat reminded me it was the only way out. I needed to bust the back window with something and squeeze out.

The pain and shock of what was happening consumed me. I was going to burn alive, and oh God, the dumbest things ran through my mind. Like poor little Hermie, and my dad's snow globes. I managed to crawl on the bed and I struggled to breathe. Oxygen was running out and I began coughing as my chest tightened, which made me dizzy and nauseous. I knew I was in mortal danger, but between the pain and inability to breathe, I became disoriented. I pushed my face into the mattress—my eyes stinging, lungs burning.

An explosion rocked the trailer and a force of energy burst into the room.

"April, I'm coming!" Reno shouted.

"No, no, no," I murmured, not wanting him to be there. Not wanting him to get hurt.

"Get up." He yanked my arm and when the weight settled on my foot, I screamed so loud that I blacked out.

CHAPTER 20

After Reno had spoken with his pack about April, he let his wolf run on the property. After shifting back, he'd spent the rest of the afternoon thinking about her and then decided to head over to her house late that evening. His wolf demanded it. She had sent him a message on the phone that she was spending the day with Trevor and they were going out for some Mexican food before heading home. On the main street near the turnoff, he thought he saw Trevor's car speeding away.

As he eased up the road, an orange glow illuminated the dark sky in the distance. He blinked from the headlights of an oncoming vehicle, and an expensive car blew past him. Reno glanced in the rearview mirror and slammed his foot on the gas. Something wasn't right, and the closer he got to the trailer, the more he knew why. He sent a message to Austin:

LEVEL RED. APRIL.

Reno went cold with dread when he saw the trailer burst into flames. A window on the right shattered and fire licked at the roof like the devil's tongue. The fire engulfed the right side—not so much on the left from what he could tell.

"Jesus," he breathed, feet barely touching the ground as he tore open the door. He had only seconds before it consumed the entire thing.

Flames and thick smoke poured out with the introduction of fresh oxygen and then receded. Reno didn't hesitate.

He ran through fire.

Heat seared his skin and he grimaced from the intense burn on his arms. His eyes teared up and he covered his nose and mouth.

"April, I'm coming!"

She was sprawled across the mattress with her legs hanging off. He tried to pull her up, but she screamed and passed out in his arms, completely unresponsive. Reno had no time to assess her injuries.

She'd burn if he carried her out. There wasn't time to think about why she hadn't busted out the windows, so he wrapped the blanket around her tight and rolled her up like a burrito—not an inch of her from head to toe exposed.

"Hang on, princess," he whispered.

Lifting her in his iron grip, Reno turned around and walked through fire. It singed his hair immediately and burned his face and arms. He kept his eyes closed and head turned away, focusing on walking steadily so as not to fall. It slowed his pace to a painful degree, but he managed to continue holding his breath, enduring the heat as he went for the door.

He nearly fell down the steps but caught his balance and staggered several yards away from the danger. Reno dropped to his knees and patted out the flames from the ends of the blanket, quickly tearing it off.

"April," he gasped, patting her cheek. His world was about to come crashing down if she didn't wake up.

Reno struggled for breath, skin peeling off his arms. But all his worries melted away when he saw her eyes flutter. She'd live, and that's all that mattered. Reno fell to the ground beside her and everything went dark.

"The patient needs rest," a woman's voice spoke from a distance. "I'll be back to check her vitals. Do you want me to bring you a blanket?"

"No," I heard Lexi say. "I don't plan on sleeping until my sister wakes up."

Sister? Why would she say that? I wondered. *I must be dreaming.*

As a door clicked shut, I slowly opened my eyes. "My arm burns," I croaked.

Lexi leaned in close. "Shhh. The nurse mixed something in with the potassium drip—it should stop burning in a minute. How are you feeling?"

I licked my dry lips and looked around. "Where am I?"

"The Four Seasons?" Lexi smiled and brushed a strand of hair away from my forehead. "The hospital. They had you on oxygen for a while and said if you have any trouble breathing to let them know right away. You had me worried out of my mind. Reno sent a message to Austin that sent him running out the door without his shoes."

I tried to sit up. "Reno?" Then a memory flashed through my head of seeing him inside the trailer. Tears blurred my vision. "Is he okay? Please tell me he's not hurt… Oh God…"

"He's better," she said gravely. "Austin got there in time, but Reno sustained serious burns. Austin made him shift. That's how we heal; shifting back and forth from human to animal works a magic through our body. Something that bad, well, Reno needed to do it several times in order to heal. Once he was in wolf form, Austin had a hard time forcing him to shift back because Reno's wolf guarded you as if he was your protector."

"Where is he?"

"I don't know. He took off an hour ago and said he'd be back. I want to apologize, April. Reno explained everything. If you had told me someone was threatening you, I would have given you that money. I know why you kept it to yourself, but sometimes it's okay to let people know you don't have everything under control. Nobody's perfect, and it doesn't say anything bad about you. We all have things going on in our personal life, but you can't carry that burden alone."

"I shouldn't have taken it," I said in a raspy voice, feeling a stiff board and tape on my index finger where they were monitoring my pulse. The discomfort in my foot became a dull ache when I bent my knee and tried to move.

"Your doctor took an X-ray and said he thinks there's a hairline fracture in your foot. But it's definitely sprained and bruised up." She leaned over my bed and held my hand. "He wants you to wear one of those ugly boots with crutches. After they ran the CT scan to check your head, they gave you a mild painkiller. *Thank God* we have insurance because this is going to cost a fortune. I'll help with the expenses your insurance doesn't cover, so don't worry about a damn thing."

"I can't ask you to do that."

"I don't care," she said matter-of-factly. "You've never once asked me for anything and all this time, you were the one who needed help the most. Accept my help, April. I'm giving it to you and that's final. Dammit."

I smirked at her stubbornness and she smiled at mine. "I'll pay you back."

"No, you won't. This isn't a favor; this is me helping out a friend and you accepting. That means no paybacks. Who did this to you?"

I turned away.

Lexi's voice lowered. "Reno thought it was Trevor."

My eyes widened and I tried to sit up but she pushed me down. "He didn't go after him, did he? It wasn't—"

"Chill out, babe. No one's coming after me," a good-humored voice said from the doorway.

His oxfords crossed the floor to the left side of the bed and Trevor bent over and kissed my cheek like he meant it. He did it super-softly this time and sighed, pressing his forehead against mine. Lexi walked to the foot of the bed and squeezed my left toe—the one that wasn't hurt.

"We're going to kill the asshole who did this to you. All I need is for you to give me his name," Trevor said.

I looked up and saw Reno looming in the doorway, quietly watching us.

"Sanchez," I whispered. "His name is Sanchez. He sprayed a canister of lighter fluid or something onto the sofa and walls. Before I could get up, he stomped on my ankle and I was paralyzed with pain. Then he shut the door. He didn't douse me in that stuff because he wanted me to be afraid for as long as it took. I should have tried to get out the door—but the fire—I was scared and confused."

"You did good, babe," Trevor said, brushing his hand over my forehead. "He was probably holding the door shut, knowing you'd try to get out. Running to the back bought you some time."

I lowered my eyes. "I was going to try to smash the window but I couldn't breathe… everything began to spin and—"

"It's ok, honey," Lexi soothed. "The doctor said you have a nasty bump on your head. You were awake when they brought you in, but not lucid. I'm guessing you don't remember."

I shook my head. "All I remember is not wanting to burn alive."

Reno's eyes were blazing like the fire that had consumed my home, and I could almost feel the tension snapping like one of those live wires on the road after a storm.

Lexi must have felt it too, because she shuddered. "I'm going to talk to Austin," she said. "Do you need anything?"

I shook my head and Reno whispered something to her at the door before she left.

"So, you two are on speaking terms?" I asked Trevor with a faint smile. My best friend on my left, my best *I-don't-know-what* on my right.

It was a rhetorical question and I looked at Reno, searching for injuries.

"I'll be back," Trevor whispered against my cheek. "The cops want my statement and all that. I'm heading out to the trailer to see if anything is salvageable before we track down the soon-to-be-dead man who did this. The firemen got there pretty quick, so there might be something."

"Your guitar is gone," I said wearily. "I'm sorry. All your stuff—"

"Yeah, like I give a shit about my junk, April. Won't be the first time I've had to start over. Just let them take care of you and hopefully they'll discharge you this afternoon. I'll pick you up and we'll stay with… well, I'll figure something out."

Trevor disappeared around the corner and shut the heavy door.

"Are you okay? Did you heal all the way?"

"Don't you worry about me, princess." Reno leaned down and cupped his warm hands around my face. "But when you feel better, we're going to have a talk about your friend kissing on you. I got a problem with another man's lips on your body."

His thumb gently stroked my cheekbone and I smiled into his palm. I didn't have words for a man who ran through fire to save me.

How do you show someone your gratitude for burning alive to save your life?

His eyes floated up to the plastic tubes going into my arm, the machines, and when he eyed the space beside me, I scooted a little to the right.

Reno walked around to the left side and tested his weight, slowly easing himself on the bed and turning on his side, draping his arm around my stomach. His nose touched my neck and I relished the warmth of his body so close to mine.

"Is this all he did to you?"

My stomach knotted. The sharp edge in his voice terrified me. "Yeah."

He looked at me softly, not like he had before. Why had I been so afraid of this man when we first met? I'd never dated a tough guy before, so I'd never had a clue they were all soft inside. Reno redefined what a man was in my eyes.

"You're more beautiful without makeup on your eyes. You know that?"

Which meant I was lying there without a speck of eyeliner. Not that it should have bothered me, but I must have looked like a hot mess.

"How long do I have to stay here? I can't afford this." I coughed a few times and cleared my throat.

"Don't think about that right now. Just get better," he murmured against my neck, kissing me tenderly. "I'm going to take care of you."

Those last words lingered in my mind. I wanted to be with Reno, but I also wanted a fresh start. I couldn't enter a relationship with him with all this debt, a man trying to kill me, being homeless, and not having a job. It wouldn't be fair to anyone. He'd almost died for me and I needed to sort out my problems so nothing like that would happen again—I owed him that much. If they never caught Sanchez, then Reno would always be in danger.

I listened to the sound of the machine pumping fluids through the IV and closed my eyes. "I can't do this with you."

"Shhh," he said. "Close your eyes and sleep. We'll talk later."

"When they let me go, I'm going to figure things out with Trevor. I don't want you to get hurt again."

Reno drew in a deep breath and sat up, leaning on his right elbow. "It's about time you learned a little fact about your friend. Trevor is a Shifter."

"Don't do that, Reno. Don't make up lies to try to turn me against my best friend."

"How do you explain the night we found him beaten and he healed? Your friend had a compound fracture in his arm; that kind of injury doesn't just mend with a little peroxide."

"It's not possible. I've known him forever."

He quietly huffed out a laugh and looked up at the chalkboard where the nurses wrote their names. "He's in the closet."

My eyes went wide. "How did you know?"

Then he glanced at me with a quizzical brow. "Are we talking about the same thing?"

"What are you talking about?"

Reno rubbed his face and then dropped his hand on mine, quickly moving it when he felt all the tubes. "He's turned his back on his own kind. Trevor's a Shifter. When we get close enough, we can usually sense someone who is Breed. Trevor was easy to peg in the grocery store because of how territorial he was. There's a subtle body language and something you notice in the eyes of other Shifters when we're acting on instinct. Austin forced him to shift that night and Trevor was madder than a hornet's nest. I've seen his kind before. He doesn't want to be part of our world. He's living in denial, trying to be human. I don't know if he lets his wolf out—if not, that makes him unpredictable and dangerous. Our wolf *has* to come out; that's just a fact of life."

"It's impossible. There's no way I could have known him this long without noticing my best friend is a wolf. I would have… I…"

How could I have known Trevor was a Shifter? None of it seemed logical, but it's not as if they had a membership symbol stamped on their foreheads.

"Even after shifting, he denied what he was," Reno continued. "He called us lunatics, but he knows. He *knows* what he is. He's in the closet and living in denial. It's a sad fucking thing to behold because I'm proud of what I am. If you want to stay friends with him, then you have a right to know your safety will be compromised. We can't control our animal and I've got no idea what his pattern is. That makes me uneasy. If you won't stay with me, then so be it. But you sure as hell aren't staying with him. Over my dead body, and that's the deal."

I'd never lived with Trevor, but we'd crashed together a time or two. I suddenly thought about him storming out on the occasions when his temper flared or when he was hurt. What Reno said made sense: Trevor's wolf wanted to come out and he couldn't be around me or I'd find out what he was.

"Unbelievable," I whispered. "This just isn't my life. How strong are these drugs they're giving me?"

"If I were you, I wouldn't confront him on it. He's not ready to face his demons, and I don't want you pushing his buttons. Sorry, but I don't trust his wolf. That's just the way it is."

The IV pump by my bed clattered and I feared it would be impossible to sleep because of the noise.

Reno leaned in and kissed me on the mouth, gentle and sweet. Then his lips reverently kissed my cheeks, nose, and forehead.

"What do you want? Name it and I'll get it for you," he said, brushing a finger lightly over a dark bruise on my right arm.

My eyelids drooped and my mouth barely muttered, "Cookies."

CHAPTER 21

My doctor advised me to wear a large boot for three weeks and then come back for X-rays to see how it was healing. I had to keep it elevated when sitting and not put any pressure on it. The crutches were tiresome and hurt my arms. I practiced in my room for a little while before Lexi helped me into the bathroom to get dressed and remove the round adhesives they'd used for the heart monitors. They were all over my chest, and they left red marks when I peeled them off.

A knock sounded on the bathroom door.

"Just a minute," Lexi said.

"Open up," Reno insisted. His voice raised the tiny blond hairs on my arms. She unlatched the door and as soon as it opened, he cupped her arm and pulled her out.

"Wait a second!" she complained. "Don't manhandle me."

Reno ignored her and shut himself in the bathroom. "Let me see," he said, kneeling down to look at one of the stickers I was struggling to pull off from beneath my breast. He splashed a little water on it and peeled it away, dabbing my skin with a cool rag.

"What did he say about your head?"

"That it's empty, just as I'd suspected all along."

He smiled. "I see you have your rapier wit back."

"I had a mild concussion. It was precautionary to keep me here, but I'm glad he's letting me go home."

Then I got the big picture as Reno knelt there, caring for something as trivial as a red mark left on my skin by an adhesive.

Reno could heal.

He had sustained serious burns in the fire and yet was fully recovered, while I was in a walking boot with bruises and a few scars from the IV. I had no place in his complicated world. How could I expect him to hang around and watch me get hurt, or what if I got cancer someday?

Maybe I shouldn't have been planning our future when we'd only been seeing each other for a short time, but it felt like it could go that way if I let him in. He seemed willing, but I don't think he'd taken into consideration what he was getting out of this deal. We were pulling on a wishbone and he'd gotten the short end, while I was getting the fairy tale.

I ran my fingers through his bristly hair and down to his pensive brow. Reno's weathered face had lines etched in his cheeks and forehead, but it didn't make him look old. It made him look rugged and sexy, like a man who expressed himself. He glanced up at me with smoldering brown eyes and I realized what made him so attractive to me—his commanding presence combined with a softness whenever he looked at me. My fingers traced the deep lines carved in his cheeks, and when he smiled, they became pronounced. Reno appealed to me in so many surprising ways.

"Have you led a hard life?" I asked in a quiet voice.

He tipped his head side to side. "I've seen my fair share of death and war. I guess that toughens a man."

"Why did you go to war? I mean, doesn't that require being enlisted, and how did they not discover what you were?"

"We can get fake identification, social security numbers, you name it. The Breed look after their own. I believe in fighting for what's important, April. I didn't always think so. When I was young, I had a foolish heart."

"Is that when you smiled more?" I asked, grazing my finger over the laugh line in his cheek, trying to imagine the young man he'd once been before the pitfalls of life had caught up with him.

Reno stood up and threaded his fingers through my hair, studying the roots. "You should grow out all this shit. I'd like to see the real you. I bet you're a knockout." He straightened the brown T-shirt that Lexi had lent me.

"Are you saying I'm *not* a knockout?" I grinned wryly and Reno struggled for words. "I'm just teasing. But feel free to remove your foot from your mouth anytime."

Reno bent forward and wrapped his strong arms around my waist. I draped mine over his neck as he lifted me up and walked into the room. "Got everything?"

I sniffed out a short laugh. "I don't think I came in here with anything."

"Yeah, you forgot something," he said with a smile in his voice. Reno set me down and picked up a package of cookies he had bought from the vending machine. "For the ride," he said, putting them in my hand. "I'll get the nurse and tell her you're ready."

After I signed the papers and was wheeled out front, Reno lifted me out of the chair and carried me to the passenger side of his blue truck. The crutches were tossed in the back.

"Where's Trevor?"

"Trevor isn't taking you anywhere. You're coming home with me," he said in a thick, leathery voice.

"No, Reno."

"This is temporary until I get a hold of Sanchez and knock his lights out. You're not safe anywhere else."

The engine rumbled angrily when he turned the ignition.

"We can't leave without Trevor."

"He's not coming."

"Whose decision was that?"

"His."

I tugged at the plastic bracelet on my wrist that had my name on it.

"He blames himself. Admitted he shouldn't have left you alone, and he was right."

"It wasn't his fault," I argued.

The timbre in his voice grew harsh and punctuated his aggravation. "Someone used a tire iron to beat the hell out of him with *you* in mind. Trevor knew damn well that it wasn't safe to leave you alone last night."

"It was only going to be for fifteen minutes."

Reno leaned over and cupped my neck, tapping his forehead against my cheek. "Yeah. Fifteen minutes and I almost lost you."

He was tugging at my heartstrings. A man who owned a

motorcycle and a gun bowed his head, melting me with his kindness. The more time I spent with Reno, the harder it was going to be to leave. How could I have fallen so fast for a man who led such a dangerous life?

"I'll stay until Sanchez is caught, but then I have to leave."

A horn honked behind us and Reno pinched my jaw, studying my face. "I wish you'd let me in."

When we arrived on the property, my nerves were rattled. Lexi had forgiven me, but I didn't want to face Wheeler and wasn't sure how Austin really felt about me staying with them.

The October sky was overcast and drizzle smeared across the dirty windshield. Reno draped his jacket across my lap and turned the heater on. The soft leather felt nice against my skin and it smelled like him. I thought about our bike ride that day and smiled.

The truck bumped around on the dirt road as we eased up their long driveway. When I saw a group of people waiting for us out front, butterflies waged war in my stomach and I unbuckled my seatbelt.

Lynn and Maizy were on the porch steps. Maizy blew a few bubbles from a yellow wand, but the tiny sprinkles of rain were popping them before they could take off. She wore a red raincoat with a wide hood, a striking image that stood out in all the dreariness of mud and fog. Lexi and Ivy weren't far behind us in her car.

When Reno exited the vehicle, I tilted the visor down and glanced in the mirror. I hadn't brushed my hair or teeth, or put on a speck of makeup. I had a small cut on my cheek, but no bruises. Reno spoke privately to Denver, Wheeler, Ben, and Jericho a few feet ahead. They simultaneously looked up at me and Wheeler pivoted around, walking to my side of the truck.

Oh crap.

I tensed when he yanked my door open. My heart raced, and I kept my hands crossed around my waist as he leaned in and tossed Reno's jacket to the floor.

Before I knew what was happening, Wheeler hooked his right arm beneath my knees, his left behind my back, and lifted me out of the truck. He glared at me with a black eye and I looked at him, dumbfounded, too afraid to ask him why he was being so helpful.

Reno reached for the crutches and a small bag in the back and walked toward Lexi's car when she turned up the driveway. The drizzle tapered off, replaced by a gentle breeze.

I rested my head on Wheeler's shoulder and drew in a deep breath. "You smell like beef jerky."

His arms tightened when we reached the steps and Lynn patted my arm. "Anything you need, hon, just let me know and I'll get it for you. I'm cooking up some beef stew for dinner. You just get some rest."

Wheeler proceeded up the steps and a few bubbles from Maizy's bottle floated around us. One popped on Wheeler's nose and he sniffed, shaking his head.

"Do you hate me?" I asked him. "I wouldn't blame you."

"That what you think?" he said in a curt voice, moving up the stairs.

Wheeler's looks were brutal compared to Ben's, but they were both strikingly handsome in different ways. His jaw was strong and he had sharp cheekbones. A shadow ran down both sides of his face from his carved bone structure, but all that seemed less pronounced because of the circle-beard goatee. He had squinty eyes, but in a good way.

"Reno almost died because of me."

"Reno makes his own decisions. If you're asking if I hate you, then no. But I'll be honest—I sure as hell don't trust you all the way. That's something you have to earn, and when you stole that money, it proved you were more concerned about saving your own ass than the consequences of your actions. What if you couldn't get that money back? What if that was just enough to get Lexi in trouble with paying her bills?"

"I can't take it back, Wheeler. I'm sorry I ever did it, more than you know. It's a mistake I'll have to live with. I'm not trying to get you to accept me; just don't take it out on Reno. I'm only staying here until Sanchez is caught and turned in."

He laughed and leaned down, opening a door. "Sanchez isn't going to jail."

"Why not?" I lifted my head and he looked down at me with pale brown eyes that were as bright as amber but warm like honey.

"Because he's going into the ground."

Wheeler leaned forward and deposited me on the bed.

"Whose room is this?"

"Yours."

When I looked to my right and saw a giant poster of Billy Joel, a laugh burst out. "Oh. My. God."

"I think 'what the fuck' was my choice of words, but yeah. Reno's had the room closed up for the past couple of days, bringing stuff in."

I sat on a lavender bedspread with tiny black designs, and the same mirrors we'd bought for my trailer decorated the walls. "Can I see that?"

Wheeler lifted a small snow globe from the dresser and handed it to me. It wasn't one of mine, and my eyes glittered with tears when I thought about what I'd lost. It was the sentimental stuff like this—pieces of my father that I'd never have back. I shook it and snow swirled around a small cottage surrounded by fir trees.

"What did Reno say to you when we drove up?"

Wheeler averted his eyes. "He said you saved his wolf. Is that true?"

I nodded.

"Maybe that's why I trust you a little bit more than I did before. If he had tried to shift with a screwdriver lodged in his flesh, it might have killed him. I don't take that shit lightly. We're Shifters, and saving one of our brothers means something. If you're his woman, then we have to respect that choice because he's family. And we don't turn our back on family."

I handed the trinket back to Wheeler when Reno appeared in the doorway.

They didn't say anything to each other. Wheeler swaggered out of the room, but not before Reno gave him an appreciative pat on the shoulder.

"Is this okay?" Reno asked.

He bent over and elevated my legs onto the bed, forcing me to turn around. I propped a pillow behind my head and he stuffed one underneath my right calf.

Lynn breezed in and set a glass of red juice on the table with a plate of cheese, crackers, and grapes. "You need anything, hon?" she asked smoothly, looking at me with faded blue eyes. "I'm so sorry to hear about your home, but we're glad you're okay and that's all that matters."

"Thanks, Lynn. I just need some rest." The reality hit me like a ton of bricks that I didn't have a home.

"Come on, Reno. Out," she snapped.

"Lynn, with all due respect, you'll need a fucking bulldozer to get me out of here."

She sighed impatiently and looked at me in a motherly way. "What this girl needs is sleep, and don't let her move that foot around. April, when you need to take a shower or do anything, just call." Then she glared at Reno. "I don't care what you two have going on—if she needs to use the toilet or shower, that's where I draw the line. You let the women help out with that."

He smirked hard and walked around to the right side of the bed as she closed the door. Reno kicked off his boots and unlatched his belt. I giggled a little when I heard it hit the floor.

"What's so funny?" he asked, not expecting an answer as he scooted next to me on my right.

"I can't believe you put that poster on the wall. Why did you decorate this room? Was your secret plan to kidnap me and hold me captive?"

He leaned back and situated himself so that his left arm slipped beneath my neck while his right hand stroked my stomach. "I wanted you to feel at home when you came to stay the night here. You wouldn't like my room."

"Why not?"

He shrugged. "I don't know. It's plain."

"So is vanilla ice cream, but it's my favorite flavor."

Reno deepened his voice. "Why did Sanchez call you Vanilla in that note?"

I bit my lip. "He was inside the store asking for vanilla candy and that's how it started."

His eyes became brutally sharp. "Austin hooked up surveillance outside the building months ago. Tell me what day and time he came in, and I'll get the footage. I want to know what that animal looks like."

"I have his phone number. You can always call him."

"Maybe I don't want him expecting company," Reno suggested in a way that sent a shiver up my spine. He stroked my stomach possessively. "I'm not going to sugarcoat it for you, April. Sanchez is mine. He put his hands on you, and he tried to set you on fire. That officially earned him top billing on my hit list. Do you want to tell me what he looks like or what kind of car he drives?"

Reno's touch was soft, but his face was granite. He looked down at me with cold eyes and a tight mouth. Those bullwhips of electricity were snapping in the room again.

"I think he drives a silver BMW. He's got black hair that's spiky, and one of those chin patches," I said, pointing below my lip. "He's a little taller than me, but not much."

"Any tattoos or scars?"

"A teardrop by his eye and a scorpion tattoo on his… I can't talk about this right now. I'm sorry—I'm still shaken up."

I relished the feel of Reno's powerful body, the sound of his breath, and the smell of his skin. It felt comforting to lie next to a man like him. Safe. I stroked his stubbly chin and he kissed my fingertips as we listened to the rain falling outside.

"Is there anything you lost that can't be replaced?" he finally asked.

Hope? It's what I wanted to say. Reno's family might have brought me in, but I'd never felt so lost. "Just the snow globes and my fish, Hermie. The snow globes were sentimental, you know? I love what you gave me, don't get me wrong, but it's not the same."

"Why not?"

"Because my dad gave them to me. They were special because he chose each one for a reason, and he actually made them himself."

"Talented."

"He was. Are your parents still alive?"

Reno's mouth pressed against my temple, and then he resumed staring at the ceiling. "They move around a lot. Last I heard, they found a pack up in South Dakota that might take them in. It's harder the older you get to be taken in by a Packmaster. They carefully consider every candidate's worth and what they can offer the pack. Most will turn down an aging couple. But our parents have wisdom and experience that would be an asset to any damn pack."

"Why is it so important for you to have packs instead of living alone?"

"There's safety in numbers for wolves—we have family to look after. It's instinctual; I don't know how to explain it. Some of our animal traits bleed into our human ones, I guess."

"How come you guys don't let them live with you?"

"It's not our way. The parents can't live under the same roof if the Packmaster is their son. I've only seen it happen once and the entire pack was dismantled. When our children become adults and go through the change, they have to leave the pack. They're not allowed to mate within the pack and stay."

"Why not?"

"More than one male might have feelings for a female and if she chooses one over another, it becomes problematic. It's also how new blood is maintained so that inbreeding never occurs. The men want to go out and find their own family, just as the women do."

"Do your parents visit?"

I felt his smile stretch across my temple. "Are you asking to meet my parents?"

"No," I blurted out.

Kind of lying. Kind of not.

He turned on his side and his voice softened around the edges. "Sounds like you are. You sure you don't want to meet my mom? You'd love her. She can shoot a bow and arrow and cook a mean chili. I can call her to fly down on a moment's notice."

"Don't you dare," I whispered, looking up at his amused eyes.

"You're right. I don't know what she'd think about her son dating a woman with a poster of another man at the foot of her bed."

A laugh pealed out of me and Reno perched up on his elbow, smiling wide. A rumbling laugh rolled through his chest and he looked at me in a way that gave me second thoughts about decisions that were rattling around in my head.

Then his hand smoothed down the cotton sweats Ivy had lent me, and I released a shallow breath.

"Is your foot bothering you?" he asked, lightly stroking his finger between my legs.

"Not anymore."

CHAPTER 22

OVER THE COURSE OF THE next month, Reno's visits to the house had become more infrequent. He'd moved to their second home so he could focus on hunting down Sanchez. That's how long I'd been living in the Weston house. Weston was the name of Lexi's brother who'd died years ago, someone she had never spoken of before, but Lexi opened up to me about her life during my stay. Since she wanted to spend more time with me, she offered the part-timers at the store a few extra shifts, which they eagerly accepted.

Lexi began pursuing her vision for Sweet Treats and Austin loaned her the money to expand. I told her I didn't feel right going back after what I'd done, but she adamantly refused to let me go. I helped her review inventory to determine what wasn't moving, and we reevaluated her strategy as a business owner.

"So here's what I'm thinking," Lexi began, propping her feet on an ottoman while fishing around in a bag of Doritos. "Austin wants me to move my business to the Breed side of town, but I'm concerned about the risk. We have regular customers and the store is in a prime location. What if we relocate and nothing sells? I'm going to scout the area and check out some of our competition to see what's going on. Seventy percent of our sales come from children, and not all Breeds can have children. I'm just not sure if there will be enough to keep the business afloat."

I reached down and scratched the bandage on my foot. After the last X-ray, the doctor had said it was healing remarkably well and told me to keep using the crutches.

"So your plan is to check out the local businesses?" I asked from the beanbag chair. I'd grown to love the cozy feel and ambiance of hanging out in the game room.

She crunched on another chip. "I'm going to open up a bakery."

I clapped. "Woo-hoo! It's about time."

"I want you to run the candy store and I'm going to run the bakery."

My jaw dropped. "Wait, what did you just say?"

"You know that store inside out, April. I want to give it over to you. Charlie left me the business and money, but maybe it was just because I'd been there the longest."

"You can't do that."

She laughed and crunched on another chip, licking the orange dust from her finger. "Oh, can't I? Look, I'm the one taking the risk with the bakery. I have no idea if these immortals are going to want cookies, and I plan to keep it open twenty-four hours a day, which means I'll have to hire someone who can bake. I'm thinking about a Vampire because they don't need to sleep. Austin says 'hell no,' but he's not the boss of me."

A throat cleared in the doorway and Austin leaned against the doorjamb. I caught Lexi biting her lip as he gave her a loaded glance.

"No Vampires," he said firmly.

"Austin, I need someone I can depend on who doesn't have a family to go home to, who can work all hours and—"

"Ladybug, I'm not having my woman working in the middle of the night with a Vampire. They may not require blood to survive, but it's too much temptation for them to work in close proximity to someone as tasty as you," he said with a dark laugh.

There was that chemistry, quietly zinging back and forth between those two like Ping-Pong balls.

"Who's up for horseshoes?" Denver yelled out from the hall.

Austin moved aside when Denver appeared in the doorway and reached for the top of the doorframe while cocking his eyebrow. His dark blond hair looked messy, like he'd just woken up. He gripped the frame and it punctuated the muscles in his biceps.

"It's too cold to play outside," Lexi complained.

"I smell bullshit," he said. "Sounds like you're afraid of losing."

Her face tightened.

"C'mon, Lexi. Put on your big-girl panties and see if you can swing with the men."

She angrily rolled up her bag of chips and Denver sauntered off with a wide grin.

"Lexi, you're just going to get yourself worked up," Austin said. "Last time you gave me the silent treatment for two days."

"That's because you took his side," she said sharply, walking toward him as I rolled over to stand up.

Austin grabbed her ass and kissed her hard. While they swapped tongue, I gathered my crutches and managed to climb to my feet.

"I took his side because you were cheating." He lightly patted her backside.

"How do you cheat at horseshoes?" she said gruffly, wiggling out of his arms and vacating the room.

Austin shook his head and centered his eyes on mine. "By screaming every time it was his turn to throw. Denver bought a bag of earplugs this morning, so I have a feeling this is going to get ugly real quick. Want to join?"

"Sure."

When I made it to the hall, Austin took the crutches from me and handed them to Wheeler, who headed downstairs. Then he threw me over his shoulder, and with a squeak, I held on to his back.

It was weird, but that's how they moved me around the house—like a sack of potatoes. I could walk on the crutches just fine, but anytime I got near the stairs, one of them would appear and end up carrying me up or down. I accepted their kindness without question. It was evident that Shifters respected women, looked after them, and had healthy relationships with the girls in their pack. They heeded their advice and treated them as equals. The only hierarchy going on had to do with the Packmaster, but Lexi said she was an alpha female and had some pull.

Over the past few weeks, I'd been growing out my platinum hair. I'd decided to change some things and give myself a fresh start. On the night of the fire, Trevor had found my purse in the back seat of his car when he arrived at the restaurant. It had slid beneath the passenger seat and only the strap was poking out. So he sent it over to the house along with my phone.

Yeah. *Sent.*

As much as I pleaded with him, Trevor refused to visit me at the house. So Lexi drove me into town quite frequently and I'd meet up with him for coffee at the bookstore or lunch. No matter how many times I kissed him and told him how much he meant to me, he'd pull away as if I'd rejected him by choosing to stay with Reno's family.

I couldn't talk to Trevor about Shifters, even knowing that he *was* one, because I'd given Reno my word and wanted to earn back his trust. Trevor must have sensed Reno and his family were Shifters too, and that's why he'd never liked them. I started to recall things he had brought up in conversation that hadn't made sense then but did now.

Austin carried me downstairs and out the front door, setting me down at the foot of the porch steps. I followed behind him on my crutches, frowning at the mud that began to stain the rubber bottoms. Now I knew why they always piled their shoes by the door.

Jericho was sitting on the hood of Denver's faded yellow truck on the left side of the yard. Denver and Lexi were milling around, preparing to throw. Austin snuck up behind Lexi, turned her around, and zipped her jacket all the way up to her neck.

It was a crisp sixty-two degrees, but with the breeze and no sun, it felt a lot cooler. Lexi had been lending me her clothes, so I wore a beige knit shirt with quarter-length sleeves. It didn't really go with my grey sweats and sneakers, but I didn't want to impose by getting picky about fashion.

Lexi threw the horseshoe and spun around, letting out a holler.

"Doesn't count," Denver said.

"The hell it doesn't!" she protested.

He threw out his left arm and pointed at the pin. "That was a woody. It doesn't count."

"What's a woody?" I asked Jericho.

He arched his brows suggestively and I shook my head.

"Austin, tell him it counts," she said, hands on her hips.

"Sorry, Ladybug. He's right."

She glowered and began to retreat. "I've changed my mind."

Austin snatched her wrist and spun her around. "Since when is Lexi Knight a quitter?"

"He takes it too seriously. I just want to have fun."

Jericho leaned toward me and lowered his voice. "This happens every time. Lexi hates losing. Austin said when they were kids she used to cheat her ass off at checkers by distracting him and moving the chips around."

"So why did Denver invite her to play?"

He reached around and tied his long hair back, but a loose strand slipped in front of his face. Jericho smiled with his jade eyes. "Denver likes to ruffle feathers; it's his hobby, in case you hadn't noticed. He has a way of getting under your skin because of how casual he is about things. Most of us can kick his ass at horseshoes, but he's a sport about losing, so this is actually fun for me to watch."

"You should let her win," I whispered.

"April thinks we should *let* Lexi win!" Jericho shouted and laughed all at once.

Oh yeah, these men were pure evil, trying to stage a catfight. I hit him in the shoulder with my crutch and Lexi turned around as if I had betrayed her.

"Sorry, Lexi," I said with a shrug. "Maybe it's just not your game."

"I'd like to see *you* try it," she dared.

"Fine." Challenge accepted.

Denver gave me a brief rundown of the rules and how to score points. Then he threw his horseshoe and it spun around the peg.

I handed my crutches over to Lexi. "Okay, go easy on me because I have a disability here," I said with a wide smile. All eyes were on me. *Careful not to smack someone in the head with that thing*, my inner voice teased.

When I swung my arm forward, the horseshoe hit the ground and rolled off to the right.

Austin whistled with his fingers and Jericho clapped. I had to laugh because that was a truly embarrassing first attempt.

Ben leaned against the truck and I caught him staring at my ass. It made me uncomfortable, and I flushed as Denver handed me a heavy horseshoe.

"I'll let you practice and throw a few," he said.

"Swing low," Ben suggested. "You need to bend over a little."

He was drunk by the glazed look in his eyes, and it was only three in the afternoon. I didn't care for Ben, and even though Wheeler had a sharp tongue, I felt like I could trust him. The rest of the house favored Ben because of his light humor, but underneath, I don't know. I couldn't put my finger on it.

Jericho smacked him in the back of the head, a look of annoyance on his face. Ben instantly shifted into his wolf and growled before trotting off. Wheeler leaned against the house, watching Ben's wolf from the corner of his eye.

I swallowed hard and tossed another one. This one cut short and hit the ground with a thud.

"Do you guys want to play laser tag tonight?" Denver suggested, stuffing his hands in his pockets and glancing toward Jericho.

"Sounds like fun," Lexi piped in, her voice mysteriously cloaked with politeness. "Can I be on the opposite team as you?"

"Yeah, but dickhead's on *my* team."

Dickhead was Denver's nickname for Jericho. It didn't seem to bother him.

"Well, I'm *not* having Ben on my team," Jericho announced. "He'll be tanked by then."

While they rattled on about their plans, I threw another horseshoe. This one landed on one of the wood planks that bordered the pit and I frowned.

"What about Mom and Maizy?" Lexi asked.

"Bring 'em along. Your mom can go in the arcade with Maizy while we mature adults are left to our devices," Denver said, tucking his hands beneath his armpits.

"What about..." Lexi didn't finish her sentence, but she didn't have to.

Austin's eyes skidded over to mine.

"I'm fine," I said. "If they have a place to sit, then I'm good."

Reno's badass motorcycle roared up the driveway, the engine throttling, but I couldn't see around the cars. The blue truck belonged to everyone, but the gunmetal-grey Chevy Camaro belonged to Wheeler. It was a classic beauty and he'd spent many mornings washing mud off the tires.

A thrill moved through me every time Reno drove up on his Triumph. We hadn't been intimate outside of a little friendly touching since my arrival. Lexi said Shifters respected privacy and, if asked, would travel to the other end of the house when they were doing the deed. I wasn't about to announce to anyone we were doing anything. I was a guest in their home—what kind of impression would that make on a family I was trying to make amends with?

Reno appeared, looking dangerously handsome. I loved it when he wore all black. Today he had on black cargo pants with a tight shirt that fit his body so perfectly, and the way it outlined his sculpted arms was downright sinful. Long sleeves, of course. His jaw was covered with stubble and he had on his mirrored aviators. He kicked a small rock with his boot as he stalked forward and then stopped short, looking me over from head to toe. I could feel his hot gaze behind those glasses and my knees weakened.

"Is this how you take care of my girl?"

All eyes fell on me and then swung back to him, confused.

Reno peeled off his shirt.

"Oh, Jesus. I think I've had enough of family hour." Jericho slid off the truck and swaggered off.

Reno slipped his shirt over my head, pulling my arms through the sleeves, which were still warm from his body heat. I dropped the horseshoe on the ground so he could roll up the sleeves, which went past my fingertips.

I could have objected. But that would have meant him covering up, and I loved staring at his bare chest. He was fit and strong—slender ropes of muscle along his arms and a broad torso with just a light dusting of hair. The chilly air hardened his nipples and I smiled at him.

He smiled back.

"You guys are a bag of nuts." Denver tossed his horseshoe to the ground. "Eight o'clock, everyone. No excuses this time," he said, his voice fading in the distance.

The pack dispersed and headed inside.

"What's he going on about?" Reno asked.

"Laser tag."

"Again?"

"He went with Jericho and Austin last week and they wouldn't shut up about it. I think Lexi is itching to kick his butt *Platoon* style."

"I could kick all their butts," Reno said with a wry smile. "How's your foot, princess?"

"Better. I tested my weight on it, and I don't feel any pain."

"Keep using the crutches," he ordered, straightening my shirt and pulling the tips of my hair away from the collar. "Damn, I love the new color growing out. Are you keeping it?"

I shrugged lightly. "It's looking that way."

"Has someone been showing you how to play horseshoes?" he asked, brow slightly arched.

"I'm doing pretty good."

He glanced over my shoulder at the horseshoe by the house and the other three feet away. Then he gripped my shoulders and turned me around. I hopped in a circle and he bent down and put the horseshoe in my hand.

Every inch of Reno was pressed behind me. His fingers curled around my wrist as he gently swung my right arm forward and back, left arm tight around my midriff and his mouth lightly grazing the back of my right ear.

"Like that," he said in a caged voice. "It's all in the release." His words heated my body, and as if sensing it, he seductively ran his nose along my neck and inhaled deeply.

Tingles spread across the lower half of my body and when I shifted my hips, he moaned, tightening against my back.

Reno swung my throwing arm forward and I opened my hand. The horseshoe tumbled and hit the side of the house.

"You really suck at this," I said, deciding I needed more lessons.

Then his mouth was on my neck, and the short bristles of whiskers on his jaw scratched my skin. "Do I?"

I leaned against him and threw my head back. "Yeah. You're terrible."

His right arm journeyed south and his fingers slipped inside my sweatpants. My breath caught.

Three hard claps sounded to our right and I jumped, straightening my shirt like a busted teenager when I saw Lynn on the porch with an oven mitt tucked beneath her arm.

Reno didn't let go and I wriggled against him.

"Supper is almost ready," she announced with a hard glare. "This isn't a brothel, so let's keep that behind closed doors."

I snorted and turned around. "You are not going to get me on that woman's good side if you keep this up. She used to like me until you started spending the night in my bed."

"Good point," he said, kissing my mouth. "Next time, you come to my bed."

I placed a delicate peck on the tiny scar on his lip, something he hadn't caught on to, but that was my special little place I'd claimed as mine.

CHAPTER 23

"I'll sweeten the pot with an extra hundred," Ben offered.

Denver stood up and curled in his lips. His sharp whistle cut through the air and caught the attention of Reno, who was strutting through the automatic doors of the bowling alley.

"Shit, I'd do it for free." Jericho flipped his hair back, revealing a charismatic smile.

"Don't," Denver warned, pointing his finger. "You're going to get us kicked out of here."

"Chicken." Ben sneered as he leaned back in his plastic chair and laced his fingers behind his head.

"Shut it," Denver snapped.

Jericho stood up, peeled off his shirt, and climbed on top of the table. Denver yanked him so hard by the arm that they both went crashing to the floor.

Three girls at a nearby table stood up and applauded.

Denver sat up with a cocksure grin and jumped to his feet, winking at them.

Jericho slowly rolled over and towered over Denver with his lean body and a lone tattoo of a guitar on his left arm. He didn't have to wink. The girls were practically losing their virginity all over again watching a sex-laced smile spread across his face.

"Same old drama." Reno kissed me on the neck. I smiled at him because I loved how a tough guy like Reno wasn't afraid to show his affection for me in public. "How many rounds have they had?" he asked, taking a seat on my right.

"I lost count at three."

"Where's everyone else?"

"Austin and Lexi are checking if the room is ready. Lynn's in there with Maizy," I said, thumbing toward the arcade.

"Well, if these boys get too rowdy, Lynn should head home."

"She walked by a minute ago and I have a feeling she's all for that plan. This doesn't seem like the kind of thing Lynn does for fun, so she's probably bored. You don't think this atmosphere is bad for Maizy with all your cussing and wild behavior?"

"Shifter life." He shrugged it off, taking a sip of my orange soda. "Swearing doesn't make a child grow up to be dysfunctional—an uncaring family does. Maizy has more love and protection within this pack than she'll ever know in the human world."

"But they're not Shifters."

He sighed and set down the cup. "Lynn's brought up the idea a few times about sending her off to a boarding school when she gets older, and Austin said over his dead body. I don't know that Austin is going to win that battle because she's Lynn's daughter, and since she's unmated, he has no say. Lynn and Ivy homeschool her, but I don't think that's working out. She needs to be around kids her age, and most Shifters don't like their kids playing with humans. Did you eat?"

"I ordered some fries."

His eyes narrowed. "Why didn't you order a meal?"

"Because she's afraid someone's going to hock a loogie in her food," Trevor said from behind me. He sat in the bucket seat to my left and took a bite of his hot dog. "Isn't that right, babe?"

My cheeks heated and Reno's lips twitched.

"Don't laugh at me," I said, feeling a tad embarrassed. "I saw it on a show once. They had hidden cameras."

His lips pressed tighter, fighting the urge to laugh.

Jericho pulled his concert shirt over his head and I caught Trevor peering up at him. I'd decided bringing Trevor along would be a good way for him to get to know the guys who had been looking out for me. A weird vibe was going on with all the men that no one addressed, but I noticed the sideways glances at one another.

"Well, you just robbed those lovely ladies of a fucktastic show," Jericho said, pulling his hair away from his collar. "Never dare a musician to dance naked on a table for fifty dollars, Ben. You'll lose every time."

"Show-off," Ben murmured, taking a swig of beer.

"It's ready!" Lexi's bright voice called out from the entranceway that led to the laser-tag room. "We've got the room to ourselves for the full hour. So are we all good on teams?"

"I say every man for himself," Wheeler suggested, walking past her with Denver close behind him.

"Go on, Trevor," I said in a low voice. "You'll have fun and you can get out all your aggression in there. Admit it. You want to go Rambo on their ass."

He shoved the rest of the hot dog in his mouth. "Fuck it. I'm in," he said with a mouthful before taking a sip of my drink and walking off. I'd spent the better part of an hour talking him into it, and no matter how much he resisted the idea, Trevor couldn't say no to me.

"Come on, Reno. We need one more," Lexi yelled out, tying her long hair in a ponytail. "Ivy's playing too, so that makes an odd number."

"Go have some fun. It'll only be an hour and I'd rather you go than sit around being bored. It's not like we're attached at the hip," I said with a short laugh. "Lynn stuffed one of my paperbacks in her purse, so I'm going to catch up on my reading."

He kissed my neck, working his way to my mouth, giving me second thoughts.

"I know what you're up to, Reno. Cut it out and go play."

"You sure?"

I smiled at him with closed lips, feeling melancholy. "Yeah. I'm sure. Maybe next time I'll be able to join you guys."

"What's going on in that head of yours?" he wondered more than asked.

My heart sank. Reno kissed me and walked off, giving me another glance before rounding the corner. I could still smell his cologne on me and already missed the rough feel of his hand against my skin.

I'd been considering Maddox's offer. It seemed like a crazy

bargain, but he came from a different world. Maddox was giving me an opportunity to get my feet on the ground, and it had nothing to do with a physical relationship. I still had a substantial amount of debt to clear with him and that weighed heavily on my conscience. Lexi wanted to hand Sweet Treats over to me, but she still had to get the new store up and running, so the transition wouldn't be immediate. Even still, I didn't want to take over a business with all the debt I had incurred. We hadn't discussed details, like what percentage of the business I would own, if any. Maddox had said that each day that I delayed giving him my decision would cost me.

As for Sanchez, Reno had questioned two of Delgado's men for information. He hadn't talked about it with me and I'd learned the details from Lexi, who'd heard it through Austin. I was afraid for Reno's safety and I'd do anything to keep him from getting hurt. He would probably lose interest in me if I went with Maddox, and maybe then he'd stop searching for Sanchez. It didn't feel right to expect a man who had already done so much for me to continue risking his life.

"Miss April?"

"I glanced to my left and Maizy was sticking her tongue through the tiny gap where one of her bottom baby teeth used to be.

"Where's your mom?"

"In the bathroom. She told me to stand here with you."

"Sit down, sweetie," I said, patting the chair beside me. "Are you having fun?"

"Uh-huh. But I can't get enough tickets to get the ring I want. I spent all my money, and that means we're going home. Mr. Reno sometimes gives me extra, but he's not here."

She was upset, holding about ten tickets in her hand. I suspected Lynn wasn't letting her spend too much in there, and I knew how to work those machines from a misspent youth at the Nickel Arcade.

I had a few bills in my back pocket, so I grabbed my crutches and swung my feet toward the game room. "Come on, Maizy. Let's get you that ring."

I found one of the games notorious for spitting out obscene

amounts of tickets if you hit the right spot. A light would flash around in a circle and you had to stop it between certain slots to earn rewards. I worked my magic and within minutes, Maizy had a wad of tickets and a priceless smile.

"Is that enough?" she asked excitedly.

"Go take it to the counter and have the man count it."

She ran off before I could ask her about Lynn. I looked around at the tables and didn't see her anywhere.

The bathroom was within sight, so I went in.

"Lynn? Are you okay? I'll watch over Maizy if you aren't feeling well," I called out. "Lynn?"

I peered down to look beneath the stall doors on the right. "Oh my God, Lynn!"

I threw down the crutches and hopped to the far stall. The door was semi-closed, so I pushed it open and found Lynn slumped against the wall. Bright blood trickled down her face from a cut on her head.

"Lynn, can you hear me? Did you fall?" I shook her a little and when her eyelids fluttered, I breathed a sigh of relief.

Until I heard a click behind my head.

I turned my head and saw an unfamiliar man aiming a gun at me.

"Sanchez sent us to keep an eye on you."

Holy smokes, this isn't happening.

"Where is he?"

The man tugged on his black goatee and I couldn't read his expression because of the black baseball hat pulled over his eyebrows. I hadn't realized how important eyebrows were when it came to facial expressions. "He's killing your boyfriend."

I opened my mouth to scream and he bent over. "My friend is watching over that sweet little girl, so keep your mouth shut or we'll drive her out to the lake and throw her in."

Adrenaline poured through my body, mixing with fear and anger.

"If you want to sit and think about it, I'll put a hole in her head," he said, waving the gun at Lynn. "Now get up before someone comes in here. Just remember that my friend has the girl, so do exactly as I say."

He put the safety back on and tucked the gun in his pants. I picked up my crutches and walked toward the door, glancing over my shoulder at Lynn. He laughed to himself, no doubt thrilled that I wasn't going to be running away with this boot on my foot.

Denver stalked in my direction from the laser room and the man fell back a little. He gave me a menacing glare, and I turned to Denver, struggling to appear calm.

"Where's Peanut?"

"Huh?"

"Maizy," he said. He was sweating and had an anxious look on his face. "Something isn't right."

"Everything's fine, Denver. Lynn took her home. She... she had a stomachache. That's all."

His brows pushed together, forming a vertical crease between them. "That it? Are you sure? It just feels like..."

"Go back to your game before you run out of time. Your hour will be up soon and we came all this way," I said, trying to relax. The guy behind me had a gun, and I didn't want to test how willing he was to use it on Denver.

"When did they leave?"

I tapped my crutch on his leg. "About five minutes ago. You know Lynn won't answer her cell while she's driving. They're fine."

Denver reluctantly walked back to the game room where the door had been left open. He searched the massive building with his eyes as if Maizy might appear out of the rafters. I wondered how he could have known something was wrong, but even more terrifying was that Maizy was nowhere in sight.

"Where is she?" I hissed, turning to look at the man.

"I want you to head out those doors," he said, pointing toward the exit.

I wondered if I could knock him out with my crutches, but they didn't weigh much and it would be too much of a risk if it meant Maizy getting hurt.

Enough people had been hurt already.

"Bring Sanchez out," I demanded.

He tapped his fingers on the outside of his shirt, over the gun. I turned around, swinging on my crutches toward the door in a slow pace as I glanced over at the laser-tag entrance. I started to get visions of what could be going on in there and my heart sped up. Three of the guys had brought ski masks, fatigue pants, and combat boots to get into character. They were all armed with toy guns.

Except Sanchez.

"Everyone's going to hear it if he goes on a rampage in there," I said to Goatee, who shadowed behind me.

"Silencer," was all he replied.

My heart palpitated and my knees got weak. Because I wasn't watching where I was going, I tripped and fell on my stomach.

Goatee looked pissed, as if I'd done it on purpose. He grabbed my arms with bruising force, and I curled them against my body, trying to stay down.

"Get your hands off her," a belligerent voice said. "Is this asshole bothering you?"

Three college-aged guys, who had surpassed their limit at the bar, crowded around us. I'd seen these types before, always starting shit with pool sticks and getting kicked out.

"Mind your goddamn business," Goatee spat out.

Wrong thing to say to three drunk guys itching for a good old-fashioned fistfight. They grabbed the scruff of his collar and began to pound the crap out of his face. When his shirt rose, one found the gun and exclaimed, "Holy shit!" and took it out. A few people scrambled, searching for help.

I left the crutches behind and hurried toward the laser-tag room, putting light pressure on my foot.

I swung the door open and entered a dark hallway with doors on opposite sides. I limped to the door on the right and slowly opened it. Everything was illuminated by black lights, and a fog machine made the air dense. I heard the occasional clattering of a fake gun in the distance and feet stomping across the floor from the upper level.

Three levels, Denver had said. I quickly glanced down, glad I'd worn a color that didn't show up in the black light, although I had no idea what my hair might have looked like.

I cautiously moved through the room and hid behind a corner wall with holes that allowed me to look around.

Someone snatched my arm and I spun around to slap him when Denver caught my wrist.

"What are you doing in here?"

"Someone has Maizy. I don't think she's inside. He's probably armed."

Denver dropped his toy gun and his upper lip twitched. It was a scary look I'd never seen before. "Who?"

"Sanchez. He's in here looking for Reno."

Denver wiped his hand over his mouth. "Nobody ever beats Reno at this game. Look, I'm going after Maizy. You shouldn't be in here, but if you're one of those chicks who doesn't listen, then make sure you warn everyone you pass and tell them what's up." He unstrapped his vest and it dropped to the ground. "They'll spread the word and get everyone out without tipping him off. If you see Sanchez, scream like hell. Reno will find you real quick. You got it?"

I nodded, shocked he hadn't just told me to get out. Denver was looking out for his pack, but his priority was Maizy. Lexi had told me that he had taken over as a watchdog—a term they used for a Shifter who acts as a protector for a child or young woman. It's instinctual, and I could see it by the fire in his eyes.

Denver walked off and I made my way up the ramp.

CHAPTER 24

R ENO WATCHED IVY DASH BY and he lowered his plastic gun. Game or not, he couldn't shoot at a woman. The lights on the vest had become a nuisance, but that's how the game kept score. He had this one in the bag. Denver always stayed on the lower levels to ambush those who went back to the base to recharge, so Reno stayed up top to score more points.

The layout wasn't much different from other laser-tag places they'd been to. Reno preferred outdoor games like paintball, but the girls weren't up for that. They didn't like standing in the rain, and laser tag had air-conditioning and nachos. Each level had barriers and obstacles to maneuver around. The fog machine was a pain in the ass, as were all the neon-colored patterns splashed on the walls and carpet.

Reno regretted like hell April wasn't able to join them. After everything she'd been through, that woman was a trouper, and that was a fucking understatement. She helped around the house as much as she could and spent every morning looking for rentals in the newspaper. Not once had she complained about having lost everything, not to mention the pain of her recovery. He'd had a few sleepless nights thinking about how it could have been a hell of a lot worse. There had been several nights in the beginning when she'd moan in her sleep from the pain. Reno would bring her pain medicine, but she refused to take anything stronger than ibuprofen. Seeing that was all the fuel he needed to start tracking down Sanchez—the elusive sonofabitch.

Lexi quietly sprinted to the lower level and Reno fired a warning shot, smiling as she let out a squeal. Lexi wasn't half-bad at this game and had taken off her shoes, which made it more difficult to hear her stealthily moving around.

"Goddammit, you can't do that!" he heard Denver complaining downstairs.

Reno took another calming breath. Something didn't feel right in his gut, but he couldn't put his finger on it. Maybe a man who had seen war shouldn't be playing a game like this, or maybe it was something else.

"Shhh," a voice said from the right.

That snagged his attention. Someone had broken the rules and teamed up. Footsteps moved to his right. Reno backed up against a pillar and spied through an opening. A red laser light beamed in and he squatted down, recognizing a tactical distraction when he saw one. That meant the other party was engaging in a flanking maneuver.

He wasn't a fan of playing a sitting duck. Reno waited until he heard the shuffle of someone growing closer, then he knifed around the corner and fired.

"Fuck!" his opponent shouted. Jericho opened fire on Reno, but nothing happened. Then he pulled his black mask away and his hair spilled over his shoulders. He glanced down at his blinking vest, muttered a curse, and stalked off.

Trevor suddenly appeared and Reno raised his gun. Trevor shoved it to the side and closed the distance between them. "Maybe I'm nuts or having post-traumatic stress," he whispered, "but I swear I just saw Sanchez."

Every muscle tensed. "*What?*"

Trevor held his finger up to his lips in a "hush" signal. Reno peered through a hole in a curved pillar, scoping out the room. He couldn't make out any movement and the noise downstairs was creating a distraction.

Reno mouthed "Where?" at Trevor, who pointed toward the other ramp that led to the lower levels.

Reno unbuckled his vest and let it drop to the floor. He stripped out of his button-up shirt and released his gun from the holster strapped over his tank top. Sanchez had made one hell of a mistake picking this location for an attack—he didn't know who the fuck he was dealing with.

Shadows moved about the room and Reno had to be careful not to target the wrong person. This could end badly if he had to fire off his gun in a human establishment. Reno had taken out one of Sanchez's partners during a confrontation two weeks ago when the man pulled a gun and began shooting. After that, Sanchez had taken his focus off April and targeted Reno, which was exactly what Reno wanted. It's why he'd been avoiding the pack—he wanted to hunt him down.

Reno crept up a ramp and charged forward to cover Ivy's mouth.

"Get out," he whispered in her ear. "Trouble. If you see the others, tell them *level red*. Don't stop to look back. Just get the hell out of here as quick as you can and be on standby to call a Packmaster for backup if we need it."

Reno unstrapped her vest and Ivy took off, crouching low as she made her way down the ramp.

Reno went in the opposite direction, toward the left side of the room, gun in hand, making his way down. Only in wolf form could he easily sniff out Sanchez, but Reno didn't have control over his wolf and might get shot, or get someone else shot. Not to mention that after shifting back, he'd be walking around as naked as a jaybird. They had to exercise extreme caution around humans since there were strict Breed laws. Everyone knew the risks of what could happen if the rest of the world found out they existed. War.

Halfway down the ramp, he did a quick scan of the room and leapt over the railing, crawling toward the back of the room. He could hear Denver hollering somewhere and the sound of laser guns firing.

He made eye contact with Austin, who quickly understood they were in danger.

Maybe it was the look in Reno's eyes, the fact that he was on all fours, or maybe the Beretta in his hand. Austin unstrapped his vest. He was ten yards in front of Reno and all Reno could do was mouth Sanchez's name. Austin must have been a hell of a lip-reader because his eyes sharpened and he started scoping the outer perimeter of the room.

Lexi's wolf scurried in and skidded to a halt next to Austin.

Something must have spooked her to shift in public, but she was also new and not always in control of her animal. Reno recognized her silver fur and white face with black-tipped ears. Austin mouthed a profane word and rolled his eyes as he curved his arm around her neck to keep her still.

It grew eerily quiet. Footsteps tramped overhead and Reno's eyes tracked the movement.

Reno crouched low and ran across the room to the ramp that led upstairs. Austin remained in human form so he could control Lexi's wolf. A good man fought to the death for his woman. Her wolf was too green and leaving her behind to hunt for Sanchez could endanger her life.

Wheeler crawled into sight and sat with his back against the wall. He pointed at a divider to the left and Reno turned his attention that way.

Reno cupped his wrist that held the gun, scanning the room. That's when he heard the distinct click of a trigger release. Metal snapped on the plastic wall beside his head.

He hauled ass in the opposite direction and dove behind a pillar. As Reno made his way up the ramp, he heard another muffled clack.

When he reached the upper level, he flattened his back against a wall, looking at every shadow in the foggy haze. He couldn't risk firing his gun haphazardly or the humans would hear and come running into danger. If he was going to use his gun, then the bullet couldn't miss.

Pain sliced through his calf and he winced. "Fffuck," he hissed. *Sanchez had a silencer.*

Amid chaos, he peered through a small opening and saw her.

April.

She limped up the ramp, her determined eyes wide and alert. When she reached the center of the room, every muscle in Reno's body tensed like a cord being pulled taut. Dammit. She was going to offer herself to Sanchez to save his pack. Reno knew it would draw Sanchez out of the shadows and could work in their favor, but one wrong move could mean life or death.

"Sanchez, if you want me, here I am," she yelled in a confident voice.

Walking up the ramp in my boot was an arduous challenge, but I finally made it to the second level. Ivy had rushed by, imploring me to get out. The blanket of fog made it difficult to see in the semi-dark room, but I kept my eyes alert. My stomach twisted into a nervous knot while I tried to decide if I was looking for Reno or Sanchez. But in my heart, I knew what had to be done to end this. Sanchez wasn't after Reno, so I needed to lure him out to give the others a chance to get out safely.

I peered over the railing and my breath caught. Austin had his strong arms wrapped around a silver wolf and his eyes sliced over to mine. He pointed for me to get out and I shook my head. The wolf was struggling to get free and he tightened his grip, whispering into her ear. That wasn't just an ordinary wolf—that was Lexi, my good friend.

When I caught Austin's eyes floating up to the ceiling, I knew Sanchez was on the upper floor. Instead of crossing the room, I moved toward the walkway in the back that led to the next ramp up. When Wheeler saw me moving about, his eyes blazed, but I ignored him and kept moving.

A strange sound popped and it made my heart squeeze in my chest. When I reached the top, I decided to end the game.

"Sanchez, if you want me, here I am," I shouted, uncertain which level he was on. I floated behind a wall and peered through one of the gaps. "Looks like you underestimated me. If this is all about pride, you'll never get it back. You can kill me, but you've still lost."

I moved around the wall and winced when my foot began throbbing. "Did Delgado find out what you've been up to?"

"As a matter of fact, he did." Sanchez appeared out of nowhere and snatched at my right arm, throwing me off balance.

I let out a squeak and staggered as he dragged me to the center of the room.

"I should have done you in a long time ago, Vanilla. But I couldn't get near your piece-of-shit trailer because of some mongrel.

Got him with a screwdriver after he bit my arm, but he kept hanging around and I couldn't get a shot at him. So I came to your shop. Never thought you'd actually come up with the money."

"Take your hands off her."

Reno emerged from the far end of the room. He moved through the fog like a man serving a death warrant. I noticed a dark stain on his pants below the knee and the level of fear in me spiked. He aimed a gun at Sanchez, holding his wrist steady.

"Should have known you were the one with the screwdriver," Reno said, his voice so in control it was volatile.

"Sorry about your pooch," he said insincerely. Sanchez jerked me closer and hooked his left arm around my torso, latching his hand on my right breast. His voice held a smile. "Have you seen these pretty tits of hers?" He placed the gun against my temple and squeezed my breast painfully.

A muscle in Reno's jaw tightened, but he held his gun steady.

"Yeah, I thought so," Sanchez continued. "I like that little mole right in the middle—I'd call that a bull's-eye. You got yourself a real winner here with this one. She's very business savvy, but it didn't take much for her to show me her titties."

No, I wasn't playing *this* game either.

I gripped his elbow, pulled it up, and sank my teeth into his forearm. Hard.

Sanchez slammed the butt of his gun against my temple. Guess he didn't hit hard enough because my teeth went deeper into his skin. "Motherfucker!" he shouted.

"Just for that, I'm going to knock out your teeth before I kill you," Reno said in a malevolent voice, his body rock solid.

I stopped biting and chills swept over me as I looked at Reno's cold expression. Sanchez yanked me against him and extended his arm. Seeing the gun aimed at Reno seized my heart with fear.

This wasn't like the movies where there was a big standoff and a lot of negotiating. Sanchez didn't have a good hold of me, so I pried back his fingers and twisted my body around until he let go. He got a handful of my hair and I yelped, kicking him in the shin. Reno surged forward and at that very moment, Trevor appeared and rushed in front of him. Sanchez fired his gun and it made a muffled crack.

"No!" I screamed.

Tiny flashes of glittery light sparked the air and I almost fainted when Trevor fell to the ground, taking a bullet for Reno.

Before Sanchez could fire off another round, I struck his arm, hoping to throw off his aim. He yanked out some of my hair during the struggle, and before I knew it, Reno was on him. He wrested the gun out of his hand, tucked his own weapon behind his back, and slammed his granite fist into Sanchez's mouth. A tooth fell out along with a stream of blood.

Sanchez let go of my hair.

While I heard the pounding of fist to bone, I dove to the floor and smoothed my hands over Trevor's chest.

"Trev, can you hear me? Somebody help us!"

He smiled lazily, sexily, sadly. I brushed the hair away from his eyes as my tears splashed down.

"Don't cry, babe. Your nose swells and you look like Rudolph."

The sound of footsteps trampled into the room.

"You got him?" Austin shouted. He still fought to keep Lexi's wolf under control as she lunged toward Sanchez. Her lips were peeled back, revealing her sharp canines when she snapped and snarled. "Lexi, *no!*"

I threw my attention back on Trevor.

Jericho stalked forward and fell to his knees. "Where's he hit?"

Wheeler's strong hands coaxed me up and I fought against him. "Come on, you don't need to see this."

"See what? Let me go! Trevor needs help!"

Trevor looked up at Jericho. "Get her out."

"No, no, no!"

Wheeler's arms locked around me tightly and he lifted my legs, carrying me out of the room at a quick pace. I stretched out to see around his shoulder and watched Austin kneel down beside Trevor.

"What's he going to do?" I whimpered, not knowing enough about Shifters to abate my fear.

Wheeler lowered his eyes to mine. "Save him, if it's not too late."

My bad mojo was like a hurricane, injuring everyone within its path.

Wheeler yelled out as we went down the second ramp. "Ben!"

I squinted from the bright lights as the cool air hit us with a swing of the door. The sounds of bells and arcade music blasted, but it was a weeknight and not that busy. The attendant had taken off, assuming that we would be another half hour. Wheeler kept walking toward the exit and pushed it open with his shoulder.

I wiggled to get down when I saw Lynn sitting on the curb. Denver held Maizy and her arms were wrapped around his neck, her head on his shoulder.

"Is it secure?" Wheeler yelled out.

"The bad guy is over there," Maizy declared, pointing her finger toward the right. "Denny, I'm cold."

Wheeler spun halfway around and I glanced at the side of the building and saw a man lying unconscious on his stomach. By his bruised face and the bloodstains on his shirt, Denver had taken care of that problem. I couldn't have imagined what that scene must have been like—Denver coming out to find Maizy in the clutches of a dangerous man.

"Is everyone okay?" Denver said in a quiet voice.

Wheeler set me down, and while they talked, I went to Lynn. "Do you need to go to the hospital? Lynn, let me see your head."

She was holding a wad of paper towels from the bathroom over her head to stanch the bleeding. "I'm not sure I need to go to the emergency room, but I may need stitches."

"Well, we can't wait until the morning. Let me see."

Her fingers and arm were covered in dried blood. Lynn had always maintained her appearance—perfect makeup and her clothes modest and ironed. It was hard to see her pasty complexion smeared with blood that was matted in her blond hair. She was a good woman and didn't deserve something like this happening to her.

"Wheeler, she needs to go to the hospital right now. Can you take her? This shouldn't wait until the morning. She was unconscious when I found her and might have a concussion."

Wheeler cursed under his breath and looked at Denver. "I'll use the truck. Tell Austin where I am… and where the fuck is Ben?"

"Where do you think?" Denver said. "Five minutes into the game, he slipped out the door. I saw him in the back room playing cards when I was looking for Maizy."

"You have got to be shitting me," Wheeler said in a flat voice. He bent over and helped Lynn to her feet. She wobbled a little and I gave Wheeler her purse.

Maizy looked up and her lashes were wet. "Mommy, can I come?"

"No, Peanut," Denver said. "Your mama needs to get fixed up, so you're coming home with Denny." He spoke in an easy and relaxed voice, keeping her calm as worry filled her eyes. "I think we should put on your favorite movie tonight. Let me see, what was that movie called? Oh yeah, *King Kong*."

She smiled a little. "That's not it, silly."

Wheeler helped Lynn to the truck and Denver lingered.

"Go on and take her home," I said. "Everything's under control. I think."

"What's that mean?"

My lip quivered and I sat on the curb, still shaking. "Trevor." I hugged my knees and dropped my forehead on them, tears spilling.

The door behind me clicked and heavy footsteps approached. Reno came into view only briefly before he scooped me into his arms and carried me toward his motorcycle.

"Where's Trevor?" I whispered against his neck, trembling with fear.

"Austin had us clear out. He wouldn't shift with us in the room. He's in the fucking closet, and he needs to come out."

I laughed against his shoulder.

"Is that funny?"

"Kind of, yeah."

Reno didn't kiss or coddle me one bit. He put me in his leather jacket and fired up the engine of his Triumph, waiting for me to hold on tight so we could ride off on his badass bike.

"Your leg is bleeding," I said. I didn't have a helmet, so Reno could hear me fine.

"Don't worry about me, April. It's not the first time I've been shot."

Heads turned as they always do whenever a motorcycle drives by, and I placed my right cheek on his back and nestled into him. He didn't voice any complaints.

I realized that when romance novels happened in real life, it didn't feel as thrilling. Bad guys sometimes won, people you loved got hurt, and maybe stuff like that would ruin that fragile piece of strength left in you.

By the time we got to the house, I was shaking from the cool air. When Reno didn't see Denver's yellow truck in the driveway, he sent him a text message. Denver replied and said he'd taken Maizy to the movies so she'd fall asleep and stop worrying about her mom. I can only imagine what a frightening experience that was for her and how she was probably crying on the way home. I admired the way Denver looked after her, and not because he had to, but because he loved her.

The wood floor creaked as Reno carried me inside the house and set me on my feet. He flipped a switch and a small lamp lit up the corner of the living room to our right. I sat down to remove my sneaker and walking boot, adding them to the pile of shoes they kept in the corner. They didn't always adhere to the rules, but they made an effort since the outdoor mud created a mess. Reno helped me up and unzipped the oversized leather jacket he'd made me put on, tossing it on a chair to the right.

"Maybe you should leave that on," he said absently, staring at the boot.

"It's fine. My foot needs to breathe before it swells up. Should we call Austin?" I asked, anxious to get a status on Trevor.

As if on cue, his phone rang.

"Reno," he answered. "Yeah, we're here. Did Denver call you? … Good, then you might want to get in touch with Wheeler and see when they'll be back. You know how long they make you wait in those damn human hospitals. … Right."

His eyes locked on mine while Austin continued talking on the other line. Reno watched me, listening astutely.

"No sweat. Later."

"Well? What did he say about Trevor?"

Reno set his phone on a small table and kicked off his shoes. "Your friend is fine."

I exhaled a sigh of relief, covering my eyes for a second. *Thank God.*

"It wasn't without a fight. He refused to shift with anyone in the room. Austin cleared everyone out except Jericho, and even then, he had to force his alpha magic on him. It took a few shifts to heal up his injuries, but he's all right. They rented out the laser room for another hour so they could clean up the mess. Prince is helping them out."

"Prince?" I smiled at the name.

"A Packmaster from our old territory. He and Austin have a respectful alliance, although we seem to be too much in his debt these days. Come on, let's get you upstairs."

"Wait, Reno. We need to talk." I pressed my back against the wall, scared as hell at what I was about to say to him. When he stepped forward, I held out my arm, my hand flat against his chest. "Please. I can't do this anymore."

"Sanchez is taken care of," he said in a stony voice, pushing his body against my hand. "I personally made sure of that."

I shook my head as he drew even closer. "It's not just Sanchez. What if Delgado comes after me?"

Darkness swirled in his eyes and he placed his hand over mine. I could feel his heart pounding against his chest in a steady rhythm. "If anyone ever touches you again, they'll answer to me. That's a promise. No one comes after you without coming through me first."

I jerked my hand away, startled by his declaration to protect me. "That's my point. It's not worth the risk. We barely know each other, and you can't keep sticking your neck out for a mortal. These are my problems and I need to fix them before I get involved with anyone. It's not fair to you and it's not fair to me. It's not fair to *us*."

Reno dropped his hand and stuffed it in his pocket, fishing around. "What are you saying?"

My heart constricted and I bit the inside of my lip to keep from breaking down. The nearness of him made it difficult to be candid.

"I'm not part of your world. I'm not even part of Trevor's world, even though he wants to live in mine. I'm bad mojo, and that's just the way it's always been. Everything—my whole life. Rose was lucky. She found a great guy and got out of this mess before it touched her. It's not just the debt, Reno. I've had bad luck following me my entire life. Did you know that when I was twelve I was taken to juvie? I was arrested with a few friends for joyriding. Maybe it wouldn't have been such a big deal if we hadn't crashed into a department-store window. My mom had to pick me up from the station, and do you know what she told me years later? That she met her first dealer because of me."

Reno's lips curled in and he shook his head.

"She blamed her addiction on me because of all the trouble I'd put her through—all the embarrassment. She said I was worthless and lavished my little sister with all the affection she refused me. I spent two months in juvie, and the only one who came to visit was my dad."

Then the tears came and I wiped my face, reliving the visceral pain of my mother's rejection. "I was so scared he would end up hating me, so I tried to be a better daughter. My trailer is paradise compared to where I used to live, Reno. So you think I look like some sweet girl, but I also made my dad go buy chicken."

"What are you talking about, April?" He stepped forward, still moving his hand around in his pocket. "I don't follow what you're saying. Look, a lot of shit went down tonight—"

"No," I said tersely, still crying. "I made my dad pick up dinner that night. He didn't want to go because of the rain and said he'd make some macaroni, but I begged him for fried chicken. I even pulled out the *pretty please with sugar on top* routine. Because of me, he left the house and that was the last time I ever saw him. Do you understand how hard it is to know that because of you, someone else died?" I gasped and wiped the tears, remembering the words of blame my mother had said to me. "The last thing I said to my father was 'don't forget the rolls.' What kind of last words are those?" I covered my eyes and gathered strength. *You can handle this*, my inner voice whispered reassuringly. "All these years later and it still hasn't sunk in. I wish I could have told him I loved him and how he meant the world to me. They found his car in the river. It didn't hit me then like it does now that I'll never have a father to walk me down the aisle. I've brought nothing but pain to everyone I've loved. My last boyfriend slept with other girls because I pushed him away. But maybe I push a little because I'm scared of getting hurt. I didn't give him what he wanted, so he got it somewhere else."

Reno pulled his hand out of his pocket, holding it in a tight fist as if he wanted to hit something. "What's his name?"

I sniffed, looking down at his fist. "What's in your hand?" Something red poked out from the side.

Reno surreptitiously slid his closed fist into his pocket. He put his left hand on the wall above me and leaned in tight. "Listen to me and listen good. You're not bad mojo, April. You were a young girl who had a shit life. You've paid your dues and then some. That's the luck of the draw, and it pisses me off to hear that your ex treated you like mud on his boot."

"But that's not—"

"Quiet," he interrupted.

I blinked in astonishment—Reno had never spoken to me that curtly. His eyes looked like static and I tried to hold his gaze. But then I saw something soften in his features, and his brown eyes melted like dark chocolate.

"Yeah, you fucked up a few times. But I'm not going anywhere. That's what makes me different from every other guy you've met. I'm a Shifter, and we don't walk out on our women. You're not your mother. You're human. You make mistakes. So you made a few bad choices. Does that mean you don't deserve happiness? Why are you setting me up to be 'that' guy? Something you may not know about me is when things get tough, I get tougher."

"You can't fight my battles."

"Dammit, April. Let me in!"

"I once told Trevor that I wanted to be taken care of, but you know what? He was right. You'll never learn to stand on your own feet if someone else is holding you up. I have to fix what's wrong in order to deserve what's right. I don't expect you to understand it because you can be so damn bossy!"

His lips twitched. "You done?"

"*No*," I said, finally getting my second wind. "You don't seem to understand that this isn't going to work out. What happens when I turn forty?"

"Then we have a kickass party," he said softly, his eyes roving down to my mouth.

"And you'll still look the same."

"Maybe I won't. I'm an old wolf, April. The years are catching up with me." He sighed and lowered his eyes. "I had a woman a long time ago and she left me for another Shifter because I couldn't get her pregnant. She went into heat four times and nothing. Maybe that doesn't mean anything in your human world, but that's a big deal in mine. I never told my brothers because that's not the kind of thing a man wants to spread around."

"How do you know you were the problem?"

"Because she got pregnant right away with the new guy."

I knew Reno had a past, but it hurt to see it still followed him. Now I understood how he felt about my ex because suddenly I wanted to find that woman and wring her neck.

"I've always wanted a good woman, but it just never played out that way. The older you get, the tougher it is with Shifters. The women go after the young, virile men if they can't mate with an alpha."

I smirked and touched the sleeve of his shirt. "You're virile."

"Getting women isn't a problem; it's keeping them. I don't tell them I'm sterile because I don't ever let it get serious enough that I have to. But I'm telling *you*," he said, his voice softening.

"You can't get serious with me, Reno. I'm mortal. I'm not going to live hundreds of years like you will."

"You don't think it kills me to know I'll have to watch you get older? I know a Mage who owes me a favor—I can find a way to bring you into our world."

"But I don't want to be one of you. I like who I am. I don't even know what the heck a Mage is, but I don't think I'd be okay with becoming something I'm not… just for love."

I clamped my mouth shut and the energy in the room became electric.

Reno tilted my chin up and his sexy mouth stretched into a smile. "Did you just say what I think you did?"

"That I don't want to be an immortal?" I said coyly.

His thumb stroked my jaw and insatiable desire bloomed throughout my body. "No. That last word you just said. *Love.*"

My lips had barely parted to conjure up a good argument when his mouth crushed against mine. It wasn't rough and demanding, nor was it soft. Reno explored my mouth with his lips, working his way to my chin where he planted a soft peck. The feel of his bristly face and soft mouth became an argument that I couldn't win.

"You want to say that again, princess?"

Oh, boy! Do you! my inner voice screamed excitedly.

I gave her the middle finger.

"No. I didn't mean it that way, Reno."

His warm hand slipped beneath my shirt and caressed my back. That was the moment my spine turned to jelly and I was all his.

"Sure didn't sound that way." He unzipped my black pants and they dropped to the floor. I stepped out of them and kicked them aside. The house wasn't so quiet when it filled with the sounds of wet kisses, quickened breaths, and soft moans. Reno filled me with desire and I soaked him in like a sponge.

"They'll be back soon," I whispered. My heart raced like a greyhound on a track.

"They'll be hours," he promised through a kiss, stroking my tongue with his in slow, possessive motions. His thumbs hooked around the thin string of my panties on each hip and he pulled them down.

Reno's body felt solid beneath my touch, like granite. I'd never felt a man so fit. I reached up and held on to his broad shoulders.

"Princess, that's not where I want your hands." His forehead tapped against the wall and his breath heated my ear. "Unbuckle my belt."

A rush of exhilaration heightened my craving for more. It was his voice—the one I couldn't resist. I stood before him fully exposed from the waist down, feeling even more desire than I had our first time.

I separated the leather from the latch and waited. I knew Reno liked to be in charge and part of that was giving detailed orders. I could have just unzipped his pants and continued with the obvious, but that would have taken away his illusion of control.

"Undo my pants," he said in a raspy voice.

I stared at his shoulder, using my hands to feel my way to the button, and then I slowly dragged the zipper down. I knew how much he liked slow motions, so I took my time.

His breath felt like an Arizona wind against my neck. He shifted his head so that his lips were grazing along my earlobe. "Tell me what you want."

Would he do anything I asked of him? I remembered our first night together, and yeah, he would.

"Shift."

He jerked his neck back. "What?"

"Reno, your leg is bleeding and you're in pain. If shifting heals you, I want you to shift."

He stepped back, breathing unsteadily as if he'd run a marathon. "My wolf—"

"Won't hurt me. We're on good terms and I'm not afraid of him. Please, heal yourself."

Something wild spun in his eyes and without a word, Reno shifted in a liquid movement of flesh to fur. Standing before me on a pile of clothes was that beautiful wolf with the dark mask on his face. He groaned deep in his throat and I rubbed his soft ears. "Oh, sweet boy."

When he abruptly shifted back, Reno stood before me naked. I admired his impressive body, feeling a deep yearning to know every part of him. He brazenly reached down and slid his hand between my legs, working me over with skilled fingers. When I moaned, his actions were quick. Reno lifted my left leg and I felt the blunt press of him against my core, anchoring into position. He slipped inside me so fast I made a strangled moan in the back of my throat. I'd never imagined being taken by a man in such an uncompromising and primitive manner.

Reno lifted my other leg and held me against the wall, crashing into me like a violent collision as he went every bit as deep as he did hard. Something wild took hold—I'd never felt so much passion and became consumed by it.

"Look at me," he said when my head fell back and my eyes closed. "April, *look at me when I take you.*"

A turbulent power rolled in his voice, and I wondered how he could sound so in control when his body felt anything but. I glanced down and as soon as our eyes met, something happened.

A connection formed that had nothing to do with sex. Feeling him deep inside me while we gazed at each other made it like nothing I'd ever experienced.

I couldn't take my eyes off him. Our lips almost touched as we moaned and blew heated breaths against each other. Reno rocked his hips faster and faster until it felt so out of control I cried out. My nails bit into his back and all I could feel was the animalistic passion between us.

His simmering eyes looked wild as they devoured me, pupils dilating each time I let out a gasp. I felt my climax coming on and he must have sensed it closing in fast. Reno's movements became skilled as my legs clenched against him, a ripple of tension and pleasure moving through me. This wasn't about control where every move was premeditated. This was carnal desire in the raw.

"That's it, baby. Gimme *everything* you got," he demanded as he drove impossibly deeper. His whiskers scratched torturously against my throat while his mouth journeyed toward my ear—each word a penetration into my fantasies. "Don't hold back. Jesus… I can feel you tightening around me," he said in a ragged breath.

My breath caught and every muscle contracted when I came in his arms. Over and over. Reno kept pumping into me, and when my legs began to tremble, he held me firmly in his grasp, hands splayed beneath my thighs. His eyes widened as I gripped the back of his neck and arched my body, caught up in the animalistic desire I felt for this man. Reno let me ride out the wave of pleasure before he stilled.

I blinked away a few bright flashes of light and rested my cheek on his sweaty shoulder. Spent and out of breath, I planted a tender kiss against his skin and felt him shudder as I blew a cool breath of air on his neck.

Suddenly, I felt him move inside me, still fully erect. "Reno?"

"Yeah?"

"You can finish."

"Nah."

I lifted my head and looked at him. His hair was somehow smashed in different directions. I didn't remember doing that with my hands, but I must have.

"What do you mean by *nah*?"

He turned to walk toward the stairs, still carrying me. "I like being inside you, princess, but two minutes ain't nearly enough."

"Reno?"

"Yeah?"

"You're coming back down to get my panties and your clothes before they get home, right?"

"Nah."

I jerked my head back. "What do you mean by *nah*?"

"I'm too busy admiring your flowery petals," he said in a drop-dead serious voice.

I busted out laughing. "Have you been reading my books or are you making fun of me?"

He stopped and his eyes glittered with amusement. "Maybe I'm trying real hard to be the guy in those books for you, April."

Damn if that didn't sucker punch me right in the heart.

When a car door slammed, both of us froze.

"My clothes!" I screeched, wriggling my legs frantically until he put me down.

"April!" Trevor shouted from outside. His footsteps hammered up the porch steps and I panicked.

I scrambled toward my clothes and grabbed my pants just as the door swung open. My eyes went wide as I held them in front of me.

But not as wide as Trevor's.

Then they narrowed and sliced over to Reno. "Guys like you are a dime a dozen," he began. "You'll fuck anything in sight. Barely got the door closed and couldn't wait to get off. Even though she's hurt, even though she just went through some traumatic shit tonight. You're a real piece of work, you know that?"

Reno walked coolly over toward us and lifted his pants from the floor, yanking them up. Trevor curved his arm in front of me so that I was behind him.

"Get dressed, April. We're leaving."

"Over my dead body are you taking her out of this house." Reno zipped up his pants, not even bothering with a shirt. He moved so slowly that I got dressed even faster.

"Trevor, please don't start anything," I said in a calm voice. "Are you hurt?"

He gave me a sharp glare. "You didn't look too concerned about my well-being when I walked in the door, babe."

"Then why don't you tell me how you healed from a bullet wound?" I said coldly, loudly, putting my hands on my hips.

His nose twitched and he slanted his eyes toward Reno. "You want to know why girls like you are so damn sexy to guys like him? You're submissive."

I expected Reno to lunge at Trevor, but he didn't. That's when I knew Trevor was right.

CHAPTER 25

"**H**OW'S YOUR FOOT, BABE?"

Trevor turned down the small TV in our motel room and crawled into bed next to me, switching off the lamp. After we left Reno's house, Trevor swung by a gas station and bought a small bag of toiletries for our stay at the motel. It wasn't the finest digs in town, but it was a step up from some of the places I'd lived in as a small child.

"Are you still giving me the silent treatment? Let's see, your record is twelve days for beating up your ex after you came crying to me the night you left his sorry ass."

"Fourteen days," I murmured against my pillow. "And you did more than beat him up. You terrorized him."

Trevor curled up behind me and brushed back my hair with his fingers. "I'm sorry I had to pull you out of there, April, but you need to understand that someone like Reno isn't good for you. Guys like him just don't give a shit about girls like you, and you're a gem. You're like those little glass snow globes your dad gave you—fragile and beautiful. He just wants to keep shaking you up until you're confused, but once the snow settles, you'll see he's still on the outside and not the right guy for you."

"He makes me happy."

"You can find someone better to make you happy."

"It's not what you think."

"Nothing ever is."

I rolled over to face him and stared at his soft lips. It was the one thing about him that no one took notice of, but he had a great mouth. Maybe it's because his smile was always genuine, never forced or phony, never mean-spirited or mysterious. When Trevor smiled, it was just *all* Trevor.

"I know what you are."

His expression went rigid and he rolled onto his back, grabbing the clicker and turning up some stupid movie with alien explosions. "Tired, that's what I am."

"Trev, I've known you long enough that I can tell when you're lying. I can't force you to confide in me, but we both know what I'm talking about. I'm not going to back you into a corner, but when you want to talk about it, I'm here. That's all I wanted to say."

"Don't know what you mean, babe," he said in a distant voice, tucking his hand behind his head. "I booked the room for the week. They have pretty good monthly rates—cheaper than some apartments. Not bad for a couple of drifters without any junk to haul around. I'm hoping I land a job soon."

"Where did you apply?"

"One of them is a shoe store; the other is a pizza shop."

"Trev?"

"Huh?"

"You don't like sneakers and you hate pizza."

"Doesn't mean I can't sell the shit out of them."

I smiled. Yeah, he could.

"Hold on to your panties!" he exclaimed, swinging his legs off the bed and reaching in the closet. "Wait until you see this. I went back to the trailer and found a couple of odds and ends that weren't incinerated too bad. Check it out!" He whirled around.

Trevor handed me an e-reader and I turned it over in my hands, dumbstruck. He gloated and sat on the bed, peeling off his socks.

While he did that, I held it to my nose and could still smell the plastic packaging. "This isn't mine. You just bought this, didn't you?"

"Dime a dozen, babe."

"I can't take it."

"And I refuse to have a birthday present I bought for you sitting in the ashes of your past. You're my sexy nerd girl and I'm always gonna be here to make sure you get your book fix."

I laughed and fell against the pillow as he walked around the room. "I guess if I'm going to be a junkie like my mom, then at least my drug of choice is words."

"That's not funny."

I set the gift on the nightstand. "Thanks, Trev."

"Just don't say you owe me, because that's not the deal with us."

No, it was never the deal with us. Trevor was the exception to the rule. He never made anything he gave me feel like it was more than I deserved. But he did make it seem like my gratitude was more than *he* deserved.

I'd thought Reno would destroy Trevor with a series of punches, but their confrontation never got physical. I wanted to cry because he kept saying I was his girl, and he wasn't letting me go.

I never imagined I'd be the girl who would sabotage a relationship, but that's how it unfolded. In the end, it might have destroyed me to love a man like Reno.

Maybe twenty-three was too young to have all the answers. Trevor had hit the nail on the head when he told me that sometimes when you hold on to the fantasy, all you end up with is the reality. I loved Reno, even though I hadn't declared it aloud to him. But I was the daughter of a drug addict, a traveling circus of debt, and a girl with a rocky past who didn't trust men. I didn't have skeletons in my closet—I had a boneyard.

Trevor carried his own demons, and we both had a quiet understanding that we couldn't fight each other's battles or change who we were. But Reno had fought my battles and that scared me. I'd never had anyone put his life on the line for me. Despite Reno's badass physical appearance and demeanor, he was a decent man with an amazing family. A man with integrity who'd fought in wars that weren't his to fight, and here he was, trying to fight my battles too. A man who swallowed his pride so his baby brother could lead the pack. Why? Because he had integrity and respected rules. Maybe he saw me as a shy girl with pretty eyes and a pocketful of dreams, but the reality of who I was would eventually sink in. Reno could have saved me from debt, but I didn't want to be saved. I wanted to save myself so that one day the man I finally ended up with would respect me as a woman.

I wanted to be the sail in his ship, not the anchor.

My phone rang and I rolled to the left side of the bed. I sighed heavily when I saw the name of the caller. "Hi, this is April."

Trevor clucked his tongue and tossed the remote on the bed, then stalked toward the bathroom. He thought it was Reno calling.

"It's Maddox. I stopped by your place for a spell and noticed it's not there anymore. It looks like you ran into some trouble. Is that trouble taken care of?"

"Yeah," I said in a low voice. "I think."

"If you come with me, I'll make sure you don't have that kind of trouble again."

"The guy who was stalking me is taken care of, but I'm not sure if that means his boss will try to come after me or my friends." I paused for a beat. "If I agree to your proposition, will you make sure my friends are safe?"

I heard him sucking on his teeth as if considering. "I can only surmise you haven't nipped that problem in the bud. What's the name of the man after you?"

"Delgado."

A soft laugh filled the line. "Yeah. That'll be taken care of. I've got connections and he's easily bought off."

"What are you?"

A scratchy growl filled the silence. "Are you asking what my animal is? Well now, that's not something I tell just *anyone*. I'm lethal, woman. But nothing you need to worry your pretty little head about. I control my animal and I won't shift around a human unless they have it coming. If you stay with me, you'll have my complete protection. Are you sure about this?"

Hell no, you're not sure, my inner voice shouted.

That was fear talking. In the real world, problems didn't magically disappear—they multiplied like gremlins. I owed Maddox more than fifty grand and didn't have a dime in my pocket, not to mention I was homeless and without transportation. Trevor would never be able to get his feet on the ground if he had to take care of me too. It was time to start making tough decisions.

"This is a business arrangement, Maddox, and I want to verify our verbal contract before you put it in writing. According to your terms, I can leave whenever I want. That means you can't hold me by force. If I leave, I don't want to be looking over my shoulder because you're stalking or harassing me. I won't agree unless you can promise me that even under your protection, I'll still be able to pay off my debt. I don't want that to be the tie that binds me to you. Someday I'm going to want to leave, and I want to be free and clear."

"Hmm. I can arrange something between us if that's what you want. But why not just stay on the outside if all you want is to pay me back?"

"I gave it some thought. I'll have a better chance at paying you back quicker if I don't have any bills or rent to worry about. Plus I'm sure you can find me a better-paying job than what I've been doing. You said you have connections. Can we come to a compromise?" I said, making a business proposition.

"I don't mind you going to school, but I won't have you working a job."

This wasn't going to be easy. "Instead of an indefinite stay under your care, what about five years and you'll clear what I owe?"

"No, I can't agree to that. But ten years and you sleeping in my bed, I'll consider those terms."

"Absolutely not." I sat up and tugged at my hair. "What about seven years, no sex, and I'll work my ass off to pay my debt by cleaning, cooking, doing your taxes, whatever you want."

His laugh sounded like a crow and he quickly put a cap on it. "You're quite the negotiator. I'll agree to that, but you don't have to worry about the taxes. I don't have a relationship with Uncle Sam."

"Promise you won't push me into sex? How do I know I can trust you?"

"Because I'm giving you my word, and that's the best thing I've got. You'll have it in writing, but I'm not an animal. Not to mention it's a little insulting to insinuate I have to force a woman to sleep with me. I got problems, but that's not one of them."

"That includes kissing and anything physical."

He chuckled a little, but his voice was sincere. "Sure thing. But if I need you as a date, I'd like it if you uh… well, if you put out the vibe that you were sleeping with me, I'd appreciate it. I'm a man who likes leaving an impression with my business partners; it'll look bad if I have a pet who doesn't cuddle up with me at night."

"Fine, as long as we adhere to the previous rules. I'm not going to make out with you in public to prove something, but I'll give people the impression we're intimate. Can I date?"

"No, I went over that already."

"What if I see them but don't sleep with them? Just go out to a movie or something?"

He paused and sighed through the phone. "No. If you're my pet, then you're no one else's. That's a hard-and-fast rule because no man will respect me if you're gallivanting across town with other men. I get that you're human and this is a hard thing to wrap your head around, but it's a legitimate offer that's only going to come around once. I'm not just offering you a chance at a clean slate, but if you want to further your education, I can help. That'll come out of my pocket. This isn't a self-serving relationship, and I'll want to see that you're happy."

"April, do you need the bathroom? I'm about to take a shower," Trevor yelled out.

"No, I'm good."

He shut the door and I slid back under the covers, turning on my right side.

"Including *him*, whoever that was," Maddox said firmly. "Platonic means nothing in my world."

"Except with you, right?"

"The door's wide-open on that topic. You'll have seven lonely years to make up your mind, and how old will you be by then? That's a long time to go without being loved by a man. You may not want me now, but you'll cave eventually. That's not a threat—it's just a fact. Don't beat yourself up over it; I'm not that bad of a guy. Just so we have it out in the open, I don't lay a hand on women. I find a man contemptuous who would strike a female, so you can put that fear to rest. I'll treat you fair and no one will mistake that you're mine. That means you'll be protected and won't have to worry about anyone else messing with you. I mean it. No one touches you. All right, we've exhausted enough time going back and forth on this, so decide now. If you're good on the deal, then I'll send someone to pick you up. Give me your address."

I heard Trevor singing a Thirty Seconds to Mars song when I slid out of the bed and put my clothes on. He liked his long, hot showers and wouldn't notice I was gone until I was really gone. I had to keep reminding myself that the Breed world didn't work the same way as mine, that this was a business proposition. More than that, it was an opportunity for me to get my head together and start over. Maybe Maddox thought I'd cave in to sex, but that wasn't happening. As we spoke, I scribbled a short note for Trevor and left it on the bedside table.

"Maddox, I want you to draw up a contract with our agreement. Laugh all you want, but that's nonnegotiable. You guys may hide from the human world, but I'll drag you into a court of law if you breach the contract, and I know for a fact that would put you in some serious hot water with your own Breed laws. I'm at the Western Lodge Inn. Have you heard of it?"

"I got a guy who can be there in five minutes. Wait out by the lobby and he'll pick you up."

Maddox ended the call and as I walked by the bathroom door, I leaned forward and kissed it.

"Bye, Trev," I whispered.

"Mom, you need to go lie down." Lexi was clearly frustrated. "You heard what the doctor said."

Lynn stood in the lounge room with a bandage on her head after getting a bunch of stitches in the emergency room. Reno felt sick about the whole thing. "I want to know what happened to April. Hon, I can't go upstairs and sleep after everything. I need a drink."

"You don't drink, Mom."

"I still need a drink."

"Lynn," Austin said.

She cleared her throat. "I told you not to call me that."

Austin scratched his jaw and a smile ghosted his lips. "Mom, you need to take it easy. We'll sort everything out down here and fill you in tomorrow morning." He glared at Reno. "Lexi'll cook breakfast and bring it up to you."

"That's right, Mom. French toast and bacon—your favorite."

Reno hadn't spoken a word since they had walked in the door. He just sat back in his favorite brown chair with a beer in one hand and his good-luck charm in the other, wondering what the hell he'd done to drive April away. Reno knew nothing about human women outside of what he'd seen on television, but it sure as hell didn't feel right letting her walk away. What could he do? He had tried to get her to talk to him, but he didn't want to risk pushing her further away with an aggressive pursuit.

Denver dragged his bare feet across the living room floor, wearing his favorite sweats and no shirt. After reading *Peter Pan* with Maizy and putting her to bed, he'd gone into the kitchen to forage. "Maybe next time we should all take *real* guns. That would have been kickass," he said, eating soup right out of the can.

"Your aim is so bad you can't even hit the toilet," Lynn blurted out.

Jericho barked out a laugh and grabbed his smokes off the table. "I'm heading upstairs," he said, still laughing. "She got you good, brother. I'm sleeping in tomorrow, so don't come knocking." Jericho left the room and the stairs creaked as he disappeared out of sight.

Denver ignored them, eating another giant spoonful of chicken and rice. "Would've been easier to take down the asshole who grabbed Maizy if I'd been armed like Reno was. Just sayin'."

"I don't like guns." Lynn glared at Reno.

Months ago after Lynn had been kidnapped by her ex-husband, she'd remained in a state of denial, still excusing the man's actions. Then one day, reality had hit her like a runaway freight train, and she'd smashed every plate in the kitchen. She'd finally come to terms with the fact that a man she'd loved had almost killed both of her daughters and was indirectly responsible for the death of her son.

After that, Lexi bought a bag of paper plates, and they ate on those for a few weeks until Lynn sought counseling. Lexi went with her for support but also found it helpful to talk out her own feelings even though she couldn't disclose details about Shifters or her father's death. Humans didn't cope as well as Breed did when it came to traumatic shit. Part of it was having lived long enough to learn how to shut off pain, but it also had to do with the spirit and strength of their animal.

Pain sliced through his gut when he thought of April looking at him over her shoulder when she walked off the porch. She'd stumbled clumsily, but April didn't have a clue that he thought she was adorable as hell. He didn't make a big deal of it when she bumped into things. In fact, it made her even more fascinating to him. She was different on so many levels from Shifter women. April was like one of those Rubik's Cubes that no matter how many times you twisted it around, you couldn't figure it out.

"Where's April?" Austin asked for the umpteenth time.

Reno tightened his jaw.

"Guess she didn't want to be your bitch," Denver muttered matter-of-factly.

Reno was out of his chair in a heartbeat. The soup splattered on the floor and he seized Denver's throat.

"Cut it out!" Austin shouted, wedging between them. "Dammit, Reno, you know he didn't mean nothin' by it."

"Maybe not," Reno bit out, giving Denver a hostile glare, "but you ever call her a bitch again, no Packmaster will be able to stop what I'm going to do to you."

Denver wiped the soup off his arm and shook some of it off his foot. "When the hell did *bitch* become a bad word in this pack? Maybe you need to lighten up, big brother. Humans don't like all that serious Terminator shit. Someone tracking our ass down is just another day in the life of the Cole family. But April goes out for laser tag and finds herself in the middle of a showdown. That's some heavy shit. And why don't you explain how you helped her cope when you got home? Did you give her a beer? Watch a little TV? Yeah, we all saw the panties by the door." Denver waved his hand and walked away. "I'm outta here."

"I need everyone upstairs except Reno," Austin said in an authoritative voice. That was the tone he used as an alpha, the one that every Shifter wolf heeded whether in human or wolf form. There was power in his words when he summoned it, and without an argument, everyone drifted upstairs and left them alone.

After Lexi shut the door, Austin folded his arms. "Talk."

Reno pinched his chin and slanted his eyes away. He didn't want to talk, but Austin was the only one in the house he could confide in. "While you guys were still cleaning up the mess with Sanchez, Trevor came by and took April away. She's gone. For good."

It took a second before Austin decided what to say. "And you're okay with that?"

Reno's eyes slid up. "Do I look okay with it?"

Austin sat across from him and touched the small cleft in his chin. Reno noticed a few spatters of blood on his dark green shirt. "I can think of at least four Shifter women who've had their eye on mating with you. Good women from respectable packs. All I'm saying is that you want someone who's going to age at the same speed. I get the fascination; we've all had crushes on a human at one time or another. They're the forbidden fruit and incomparable to our women. But you don't want to get your emotions mixed up with one of them. They don't understand our ways—they don't mate for life. Men leave their families and some want nothing to do with their own children." He shook his head. "And that's another thing. Shifters and humans can't have children together. Think about what you'd be giving up. She did you a favor."

Reno stretched his legs and laced his fingers together on his lap. "Did our dad ever tell you about Faye?"

Austin shook his head and Reno continued.

"This was long before you were born. Faye was a good bitch from a respectable pack, and we had a thing. A good thing. She was a tough woman with black hair and blue eyes—all the men had their sights on her, but she was mine. We knew right away we had a connection, and it got serious."

"How serious?"

"Serious enough that I was going to ask her to be my life mate. Turns out I couldn't give her what she wanted."

"And what was that?" Austin knitted his brows.

"Children." Reno took a deep and painful breath. "I'm sterile."

Austin sat back, staring pensively to the right. "Sorry. I didn't know."

"Yeah, that's not something I want to share with the others, if you catch my meaning. It's better that you were born the alpha. Maybe that's why the gene skipped me, little brother. Faye didn't stick around; she found herself a man who could give her what I couldn't. So that bullshit about wolves mating for life is only a standard we hold ourselves to. Maybe we honor it more than humans do, but it doesn't make us any better than them. I don't believe in destiny. I believe in finding something good and making it work."

It had taken years for Reno to get over losing Faye. He didn't reveal to Austin how her rejection broke him in ways he couldn't have imagined. That he'd pursued her hard, even after she chose another man. He'd loved that woman and the last time he saw her, she slapped him in the face and told him he was a disgrace to his own kind—that no woman would ever choose to mate with him. Faye wanted children more than love. Reno would have built a pyramid for her. And yet Faye didn't hold a candle to a human who had stolen his heart with her whimsical smile and unyielding acceptance.

Austin leaned forward, his icy blue eyes pinning Reno to the chair. "Don't be so quick to knock the idea of destiny. I've always felt a connection with Lexi. It's not something I can explain—it's a pull in my gut that tells me she's the one. When she's in trouble, I can sense it. There's something about the way we fit that doesn't always make sense, but we're like two puzzle pieces coming together. I wouldn't be a complete man without her, and that's as good as destiny for me. We've all heard the stories about soul mates and the bond between two Shifters who were born for each other. I believe it because I have that with Lexi. It's an inherent attraction that brings us together like magnets. Just give it some time and you'll find it with a Shifter. You can't have that kind of bond with a human."

Reno shifted in his chair. All the things Austin had just listed off were exactly how he felt about April. "So you're saying if Lexi had turned out to be a human and not one of us, you would have let her go?"

Austin flexed his jaw and sat back, the lamp beside him shining on his tatted shoulder. Cold weather didn't faze Austin; he ran hot and often wore T-shirts or tank tops in winter. "Lexi would have still been in our pack if she chose—that's a given. Not all humans can accept that people like us exist. I don't know if I could love someone that hard and let them slip through my hands because they have a shorter expiration date. But I don't have that choice to make, you do. April is a smart girl and she lived with us long enough to see this was the wrong life for her. Lynn still struggles with it, and she's been talking about sending Maizy away to live with her grandparents or shipping her to boarding school when she's older. She's worried we're a bad influence on her even though she's found a home with our pack. Lynn doesn't want to start over on her own, and she has a place in our family. Humans don't think the way we do. They don't get our lifestyle. They don't cope well in a crowded house full of people who aren't even related. She doesn't like having to hustle downstairs whenever I want to get frisky with my woman. I don't understand how anyone could ship their kid off, but humans do it all the time. They leave them in day care and send them to summer camp." He shook his head and ruffled up his hair. "They don't raise a family the same way *we* do—that's part of the disconnect. Maybe April wants a family and that's something she can't have with a Shifter. We live in a dangerous world, Reno. Do you think it's fair to ask a human to give up family and normalcy to live with Breed?"

Reno released a heavy sigh and rubbed his face. April was adamant about not wanting kids, but she was only twenty-three. Does a person really know what they want at that age?

Then it hit him like a sledgehammer.

She didn't want to commit, plain and simple. A female Shifter her age wouldn't hesitate to settle down with a good man, because Shifters were tenacious and decisive. Humans were uncertain about their feelings and always changing their minds. She didn't want to live in his world, but she also didn't want to force him into making a choice between love and family. And she was right. It would have torn him apart. April could have taken advantage of his hospitality, but in the end, she'd walked away with nothing. Maybe it was for the better. She would have never found happiness if she'd felt indebted to him.

That night, Reno let go of hope that two star-crossed lovers from different worlds could make it work.

CHAPTER 26

SEVERAL WEEKS HAD CRAWLED BY after I left my old life behind and moved in with Maddox. He lived in a quaint house compared to Reno's—a five bedroom, two bath. The kitchen was outdated and I stood taller than his fridge. My favorite place was the tranquil patio in the back with a tin awning. It wasn't so tranquil on rainy nights when the water hammered against the tin roof, but the house was nestled deep in the woods on a large stretch of private property. Lantana bushes ran along the side of the house, and a covered hot tub sat out back. Maddox said he only enjoyed running it in the summertime.

True to his word, Maddox set me up in my own room and didn't make any sexual advances. Per my request, he had drawn up a contract. The first week, I was timid about our arrangement and kept to myself. I cried in my bed late at night until one morning, he took me out to the back patio and we had a long talk about how Shifters lived. Having human pets wasn't the norm, but it wasn't a deviant lifestyle either. Many humans were willing because they were fascinated with their world, and for a Shifter, it often showed status since most were wealthy and respected. Maddox craved companionship and I needed to get my life in order. I became optimistic about my future for the first time in a long while. Maddox supported my desire to go back to school and said if I wanted anything else, that he'd pay and it wouldn't be included with my debt. I had a feeling his reward program was merely an incentive to stay with him longer. I began to see that Maddox was just a lonely guy.

I never went back to Sweet Treats. I couldn't face Lexi after her mother was attacked and sister grabbed, not to mention I didn't want to run into any of the Cole brothers. I was certain they were relieved to have normalcy in their lives again.

Fall was in full swing. The tips of the leaves on the trees appeared to be dipped in gold, as if the sun had frosted them with its light. On Thanksgiving, we had a simple meal of deep-fried turkey, cornbread dressing, green beans, salad, and a bottle of wine. Maddox wasn't big on holidays, but he surprised me by cooking the turkey because he knew it was a big deal to humans. Little did he know my last Thanksgiving meal had been a frozen TV dinner.

Maddox didn't beat around the bush with his expectations. When he wanted me to keep him company, I joined him. Most of the time he worked jigsaw puzzles at the table and I'd conceal my frustration by separating the pieces by color while he assembled them into a picture. I never saw his animal and didn't want to. No one shady ever came around, and he did most of his business over the phone or away from the house.

Then he'd come back, kick off his dirty boots, hang up his hat, and sit on the back patio with a tin can and a bag of sunflower seeds.

"How long are you going to stare at that book?" he asked, slumped down in the tattered chair in the living room next to the sliding glass door. "I never saw a woman read so much."

"You should try it sometime," I suggested from the green sofa.

He dismissively blew out a breath of air. "Books are a waste of time when you can live the real thing."

"Not everyone's life is an epic fantasy," I said, touching the choker around my neck.

Maddox had given me the necklace on day one of my arrival. It was a black cloth choker with his name in silver. The material was thick, and he was right—it had a trendy appeal, something any young girl might be wearing to the mall or a club. Except in the world of Shifters, it was a declaration of status.

I discovered this the first time he took me out in public. We went to a Shifter bar on the Breed side of town where humans weren't allowed inside. Quite a few men approached me, but when I turned to look at them, they abandoned ship. Some laughed and shook their heads, while others gave me a look of disgust.

I wondered if they kept pets because of their history. Maddox told me Shifters had only recently acquired their freedom. Before that, they were treated as slaves and sold to other Breeds for manual labor. Sometimes if their animal was trainable, they'd work as guards to protect property for the wealthy and powerful. The women weren't so fortunate in how they were treated. Wolves eventually formed rogue packs and gained power in numbers. Shifters had fought for their independence and the right to own land. Slavery was still fresh on their minds since they lived a long time and many had once been slaves themselves. Maybe some collected human pets to erase the submissive chip on their shoulder—so they could feel superior to someone since they were still treated as lower-class citizens.

It was a world I understood little about, even though I was smack-dab in the middle of it.

"You know, I can pay for a salon," Maddox offered, staring at my roots. My hair had grown out a couple of inches and the platinum dye was fading. Now my natural color of fresh blond was taking over—a color I hadn't seen in years. Still light, just not white.

"I'm growing it out," I told him. "It's time for a change."

"Speaking of change, why don't you put on something dressy tonight? I have a business meeting at one of the Shifter bars and I want you to come. We need to look a little social, so wear something fun."

Jeez, like I had a choice.

"Maddox Cane, in the flesh." A man greeted us with an insincere smile, his voice as rusty as nails.

"How's life treating you, Randall?" Maddox scoured the man with his gaze. Randall looked like Mr. Clean without the bushy eyebrows. I wondered if he oiled down his head because the light glistened against his smooth scalp.

He smiled invitingly as we approached the cluster of wooden tables in the Breed bar. I knocked a chair over and heard a few chuckles when I bent down to pick it up.

Randall's eyes narrowed on the choker around my neck. "Well, Maddox. I see you've been busy. She's a pretty one. How old?"

"April, go to the bar and order a whiskey neat for me and something fit for a pussy. What's your drink of choice, Randall?" Maddox antagonized his friend in a way that led me to believe he was daring him to insult me.

Randall smiled, but not in a pleasant way. "Martini," he said, taking a seat in his chair.

If these two were frenemies, then Maddox had brought me along to make him look good.

"Get whatever you want," Maddox said with an invisible smile buried beneath his scruffy beard.

I cut through a crowd of Shifters and tried not to make eye contact. Breed bars made me uneasy—the men didn't hang back and do all the flirty stuff from across the bar like humans. They'd come right up to me and say whatever lascivious thing was on their minds.

Until they saw the choker.

To avoid any awkward situations, I pinned my hair back with a few long strands hanging loose. Amid the crowd of women wearing painted-on dresses, do-me heels, and bustier tops, I must have looked like a joke in a pair of jeans, a white knit top that fell off one shoulder, and a pair of simple black heels. In my book, the right kind of heels could class up any casual style.

Men were eagerly eyeing the pool table where a few women looked as if they were debating whether to play. Only in recent weeks had I realized my mistake of playing pool at Austin's house. In retrospect, I must have looked as if I were inviting every man in that room to mount me.

"Well, well. Color me dazzled," Denver said from behind the bar. I looked up and expected to see a boyish grin on his face but was met with a persecuting gaze.

Crap. He *worked* here.

Denver leaned on his forearms, which made his biceps firm up. Black sleeveless shirts seemed to be the dress code in this bar for all employees. The logo on the breast was a wolf howling inside a moon with the bar name "Howlers" written below it.

"I need a whiskey neat, a martini, and something *strong*."

"I just bet," he said, eyes sliding to the table where my party sat.

"Are you going to be a dick or give me a drink?"

"How about both?"

"What's between Reno and me is between Reno and me."

"Doesn't seem to be much between you two these days but distance. Now why is that?"

My heart began to race with anger. "Fine," I said softly. "I get it. I'm obviously not up to your standards, being that I'm just a human trespassing in your world. Reno's better off without me."

"So you can be owned by that asshole?" He pointed to the table. "You seriously want to stand here and pretend like I'm not offended that you left a man like Reno for a douchebag who takes in pets? You'd rather be another man's pet than date my brother," he said through clenched teeth.

I grabbed his finger and pushed his hand on the table. "Don't point your finger at him. You have no idea how dangerous that man is."

Denver drew in a sharp breath as he stood up straight and went to fix my drinks.

My thoughts drifted back to Trevor. We'd exchanged e-mails over the past few weeks, but he was upset with me, and the replies were always short. Since he didn't want to admit he was a Shifter, I didn't divulge the details of my living situation. But I had a feeling he might have figured it out.

To my knowledge, Reno knew nothing about Maddox. We hadn't spoken since the night I left, and I'd never forget the look on his face as I walked out the door. I tried to erase it from my memory, but it burned in my heart like a brand, marking me. I had no doubt Reno had moved on with his life—a man like him could have any girl he wanted. He'd never gotten over that woman who left him for another man, and that's what hardened his heart. It sure toughened mine when my ex made it clear that I wasn't enough of a woman for him.

"Here you are," Denver said. "Whiskey, martini, and a Devil's Eye."

I warily looked at the red liquid. "Devil's Eye? What's in it?"

"Sin."

I quickly downed the shot and immediately shivered. A rush of heat moved through my body and suddenly, everything became sharp and vivid.

"You're a bag of nuts," he said. "Better make that your only drink tonight. Most people barely survive one, and I've never given it to a human before."

"Super." I smiled and gathered up the two drinks, then sauntered back to the table.

Yeah. I *sauntered*. Suddenly it felt good to loosen up and enjoy myself. I was a young woman who had spent too many years trying to be the responsible one. I avoided having fun because I didn't feel like I deserved it. Who thinks that way at twenty-three?

"Here you are, boys." I slid the drinks on the table and plopped down in my chair. My face felt like warm cinnamon and my tongue tasted cherries. Whatever was in that drink was like nothing I'd ever experienced.

"Honey, you okay?" Maddox whispered, eyes brimming with concern.

Randall grinned wolfishly and reached for his glass. "Looks like that one's had her first taste of Devil's Eye. You can always tell by the red rim around the irises. Better keep an eye on her; they don't call it Devil's Eye for nothing. I've seen a few bar fights break out because of it. Last Thursday, a Packmaster got a little too frisky in the back room with a woman who wasn't his mate, not to mention his Breed," he said with a hard laugh. "That shit is *bad* news."

Maddox swung his attention back to Randall and leaned in privately. "Have you heard of a man named Delgado? He's been a thorn in my side for the last ten years."

"Breed?"

"No. Human. He's cutting in on my action and not running his deals smoothly. There was an incident a month ago where one of his men went rogue."

"What business did you have with him before?"

"None," Maddox said coolly, and I listened out of vague curiosity. "He's expanded and now I hear he's dealing drugs and bought a few strip clubs."

"So? Not my problem."

"*Breed* strip clubs."

Randall leaned in, his head shining beneath the lamp. "We don't sell to humans."

"Someone got paid a shitload of money and skipped town. That now makes Delgado *our* problem."

"Is that why I'm here?" Randall sipped his martini and looked at his watch. "Or did you just miss my handsome face?"

"No," Maddox said, leaning back and putting his hat on the table. "That's a sidebar. I got a Shifter who's been asking questions about me and sticking his nose in my personal affairs. He's a wolf, and you know I don't like to get tangled up with packs. He laid out a *not so subtle* threat and wants information on one of my old clients. Since you're my partner, this involves you too."

I rolled my eyes. "I'm going to mingle," I said, kicking back my chair.

Maddox caught my wrist. "Maybe you should sit."

"I want to put some music on, and they have a jukebox in the back. Let your pet take a walk."

"Whoa!" Randall exclaimed with a boisterous laugh. "Looks like you got this one nipping at your heels there, Maddox."

"Don't wander far," Maddox said, giving me a curt nod.

I couldn't hate him. As much as I tried, he was good to me. I'd never felt controlled or bossed around by him, and his assertive behavior was derived from concern. That much I could see in his grey eyes.

I touched his shoulder and walked down the length of the bar toward the jukebox—a popular music player that most of the Breed bars had. There was something nostalgic about them, and this one was free.

I leaned over the machine and began my search.

"Hot damn." Someone hissed from behind.

I peered over my shoulder to get a look at him. "Take a picture; it'll last longer."

His eyes widened and he stalked in my direction, his flannel shirt and bushy sideburns a dubious fashion statement.

Great going, April! Your mom would be proud, my inner voice said with derision.

"I'm Stu, and you were just about to give me your number," he declared, leaning next to me on the jukebox.

"Sure thing!" I exclaimed, twisting around to face him. "It's right here." I pointed at my choker. "Sorry, you got a busy signal. Try again later."

A sexy smirk slid up his cheek. "Human, huh? Interesting. Never been with one, but you seem just as feisty as any of these other Shifters."

I frowned a little, wiping a strand of hair away from my face. "I don't think you get it. I can't talk to you."

He slowly bit his bottom lip and held it that way for a minute, looking down the length of my body in a way that made me turn back and review the song selections again. Shifter men were persistent, but this guy was just an asshole.

Stu leaned in close. "Feel like being a bad girl and breaking a few rules? He'll never find out."

I pushed a button and loud murmurs were drowned out by the classic "Who Made Who?" I turned around and leaned on my elbows, scoping out the room. I almost slid off the jukebox at what happened next.

On the first beat of the song, the main door swung open and Reno Cole walked in.

A black leather jacket hugged his body, unzipped so I could see a charcoal-colored shirt beneath. His jeans fit him in a way that should have been rated *S* for sexy, and his polished motorcycle boots looked ready to kick some ass. His brown hair was neatly groomed and the lines in his jaw looked fierce, even from across the room.

My heart seized in my chest and a cold sweat touched my brow. Pool balls cracked on my left and a blonde at the bar swiveled in her seat, targeting Reno as her prey. She had on cherry-red pumps and a white pencil skirt. She swung her hips as she made her way toward him and then suddenly turned around as if she were giving him a modeling show. Shifter women turned their backs to men they were interested in. It's something I started noticing on our trips out, except with the waitresses who always kept that kind of behavior in check.

But Reno paid no attention. His eyes scanned the bar and my throat became as dry as the Sahara Desert. My elbows were glued to the jukebox, and the idiot in the flannel shirt kept yammering on about taking a walk to the parking lot. But I couldn't take my eyes off the striking man across the bar. Maybe it was the drink, or maybe it was the fact I thought Reno was the sexiest man I'd ever seen, but I got warm and tingly.

Reno reached in his back pocket and pulled out his phone. His eyes swung to Denver at the bar and suddenly shot straight ahead, landing on me. I glanced over at Denver and when he hung up his phone, it all became clear.

"Holy smokes, this is bad," I murmured.

Stu stepped in front of me and blocked my view. I tried peering around him, but he dodged his head and smiled, trying to make some eye contact.

"You're hard to get."

"I'm taken," I said, looking up to show off my collar again.

"Yeah, which one is the big and bad Maddox?"

"That would be me," Maddox said in a voice that made my blood run cold. He was wearing his hat, which made him even more menacing because it obscured his eyes.

The Shifter stood up straight and turned his head to look at Maddox, who showed off his mean face. I knew the man to be gentle, but anyone who pissed him off got the jagged edge of the knife.

"See that collar?" Maddox reached for my wrist and gently wrapped his fingers around it. "That says she's *mine*."

"A little young for an old dog like you," the man taunted.

Maddox looked at him like a predator, tugging me real tight against his left side. "I ain't no dog, and you should watch your tongue or I might be tempted to cut it out and feed it to you between two slices of bread."

I grimaced as the Shifter's eyes darted between us. It didn't look as though he wanted to take any chances on calling his bluff, so he shook his head and walked away.

"Why do men always have to lay down vicious threats?" I said, still buzzing from my drink.

He stroked his finger across the collar on my neck. "I don't make threats. I simply state the facts. I want you to come back to the table and sit beside me. I have some business to take care of, so come grace us with your pretty smile."

It was hard to look pretty when Maddox insisted that I wear heavy makeup. I think he wanted me to look older than I was. He always made sure that when we went to a Breed bar, I had my lashes curled and cheeks blushed.

Maddox had been including me in on meetings I had no business attending. It might have been strategic so I'd need his protection, or maybe he was beginning to trust me. I was more inclined to believe the former.

He led me to the table with a gentle tug. When I froze mid-step, he peered over his shoulder and chuckled.

Maddox had no clue that I knew the man sitting at our table. *Intimately.*

"Sorry about that, gentleman. Men can't seem to help themselves, but she's as loyal as they come."

Reno was sitting in the chair in front of us but hadn't turned around. I smelled his cologne and felt a pang of regret as memories flooded my mind of that wonderful night we'd curled up in my bed, listening to blues while it rained outside. When he casually glanced over his shoulder and looked up at me, it felt as if I'd been stung with quiet judgment. I wanted to tell him I wasn't sleeping with Maddox, but what did it matter?

"This is my girl, April. Show some manners or I'll have words with you, Cole. Let's get down to business," he said, settling in his chair and kicking mine out on his left.

Thank God for Devil's Eye or my nerves might have resulted in me flipping the table over. Instead, I coolly sat in my chair with Reno directly across from me, Maddox to my right, and Randall to my left. I kept my hands folded in front of my chin, obscuring my collar.

"I still want to see her ID," Randall said, snorting into his glass as he took a drink. "I thought you went for the cougars."

Maddox narrowed his steely eyes and patted my leg, turning his attention to Reno. Little did he notice that every muscle in Reno's face had turned to marble, and I barely saw his lips because they were so tightly mashed together. He tipped his head at me in a gesture that spoke volumes.

Reno didn't know me.

At least as far as Maddox and Randall were concerned.

"So what's your business with me, Cole?"

Reno rested his right arm on the table and lifted two fingers to a waitress named Rosie, signaling he wanted what Maddox was having. "Did you know a human named Charles Langston?"

Oh my God. They were talking about Charlie, my old boss.

Maddox twisted a few hairs on his beard. "Anything's possible. Want to tell me why you're askin'?"

"I'm a PI and he's one of my cases. Langston had payments going into your pocket, and now he's gone missing."

"Dead is the word I think you were searching for," Maddox corrected, leaning back in his chair and putting his arm around me.

I thought I saw Reno flinch, but he kept his eyes locked on Maddox. "What was he paying you for?"

My eyes glazed, and I smiled at Randall who silently chuckled and sipped his drink.

"Charles took out a substantial loan. Sonofabitch died before finishing out his payments, and I got no family to call on for the rest. Ain't that a bitch?"

I stayed quiet since Maddox didn't seem aware that I knew Charlie, but I was itching to say something.

"Honey, why don't you go and make the boys jealous for a little while?"

In other words, *get lost.*

"I'd rather keep you company," I insisted, placing my hands on the table.

Maddox brushed a fallen strand of hair away from my neck and tilted up my chin, exposing the collar I'd been desperately trying to hide since I sat down. I jumped at the sound of Reno's chair scraping against the wood floor. He loomed above the table and spoke aggressively. "I need to get a stronger drink. Get rid of the girl and we'll talk."

He looked scary mad. My face flushed from the intensity of his gaze, which wasn't on my eyes but on the fabric wrapped around my neck, which he hadn't noticed before. With recognition in his eyes, Reno now understood that I'd left him to become another man's pet.

"Go on, April. Get." Maddox yanked my chair back. When it came to business, he didn't mess around, and the look in his eyes put a fright in me.

Realizing I wasn't going to win this argument, I left the table.

CHAPTER 27

When Reno entered the bar, he'd been gearing up to fight Maddox for information on Charlie. He'd had no idea he would end up wanting to kill the man because of April. Reno hadn't seen her since the night she left the house. When Denver gave him a quick ring on his phone and told him to look straight ahead, Reno almost lost his cool.

Seeing that damn choker around her neck had incited an explosive reaction that had him out of his chair, two seconds from pulling out his gun and taking care of Maddox. Buried feelings resurfaced for April—protective and territorial feelings. Maybe a human would have turned the anger on her, but it incited a deep-seated instinct to protect what he loved. That's when he knew he hadn't gotten over April.

He wanted his woman back.

Reno needed to cool off before talking to Maddox, so he left the table and ordered a cold draft at the bar. April wandered over to the jukebox again and switched the song to Billy Joel's "Big Shot." Denver made a snide remark about it, paired with an eye roll.

Before Reno returned to the table, he glanced over his right shoulder. Damn, she looked *hot*. Not with all that makeup on her face—Maddox must have had something to do with that. The April he knew was a natural beauty. Her white shirt had slipped off her left shoulder, revealing she wasn't wearing a bra. And the way she turned around and tilted her hip while looking at the jukebox made him want to throw her over his shoulder and haul her out of there, caveman style. It pissed him off to see the other Shifters in the bar checking her out, especially the dead man in the flannel shirt. Her choker would keep most of them away, but not all. Rogues especially.

Reno cursed under his breath and made it back to the table without taking any lives. Even his wolf wanted to take a bite out of every man who was memorizing her ass.

Maddox stood up. "Let's take this outside."

"Fine with me," Reno lied, wanting to stay at the table. April wasn't acting herself. It didn't seem like her to get drunk. Then again, it didn't seem like her to wind up as a Shifter's pet.

"Finish up your sissy drink," Maddox said to Randall. "I'll fill you in later."

Reno followed Maddox down a narrow hall and out the exit door. As soon as the door closed, Maddox took off his hat and turned around.

"What the fuck is your interest in my former client?"

"Maybe I got reason to think Langston isn't dead," Reno said, sliding his hands in the pockets of his leather coat.

Maddox quirked a brow. "Now you have my undivided attention. What makes you so sure he's alive?"

"Let's just say that after a little digging, there's a guy who works at the crematorium who will tell you anything after six beers. The record was falsified and I think his lawyer had something to do with helping him out."

"*Sonofabitch*. Years ago, Langston got into a sticky situation where he needed help."

"What kind of help?"

A motorcycle engine fired up and sped down the road, briefly catching their attention. Maddox sucked on his teeth for a second before answering. "He got drunk and hit another car, killing the guy. Let's just say I got a reputation around this side of town for helping people in need. I took care of his problem—had the car launched off the side of a bridge to conceal some of the evidence because the idiot got out and tried to help the poor bastard, who was already dead. Fingerprints everywhere, not to mention the paint from his car. I gave Langston a new identity and his life back."

"That's what he was sending you payments for?"

Maddox smirked and looked up at the sky. "If that bastard is still alive, I'm going to kill him myself. No one skips out from owing me."

Reno stepped in close. "Seeing how that personal loan could land you in a world of trouble, I'd suggest you cut your losses. I don't want to hear about you showing up at the new business owner's doorstep for payment due," he said. "Let's just say you'd be treading on my territory." Reno knew how guys like Maddox operated and didn't want him coming after Lexi.

Maddox dropped his hat on the ground. "Are you threatening me, boy?"

Reno's lips curled in and he spoke through clenched teeth. "I'm not sugarcoating it. You fuck with anyone in my pack and I'll take you out. How 'bout that?"

In a flash of magic, Maddox shifted and his clothes fell to the ground. *Holy mother*, he was a mountain lion. One of the biggest Reno had ever seen, with a muscular body and ravenous fangs. Shifting inside Breed establishments was against the rules, but they were on the streets where rules didn't exist.

Reno pulled out his gun and aimed it at the wildcat. "Still feeling confident?"

My eyeballs felt like they were vibrating in my skull. The music buzzed like static against my skin, and reality began to feel like needles prickling my nerve endings.

I shouldn't have drunk the Devil's Eye.

As quick as I could, I made my way down the hall to the bathroom. I wasn't sure if I was going to be sick or not, but a little water splashed on my face wouldn't hurt. What I really wanted to do was wash off the makeup that was beginning to feel like a mask, hiding the monster beneath. Whatever was in that drink should be declared illegal.

"Yeah, but honey, I *love* a hard man," a blonde said, reaching in her bra and arranging her breasts closer together. Once enough cleavage to crack walnuts was produced, she stretched her tank top lower and tucked it into her jeans.

"A Shifter like that is a waste of time. He looks like trouble, Nadine."

The blonde cackled. "*I'm* trouble. I bet his animal is a wolf by the way he sized up the room when he walked in. Did you notice that? I love a man in black boots—betcha anything he owns a bike. I'd love to ride him on that bike."

I raised my brows, realizing they were talking about Reno. Nadine slid an ugly stare my way and I must have made a facial expression because she narrowed her beady little eyes. Ignoring her, I bent over the sink and turned on the cold water. The faucet squeaked and a gush of tap splashed against the porcelain sink.

"Come on, Chelsie. Let's get out of here. Looks like someone's mangy pet ran away. I wish they would ban those humans from Breed bars. It's appalling how they get a free pass because of their *slut* collar."

As much as I wanted to engage in an argument with her, it felt like my head was about to explode. Not to mention I'd learned not to mess with Shifters on a whim. It might have been against the rules for them to shift inside the bar, but sometimes rules got broken, and I didn't have a clue how to fight a werebitch.

The click of their pointy heels against the tile faded away as they left the room. The cool water slid over my hands like liquid stars and I stared at it—mesmerized. Maddox had warned me about house specialties when it came to alcoholic drinks—most Breed bars served strong concoctions made from magic and unknown ingredients.

The next thing I knew, a hand was cupping my breast and a body pressed down over my back. My heart raced because Maddox had never put his hands on me that way.

I looked up in the mirror and saw Stu, the flannel shirt-clad Shifter with an overactive libido.

"Get off!" I yelled, elbowing him as hard as I could.

"'Zactly what I'm trying to do, little human."

His hand slid down to my jeans and brushed over my zipper. My back stiffened and I tried to stand up, but he was too heavy. Maddox had warned me about overzealous rogues who had a thing for humans.

"Let go of me," I demanded.

"Shhh." He unlatched my button and settled his weight on me, pressing my stomach painfully against the edge of the sink.

That's when things got fuzzy and survival instinct kicked in.

I rammed my elbow into his ribs twice. Stu grunted in pain and then corralled me into the corner stall. I tried to get around him, but he was crowding the door.

"I hear Devil's Eye makes you horny," he said. "Never tried that shit, but I've seen the aftermath."

He reached out to touch me and I slapped his hand. Stu gave me a sardonic smile. "Look, I don't want to have sex with a human," he said. "That's not my thing; I have standards. I just want to touch you. Maybe you can touch me back."

"Maybe I can *scream*." The last word trailed off into a scream. He lunged and covered my mouth, flipping me around and pushing me against the wall. His body pinned me until I had nowhere to go.

This isn't happening, my inner voice whined as I heard him lock the stall door. Didn't the women in this bar ever have to pee? Oh God, I was starting to have a panic attack. The idea of him touching me—I just couldn't deal with it. I could only breathe out of one nostril because his hand was covering my mouth and pinching half my nose. My body began to shake and I suddenly felt like that helpless little girl in the dark bathroom.

Damn him.

I wasn't that helpless little girl anymore. I thrashed and struck him, scraping my nails down his face. It became a mad struggle. When his hand loosened, I bit his wrist.

The metallic taste of blood filled my mouth and he yanked me by my hair to pry me off. Feral sounds escaped my throat, and I began to have an out-of-body experience.

He shoved me to the floor and I landed on my knees. "Man, you sure got some fight in you. I wouldn't have expected a human to be so goddamn feisty. Look, just give in to the Devil's Eye, and let's have a little fun before someone walks in on us."

Before I could punch him in the groin, the stall door shook violently and I heard Denver shout, "Open the goddamn door!"

His fingers gripped the top of the door and the lock broke. When the door swung open, Denver's indigo eyes were volcanic.

I no longer noticed his sexy blond hair in a messy tangle, nor his toned arms and mischievous smile. The scar on his forehead seemed pronounced, but I barely had time to blink before he grabbed a fistful of Stu's shirt and pulled him out.

"You've got a set of brass balls coming into my bar and pulling this shit." Denver hauled him by the collar to the center of the room. Stu swung his arm and clocked Denver in the jaw.

That's when the fight began. The two men began to pound the hell out of each other—Denver was thrown against the sink before he kicked his leg back and hit the guy in the balls. When Stu bent over, Denver shoved him against a stall divider and it was back and forth. The paper-towel dispenser broke off the wall, and Denver almost lost his balance when he threw another punch.

I leaned over and spit, repulsed by the man's blood in my mouth. My hands were shaking, and a cold sweat broke out on my forehead from the drink.

I thought the demons were unleashed, but I hadn't seen anything until Reno walked in the room. His eyes looked turbulent as they scanned down to my jeans where the button was loose.

"Don't fuckin' do it, bro!" Denver yelled out.

Reno's eyes rolled back in his head for a split second, his fists clenched, and his biceps twitched.

"Brother, if you shift in here and… Jesus effing…"

Denver punched the man in the eye, still engaged in the fight. He'd already acquired a shiner and a busted lip—his hair was all messed up, and he still looked better than the other guy.

I crawled toward the wall and curled up my legs, staring at Reno. He stood absolutely still. If his wolf attacked someone, it could lead to serious trouble with the local Packmasters. If he killed someone, well… I didn't even want to think about it.

Reno's brown eyes settled on me once more. I wiped the blood from my mouth with the back of my hand and spit on the floor.

He stalked toward me with a lack of mercy in his expression.

Denver slid across the floor on his butt and groaned. Without breaking stride, Reno approached the man in the torn flannel shirt.

The Shifter threw a hard right hook and hit him in the jaw. Reno didn't flinch. He grabbed a tuft of Stu's hair and gripped the back of his neck. Reno jerked him over to the sink and I looked away before he smashed the guy's forehead against it.

"How 'bout that? You like hitting women?"

"He didn't hit me," I murmured.

"Don't fucking defend him," Denver accused, holding his side.

The Shifter collapsed to the floor with a nasty lump on his head and lost consciousness.

"I'm not defending him, but this is *his* blood on me, not mine. He just felt me up."

Reno's eyes sliced through the room like a sword. The skin on his neck and face turned red, and I suddenly remembered telling him about that incident I'd gone through as a kid. Instead of coming over and seeing if I was okay, he kicked the Shifter.

Over and over.

"He's down," Denver shouted, pulling Reno back by the arms. "Let me clean up this shit before the manager finds out and I get my ass fired."

Reno didn't hear him. He shoved Denver across the room and delivered another punishing kick, this time to the man's groin.

This was too much violence for me to take and I got up and staggered toward the door, still intoxicated and dizzy.

"You okay?" Denver asked, taking my arm and swiping back my hair. I caught a glimpse of myself in the mirror. My eyeliner was streaked and I had lipstick smeared across my face where I'd wiped the blood.

I rushed to the sink and wet a paper towel. "He's going to flip out if he sees me like this," I said, frantically wiping my face clean.

"See you like what?" I heard Maddox say from the doorway.

Denver held Reno in a viselike grip, struggling to pull him away from the unconscious Shifter.

"Let's go home, Maddox." I rushed toward the door with my head down.

Maddox stuck his arm out and blocked my exit. "Look at me."

"I want to leave."

"Look. At. Me."

I lifted my head and his face relaxed. Maddox had a different look when he got pissed that was opposite from most men. He did this thing where he sucked on his front tooth, or sometimes he'd squint and rub his eye.

"Is this how you take care of your women?" Reno shouted.

Accused.

Provoked.

Holy smokes, this was going to get ugly.

"Please, Maddox. I want you to take me home. I'm not hurt—this isn't my blood." I glanced down at the spatters on my shirt.

Maddox scratched his chin and looked at the pulp of a man lying on the floor. Then he flicked his eyes back to Reno and then to me.

"If I didn't know better, I'd say you two know each other." He hooked his finger beneath my collar and tugged me forward just a little bit. "You know him?"

I shook my head. Smart thing to do. Maddox was possessive and I'd rather he remain in the dark about my history with Reno.

"The bartender heard a ruckus and they both came in to help me out."

His nostrils flared. "Just remember who you belong to," he said in low words. "I treat you good."

"You treat me so good that you left me drunk in a bar full of horny men. I feel special."

He sighed hard and let go of the collar. "That's just the alcohol talking, so I'll let your sassy talk slide."

Reno had started to say something when Denver interrupted, "You're an asshole for the way you treat your pet. You didn't even bother keeping an eye on where she went? This is a Shifter bar; you know assholes in here are fascinated with them. Word gets out on that kind of thing and men lose respect for a Shifter who can't keep his own safe. I think it's time for you to get out before I call the manager and explain what happened. Jake doesn't like drama."

Maddox pointed his finger. "Boy, you—"

"Don't," I pleaded, gripping his wrist. "Please," I whispered. "Take me home."

Maddox's eyes softened and he tapped my nose with his finger before wrapping his arm around me.

I wanted to glance over my shoulder and get one last look at Reno. I'd never thought I would run into him again, and this was the worst way it could have possibly happened.

Seeing his explosive reaction made me realize he still cared about me. Or *did*. Reno would never respect me after this incident, not that I expected we'd get back together. But this solidified it.

Permanently.

CHAPTER 28

Two weeks before Christmas, my life had returned to normal after the brawl at Howlers. I hadn't heard from Reno, and Maddox didn't bring it up. He'd brought me home, cleaned me up, and sent me to bed. He'd also apologized for having left me alone in a Breed bar, which wasn't always a safe place for a human to be in alone. Shifters were aggressive, but the vast majority of them would never put their hands on a woman. He said it wasn't my fault—that no woman could do anything that deserved that kind of treatment.

I still slept in the front bedroom and nothing had changed in regards to our relationship. I kept him company and he put a roof over my head.

It wasn't all bad. We laughed at old sitcoms and Maddox enjoyed reading me articles from the paper, making comments about human politics. Sometimes he'd tell stories about his younger days, and I began to see a gentler side of him. Deep down, Maddox was a gem, and I truly enjoyed his company.

One evening after sunset, Maddox led me into the kitchen and sat me down. The lights were off and only a pine-scented candle illuminated the room from the center of the table. Sometimes he liked to eat by candlelight. He often showed off his culinary skills by cooking stew, even though I didn't care for the gamey meat he often used in it.

"What's for dinner?"

He removed an object from the kitchen drawer and circled around behind me. "We're skipping the meal unless you change your mind. Although, I'm hoping you change your mind. Do me a favor and close your eyes."

I nervously shut my eyes, feeling his hand brush my hair away from the back of my neck.

"You should dye it the way it was. I liked it that way," he murmured.

Something cold and hard touched the nape of my neck and I swallowed thickly.

"Hold still."

Snip.

My collar fell free and landed on my lap.

I clutched it in my hand and looked up. "What's going on?"

He tugged at his beard and patted my head. "You're a doll, but this isn't going to work out. You're too young for an old dog like me, and I got needs you're clearly not going to be filling anytime soon."

"Can we talk about the payment plan? I need time to find a job, Maddox. And a place to live. We have a contract and you can't let me go." I started to panic. "I've already cleared two thousand off my debt from the odd jobs you've given me—but I still can't afford the rest."

Maddox strolled around the chair and sat to my right. He laced his fingers together and blew out a short puff of breath, causing the candle to flicker. "We're square."

"Um, no we're not."

"April, there's no way in hell you'll ever be able to pay what you owe. My interest rates are too damn high for a human like you. It would take too long, and after spending time with you, I'd rather cut my ties. It's just not going to feel right seeing you on any kind of level."

"So that's it? All this time I thought everything was fine." Suddenly for some reason, I felt insulted. "Just because I won't sleep with you? Are you really that shallow?"

"Are you really that naïve? How many Shifters do you think keep pets that don't service them in the bedroom?"

"I'm not a service. I'm a person."

"Yeah," he murmured, resting his chin in his hand and staring at the candle. "This was just a business transaction, honey. I made a promise that it wouldn't go that route, but it's not easy. When you wear those little black shorts around the house before bed… *hell*. Sex with other women means I have to rent out a hotel room, and that's not my scene. How do you expect me to sleep in my bed knowing you're just a few doors down the hall? I toss at night, April. It's hard on a man. You're too damn ripe for the pickin' and I can't go on playing house anymore. I thought companionship was all I needed, but I was wrong. I need the whole package."

"So you're just going to throw me out on the street?"

"As far as I'm concerned, you don't owe me a dime. You're free."

I let the words resonate. *Free.* Not just from Maddox, but from all the strings that held me to my past. The ones that had twisted my life into knots and kept me bound.

He cleared his throat. "You still want dinner? I can heat up a pan of lasagna or you can go pack your bags. You can have anything in your room, even though you haven't let me buy you a damn thing."

A tear rolled down my cheek. I'd hoped for this moment but never imagined how strangely fond I'd grown of Maddox. He played it off as if it were about the sex, but I knew him better than that. Somehow, I had crept inside his heart and he'd begun to care. I got up from my seat and stood behind him, slipping my arms around his neck.

"Thank you," I whispered against his wavy hair. "No matter what anyone says, Maddox, you have a heart of gold."

"Stay out of trouble, little girl. If any man puts his hands on you, then you come see me and I'll take care of it. Stay away from lenders, you hear?"

I nodded against his shoulder.

"Go on," he said in a soft voice, reaching around and patting my back. "Before I change my mind."

And just like that, I was free.

After the incident at Howlers, Reno spent two weeks running a background check on Maddox, hoping to find something that would get him in trouble with the authorities. Only then would April be free, whether she wanted it or not. Why the hell would she become another man's pet? The thought twisted into a painful knot in Reno's mind as he thought about the two of them having sex.

Reno had come close to shooting Maddox's animal, but Denver had come out and dragged him back inside the bar, leaving Maddox to shift back and get dressed. Reno had gone into the men's room to cool off when he heard a ruckus coming from the adjacent bathroom. When he saw April on the floor, something dark had not only splintered *his* heart, but his animal's heart as well. Reno's wolf had thrashed at his skin to come out, and he'd fought hard to keep him tethered. Murder would not only lead to his arrest by the higher authority, but it would shame his pack if it couldn't be justified. The odds were against him since Breed establishments were neutral ground with strict rules.

And murder was exactly what would have happened. Instead, he'd unleashed violence.

During the weeks that followed, Reno's investigation on Maddox came up clean. He ran a legit business and dealt with the right people. Loan sharks weren't illegal, but sometimes they did illegal things. Maddox's record was so clean it squeaked. Unfortunately, without any evidence, he couldn't do anything about the questionable loan made to Charles Langston. Maddox had meticulously covered his tracks, and there were laws against slander that kept Reno's hands tied.

Maybe April didn't want anything to do with the likes of Reno, but after that night, he knew with absolute certainty it had *nothing* to do with him being a Shifter.

Eventually, he could no longer sleep without knowing what their arrangement was all about. So Reno had called up Maddox to confront him and find out the truth. And the truth is exactly what he got.

Holy hell, that woman had given up her freedom to get out of debt. That amount of money was a drop in the bucket for Reno, who had been stashing his income away for years. But for a young girl like April, it must have seemed like quicksand. He didn't want her to lose sight of her dreams, becoming a woman he'd no longer recognize.

So Reno cleared her debt. Every penny.

At first, Maddox wouldn't accept his money but wouldn't give a reason. Reno didn't relent. He called him two days later, and after a heated discussion, Maddox said he'd do it for double the amount. Maybe he'd been testing him, but Reno had never flunked a test in his life.

He'd paid the full amount, but he had conditions of his own. The first being Maddox wouldn't tell her about their arrangement. She could never find out about Reno's involvement under any circumstance. April would then feel like she owed Reno, and he wanted to give her something she'd never had: financial freedom. A person deserved a clean slate in life at least once, and she had more than paid her dues. The second condition was that Maddox had to cut her loose immediately and tell her it was for personal reasons.

Maddox thought Reno was a crazy sonofabitch, as he put it, but he'd agreed. All men have a price. Reno had received the call the other day to confirm it was done, but Maddox had no clue where she'd gone.

Reno tapped into a few resources to track her location; he wouldn't sleep easy until he knew she was in a good place. He found her sister's number and called under the guise that he was a friend who owed her some cash. Rose said she hadn't heard from April in a month and feigned concern. She also told Reno if he happened to run into April, to let her know she was canceling her Christmas trip and going to Vegas instead. Rose didn't seem worried about April's whereabouts, but she was young and a little full of herself.

Jericho spun a silver lighter in a circle on the bar in their game room. "You gonna play with yourself all day or help Ivy put up the tree? I don't see why they couldn't get one of those shiny plastic ones at the store," Jericho grumbled. "That thing they hauled in is so fresh I thought I saw a squirrel's nest in it."

"Why don't *you* put it up?" Reno muttered from the beanbag chair that was too damn small to fit his frame.

"Because I have a gig tonight and I'm not breaking my neck over a commercial holiday that bleeds your wallet dry."

Reno still had his hands locked behind his head as he stared up at the ceiling. "I seem to recall a different Jericho who once got up in the middle of the night and stole all the neighbor's lights and put them on Dad's house."

Jericho chuckled with a look of nostalgia. "I think Dad was more pissed I was on the roof than the fact I stole the lights."

"You were eight."

"Yeah, well." He took a long drag of his smoke and looked reflectively at the cigarette. "Time changes people. We're only putting it up because of Maizy."

"She's a kid. Let her enjoy it while she can. That's what pack life is all about, Jericho. Family. Kids. We have to do right by them."

"Mr. Reno!" Maizy yelled out. She stomped into the room, out of breath and grinning excitedly. "Miss Ivy wants me to tell you that she's... that she wants you to help put up the Christmas tree. Mommy has our decorations in a box and are you coming?"

Reno swung his legs around and sat up, looking at Jericho. "Where the hell is Austin? I'm not up for this."

Maizy flew out of the room. "He's coming!" she yelled.

"Christ," Reno muttered. The twins had volunteered to cut down the tree and Denver had hauled it to the house in his truck, leaving Reno with the final honors of getting sap all over his hands to stand it up.

When Reno ambled downstairs, he couldn't help but smile at Maizy. She was wearing a red dress and sitting in the middle of the room, surrounded by a string of white lights and tapping her wand on the floor. The women had moved the furniture, cleaned, and decorated the house.

"Great timing," Ivy said, out of breath.

She didn't have on her usual skirt or dress today, but a pair of baggy overalls and a beige sweater. Ivy still wore a braid—it was her trademark. None of the men in the house had ever seen her hair loose, but they never asked why. Women were a mystery unto themselves.

Reno pulled out his pocketknife and began to cut away the rope.

"I broke off some of the lower branches, but I don't know how to get it up on the stand," she said.

"Jericho, give me a hand," Reno barked out, lifting the tree by the top. "I need someone to hold the other end. Grab the trunk and ease it into the middle. Once it's straight, you need to screw it in until it's tight."

Jericho chuckled and swiped his tongue across his bottom lip. "Hmm, that sounds *all too* familiar."

"Where's Austin?" Reno repeated, feeling an itch on his neck where a bristly needle was rubbing.

Ivy held the base of the stand and looked up. "He went with Lexi and Lynn to pick up some ornaments for the tree. Lynn said the ones she had reminded her of… well, you know," she said, eyes darting toward Maizy.

Yeah, the bastard of a man who'd fathered that child and left her. What a pathetic excuse for a human.

"I say we don't need a tree. Just put Peanut in the middle of the room and wrap her up in lights," Denver suggested.

Maizy poked her tongue out as he eased into a chair with a wide grin.

"You got it?" Reno yelled out. "When I push it up, I need you guys to stabilize the base and tighten the pins."

Someone had already cut the trunk and prepped it. He slowly eased the tree up and Jericho secured the bottom. After a few minutes, they had it righted and Ivy plopped backward on her butt and wiped her hands off.

"What's wrong?" Denver suddenly asked.

Everyone turned to look at Maizy—her blond hair illuminated by the white lights and her mouth turned down in a pout.

"There's not enough," she whined, holding the small strand of lights and gazing up at the monstrous tree.

Denver shot to his feet and opened a small closet by the front door, then pulled out his jacket. "Come on, Peanut. Let's go buy you some twinkle lights."

She stared at him dumbfounded.

"Get your coat and shoes," he said in an animated voice. "I'm taking you to the store so you can pick out every pretty light in any color you want. Skedaddle!"

Her face lit up and she flew up the stairs. They might have been a pack of males, but wolves had an instinctual reaction to look after children and make sure they were happy. Yeah, maybe that little girl got spoiled now and again, but she'd grow up knowing every last one of these men would bleed for her.

"Damn. My wolf has to go for a run before I head out tonight," Jericho announced, kicking off his shoes and peeling away his Pink Floyd shirt. "If I'm not back in an hour, come find me. I can't be late. I go on stage at midnight."

In a fluid motion, Jericho shifted into a brown wolf mixed with cream and orange. His milky green eyes wandered up to Reno, who opened the front door and let him out.

"You going too?" he asked Ivy. She rarely let her wolf run with one of them. Ivy had gone through the change not long after her arrival, and Austin had carefully introduced her new wolf to the pack, as was custom. But since then, Ivy's wolf kept to herself.

Despite her demure behavior, Reno liked Ivy. Lexi's sass kept everyone laughing, while Ivy kept the men grounded. He didn't know much about the pack she came from, but he wondered how they treated their women because of some things he noticed, which were uncharacteristic for a female Shifter. For one, Wheeler had walked by her once while yelling at Reno and lifted his hand angrily as he drove his point home. Ivy had flinched. No one said anything about it, but Reno and Austin made a mental note. She was outspoken with her opinions and the men didn't seem to intimidate her otherwise, so Reno couldn't be certain if her pack had abused her. He'd never met such a graceful and easygoing woman, but her wolf was skittish and easily frightened.

Reno heard his phone ringing upstairs. When it stopped, the house phone rang.

"Reno?" Ivy called out from the kitchen. "Someone's asking for you."

He crossed the room and took the phone, then leaned against the wall. "Yeah."

"I think April's trying to kill herself."

Reno's heart stopped and he almost dropped the phone. It was Trevor. "Is this your idea of a sick joke?"

"I need your help. Long story short, April's mother overdosed and April's staying in her motel room."

Blood pounded in his head and he almost couldn't hear Trevor. "Where is she?"

"Holed up in a dump by the sound of it," Trevor said in rushed words. "She's drunk or something and babbling incoherently. I don't know how long she's been there, but she won't tell me where it is. I have her cell number, but she's not answering anymore. Look, she told me you were a PI. I've called all the motels I can think of, but I don't know what the fuck her mother's first name is or if she was the one renting out the room. Dammit! I'll pay you whatever."

"I already have her number and mother's full name, as well as the man she usually stays with. I'll have her location in less than fifteen minutes. And Trevor?"

"Yeah?"

"Keep your money."

Trevor's voice leveled out and dropped an octave. "I'm coming with you, so call me back."

CHAPTER 29

YOU DON'T OFFICIALLY HIT ROCK bottom until you've lost it all. I'd spent years despising my mother, and after I'd been given a fresh start, I wanted to mend the rift between us by trying to understand why she chose the life she did. Why she left Rose and me with our grandma after Dad died, and why she never once showed any interest in turning her life around. Tracking her whereabouts wasn't difficult because there were only two places in town where she stayed.

This motel housed drug addicts. Every so often, the cops would organize a bust to make a public example, but it never stopped anyone from dealing and using.

My mom resembled nothing of the woman I once knew. Her body was frail and she didn't look over ninety pounds. Her once beautiful blond hair was now thinning and dry. She had track marks all up her arms and in other places on her bruised body. Two of her teeth were missing and she behaved erratically—talking to herself and twitching, as if incapable of sitting still. I tried sobering her up with coffee, and she kept asking if I had any cash she could borrow. I wanted to buy her groceries and new clothes. I wanted to make her better again so she'd leave this life and stop using.

But you can't make a user clean.

Mom made a call and thirty minutes later, someone brought her drugs. She had plenty of prescription drugs in the bathroom—either stolen or bought—but they weren't enough.

I cried. I'd never imagined it was possible to feel so much empathy for a woman who had abandoned me. I mostly cried for the woman and mother she could have been but chose not to be. I cried because deep down, I just wanted to feel my mother's arms around me and know her love.

Then things went from bad to worse.

She refused to talk about the past and seeing me must have made her shoot up more than normal. I went into the bathroom and broke down, ready to finally walk away for good. But it was so hard. All I'd ever wanted was for my mom to love me. I just wanted to be good enough for her. How could I walk away from the person who gave me life?

That was when it hit me how much our lives ran parallel. But I had something my mom never had.

Hope.

That single word was all encompassing. It bled into our lives as something that divided us—a concept she turned away from. It proved that despite our similarities, we were on different paths because of the choices we'd made.

When I finally emerged from the bathroom, my mom was lying on the bed, arms stretched wide. Her eyes were rolled back and vomit slid down the side of her hollow cheek as she convulsed.

I tried everything to resuscitate her. Despite my efforts, my mother died in my arms. The paramedics didn't go above the call of duty to save a junkie—nothing beyond a few chest compressions.

What made the situation unbearable was that I told them I didn't know her. I didn't want the burden of having to pay for her funeral or cremation.

Exposed for what I was, guilt consumed me. I had sunk so low that I sent my own mother to an unmarked grave to save me the expense. After they took her body away, I spent the next three days in her room, overcome with grief. What kind of person had I become? She'd abandoned me and in the end, I had abandoned her. Loving someone is being selfless, and what exactly had I done in our relationship to demonstrate that I was anything *but* my mother's daughter?

I took another swig of whiskey from the bottle, wiping my wet cheeks while sitting on the bathroom floor and staring at a pile of pills on my lap. I'd always been the strong one who kept going when the world went to hell. People looked at my bright hair and smile and never knew the life I led or the painful past I had survived. No one ever wants to look that deep. But it didn't matter because I didn't want anyone's pity; the challenges life had thrown at me had only made me want to fight harder to overcome them.

All I'd ever desired was respect. I didn't want to be judged for where I came from, but where I was going.

"Oh, Reno." I wept as memories assailed me. "I wish I could do it all over again. I didn't deserve you."

Truly, I didn't. Part of me wished he cared about me as much as I did him, but he could never love a human. I'd learned a lot in my short stint in the Breed world—most looked upon humans as third-class citizens. I was just a curiosity to him, and men like Reno didn't pine over women who left them for another man. They got over it and moved on. They sought out gregarious, flirtatious women who had their lives together and balances in check. I, on the other hand, was Romance Novel Girl, living in a fantasy world.

"I always knew those books would be the death of me," I murmured.

My long legs stretched out wide in front of me. My jean shorts disappeared beneath my oversized black shirt, which was heavy between my legs from a pile of multicolored pills. I wanted to see what my mother had chosen over me, so I'd spent the last hour staring at the tiny pills and tossing them into the toilet one at a time.

It was therapeutic.

"April! Open the door right now!" a man's voice demanded from outside. Not outside the bathroom door, but even farther. Whoever it was hammered on the door several times while I took another swig from the bottle.

I hadn't truly grieved her loss, and this was my night to get it all out of my system before I moved on. It wasn't as easy as I thought it would be. I didn't have the heart to call Rose and tell her our mom was dead, although she probably would have just hung up. But the memory of the woman who gave life to me lying lifeless in my arms shattered me.

I tossed a pill into the toilet and spouted off another reason why I hated her. But I was honestly running out of reasons. The main ones had already been addressed, and now I was left with some of the good memories, which made it harder to let go.

A loud crash sounded in the other room and I drunkenly lifted my eyes. The bathroom door swung open in front of me and hit the wall with a thud.

"Hi, Trevor."

His eyes were wide and staring at the pills in my lap.

"Babe, *what did you do?*" he breathed, moving quickly until he was kneeling on the floor.

"You're so handsome, Trev."

He gripped my jaw and forced my mouth open. The next thing I knew, Trevor shoved his finger down my throat and forced me to gag.

"Stop it!" My words were garbled.

But his hand wrapped around the back of my neck and he pushed his finger in deeper. I bit his knuckle and shook my head until he let go.

"April, *how many?* How long ago?"

"You're crowding my space," I argued.

"Get out," a man's voice commanded.

"What is this, a party?" I ran my fingers through Trevor's perfect hair.

A few pills scattered across the floor and when I glanced up, Reno filled the doorway.

"Why is he here? He's not really here, is he?"

Trevor grabbed my wrist and shouted, "How many did you take?"

Then he was gone.

Reno had yanked him back and had taken his place. His hands cupped my cheeks and he examined my eyes. Then he felt my pulse. Reno held up a few pills and studied them. "Did you swallow any of these, April? Answer my question or I'm going to force you to throw up and take you to the ER where they're going to pump some vile shit into your stomach."

"I'm…"

He glanced in the toilet and then looked at Trevor over his shoulder. "Leave us alone and shut the door."

"Are you crazy? Call an ambulance!"

"She didn't take these," Reno said decidedly, brown eyes still on mine. "Did you?"

I shook my head. He knew me too well. As drunk as I was, I didn't have it in me to cross that line.

"Two minutes," Trevor growled.

The door closed and Reno took a seat in front of me, moving the bottle aside and taking handfuls of the pills and tossing them in the toilet, which was already full of them.

"My mother's dead," I said in a broken voice. No more tears were left to spill, but my heart burned with raw anguish. I'd never felt so gutted—so lost.

Reno leaned in and kissed me softly on the cheek. God, I'd missed him more than I thought. He smelled so good—like pine trees—and I wanted to rewind and do it all over. I'd ruined what we had and there was no erasing my past. I hated hindsight—I wished I could back a truck over it.

"I'm sorry," he breathed against my skin. "But what is this about? Where's the girl who has it all together? Where did she go?"

My head rolled to the side and I looked away. "I turned my mother into an addict because I was a stupid kid. I should have been a better daughter."

He brushed my hair away from my face and leaned in so close that my leg had somehow wrapped around his waist.

"You told me when your mother started doing heavy drugs. Juvie. But did she drink before then?"

I didn't answer and he gripped my shoulders.

"Dammit, April. *Let me in.*"

"Yes. She'd hit the bottle now and again but was never a user. Maybe some weed—I don't remember."

"You don't get it. She was already an addict. She just traded out the booze for something stronger. It wasn't you that drove her to fuck up her life the way she did. She couldn't cope with her problems and tried to dull them away. Maybe she had a messed-up childhood or something dark you never knew about her. Don't blame yourself for what that woman did to you. You're entitled to a night of hitting the bottle after all that you've been through, and I'm cool with that. I'll sit here and have a drink with you. I've been through some rough shit in my life and hit some pretty low points; those who have been there know what it's about. Those who haven't, judge. I'm not here to judge you, April. You've got some personal demons you need to battle and I want you to win. Do what you need to do in order to deal with this and get past it. But don't shut me out."

"I wish I hadn't screwed things up with us."

"Yeah, well. People fuck up. Doesn't mean you go through life punishing yourself for it," he said in bristly words, brushing the last few pills away from me. "I'm not perfect by a mile. I got a toolbox full of issues and I'm not a big talker, so that shit mostly stays locked up."

I lifted my eyes. "You're not a big talker? Everything you say to me changes my life in ways that you don't even realize. You fix me with your kindness."

His eyes melted and he held my left hand, brushing his thumb over the top knuckles. I studied his features and admired the man before me. His eyes were coffee brown and not wide, but narrow and kind. And his masculine nose and jaw didn't seem to stand out as much as those carved lines in his cheeks or the tiny scar on his lip that used to be mine. He had recently shaved and I touched his smooth chin, pinching the tip and feeling a pang of guilt that made me let go.

"Don't," he said, capturing my wrist and bringing it back up to his face. "Keep doing that."

I outlined his thin mouth and scratched my fingers along his short sideburns, noticing how attractive his widow's peak looked on him. When I pinched his earlobe, he smiled, deepening those lines in his face. What a handsome man Reno was when he smiled.

"I have a confession," he said, and I got the feeling by the way he was averting his eyes that it wasn't something he wanted to admit.

"You regret having slept with a human?"

Reno reluctantly reached in his pocket and opened his fingers. I glanced down at his hand and saw a familiar red item settling in the crease of his palm.

"My cherry earring," I said, nonplussed. I lost it months ago and they were my favorite pair that I wore to work. "How—"

"Six months ago, you drove by the house with Lexi and I was outside playing horseshoes. I thought I was hallucinating when I saw you step out of the car. Damn, I couldn't even speak when you looked at me with those hazel eyes. You were like an angel fleeing from a devil when you ran to your car and sped off. I found this on the driveway and…"

"What?"

He tucked it back in his pocket and lowered his eyes. "I've carried it with me ever since. A good luck charm I never leave home without. Ever. Austin caught me off guard once with an emergency and halfway down the road, I turned back around to get it."

Holy smokes. "Some luck," I muttered.

"Yeah," he said with a dazed smile, gently cupping my face with his warm hands and centering his eyes on mine. "Brought you back to me, and I'd say that's pretty damn lucky. I don't think you're aware of one important detail, and I'm going to clear the air so there's no confusion. You're my girl and I'm putting my claim on you. Maybe I still need to earn it, and that's fine, but you're not walking out of this room without knowing what you mean to me. You've got my heart. You've got my loyalty. You've got everything a man can give a woman, including my love. Yeah, that's right, princess. Love. The first time I saw your eyes, my chest squeezed so damn tight I couldn't breathe. But what sealed the deal was the first night we slept together. And I don't mean the sex, but lying next to you in bed and talking. The same feeling I get when I'm on my bike and thundering ninety on an open stretch of road, I get when I'm with you. I feel alive when you're in my arms, and that's a helluva thing for a man like me to admit. Trevor was wrong when he called you submissive, and he knows it. When life keeps kicking a man down and he gets right back up, that's strength. You're just finding your way in this world and keeping your chin high, and that's what attracts me. You're a proud woman and I love you because you ain't perfect. I've never felt like this, and I'm not about to screw it up by letting you go."

"You don't mean that."

Please God, let him mean that! my inner voice screamed with giddy excitement. I didn't want to imagine that he was just messing with my head. It would kill me, because I still had strong feelings for him I couldn't erase. Reno was a man I wanted to know everything about, who not only made me feel safe, but happy. Nothing I told him about my past shocked him, and it made me want to open up to someone for the first time. Even Trevor didn't know all the details of the baggage I carried around.

"I say what I mean. How 'bout that?"

"You don't think I'm broken?"

His forehead touched mine. "We're all broken. Don't you see that? We're just pieces of ourselves, trying to fit with someone else to become whole. You and I fit."

"I don't want anyone talking down to me because I'm a human."

"And I won't let any man utter an unkind word to you without my fist breaking every bone in his face," he said in chilling words. "You have my word on that."

"Don't you want to ask me about Maddox?"

"Not really. I'm not your judge and jury." Then he looked up in my eyes, just a breath away. "I *do* want to know what happened between you and Sanchez." His eyes became a smoldering inferno.

"He's dead now and it doesn't matter. Nothing happened."

"Nothing between us, April. No secrets. I can't be with a woman who has shadows in her life she won't let me see."

I licked my lips and lowered my eyes to his mouth. "I owed him, as you know. We were at the warehouse and part of the payment he wanted was for me to take off my shirt. Nothing happened. He just stared at me and... *you know*. I was scared to say no to him because we were alone and he had a knife."

His eyes closed as if he were processing it and every muscle in his face hardened. "You'll never be alone, princess. I'm going to protect you. No scumbag will ever treat you like that again," he promised, softly kissing the corner of my mouth.

God, the way his lips moved across my jaw. Some of the alcohol buzz was dissipating and I felt intoxicated with bliss.

"Tell me something about you," I asked of him. I had to know more than just the man I saw, but a glimmer of who he once was. "Something no one else knows. Tell me about *your* shadows, Reno."

His eyes closed heavily before he spoke. "I lost my faith in humanity when I served in the war."

I spoke cautiously. "What happened?"

"Second World War. We liberated the camps and I've never seen anything so goddamn horrific before or since. The bodies stacked on top of one another, the women crying… I can't… I still can't talk about it. I've buried brothers who were just kids themselves, but nothing compares to all the innocents who died. Those children… All these years later, and that's the one thing that gives me nightmares."

This strong man fought his emotions as his lips thinned into a mixed expression of anger and pain. His eyes opened and glittered with tears, and I was finally beginning to see his shadows. Maybe Shifter men didn't allow themselves to feel sorrow or weakness, but it dwelled beneath the surface just as hot and alive as lava beneath a volcano.

I brushed my fingers through his hair. "It's okay, sweetie. You don't have talk about it. I understand. Sometimes just knowing something is more meaningful than the details. Maybe war veterans don't feel like heroes, but you are. It wasn't even your battle to fight as a Shifter, but you did what you thought was just. That's admirable. That's the kind of quality that makes you such a good man."

His eyes opened and were glittering with pain. I gently touched his hand, realizing my soldier carried his battle scars inside. Maybe words couldn't comfort a man who suffered from emotional trauma, so all I offered him was a kiss in the palm of his hand. "I can't begin to imagine all you've seen in your life."

His rich brown eyes settled on mine. "Darkness was all there was until I first saw you. I see a future when we're together. I feel it in my gut that this is right."

"I won't live as long as you will," I reminded him.

"We can argue about why it won't work out, or we can make it work. You decide."

With his lips pressed to my neck, I closed my eyes and let a little more hope back into my life. I wasn't falling for Reno. I fell for him the day he fixed up my trailer. That's when I saw the kind of man he was, and it had nothing to do with the things he purchased but rather the sentiment behind his actions. Reno had a generous heart and wanted to take care of a girl without any expectations, just to give her a little piece of happiness in this world. War may have robbed him of his faith in humanity, but he had restored mine.

"Grab your things. I'm taking you home," he said in a voice that left no doubt.

I wrapped my arms around his neck.

"Didn't you hear me?"

I placed my mouth against his ear and said in a private voice, "*You're* my thing, Reno. My very best thing."

His arms were everywhere, embracing me and bringing me home. "Wolves mate for life, princess. You up for that?"

"I'm not a wolf."

"No, you're not. You're an angel." Reno lifted me off the cold tile, securing me in his strong arms as my legs hung down. "Tonight, you're sleeping in my arms and we're going to do some spooning. But I'll be damned if I'm going to have a poster of Billy Joel staring at us."

A flurry of laughter flew out of my mouth. I kissed the tip of his nose and looked down at him in awe. When he smiled, he looked charming and boyish, and now I knew why Trevor was reminded of the actors he'd seen in the movies. I finally realized that I'd found my storybook romance. Reno didn't have a white steed or a princely title, but he had my heart.

I'd been so fixated on having a home that I'd never realized how a person could be the very thing I was searching for. Reno was home, and I was finally ready to go.

CHAPTER 30

"Don't be nervous, Trevor." I smiled at him from the passenger side of the car and he glared at me like grim death.

"Easy for you to say, babe."

We'd been sitting in a parked car in front of Austin's house for the last five minutes. Two days had elapsed since Reno had brought me home from the motel. While he set up my own room, I found my way into his bed on the first night and declared it our room.

Ours is a better word than *mine*.

I'd done most of my mourning in the hotel and tried to leave the pain of my old life behind. I knew I'd always carry the guilt of losing my mother, but I'd lost her years ago. I just hadn't come to terms with that fact. Reno didn't talk when I cried in the middle of the night, and he filled an emptiness that had been a part of me for so long. I drew strength from him and looked forward to our days together because I knew they'd be filled with laughter.

"I don't know why you're so worried. They like you."

Trevor snorted. "Yeah, I got that warm fuzzy feeling when your boyfriend pounded me in the face."

What Trevor didn't know was just how *much* the Cole brothers respected him. He'd taken a bullet for Reno, and saving their brother is not something they took lightly. I still hadn't been able to say a thing to him about being a Shifter because of my promise, but Reno told me today that it was time to confront Trevor to see where he stood. I'd spent all afternoon with him at the movies, bookstore, and then wasting hours in a coffee shop eating pastry and talking about life. Just like old times.

"Are we going to live in your car?" I asked.

"Sounds good to me. Is this really that important to you?"

"They invited you for dinner, Trevor. And you're one of the most important people in my life. I want you to be part of my new life, and I know it's not easy to accept all the changes, but we're friends for the long haul, right?"

He took my left hand and kissed the top of it. "April Showers, always showering me with love." He sighed dramatically and popped open his door. "Let's get this over with. Hold on to your panties—it's going to be a bumpy night."

We got out of the car and I stuffed my hands in my coat pockets as the chilly wind blew from behind me. I began to wonder if something was wrong because the lights were out inside the house. I hoped it meant a candlelight dinner and not that someone forgot to pay the bill. He held my hand tightly as we walked up the porch steps and took a slow stroll to the door.

When it clicked open, Reno filled the empty space and then closed the door behind him. Trevor backed up when Reno folded his arms, and I feared he might turn around and run to the car.

Then a smile curved up Reno's cheek and he winked at me. "Good to see you, Trevor."

They nodded at each another the way men often do and Reno's brows stitched together. "Well, let's get this over with."

On that note, I officially began to get nervous. Reno had promised me he'd be on his best behavior, but this was already kicking off to a cold start.

Which speaking of, a bluster of wind rattled the trees and spun some of my hair around. I moved my long bangs away from my face and tucked them behind my ear. Reno reached forward and touched a long strand. "I'm glad you grew it out. You look beautiful."

I bit my lip because my smile was borderline comical, and Trevor looked down at me and huffed. "Well, I like platinum. Just so you know."

I lifted my shoulder. "Always good to try something new."

"Get inside. Dinner's getting cold," Reno ordered. He opened the door, allowing us to walk past him. I walked in ahead of Trevor and wondered why Reno was suppressing a grin.

"Why are the lights off?"

Trevor bumped into me as I stood in the center of the room. Not even the tree was lit.

"Surprise!" The light flipped on and my heart stammered in my chest.

Everyone in the pack surrounded us, but that wasn't the surprising part.

It was the banners hanging everywhere with wolves on them.

Denver leaned over and flipped on the stereo, which was to our right in the living room. A Diana Ross song came on—"I'm Coming Out."

"Oh. My. God," I said, whispered, or exclaimed. I couldn't be sure which because the sound of disco music filled my ears as I looked at all the banners.

Maizy was sitting beneath the Christmas tree to the right of the stairs, holding a stuffed wolf.

As the music thumped against the floorboards, Trevor backed up. The door closed behind us and Reno blocked it.

"Trevor, I think it's about time we had a talk," Austin began. "I think we all know what's up. Some of the guys had an idea to throw a party and damn, I don't know if they're just crazy or stupid. But we're here to support you and let you know that we… I want to extend an invitation to you to join our pack."

Trevor's hand began to sweat and he let go. I gripped his jacket in case he got the bright idea of knocking Reno down and bolting out the door.

Austin approached in his jeans and white T-shirt. Lexi and Ivy were sitting on the stairs, Lynn peered in from the dining room, and the rest of the guys were sprinkled all about. Denver danced chaotically to the music and Maizy was giggling at him.

"What the hell is this?" Trevor said sharply.

"It's a coming-out party!" Maizy exclaimed.

Austin stepped forward and lowered his chin, giving off a strong vibe in the room of his authority. "It's an invitation. We're Shifter wolves and I'm the Packmaster of the Weston Pack. So far, it's just my brothers and Lexi's family, but we need some new blood. I've been keeping an eye out for candidates, and I can't think of a better choice. You've protected April as long as you've known her, shown loyalty and other qualities that I look for. I don't know why you're skittish about letting people know what you are, but to each his own. As you can see, this is a bit of a nonconventional pack. We have humans, but I've never believed in following all the rules in life. Family is family, and it's not about whether or not you fit the mold."

Austin dropped his hand on Trevor's shoulder and gave him a serious look, albeit difficult with Diana Ross shouting out. "You took a bullet for my brother. And maybe you don't give a shit about him, but you did it for April. That's loyalty. That's love. That's the kind of man I want in my pack. They're not all total dickheads," he said, his gaze skating around the room.

"Except maybe that one." Jericho pointed his thumb at Denver, who was bent over and gyrating his butt in circles.

Thank God they didn't put the wolves on rainbow banners. I couldn't read Trevor's expression. He looked like a ghost dressed in black.

He folded his arms and engaged in a staring match with Austin, not something you really want to do with a Packmaster. "Just so you know, I'm gay. So you can turn the disco off."

Denver whirled around and they all looked at one another.

Trevor laughed and wrapped his arm around me. "I also have no intention of shifting around you. So maybe you need a second to change your mind. Let's have dinner and forget this ever happened."

Austin stepped forward and jerked his head to the right, signaling to Reno. A hand gripped my arm and Reno pulled me to the side.

"Hey, what are you doing?" I protested.

Trevor and Austin were nose to nose. "Look, I don't need to rethink a decision I've already made. Gay? Fine. You want to hide your wolf? Not so fine. You know the rule. Your wolf has to be introduced to everyone in the pack before coming in. If something happens down the line and we shift to defend our pack, I don't need you turning on anyone in this room because your wolf doesn't know them. After that, if you want to stay in hiding, that's your choice. But we're not ashamed of what we are in this family, and we don't hide. It doesn't mean our wolves run with each other, and some of them are…"

"*Loco* is the word you're searching for," Jericho blurted out, staring at Denver.

"Shut it," Denver said with a snap of his fingers.

Austin cupped the side of Trevor's neck. "I don't have to know you for ten years to trust you. I've seen what I need to see. This is a chance for you to be part of a family—a brotherhood. You'll have April to keep an eye on, and I'm always looking for input on new members. We need a strong pack, and I'm laying the offer down in front of you. So make a decision. We're not having dinner for you to go back home, think it over, and pussy out." He dropped his hand and quirked a smile. "You in?"

Trevor clenched his jaw and glanced sideways at me. Reno had his arms wrapped around me from behind and I looked at Trevor pleadingly. The idea of having him in the house to be a part of my family elated me. I mouthed *please*.

"On one condition," Trevor began. "I don't listen to disco. I don't deal with jokes about my lifestyle. I don't think I need to explain why I've left Shifter life behind. I never had a problem with being a Shifter until my pack abused me on a daily basis."

"What the hell for?" Denver said in low, threatening words.

"Maizy, come help Mommy set the table," Lynn said.

Maizy set her stuffed wolf down and skipped into the kitchen.

Trevor looked between everyone in the room. "Before I went through the change as a Shifter, I knew who I was. Somehow, so did everyone else. I wasn't open with it, but let's just say they made my life a living hell. You know how Shifters feel about being all hetero and continuing the Breed by having more kids. I don't take shit for it no more. You can stand there and tell me you're cool with it, but if one person in this house roughs me up…"

"Then we'll fucking put him out," Reno said from behind. Everyone glanced in our direction and Reno stepped around me. "We're brothers. You come into this pack, and you're our brother. Anyone here got a problem with this?"

All eyes looked between one another in a silent agreement that they didn't care. Wheeler sat in a leather chair with his legs crossed, watching the scene with mild interest. Ben leaned against the far wall, yawning and rubbing his face. Those two were like night and day.

"There's your answer," Reno said.

Austin continued. "How about it? It's a good offer and we're a tight pack. You'll have protection and we need another good man we can trust."

Trevor blinked a few times and stared at his oxfords. I knew that look. He was on the verge of tears, and Trevor hated crying in front of people. He had never told me about his life or hinted to any history of physical torment. My heart broke at the idea that he'd suffered abuse at the hands of his own family.

"Trial period?" he asked.

Austin stuffed his hands in his pockets, jingling some change around. "All or nothing. I give you my word no one in this pack is going to put his hands on you. I can't promise they won't be jackasses and rile you up—that's daily life around here."

"They're men," Lexi blurted out from the stairs. "It can hardly be helped."

A laugh bubbled out of me and Trevor looked up, eyes brimming with uncertainty. The white lights on the tree twinkled, the room smelled of cinnamon potpourri, and all eyes were on Trevor. Denver shut off the music and Jericho bit on an unlit cigarette, flicking it up and down. Since smoking was only permitted in his bedroom and the game room, he had developed an oral fixation.

Trevor pinched his lip. "I'm cool with that. But if anyone crosses the line in this house, I'm gone."

Everyone exhaled at once.

"Well, hell. Let's get this party started!" Denver cranked up the stereo and changed it over to a radio station.

"Go back, I like that song!" Lexi blurted out, leaping to her feet.

"I'm *not* listening to Fleetwood," Denver announced, stopping at a Van Halen song.

As everyone resumed talking, Austin patted Trevor on the shoulder. They shared a private look and without words made a solid agreement.

Trevor now belonged in the Weston Pack.

Lynn had baked a succulent honey-glazed ham with pineapple rings and cherries on top. Ivy took credit for the steamed vegetables and jalapeño cornbread, while Lexi had baked the most savory chocolate chip cookies I'd ever tasted. She spent an hour talking about recipe ideas that had me drooling. It was also decided that after my long hiatus, I was going back to Sweet Treats to resume my position as manager.

Austin filled Trevor in on the formalities of joining the pack. Paperwork had to be signed in front of local Packmasters, but as far as he was concerned, Trevor could move in that night.

I had a fresh start with my life—a new beginning. No strings holding me back or tying me down. No financial burdens, no debt. Anything was possible. Not only that, but for the first time in my life, I felt a sense of belonging. I began to see what a functional family was all about—something I'd never thought I could have with someone who wasn't a blood relative. Reno paid for my mother to have a headstone, and I buried my remorse along with her.

Reno never questioned my relationship with Maddox, and when I'd tried to broach the topic last night in bed, he slipped his arms around my waist, nuzzled his face against the back of my neck, and told me to go back to sleep. He didn't want an explanation. Maybe I'd never find out why it didn't matter to him, but part of me liked having someone in my life who accepted my past. The only thing he had said to me on the matter was that a mistake was something you regretted. I gave it a lot of thought, and I didn't regret my time with Maddox. What I did regret was not having told someone early on about Sanchez, although I'm not sure it would have made much of a difference. No one leads a perfect life. I accepted the fact it wouldn't be the last mistake I'd ever make. But that was okay. I wouldn't have to go through it alone.

After dinner, the porch swing rocked back and forth and I curled up against Reno. I threw my legs over his lap and he wrapped a flannel blanket around us. After he took a long sip of his coffee, he set the mug down on a small table to his right.

"Got something for you," he said, breaking the silence. He reached beside him and handed me a box.

"Wait, I thought we weren't going to exchange gifts?"

He smiled and it pushed creases in his cheeks as he looked out into the darkness. "It's technically not a gift."

"Funny, it looks like a gift to me." The box was green with a felt exterior and I smoothed my fingers around the lid. When I opened it, I stared at a glass orb. "Oh, this is so…"

When I lifted it out of the box my breath caught.

"I managed to salvage one of the snow globes after the fire. The firemen put out the flames and while you were being treated, I went back to survey the scene. It was damaged, but I know a guy who's real good with his hands. He couldn't save the glass, but he refinished the base and touched up the inside."

I shook it and watched tiny flecks of snow swirl about the scene with a man walking through the woods with a child on his shoulders. What could I possibly give this man that could match the sentimental value of this gift? I placed the globe gingerly in the box and Reno set it on the table. My heart constricted and I'd never felt more devotion toward someone—more genuine respect—than I did for the Shifter sitting beside me.

"I wanted to save it as a surprise," he said, as if it were no big deal.

"Reno?"

"What is it, princess?"

I adored that he called me that. Even more, I adored the bookshelf he had built for me that morning and put in the bedroom as a surprise.

"I want to tell you something important."

He cleared his throat, tucked his arm around my back, and continued pushing the swing with the heel of his boot. "Already told you, I don't need to know about Maddox."

"No, you need to know this," I said in a serious voice.

I could barely make out his eyes as he stopped rocking and glanced down. "I'm all ears."

That put me on the spot. "Is this forever?"

His rough hand cupped my cheek and a kiss melted against my lips, warm against the chilly air. I could taste the coffee on his breath and I wrinkled my nose. He chuckled and said, "I think I need to get you fitted for a helmet so you can ride with me in the spring when it gets warmer."

"Is that a yes?"

His knuckles grazed my neck and outlined my breast, traveling down to my lap where my cold hand was tucked between my legs. "I don't know what forever is, April. I don't even want to think about the finish line while I'm in the race, because that's the end, and I don't want this to end. If that means forever, then yeah."

"So maybe it's time that I tell you."

He didn't blink and I could almost hear his heart pounding. So I gripped his hand and leaned in close, my forearms against his chest and my fingers touching his smooth jaw.

"I love you. That's a big deal because I've never told that to another man except for Trevor. My heart is the only gift I have to give to you. I love this life we have, and this future…"

Holy smokes, I was crying. Tears streamed down my face. As much as I'd rehearsed that moment in my head, it never involved tears or having to rub my runny nose.

"I just want you to know that it's a big deal for me not to just share my *life* with you, but my heart. Every piece of it, even the broken ones. I can't give you kids—not just because we *can't* have children together, but because that's not what I want in life. My past is something I'll never shake free of, and maybe some people can get over it and move forward, but that's not the life for me. You have to be okay with that because if you want a family, I don't want to deny you of it."

Reno sat up, grabbed my legs, and turned me so that I was straddling him. He wrapped the blanket around my back and slipped his arms around my waist.

"Just so we have a few things straight, princess, I'm turning your old bedroom into a reading room. When our pack gets bigger and we have to give up the room, then the lounge downstairs will be your library and you'll have your own time where you can close the door and no one will bother you. I'll put locks on the damn door if I have to. You're also going to learn to ride a motorcycle, because bikes are my life and I want to share that with you. Even if it's just taking a spin around the property, I want you to learn to handle something powerful without fear. I'm also going to show you a little self-defense because women should know how to take care of themselves."

I kissed his cheek as he spoke, making my way to the other side.

"Like I said a while back, we're done with all the belts and tying up. Obviously we both like to be in control, but we can work out our needs together. I still work as a PI, and if I have to leave town, then Trevor is going to look after you. If it's something serious, you see Austin."

Wow, he was getting serious with the talk. I told him I loved him, and he was planning out our days together.

"Next summer, I'm taking you on a trip to Hawaii."

"What?" I exclaimed and laughed all at once. "That's not necessary."

"Oh? Humans take vacations all the time. When's the last time you had one? Plus, I want to see that gorgeous body in a bikini."

"Ah, now I'm beginning to see the big picture," I said with a giggle, kissing his chin and ruffling my hands through his short hair. "I have a few conditions of my own."

His brow quirked. "Oh?"

"Every so often, I want you to skip a shave or two. I like your stubble."

"Done."

"I'm also a little messier than you, and I'll try to pick up, but don't get all neat-freak on me and start lining up my shoes. My sister has OCD and if you don't keep that under control, it can take over. I'm not saying you have it, I'm just pointing out that I've never seen a man neatly line up packages of gum on his dresser like you do. I also want you to teach me how to play horseshoes."

He smiled. "Is that so?"

"Yeah. I'm having fun learning all these new things. I want to be good at something."

"Oh, you're good at something," he said suggestively, waggling his brows. "I like it when you nibble on my ear. Maybe you can do some of that later on."

I slipped my arms beneath his and held on to my man so tight I could feel his heartbeat. His warmth surrounded me like the Pacific sun melting across tranquil waters. Reno kissed the top of my head and began rocking the swing again. Inside the house, Maizy was singing a Christmas song and Ivy joined in.

Someday I would die before Reno's time. I didn't understand Breed magic enough to speculate how his body would age, although from what he said, everyone is different and it was quite possible we could grow old together.

So I gave it some thought and concluded that I couldn't plan our relationship on sex. If I ended up sixty and he still looked thirty, the intimacy we shared would be nonexistent.

But after it's all said and done, don't you want to grow old with your best friend? At the end of the day, that's who you want to share your life and laughter with. Someone who will be there in hard times to hold you tight. Someone who will fight for your honor and support your decisions. Someone who will encourage your dreams and help you to fulfill them.

Do I think I'll be having great sex all the way into my eighties? Probably not. But I'll have someone there to make me bacon and tell me I'm beautiful. Someone to sit on the porch beside me and listen to the crickets in the summertime while we share a glass of lemon tea, talking about old times.

And I'm okay with that.

I'm more than okay with that.

I hate that I won't be there for him after I'm gone, but Reno will find himself a woman one day—maybe a Shifter. Perhaps I'll play a part in helping him become a man who is finally ready to make decisions about adoption and having a family of his own. Or maybe he'll finally realize that giving a woman babies is not what defines him as a man. The courage to love is.

Nothing lasts forever. But maybe I can carry a little piece of that happiness in my pocket for as long as I'm here.

Just like Reno carried that earring.

Printed in Great Britain
by Amazon.co.uk, Ltd.,
Marston Gate.